PRINCIPAL

PRINCIPAL

Kevin Gaughen

Principal

Copyright © 2018 by Kevin Gaughen

Cover art by Benjamin Ee

Published by the author:
Kevin Gaughen
PO Box 1517
Mechanicsburg, PA 17055-9017
USA

ISBN-10: 0986380504
ISBN-13: 9780986380501

First Edition: Published January 2018

Acknowledgments

My wholehearted appreciation goes out to the following individuals, who spent many hours helping me shape this book into what it is.

Beta Readers:
Joel K Church
Rustin Coziahr
Tobin Coziahr
Grant Gaughen
Laryssa Gaughen
Tom Gaughen
Ryan Jackson, MD
Joe Lombardo
David Lynch
Maria Elaina Martinelli
Teresa Pezzi
Franny Ryan, Esq.
Ken Sams

Mike Sams
Kathy Savage
Donald Smart
David Lynn Smith
Jeff Smith

<u>Editor:</u>
Ray

To my children:

You are your own candles in the darkness.

"The day the power of love overrules the love of power, the world will know peace."

—*Mahatma M. K. Gandhi*

Prologue

Circa 15,000 BCE, an extraterrestrial race of scientists known as the Ich-Ca-Gan traveled to Earth to study it. Upon their arrival, the Ich-Ca-Gan discovered two forms of life on the planet more evolved than the rest: human beings and the Dranthyx.

The Dranthyx, cephalopods who had descended from the common octopus, had several remarkable evolutionary advantages: the ability to breathe air as well as water, the ability to camouflage themselves as other beings (particularly humans), and superintelligence. Of note was that the Dranthyx were a ruthless and greedy species who were biologically incapable of empathy or altruism.

The Dranthyx, being much more intelligent than humans and having evolved fifty million years earlier, held a tremendous technological edge over early humans. At the time of the Ich-Ca-Gan's arrival, human beings were in the Stone Age, whereas the Dranthyx already had supercomputers and advanced bioengineering. The Ich-Ca-Gan discovered that the Dranthyx were using humans as slave labor and that the Dranthyx considered them mere livestock. The entire Dranthyx civilization and economy were propped up by free human labor, allowing the Dranthyx to live in relative ease below the water while humans toiled above it.

The original human stock had evolved from monkeys. However, using biotechnology, the Dranthyx manipulated the human genome to optimize humans for slave labor. In much the same way that humans created different dog breeds for varying tasks, the Dranthyx created three different types of humans for specific roles:

Tchogols: The Dranthyx spliced some of their own genes directly into a number of humans, creating the original Tchogol stock. Tchogols, like the Dranthyx, have no empathy, no remorse, and no conscience. Dranthyx DNA gives them a strong drive toward material wealth and power. They are designed to be ruthless, cunning, and charismatic. Due to their ruthlessness and inborn desire for domination, Tchogols are the unwitting managers of the Dranthyx slave hierarchy. As a border collie instinctively herds animals without being told to do so, Tchogols simply do what they are genetically programmed to: they rise to the top of organizations by any means necessary and rule. Tchogolism is a recessive gene, making Tchogols the least common of the types.

Saskels: Early on, the Dranthyx identified human genes for intractable behavior and independent thought. These are not favorable attributes in slave labor, and as such they had to be removed to produce Saskels, the second type of human. Saskels are designed to do tedious labor without questioning those ruling over them. Saskels have low to average mental abilities and ostensibly have the ability to reason through minor problems. However, they are genetically engineered to not trust their own thoughts and to have a deep fear of losing their security. They are terrified of having to think, or fend, for themselves. This inborn insecurity causes them to constantly seek external guidance and to obey authority, no matter how irrational or malevolent that authority is. Saskelism is a highly dominant gene, and Saskels compose the majority of the human population.

Xreths: Xreths are humans who were designed for creativity and problem solving. Xreths have both ethics and the ability to come to conclusions independently. Xreths create math, science, engineering, art. Before the introduction of the Xreth type, humans hadn't even thought of agriculture. Human technological development stalls without Xreths, and labor output declines, to the Dranthyx's detriment. The Dranthyx have kept Xreths around because the science and technology they produce benefits them. Complicating the situation is the fact that human Xreths are more creative and productive than Dranthyx intellectuals, which means the Dranthyx are extremely concerned that Xreths will usurp control. The Dranthyx consider Xreths a necessary evil, one that they monitor very closely. When the number of Xreths grows too large, the Dranthyx cull them. Xrethism is a moderately dominant gene.

Believing the Dranthyx culling of Xreths to be unethical, the Ich-Ca-Gan intervened circa 680 BCE. A global war between the Ich-Ca-Gan and the Dranthyx erupted. Fourteen of the original fifteen Ich-Ca-Gan were killed, while untold millions of Dranthyx perished in the conflict. A truce was called. The last remaining Ich-Ca-Gan agreed to not interfere in the Dranthyx culls, and the Dranthyx agreed to not interfere with the Ich-Ca-Gan's attempts to educate the human race.

In 1322 CE, the sole surviving Ich-Ca-Gan went into hiding beneath a Buddhist temple in Tokyo. He continued teaching, albeit to a select group of Zen monks.

Around 1600 CE, the Dranthyx discovered an insidious way of controlling the human population without the need for direct force: fiat currency. By creating paper money with no intrinsic value and loaning it at interest, the Dranthyx were able to yoke humanity with unsustainable debts that could never be repaid. Through usury and financial instruments, they were able to maintain complete control of the human race from the shadows. With this new slavery scheme in place, the Dranthyx painstakingly erased all evidence of their existence from the historical record and, eventually, from human memory.

The previous story in this series, *Interest*, begins in the early part of the twenty-first century. Our protagonist, Len Savitz, is a journalist living during a time of great unrest. Domestic revolutionaries are at war with the US government, and acts of terrorism are being carried out daily. Len finds himself caught up in the intrigue when his five-year-old daughter, Octavia, and ex-wife, Sara, are kidnapped by the rebels. The leaders of the revolution, a man named General Jefferson and a mysterious woman named Neith, who only speaks through an android, hold his family as collateral and force Len to do their bidding.

Neith's first assignment to Len is to travel to Ecuador. On the airplane, Len meets a Russian woman named Natalia. In Ecuador, Len finds that his daughter and ex-wife are being held captive by a drug lord. Having verified that they are still alive and well, Len is given his next assignment, to travel to Japan.

In Japan, Len meets the last of the Ich-Ca-Gan, known in the temple as the Great Master. The Ich-Ca-Gan recounts the history of the Dranthyx and how they have worked to enslave the human race. Right after the Ich-Ca-Gan warns that another large cull is imminent, Len is rushed out of the building. He sees a SWAT team attempting to raid the temple just before a large Ich-Ca-Gan spacecraft rises up out of the earth. The spacecraft disappears into thin air.

Returning to the United States, Len learns of General Jefferson's plans to sack Washington, DC, and completely usurp the existing government. He also learns that Natalia is a gunrunner who makes a living by buying weapons from the Russian government and selling them to Jefferson's revolutionaries.

Using the information Len has gleaned from the Ich-Ca-Gan, Jefferson's men capture a Dranthyx, drug it, and force it to talk. The Dranthyx confirms what the Great Master told Len: a massive Xreth cull is imminent, and billions will die.

Neith then infects Len with a virus known as the Tchogol flu and makes him get back on a plane to Ecuador with multiple layovers. On the way, Len infects thousands of people at each airport, which sends the virus all over the world causing a global pandemic. The virus kills every single Tchogol it comes in contact with but leaves the other two types of humans unscathed.

Back in Ecuador, Len saves Natalia's life. In gratitude, Natalia helps Len and his daughter escape the drug lord's island. While hiding out in Natalia's flat in Bogota, Len composes the most important piece of journalism ever written: an exposé of the Dranthyx, the Ich-Ca-Gan, and Neith. While Len is writing his story, he sees on the news that General Jefferson's coup has been successful and that he has appointed himself president of the United States.

Upon entering back into the United States, Len deliberately gets himself arrested by US immigration officials. In his luggage is a copy of his exposé. He informs the officials holding him captive to send it up the chain of command as high as it'll go.

While Len is in captivity, the Dranthyx captured by Jefferson's men visits him in his holding cell. The Dranthyx informs Len that he was freed, Jefferson has been arrested, and Neith was discovered to be a rogue, self-aware supercomputer who was summarily destroyed. He also learns that his ex-wife was killed by the Tchogol flu. Just before the Dranthyx tries to kill Len for knowing too much, Natalia and her associates attack the facility, kill the Dranthyx, and free Len.

Spurred on by what Len has written, and fearing that they're losing control of the situation, the Dranthyx are forced into a position where they must act. Further, without any Tchogols left to do the cull for them, the Dranthyx are left with no choice but to come onto land to do the Xreth cull themselves. Accordingly, the Dranthyx stage a massive invasion on the entire human world. The Dranthyx military ascends from the depths of the ocean to land on the beaches of every continent. They destroy the major coastal cities before rounding up the world's Xreths.

Len, Natalia, and Octavia befriend militia members who live in a fortress called the Freehold high in the mountains of West Texas. There, the militia attempts an armed last stand against the Dranthyx. They're unable to compete with vastly superior technology, and the Dranthyx easily conquer the Freehold. Len, Natalia, and Octavia are sent to a massive concentration camp in the middle of North America.

Len discovers that General Jefferson is alive and well in the same camp. Len is forced into mortal combat with Jefferson for the Dranthyx's entertainment. Len wins the fight and kills Jefferson. Shortly thereafter, Len, Natalia, and Octavia are rounded up and taken to the reactor, where they will be put to death.

While awaiting execution, Octavia tells her father about a dream she had the night before. In her recounting, Octavia unwittingly gives the signal that begins the Ich-Ca-Gan surprise attack. Instantly, thousands of Ich-Ca-Gan ships appear in the sky and begin a surgically precise bombardment, killing every single Dranthyx standing on dry land.

As they exit the concentration camp, Len reveals to Natalia that he planned the surprise attack with the Ich-Ca-Gan. Len incited the Dranthyx into coming ashore so that they could be slaughtered. He also says that approximately 0.3 percent of the Dranthyx population never came ashore and therefore survived the attack. Len warns that the Dranthyx could become a problem once again in the future.

Len and Natalia see a message broadcast on TV by the Ich-Ca-Gan. In it, they warn that they will not help again in the future.

When Len returns to his apartment in Pittsburgh, his landlord gives him a letter. The letter, from Neith, reveals that she is still very much alive and that every single bit of Len's adventure was part of her plan. As compensation for his troubles, Neith gives Len the coordinates to where a fortune in gold is buried.

Several months after the story ends, the Ich-Ca-Gan ships depart the Earth as suddenly as they'd arrived, never to be seen again.

Thirty-Five Years
after the Events
in *Interest*

43

"Octavia," her father yelled over the gunfire, "keep your head down!"

Panicked, she dropped to her belly behind a large rock.

What the hell is going on? Octavia thought. *One minute I'm unpacking my bags in the guest bedroom; the next, bullets are smashing through the wall. Why are people shooting at us?*

"Where are the kids?" her dad shouted.

"They're in the basement of the house, where you told them to go."

Fuck, I hope they're OK.

"Dad, what the hell is happening?" she yelled over the machine-gun fire.

Rather than answering, Len popped up above the concrete wall, took some potshots at the boats a hundred yards offshore, and ducked for cover again. Octavia saw a man fall out of one of the boats.

Her dad grabbed the walkie-talkie that he'd dropped on the ground in all the confusion. "Jeff, do you have that thing working yet?"

The people in the boats were returning fire. Three bullets came whizzing over the rock that Octavia was hiding behind. She had always thought bullets flying nearby would sound like the ricochet noises in cartoons, but, in reality, they sounded like huge, angry hornets.

"Not yet," came the reply over the radio. "I'm trying to figure it out."

"What's the holdup?" Len bellowed.

Just then, there was an explosion in the water near the beach. The boat people were launching grenades at them, and the first one had missed.

"Natalia left us an instruction manual, but it's in some language I can't read. I'm trying to figure out how to make it work," Jeff answered. "The screen says 'Calibrating.'"

Octavia's father rolled his eyes. He grabbed his rifle and, keeping his head low, hobbled over to the big rock Octavia was hiding behind and fell to the ground next to her. Octavia could see that there were several boats in the water, all of which were shooting at them. Another grenade exploded near the south beach.

This is real. We're under attack. They're launching explosives at us.

"Dad," Octavia asked, "who are those people, and why are they shooting at us?"

Her father didn't answer. He was too focused on what was happening offshore. Octavia could hear long strings of gunshots coming from all over the island. The islanders were exchanging fire with their attackers in every direction.

"It just finished calibrating!" Jeff shouted over the radio. "Should I activate it?"

"No, let's wait until we're being overrun," Len yelled into the handset. "Fuck yes. Activate it!"

Octavia heard a *ploop* sound, followed by a whistling noise. A deafening blast fifty yards to her left knocked the wind out of her lungs. She opened her eyes, gasping for air, ears ringing, to find herself covered in dirt and wood splinters. The tree she used to play on when she was a kid, the one with the tire swing, was now a crater.

"Take out the green boat. They've got a mortar!" someone yelled over the radio.

"OK, it says, 'Acquiring targets; thirty seconds remaining,'" Jeff announced.

Can I make it back to the house where my kids are? Several small projectiles smashed into the rock they were hiding behind, dusting Octavia and her father with chips of limestone. She considered the bulletproof cover the rock was providing as several more rounds buzzed by on either side. *No, they know we're behind these rocks, and they're shooting right at us. Standing up or moving seems like a bad idea.*

Just then, one of the speedboats revved its engines and came in full throttle toward them. It looked as though the attackers were going to ram the island hard enough to plow up onto the beach. Len flicked a switch on the side of his gun.

"Come a little closer, assholes," Octavia heard her father mutter.

At precisely the right moment, her dad treated the incoming vessel to a full-auto burst from his rifle. He must have hit something or someone, because the craft veered hard to the right and capsized just before hitting the shore. The old man changed magazines and then fired another long burst at the overturned boat's hull for good measure. One of the spent casings ejected from her dad's rifle landed in the collar of Octavia's shirt. The brass shell was red hot, and it seared her skin instantly.

"Ow, son of a bitch!" she cursed, flailing to pull it out.

"Jeff," her father said into the radio, "make sure it misses one."

"Why?" Jeff asked.

"Just do it," Len barked. "Let one of them go."

"OK. It's done!" Jeff yelled over the radio. "Get ready!"

Her father looked up to the big tower in the center of the island.

When did they build that? Octavia thought, looking where her dad was looking. *That wasn't here last time. How did I miss a ten-story tower?*

At the top of the tower was a cylindrical, chrome-plated object. Octavia could see it rotating, moving up and down, stopping randomly. Its movements reminded her of the robots that built cars: abrupt and jerky yet precise beyond all human capabilities. She rolled over to look in the other direction, through the small gap below the oddly shaped rock. Out in the water, the three boats that she could see from her vantage point all burst into flames simultaneously. She could hear the anguished wails of the people onboard.

What the hell just happened?

Then, the gunfire stopped. This was followed by an uncomfortable silence. Her father waited a long thirty seconds, then peeked up over the rock.

44

Daniel Barton stood at the enormous window overlooking downtown Detroit. From his seventieth-floor office, he could see for miles. The unconquered kingdom. What had once been a run-down shithole—postapocalyptic even before the apocalypse—was now a thriving, major world city. Construction cranes loomed to the horizon, building razor-thin skyscrapers that glinted in the morning light like titanium blades of rye.

Water. I should expand into water, he thought.

That was the reason they were there, after all. Rising oceans had flooded out the coastal cities. Even before the North Koreans invaded, decades-long drought and osmosis cartels had caused water scarcity in the West, which forced the population eastward. The Great Lakes region had vast quantities of water, which was its saving grace. Declining Rust Belt regions that previously had no future were propelled beyond boomtowns into cosmopolitan megacities.

The phone intercom interrupted his strategizing.

"Mr. Barton, the new hire is here," his secretary's voice announced. "Shall I send her in?"

"Please."

Dan didn't turn around as the huge oak doors to his office opened. Behind him, he could hear the footsteps of his secretary and the new girl. He always paid careful attention to how people walked. A person's walk betrayed everything about them: confidence, shame, attention to detail. The new hire's footsteps sounded careful, hesitant. Someone dutiful, hopefully. Dan turned around slowly. He eyed the new recruit. She was young. Twenty-five, maybe. Her business attire was off the rack, and she didn't look at home in it.

Straight out of MBA school and looking the part, Dan mused. *Attractive girl, though. She's got the look we need. Appearance closes more deals than anything else.*

"Elise Sutton, I presume?" Dan asked.

"Yes," she said nervously. "It's an honor to meet you, Mr. Barton." She stretched out her hand.

Dan shook it. "Thank you. You as well. So let's get started. There's a lot to go over. I understand you were at the top of your class at Wharton."

"Yes, sir. Summa cum laude."

"Good. That's what we need—brains. What do you know about currency trading?"

"My undergraduate was in macroeconomics, and my MBA thesis was on foreign exchange markets," she answered.

"Let me ask again: What do you know about currency trading?"

Elise paused before answering. She looked uncomfortable. "Not as much as you, sir. I'm here to learn."

Dan smiled. Political beyond her years. "Good. That's the right answer. I'm going to go over it with you as though you don't know anything. That isn't a reflection on you, but more about the state of academia. I hire a lot of college graduates who have fancy degrees from top-tier schools but don't seem to know anything useful. Those who can't do, teach. You know."

"Ready when you are, sir."

Dan gestured for her to follow him as he walked across his spacious office, through the doors, and out onto a catwalk above the trading floor. Below, rows upon rows of haggard-looking employees frantically made phone calls and entered data into computers.

"What people *think* we do here is trade one currency for another, taking a fee in the process."

"It isn't?" Elise asked.

"Nope. What we do is define value itself."

"OK, now I'm intrigued," she said.

"There are three major currencies in use right now in North America and several minor ones. Do you know what the big three are?"

"Land Credits, MassMoney, and, um, LaborValue?"

"Nah. LaborValue is a BS currency." Dan laughed. "No one uses that. I'll explain why later. Land Credits are the most widely used, followed by MassMoney, followed by Calibuxx. These currencies are issued by various authorities, otherwise known as *datamints*. I'm sure you know the history behind them?"

"I'd like to hear you explain it, sir," Elise said. "You know far more than I do."

"The Invasion left such a bad taste in people's mouths that fiat currencies issued by world governments fell from favor. Fiat, as you know, means a piece of paper has value simply because some government says it does, like the old euros or dollars. Even though the Dranthyx were wiped out, consumers no longer trusted fiat currency because they saw it for what it was—a control scheme. Consumers wanted something different, a form of money that was decentralized, secure, and limited in supply. First they tried using crypto-currencies. Problem with that was, they were not tied to any-thing of value. Also, the security of cryptocurrencies became a joke with the advent of quantum computing—there was counterfeiting and private key theft all over the place. The days when data security revolved around the difficulty in finding the prime factors of huge numbers are long gone."

"So how are currencies secured now?" she asked.

"Hashes, lattices, and supersingular isogeny."

Elise gave him a blank look.

"I don't understand it, either," Dan said. "It's serious egghead stuff. The important thing is that it all works, and even the most powerful computers can't counterfeit the sig-natures. Anyway, the other thing that defines a good, modern currency is a tie to something of real value. In the case of Land Credits, they simply created one land credit for each of the Earth's 150 trillion square meters of dry land area and then permanently capped the number. No more can be cre-ated. For MassMoney, they used the actual mass of the earth. Calibuxx are backed by Californium 252."

"Californium 252 is what makes the Dranthyx technol-ogy work, right?" Elise said.

Dan tried not to smirk at her grasping attempt to seem professional and knowledgeable. She seemed so out of place, so kid-like. Like a little girl who tried on her mom's clothes to pretend she was an adult.

"Yes," Dan said without cracking a smile. "It's the power source for the Dranthyx weaponry and technology. Problem is, it's a very rare material with a short half life. It's tough to produce. One Calibuxx is pegged to one microgram of Californium 252. Eventually, someone will figure out how the Dranthyx manufactured so much of it, which will implode the Calibuxx franchise. In the meantime, it's a safe bet."

"So why aren't you a fan of LaborValues?" Elise asked.

"Because that currency is backed by labor, and labor is... well, worthless. Labor has no intrinsic value anymore. We've got more people than jobs, which causes extreme downward pressure on wages. The reason, as you know, is everything is automated now. Unemployment is now over 50 percent. It's only going to get worse. Speaking of which, that you're here says an awful lot about your qualifications. We picked you out of over three thousand applicants."

"I am truly grateful, sir."

Let's see how she handles this one.

"Are you married, Miss Sutton?"

"No, sir."

"Good. Having a family is a rather unproductive use of time for someone of your caliber."

Dan watched her struggle to deal with the comment. It was like a bone going down her throat. She smiled and nodded.

Good. She can eat shit and still smile. The business world is no place for the weak and easily offended.

"Right this way to the elevators," Dan said, motioning her to walk ahead of him. "I want to introduce you to your coworkers."

The elevator door opened onto the trading floor. Dan led her into a corner office, where a tall man stood up behind his desk. "Miss Sutton, this is Randy Hughes, our senior vice president and governmental-affairs coordinator."

"Nice to meet you," Elise said, shaking his hand.

"Remember how I told you about defining value? Randy helps us make that happen. He's our chief greaser," Dan said.

"Greaser?" Elise asked.

"Skids, palms, whatever," Dan said. "An operation of our scale needs to operate with as little friction as possible. You'll get to know each other plenty over the next few weeks. This way. I want to show you your new office." Dan led her down a long hallway on the eastern side of the building, where the sun shone through the windows. As they walked, a shadow flitted through the hallway.

"Oh my god!" Elise yelled.

"What?" Dan turned around. Her eyes were wide.

"I'm pretty sure I just saw someone fall off the building."

"A person?"

"Yes!" she squeaked, her voice cracking. "He looked right at me."

"Again? I wonder who it was this time. Well, anyway, as you can see, vacancies are always being created around here, so there's plenty of upward mobility," Dan said nonchalantly. "Don't park near the east entrance; that's my advice. OK, let's get you to your office. I have a nine fifteen that's of the utmost importance."

"Octavia, stay down," her father yelled. He stumbled as fast as his old body would let him up the steps to the house. He came back out onto the porch seconds later with a familiar propellered object.

My drone, Octavia thought. *That's the one I used to play with when I was a kid!*

Len turned it on and threw it into the air. The device came alive as it fell back to earth. It stopped just short of hitting the ground and hovered obediently. Len grabbed the controller and sent the device up into the sky.

Octavia looked through the crack again. The lone surviving speedboat fired up its throttle and did a big arcing curve away from the island. Len stood on the porch, giving chase with the drone, transfixed by the little screen on the controller. Disregarding what her father had told her, Octavia stood and ran up the steps to the porch. From there, she could see clumps of floating, burning debris out in the water where the boats had been.

"There must have been thirty boats. The laser did that?" Octavia said.

"Yeah," Len said, his attention still on the screen of the drone controller. "We just got it. That thing saved our asses today. Give me a second, Octavia. I want to follow this boat to see where these assholes came from."

"You need to back off when you're following someone," Octavia said, looking over his shoulder. "You don't want them to see the drone and shoot it down. I lost three of them that way. Also, you need to adjust the trim. It's meandering all over the place."

Her dad gave her an annoyed look.

"Dad, let me do it," Octavia said in exasperation. "I'm better at this than you."

"Yeah, you're probably right." He handed her the device. "You spent your whole childhood playing with those things."

"Dad, who were those people?" Octavia asked as she piloted the remote-controlled aircraft.

"No idea," Len said while coughing from being out of breath. "They've been attacking our island for months now."

Octavia glanced at him as he lit a cigarette. She noticed his hands were shaking with adrenaline. "Yeah, but why?" she asked, returning her attention to following the speed boat.

Her father threw his hands up. "At first it was just one or two boats at a time. But the attacks have grown in size. Thankfully, we're prepared for that sort of thing."

Her father had almost finished his smoke by the time Octavia saw the boat park in a slip outside of Painesville. "Hey, look!" she said, beckoning her dad. "The old Headlands Beach Park." He peered over her shoulder at the controller while Octavia flew the drone closer to study the area.

She could just make out hundreds of crappy old boats and camping trailers. Tanks. Anti-aircraft weapons. Some sort of power plant.

"They're closer than I thought. That's quite an operation they have," Len remarked. "Can you zoom in so we can see who was on that boat?"

Octavia zoomed in, though zooming made the image grainier. A dark figure disembarked from the watercraft.

Len and Octavia stood in frozen silence, staring at the little screen.

"What…what is getting out of that boat?" Len exclaimed. "Is that a bear?"

Then the video feed went dark.

46

Len awoke at his post on the southern side of the island and found himself slumped over in a chair.

Dammit, he thought in shame. *Fell asleep again. Can't stay awake the way I used to. Hope no one saw me. Hope nothing happened.*

Len had set a policy when the attacks began: no lights at night. Everything on the island that could possibly be illuminated was shut off. Blackout curtains were put over all the windows in the buildings. All movement was restricted by necessity, and the islanders wore night-vision goggles in order to get around after dusk. Any fool with a GPS could find the island in the dark, but why make it easier by keeping lights on as well? Len rubbed his eyes and looked at his watch. The little tritium dots glowed green in the darkness: 3:13 a.m.

The structure he was in was built by Natalia's company. It was a tall concrete cylinder that reminded him of the old World War II lookout towers that he had seen on the beaches in Delaware, where his family had vacationed when he was a kid. The entrance was a heavy steel door. Inside was a spiral staircase leading up to the observation room, which was entirely spartan: a chair, a toilet, a sink, several night-vision apparatuses, a radio, and a rusty space heater with a glowing red grill. There were five such buildings on the island, plus the new tower, which was taller than all the rest: the one that housed the laser cannon. Everyone on the island took turns doing four-hour shifts in the watchtowers.

A fluttery sensation in Len's chest made him cough. The first cough felt as if it shook something loose into a bronchial tube, which caused his body to involuntarily hack repeatedly in order to expel whatever was irritating his lungs. This developed into a full-blown coughing fit that left him red-faced and wheezing. Finally feeling thick mucus come up in his throat, he went over to the sink to spit it out. To his horror, it was bright red.

This is the nastiest case of bronchitis I've ever had.

After getting his composure back and catching his breath, Len looked out through the horizontal slit, which was just wide enough to stick a gun through. To his relief, the coast was clear, and he saw no vessels on the horizon. He felt the urge to radio the other towers but thought better of it. Next check-in was at 4:00 a.m., and there was no sense in ruining the perfectly good silence until then. *Time to check the beach*, he thought. He grabbed his rifle, slung it across his back, and walked carefully down the concrete stairs, holding the rail the whole way. The pain in his hip was getting worse, and he wondered if it was the precursor to another fracture. He'd already had one hip replacement. His finger joints were swollen and painful in the cool night air, which he knew to be the arthritic result of years spent gripping judo gis and typing news stories. A lifetime of habits was catching up with him. For some reason, the only body parts that didn't bother him were his knees.

To conceal the flame, Len lit his cigarette before opening the door. Walking outside, he looked up and exhaled into the night. Heavy overcast; the clouds looked like brushed steel. The smoke from the end of Len's cigarette rose straight up into the night sky. No wind.

He walked down to the water. There was a big rock there that he liked to sit on to look at the skyline. The blue skyglow from distant Cleveland illuminated everything in an ambient, ghostly way. *No waves tonight*, he thought. He couldn't remember the last time everything was so still. The dead calm disquieted him.

He took another drag on the cigarette, using his hand to cup the glowing embers so they wouldn't be visible. Looking out on the lake again, he noticed a silhouette of something in the water. It was close, maybe ten feet away. Not too big, maybe the size of a microwave oven. It looked like a log of driftwood, but it was too dark to see the object clearly. Len got out the flashlight that he used for night watches. Its beam was dim and red, designed for deer hunters because its light didn't carry too far and deer can't see that color. He shined it at the object. His old heart nearly stopped.

The head of a Dranthyx stuck out of the water, the rest of its body submerged. Wet purple skin, yellow eyes glowing with the reflected light. Len stared at it in disbelief for a second or two. Was he hallucinating? Then it smiled at him. A hideous, nasty smile that could have curdled gasoline. Snapping to, Len fumbled to grab the rifle off his back and point it at the beast. Quickly, Len switched on the light affixed to the rifle, a dim red one like his flashlight, and put the creature in his sights. Pulling the trigger, his stomach dropped as he heard a simple *click*. He pulled the trigger again. Nothing. In a frenetic fit of muscle memory, Len banged the magazine in place and pulled the charging handle back. Not hearing the bolt slam forward automatically the way it was supposed to, he hit the bolt-release lever to do it manually. He quickly shouldered the gun and pulled the trigger again. *Click.*

Fuck! Fuck! Stupid fucking gun!

Len groped around for the walkie-talkie, but nothing happened when he pushed the button. Len pushed it several more times in rapid succession, but it didn't make the typical beep to indicate it was transmitting. He looked around in a panic, weighing whether he could get up the tower stairs to the other radio before the Dranthyx caught him. He wondered if he could shout loudly enough for someone to hear.

The creature laughed at Len's dread. That laugh—how could Len have forgotten? Like big bubbles popping in a basement oil tank. Despite the malfunction, Len kept his rifle and its light trained on the hideous animal.

"We haven't forgotten what you did to us, Leonard Savitz," it whispered. Then it winked at him and instantly slipped below the surface, leaving nothing behind but tiny ripples in the still water.

"Are you sure you didn't dream it?" Jeff asked, still half asleep. He and a dozen other people had been awoken and were now standing around at the base of the watchtower.

"Goddammit, I didn't dream it!" Len bellowed. "The Dranthyx was right there in the water!" Len pointed to the dark lake.

Jeff kept silent, but Len could see from his face, and the faces of the others, that they doubted him. He remembered that expression from when he was a child. It was the look adults would give when he told them about monsters in the closet: halfway between sympathy and bemusement. So it was at the other end of life; seventy-some years later, people were once again doubting his faculties.

Jeff and the others shared a glance.

"Len, why don't you go get some shut-eye in your own bed?" Jeff asked in his best trying-not-to-be-patronizing tone. "We'll do the rest of the night shift."

"Why don't you people believe me?"

Jeff took a ragged breath and pulled Len aside where the others wouldn't hear. "It's not that I don't believe you," he whispered. "It's just…"

"What?" Len whispered back. "I'm old. So what? I still have all my marbles. I know what I saw."

"I know you have your marbles. You're sharp as a tack. Sharper than me. It's just…I thought you said the Dranthyx had been killed off," Jeff said in a low voice, trying to avoid eye contact.

"No!" Len growled. "How many times must I explain it? We killed off 99.7 percent of them. That was thirty-five friggin' years ago, Jeff. They've probably repopulated by now."

"More importantly," Jeff said, "you keep falling asleep on the watches. How can we know for sure you didn't dream it?"

"I didn't fall—" Len cut himself off midsentence when he remembered that he had in fact fallen asleep.

Len saw Jeff chewing his lip while studying him, as if Jeff were wondering how to defuse the situation diplomatically. Len looked past Jeff at his followers, their breaths steaming in the cold night air. *Amazing that they don't believe me*, Len thought. *As if I've ever lied to any of them.*

"I believe you," Jeff said resolutely. "You've always been a straight shooter, and I have no reason to doubt you. I guess I just doubt my own sanity at this ungodly hour."

Did I dream it? The gun didn't work. The radio didn't work. Machines never work correctly in dreams.

Jeff turned to the onlookers and spoke loudly enough for them to hear. "OK, everyone, from now on we're going to double up on the watch shifts. Two per tower at all times. Those octopus bastards are out there, apparently, and we don't want this to happen again."

Len found himself caught halfway between righteous indignation and a sudden pride in his choice of a successor. *Good old Jeff*, Len thought. *Always with the savoir-faire.*

After the crowd dispersed, Len walked behind the tower to urinate. He was just about to relieve himself when he stopped cold. There, on the concrete sidewalk, was all the ammo from his gun. The cartridges were arranged into a shape—a stick figure of an octopus. Next to that were the batteries from Len's walkie-talkie.

47

"Mr. Barton, I really appreciate your taking me out to lunch like this," Elise said in between hurried, ungraceful bites of salad.

She's brilliant but a bit awkward, Dan thought. *You'd think someone so shrewd would have more insight into how they're presenting themselves.*

"The pleasure is mine," Dan replied. "Elise, I've heard you've made some excellent trades so far. The Intercoin deal in particular was rather impressive—we made a killing on that one. You have a lot of potential."

"Thank you, sir," Elise said flatly.

"But, honestly, I think you might have too much horsepower for currency trading."

"Oh?" Elise asked, looking concerned.

"Yeah. It's brainless."

"It is?"

"I was wondering if you'd like to help me on a different matter," Dan said. "Possibly temporary, hopefully permanent. However, it's an opportunity like no other."

"Um, sure." Elise's answer was stilted with forced enthusiasm.

"I want your help on the governmental side of things," Dan said reassuringly. "At Aegis. I'd double what I'm paying you now at Barton Capital."

"Double? Wow. Aegis? But what would I do there?"

"Well, Randy's my right hand, as you know. But I need a left hand too."

"I...uh..." Elise stammered with a worried look. "Mr. Barton, I'm sorry. I don't want to seem ungrateful. It's just...I don't know much about governmental stuff. I didn't go to school for public policy. I don't want to let you down."

"Don't worry. It's brainless too." Dan laughed. "I'll give you on-the-job training. Someone as smart as you can pick it up quickly—no problem."

"I...I'd love to!" Elise said, lighting up genuinely this time. "I'm always grateful for an opportunity to learn something new. Wow. Thank you!"

"You're welcome," Dan beamed. "Welcome aboard."

Elise put her fork down and shook his hand. Abruptly, her elated expression turned serious. "Do you mind if I ask you a personal question?"

"Not at all."

"I don't mean to be rude, so please don't take it that way."

"Shoot. It takes a lot to offend me."

"Why are you so involved with Aegis?" Elise asked. "I'm surprised someone of your stature doesn't find it to be a waste of time. I can't imagine it pays as well as trading currency."

Dan nearly choked on his sushi. Once he swallowed, he gave Elise a very serious look and said, "Elise, being involved in government is never a waste of time. The reason I do currency brokerage is to make a living. That's my day job, but it isn't my true calling in life. Everyone has a passion outside of work that doesn't pay well, right? Well, mine happens to be politics."

"Fair enough. What drew you to politics?"

"I'm deeply concerned about how our communities are being run. I'm worried about the lack of safety on our streets, about people having access to education, clean water, and enough to eat. I believe I can make a difference. A big difference."

"How?" Elise asked.

"Well, for starters, I'd completely change our concept of government altogether. In school, did you study the governments of the past, before the Invasion?"

"Of course."

"So you know they were nothing like they are today. They actually worked back then."

"But they were run by Tchogols and controlled by the Dranthyx," Elise stated. "They worked, but they were designed to enslave us. Isn't that how the story goes?"

"Well, that's the simplified version, stripped of all nuance. The way the history is related to you younger folks is conspiracy-minded and ridiculous, if you ask me. It's made everyone so paranoid about government that most of the developed world decided to eschew community organization altogether. The result: those magnificent old governments shriveled up and died. Now look at the mess we have. It's sad. Everyone seems to have forgotten that government was about working together for the common good."

"Things were OK for a while," Elise remarked, her mouth full of tomatoes.

Business schools need to teach these kids some table manners.

"The Peace," she continued. "Fifteen years of honest-to-God anarchy followed the Invasion, right? Most of the world had no government at all, but people got along fine."

"Yeah, but is it peaceful now?" Dan asked. "That was a flash in the pan, and we'll never see that again. You'll never see another period of time with no Tchogols. The flu didn't change the fact that the survivors carried Tchogol genes. Following the flu, there was a huge baby boom of Tchogols. Hundreds of millions of them were born all over the globe. Fifteen years later, the oldest Tchogols were teenagers, and there was a huge uptick in petty street crime. By the time those Tchogols were twenty, their transgressions had gotten serious and violent. Right now, those Tchogols are in their midthirties, and they have the chutzpah and the organizational savvy to form rogue armies that are a direct threat to our way of life."

"Like in the hinterlands," Elise noted.

"Like everywhere," Dan said. "They're everywhere. In the cities, on the lakes, in the mountains. Like cockroaches. Anyway, as you no doubt learned in school, Xreths banded together and formed security cooperatives. In the cities, everyone on a block would take turns patrolling the street. In the suburbs, people in developments would all contribute money to hire security guards. However, there's only so much good a little ragtag neighborhood watch group can do. So, eventually, all those tiny concerns started merging together to pool their resources. They hired mercenaries, they bought armaments and aircraft, they started collecting intelligence.

"They got big, but not big enough." Dan continued. "Look around. There's still crime and chaos everywhere. Pre-Invasion governments worked because they were contiguous and omnipresent. They controlled all the land in a certain area, and if you lived there, you had to be a member of that government. Most governments aren't land-based anymore, and they no longer own their citizens. It's all voluntary and membership based." Dan sneered while waving his hand in dismissive disgust.

"What's wrong with that?" Elise asked. "People shouldn't have a choice?"

"I understand that people want a choice," Dan answered with a tinge of annoyance. "Forty years ago, you'd have to pack up your whole life and move across an ocean to change governments, but now you can change citizenship without getting up from your sofa. It's great that everyone has that freedom these days. And sure, it's nice to not have any taxes because we only pay membership fees. But look at the outcome. Most of the current governments can't protect people effectively because they have no real territory. Aegis is huge in the Great Lakes region, but we can't do a whole lot to serve our members in the Rockies because most people out there are SDI members. SDI doesn't do reciprocal memberships and won't cooperate with us half the time. This whole thing is an absolute train wreck."

"If I'm not mistaken, Metteyya is a land-based government," Elise said.

"If they can defend their territory, more power to 'em. I wish Aegis would take the same direction."

Octavia came out onto the house's huge wraparound porch wearing a hoodie and holding a cup of hot tea. She put the cup down on a table and sat down in the rocking chair next to her father's. Having not seen her in a while, Len was struck by how much she looked like her late mother: tall and Scandinavian-looking. He smiled at his daughter, and they sat in silence while looking at the vivid purple clouds.

"Kids asleep?" Len asked.

"I think so." Octavia paused as a formation of young men and women marched past the house. "You have a damn army out here, Dad. How many students do you have now?"

"One hundred and three, not counting Natalia and me."

"That laser tower wasn't here last time," his daughter remarked. "The watchtowers, either."

"A lot has changed," Len said. "When was the last time you were here?"

"You don't remember?"

"My memory isn't what it used to be." Len frowned.

"Three years ago."

"Three years! Geez, kid, you ought to visit your old man a little more often!"

"I wish I could, Dad. But you guys live so far away, and it's tough to travel with kids and a job. I have plenty of time now, though. I may stay awhile."

What does that mean? Never mind; I won't pry. Maybe she had a fight with that so-called husband of hers. I never liked that guy.

"It's good to have you back," Len said.

"It's good to be back. I missed you guys. Hey, where's Natalia?"

"Off on one of her business trips. She'll be back in two days."

Len took a sip of Applewood and lit a cigarette. Exhaling, he made a choking sound, which triggered a coughing fit.

"Dad, I'm worried about your health. That cough sounds awful," Octavia said.

"It's just a cold." Len choked on the words while trying to catch his breath.

"Someone told me you've had it for months."

Len stared out onto the lake without saying anything.

"You said Natalia looks great now."

"She always looked great," Len said quietly.

"You know what I mean."

Len inhaled deeply. "I'm not doing it."

"Dad, I don't want to lose you. I've already lost one parent."

"Is that all? I've lost two."

Octavia frowned.

"I'm sorry," Len said, closing his eyes and rubbing his temples. "I don't know where that came from. Look, I know you want what's best for me. I love you too. But death is part of life. We're all headed there. I'm not sure why everyone is so damn scared of something so inevitable."

"It doesn't have to be that way anymore. Natalia could live another hundred years. You could too."

"Another hundred years?" Len scoffed. "What the hell would I do with all that time? Hell, I'm only seventy-seven, and I'm already bored of everything. I've been everywhere; I've seen and done everything. After a certain point, everything repeats. I meet the same people over and over again. There are only so many different types of personalities, you know. And every place I go reminds me of somewhere else."

"Have you ever seen Mount Everest?"

The corner of Len's mouth turned down in annoyance.

"Have you ever been to Mars?" Octavia asked.

"Of course not. No one has," Len said.

"You could," Octavia said, "if you lived long enough. You could meet your great-great-grandchildren. You'd have the time to master a hundred different skills. You could become a concert pianist one decade, a chess master the next. You could do anything, Dad."

A gentle breeze blew over them. Len stubbed out his cigarette. "I just…I just don't think life would even have any meaning if it weren't for death."

"That makes no sense."

"Light is the opposite of dark," Len said, "but one gives the other meaning. Contrast makes the image, you see. Good defines bad. Slow is the reason we have fast."

Octavia gave him a miffed glance.

"Octavia, seriously, what would life be like without mortality hanging over our heads?" Len asked. "How can there be any greatness without the time pressure of getting things done before we expire? Mozart died at age thirty-four. He probably had a sense that he wouldn't live very long, which is why he was so prolific. Had he known he'd live to a thousand years, do you think he'd have bothered with any of that?"

"Dad, no offense, but you're no Mozart."

Len laughed wheezily. "Well, OK. Bad example. I guess the point is, if we have all the time in the world, then time becomes worthless, and we'll squander it. You already see it happening. Life-spans have increased so dramatically that everyone puts off adulthood. No one gets married, no one has children, no one sticks with a career. Now we've got a world full of forty-year-olds who act like teenagers. Do you know what my grandfather had lived through by age forty?"

"You sound like you should be telling kids to get off your lawn. Honestly, I think a second youth might do you some good."

"And what the hell? I still don't even understand how it works. Natalia looks like she's twenty-five, but it's not plastic surgery? I mean, she even eats like she's twenty-five, but she doesn't get fat. I don't get it."

"They inject you with a virus that changes your genome."

"Oh," Len said. "Sounds perfectly safe. What could possibly go wrong?"

"They've been doing it for years already," Octavia said. "It works. I've had it done myself. You know I'm forty, right?"

"Yeah, I know. I was there when you were born."

"Do I look forty to you?" Octavia asked.

"No. So explain it."

"It caps your telomeres at a certain length. You can pick which age you want to be for the rest of your life. Between twenty-five and thirty is the optimal age, apparently, but they can do any age. As the seventy-seven-year-old cells in your body die naturally, they are replaced with new ones that think and act like they're twenty-seven, or whatever age you pick. After a few years, enough of the old cells will have turned over that your body will actually be that of a younger person. Then you just stay that way. All new cells from then on out will be young."

"But your parts still wear out, right?"

"Well, yeah," Octavia said. "It doesn't solve every problem of aging. Your joints will degrade from use, your arteries will still harden, your teeth will wear out. But if you keep up with it and keep fixing those things—"

"There's an old Zen koan—" Len said.

"Oh boy, here we go." Octavia sighed.

"A lowly street sweeper is pushing his broom down the street in old Japan. Some condescending jerk says to him, 'My, that's a lovely broom!' You know what the street sweeper says back to him? 'Thanks! This wonderful broom has served me faithfully for fifteen years. I've only replaced the head thirty-four times and the handle seventeen times!'"

His daughter gave him a tired-of-your-shit look.

"And let's be frank here," Len said. "You're simplifying things quite a bit. Maybe you just had an injection, but Natalia's procedure was way beyond that."

"Dad, I was still young when mine was done. Natalia's situation was different. Her body was decrepit."

"I couldn't even bring myself to visit her…" Len searched for the words, then shuddered. "In that state."

"But it worked, didn't it? I mean, she's healthy now."

Len reached over and put his hand on hers. "Octavia, look…it's been a while since you've seen me."

Octavia nodded while looking down at the wooden boards of the porch floor. The paint was peeling.

"I remember the first time I realized, with horror, that my mother was old. I saw her gray hair and wrinkles and realized that her vitality was slipping away. Losing what we love terrifies us all. I know you want to help me. But you need to understand something: nothing is permanent. Even if I do this antiaging thing, I could be killed in a car accident the next day. I could be murdered by those assholes trying to take our island. That's life. Mortality is a scary goddamn thing."

Octavia's eyes got red as she looked up at the horizon. "I wish you would at least give it a shot."

"You look at me and see an old man, don't you? But what you're really looking at is only fifteen years old."

"Huh?" She squinted at him with wet eyes.

"Cells are turning over constantly, right? Like you said. With the exception of brain cells, I doubt any of the cells in this body are more than fifteen years old. Therefore, I am fifteen years old. This body is constantly coming and going. I eat it in, I defecate it out. Bits of it are constantly coming to life and dying. Changing. People think of themselves as some sort of solid, immutable object, but that's false—"

"I don't want to do the philosophy thing with you—"

"But imagine what life would be like if a movie were just one still frame for two hours. Is that really a movie? The best people grow and change over a lifetime. It's part of the human experience. How do we grow if we stop the clock—"

"Dad!" Octavia said, wiping her tears away. "I don't want you to die!"

Len gave her a look that only a father could bake up: a casserole of pity, love, admiration, and disdain. *How can a nurse*, he thought, *someone who deals with life and death every day, not accept the reality of it?*

"Octavia, I'll think about it." He lit another cigarette.

"Really?"

"Yeah."

They were quiet for a long time as the sky turned a velvety blue color and the waves lapped the beach. After a while, Len checked his watch. "Any second now."

"Are you waiting for something?" Octavia asked.

Len pointed with his cigarette. On a neighboring island, five miles to the west, a tremendous light came from behind what looked like a hill, as if the sun were unsetting itself. Huge plumes of white smoke rose to the sky. Then came the noise—like continuous rolling thunder that was directly overhead.

"What the hell is going on over there?" Octavia asked over the din.

The powerful fireball rose into the sky. Len laughed as Octavia watched with her eyes wide, transfixed. It reminded him of when she was a young child and she'd see something unusual for the first time; her reactions hadn't changed. The rocket rose into the twilight, slowly at first, but accelerating. It passed over the house within a few seconds. Octavia leaped from her seat and ran down the steps to the yard to get a better view of the object moving across the sky. After a minute or two, the spacecraft was beyond the horizon and no longer visible. She looked up at Len with her mouth agape.

He laughed again. "That's Metteyya's headquarters," Len said. "They launch rockets every thirty-six hours, rain or shine, at either 8:00 a.m. or 8:00 p.m."

"What?" Octavia asked, walking back up the steps to the porch. "Why? What on earth are they doing?"

"No one knows. Well, I shouldn't say that. Natalia knows. She built that place for them. But she won't tell anyone what they're doing. Not me, not anyone. They made her sign some sort of nondisclosure contract. All I know is, they've launched hundreds of rockets so far. They must have put a ton of stuff into orbit."

49

"This used to be such a peaceful place to live," Len said while peering through the binoculars. "Hardly any visitors. These days it's like the Cleveland Bazaar."

Len adjusted the diopter to get a better look. A withered old man in a rowboat was braving the swells as he rowed toward Seavey Island. His bald head reflected the sunlight as he worked the oars. There was something hypnotic about the way he put his paddles in the water, patiently, sturdily, rhythmically working with the waves instead of fighting them the way most people would.

"Get a load of this lunatic," Len said, handing the binoculars to one of his students.

Overcome with curiosity, he hobbled down to the shoreline to see who was coming to bother him.

As the rowboat approached the rocky beach, Len saw the man more clearly. He was Asian, about the same age as Len. His gaunt face was covered in gray stubble, and he wore the traditional black robes of a Japanese monk. He was somehow familiar.

Len weighed for a second whether it was a trap or if the man might be dangerous. His gut told him otherwise, so he rolled up his pant legs and waded out into the lake to meet him.

"Hello," Len said, grabbing the man's boat to hold it steady so the man could step out into the shallow water.

"Are you Leonard Savitz?" the man asked.

"Who's asking?"

"My name is Mutoku. We met once, years ago."

Len, despite having difficulty recalling names and faces in recent years, remembered him instantly.

"I know you!" Len laughed.

Mutoku bowed.

Len bowed in return, then embraced the old monk.

After Mutoku and Len had dragged the dinghy ashore, Mutoku pulled his backpack out of the boat.

"So what brings you to my humble island?" Len asked. His mind flashed back to the SWAT team attacking Mutoku's temple all those years ago. The memory was sharp and indelible. "Actually, never mind. What I really want to know first is, how did you survive that day in Tokyo?"

Mutoku smiled. "The Great Master took me and my fellow monks into his ship below the temple."

"OK, but what happened then? I saw the ship fly into the air and disappear."

"We traveled to Ich-Ca. I spent a year there."

"You spent a year on another planet?"

"Yes, sir." Mutoku smiled.

Several hours later, Len stared at Mutoku in perplexity as he poured him some tea. "So what happened after that?"

"They returned me to Earth," Mutoku said while rocking back on his chair on the porch of Len's house. "I lived in India for a while, which is where I first met your neighbors."

"Neighbors?"

Mutoku gestured in the general direction of Metteyya's island.

"You know them?"

"Yes, but I knew their father better," Mutoku said.

"Who the hell are they?"

"Very, very powerful individuals."

"What is it that they're doing over there?"

"Never mind them." Mutoku laughed. "What is it that you're doing here? I'm quite curious."

"Oh hell, I have no idea. You want the short version or the long version?"

"I have time," Mutoku said.

"Well, my wife and I bought this island from a bunch of squatters after the Invasion. Before that, it was a historical monument. A century before that, it was a working lighthouse station." Len pointed to the lighthouse, then behind him at the house. "This house I live in was the lightkeeper's."

"Victorian, right? That's the name of the architecture?"

"You know your stuff. Anyway, we moved out here about thirty years ago. For a while, no one knew we were here, and it was just the three of us: my wife, my daughter, and me. But then, word got out that I lived here, and people started coming to the island to find me."

"Are you an important person?" Mutoku asked.

"I don't think so." Len laughed. "I'm just some schmo from Pittsburgh. But I wrote a famous piece of journalism about the Dranthyx, their financial scheme, Neith, the Ich-Ca-Gan, and all the other insane things that were going on back in those days. It was like a piece of science fiction that came true. So a lot of confused people imagined me to be a prophet or something."

"And you aren't?" Mutoku asked.

Len gave him an over-the-bifocals glare. "Anyway, people started kayaking out here, expecting me to be some kind of guru. I felt bad for them, because I know what it's like to be a misguided spiritual seeker. A lot of them were downright penniless, so I told them they could stay here if they helped me do some work around this place. With their help," Len said, pointing to various features visible from the porch, "we planted those orchards and the vegetable gardens, put the docks in. We built the dormitories…"

"And the meditation hall?" Mutoku asked coyly.

"Yes," Len replied.

Mutoku rocked back on his chair. "You know, I've always found the western concept of time interesting. Westerners seem to think of time as linear, going from point A to point B. Or like a rising graph indicating progress. Progress—always progress. Westerners are obsessed with the idea of measuring improvements over time."

"Is that wrong?" Len asked.

"In the East," Mutoku said, "we think of time as a loop, a cycle. History repeats itself. Everything old is new again.

Things are created, things are destroyed, then they're created again, and so forth."

Len stared at him quizzically.

"I remember our conversation when we first met. You seemed to think that Zen was"—Mutoku pretended he couldn't remember the word—"bullshit?"

"It is," Len said. "Religion is bullshit. But meditation is not. Mindfulness is not."

"And you thought that we Zen teachers were…con artists."

"You are," Len said.

"Then how is it that you're here teaching Zen? You have students and a meditation hall. Are you not a Zen teacher? Are you not also a con artist?"

"The difference is, Mutoku, I never wanted to do this. They came to me."

"Ah, of course," Mutoku said with a smirk.

"And, when they came to me, they came with their minds jumbled. They were miserable and needed help. So I showed them how to meditate and how to be mindful. I just taught them what I knew."

"You are most noble," Mutoku said, bowing sarcastically.

Len, irritated, continued. "I never asked them for money. To the contrary, I gave them free room and board because I felt bad for them. I never promised them anything absurd like spiritual attainment. I dispensed with all the ceremony: no robes, no bells, no chanting, no mythology. I cut the fat off Zen Buddhism and made it useful. I made it clear from the get-go that my approval gains them nothing, there's no enlightenment, and that we only meditate to know ourselves and see things more clearly. There's no power hierarchy here, and therefore no politics. I call them my students, but really I just show them how to teach themselves."

Mutoku laughed long and hard.

"I'm glad this is so amusing," Len fumed.

"Oh, it is. Your hypocrisy is wonderful! Very Zen-like." Mutoku laughed again.

"Thanks," Len grumbled.

"But I also have to laugh because the similarities are so striking," Mutoku said. "A case of convergent evolution, perhaps."

"Similarities to what? I don't understand."

"You'll understand soon enough," Mutoku murmured while staring out at the water. "But I'm heartened to see your progress along the path, Leonard. I can tell from talking with you that your understanding is almost full."

"Mutoku," Len whispered, shaking the old man's shoulder.

Mutoku arose from his sleep in Len's guest bedroom, bleary eyed and confused. "Huh? What? Why are you dressed like that?" Mutoku asked, referring to Len's flight suit and helmet.

"We're going on an adventure. Get dressed and meet me in front of the house. Quickly."

A few minutes later, the old monk limped out into the front yard in the dewy, predawn darkness. Len handed him a helmet like his own.

"What are we doing?" Mutoku asked.

"Pest control," Len said, opening the door to his pickup truck. "Get in."

Len drove Mutoku to the other side of the island, where Jeff and Natalia were waiting for them. Natalia was in the cockpit of an old Russian attack helicopter, which she'd purchased a few years prior for island defense. The rotor was already spinning, and the downdraft nearly caused Mutoku's robes to blow apart as he got out of Len's truck. Len could see Natalia in the dim red light flicking switches and checking items off on a clipboard.

"What's going on?" Mutoku yelled over the chopping roar.

"You're about to take a ride on the Seavey Island Air Force," Jeff answered jovially.

Len was unable to climb up unassisted, so Jeff helped him up onto the aircraft and into the rear cockpit. Jeff indicated that Mutoku should take the seat next to Len's. Mutoku, being a bit more agile than Len, was able to climb aboard without too much help.

Len checked the weapons systems. His handwritten English notes, scrawled on Post-its and pieces of tape, littered the instrumentation and covered the original Russian labels. Between his notations and the fact that Natalia had gone over it with him a hundred times already, he almost knew what he was doing.

"I'm ready," Len announced into his headset.

"Let's do this," Natalia said. She pulled the throttle out gently, and the helicopter lifted into the air.

Len looked over at Mutoku, whose eyes were wide with astonishment.

"I didn't expect this when I went to sleep last night!" Mutoku laughed. "I have never flown in a helicopter before."

"It's probably less exciting than a starship." Len chuckled.

The helicopter made a long, swooping turn around their island—a dark mass blending into a black body of water—before heading out across the open lake.

Within minutes, they were hovering off the shore of the old Headlands Beach Park.

"Ready when you are," Natalia said over the intercom.

Despite feeling Mutoku watching him, Len manned the weapons system with a surgeon's focus. He quickly counted three antiaircraft guns using the helicopter's night vision, registering each one as a target in the computer.

"You sure they can't see us?" Len asked.

"Positive," Natalia said over the intercom. "I went out of my way to buy a bird with radar-absorbing paint."

"Ready," Len said, flicking a switch and hitting buttons. From the sides of the aircraft, powerful missiles rocketed forward, illuminating the inside of the cockpit with a bright white light.

Without waiting for the missiles to find their destination, Natalia aggressively piloted the machine forward toward the pirate outpost.

Mutoku gasped upon seeing the resulting explosions on the ground. "What are we doing? This is violence! I thought you were a Buddhist!"

"So let me tell you about Buddhism," Len said as he grabbed the controller for the autocannon. "I once lived in a Japanese temple in Kyoto," he said while focusing his attention on the screen, which displayed images from the infrared cameras. White, ghostly figures ran helter-skelter against a black background. "The temple got infested with termites one time. Big mess. You know what those temples look like. Beautiful, hand-carved wood beams with ornate, complex joinery. Works of art. The bugs destroyed it. That masterpiece of woodwork became marred with frass and bore holes. The head monks let it go for too long, and we all became worried the building might collapse if the bugs kept eating away at it." On the screen, Len followed a bunch of the phantasms to a building, which he selected as a target. A red ring appeared on the building. "So, eventually, the head monks had to do something before the building was destroyed. Do you know what they did?"

"What?" Mutoku asked over the intercom while looking out the window. He seemed quite troubled by the hellish, burning chaos he was seeing below.

"They hired an extermination company," Len said while waiting for the building he'd targeted to fill up with people. "The exterminators made us all leave for several days while they put a big plastic tent over the whole building. Once it was sealed up, they filled the entire temple with poison gas to kill the termites."

When Len pressed the button, the cabin filled with a loud pounding noise as the huge rotating guns mounted below the aircraft poured hundreds of shells into the building where the pirates were taking refuge. The recoil of the autocannons pushed the helicopter backward in the air. Looking out the window, Len could see the entire structure reduced to flaming rubble. Satisfied that the target had been eliminated, he then followed some more ghost-people to another structure, which looked like a mobile home, and selected that one as a target as well.

"How many termites do you think they killed, Mutoku?" Len asked, without taking his eyes off his work.

Mutoku was too distraught to answer.

"Tens of thousands, probably," Len said as he pulled the trigger on the joystick again. Seconds later, the mobile home was a crater. "Being monks, they'd all taken a vow to never kill any living thing. In fact, that's the first vow a monk takes—not to kill. But, by calling the exterminators, they killed tens of thousands of living creatures. They broke their precepts to save the temple."

As some of the pirates tried to flee by water, Len focused his attention on their boats. He strafed the watercraft with long barrages of automatic fire, ripping the hulls apart. They hovered there just long enough to see what was left of the boats sinking.

"Let's see them attack our island now," Len said.

"This is barbaric!" Mutoku cried.

"*Life* is barbaric," Natalia interjected over her headset before swinging the helicopter around and heading back to the island.

50

While the kids slept in, Octavia sat on the porch, enjoying the view. The trees were budding, and the air was getting warmer. She heard men talking in loud voices on the other side of the house. Walking around the house to see what the commotion was, she saw workers in orange vests and construction hats moving a crane arm into position next to the lighthouse. From the crane swung a spherical black object, about the size of a small European car. It was imprinted with white Cyrillic stenciling. The boom of the crane was marked Zherdeva Heavy Industries. Octavia walked down to the construction site, curious to see what was going on.

"Don't swing it like that," a familiar voice yelled over the noise of the crane. "If it slams into the lighthouse, we're gonna have real problems."

"Natalia!" Octavia called.

Natalia turned with a start and, in so doing, also startled Octavia.

"My God!" Octavia exclaimed.

Octavia walked up to Natalia and touched her face.

"Natalia, this is incredible!"

"I guess you haven't seen me since I had the work done."

Jowls, wrinkles, and gray hair gone, Natalia's skin was now smooth and her hair black. She radiated youth and energy. Octavia couldn't stop staring.

Natalia waved her hand in front of Octavia's face.

"Sorry." Octavia laughed. "It's been too long!"

They embraced for a time and then pulled back to look at each other again.

"When did you get in?" Octavia asked.

"Last night while you were sleeping. Even took the helicopter out for a spin before you woke up. I'm surprised you didn't hear it."

"Your English is getting really good," Octavia said. "I can't even hear an accent. You're starting to sound like a native."

"I've been taking classes. I've had a lot more time on my hands lately."

Octavia glanced up and saw that the glass lantern room at the top of the lighthouse had been completely disassembled. The gigantic Fresnel lens that had sat at the top of the tower for a century or so was now sitting on the grass below like a huge discarded crystal Easter egg. The crane operators lowered the black sphere into the place formerly occupied by the tower's vintage lamp.

"You're fixing the lighthouse?" Octavia asked. "That's wonderful! It's nice to see a piece of history like this being maintained. It's been broken since you and Dad bought the place. I've never seen it lit up."

"Oh, this'll light the place up, all right," Natalia said. "Are the kids here? I'd love to see them."

"You'll see them plenty. We're going to be here for a while."

"Is everything OK?" Natalia asked.

"Not really," Octavia said. "Wanna go into town with me? I'll tell you about it over lunch. We have a lot of catching up to do anyway."

"I'd love to, just as soon as I'm finished here."

The Bazaar, they called it. The name was a joke, but it stuck. The Cleveland Bazaar had started as an informal gathering of merchants in Market Square Park in the days of chaos after the Invasion. The city was in ruins then: the railroads and highways had been destroyed. There was no gasoline, Internet, or reliable currency. People had to meet in person to trade goods to survive. It started small but quickly became enormous and chaotic. As a kid, Octavia used to love it there. The street performers, the noise, the energy, the masses of people meandering through. Thousands of merchants shouting and competing for attention. Anything that could possibly be sold was for sale at the Bazaar; there were stalls with organic vegetables, electronics, hard drugs, clothes, weapons, animals. Someone had even set up a makeshift car dealership at one end. From Mennonite farmers to people fresh off the boat, Octavia found it fascinating to see so many different walks of life interacting.

Years later, she still marveled at its frenetic spirit. Long after civilization had been rebuilt, the Bazaar continued on as an institution with its own gravity. Like city living itself, the Bazaar was no longer a necessity, yet it had developed a huge critical mass that defined its own relevance. And it was still as crazy as ever.

Octavia saw Natalia do a double take as she walked by the stand of a small-arms merchant. "May I see that one?" she asked the dealer over the din, pointing to a large, old-fashioned-looking handgun.

The arms dealer, an obese man with excessively hairy forearms, got up from his stool and waddled over. "This one?" he asked while pointing incredulously, as if to suggest the gun was unsuited for Natalia's needs. She nodded. The man reluctantly handed it to her.

Natalia pushed the release, swung the cylinder out, and turned it in her hands. She held the gun sideways and gave it some hard stares, then lifted it up to the sky and looked down its barrel. Octavia wondered how Natalia could possibly need another gun. "How much?" Natalia asked.

"Are you sure? That's a lot of gun for someone, uh, your size. Wouldn't you rather have something a little more controllable?" he asked, motioning to a bunch of miniature guns with pink grips and bedazzled parts.

"You want to sell me something or not?" Natalia asked testily. "How much?"

"A thousand LCs."

"Hah! For this old thing? No way. I'll give you four hundred."

"Four! Come on, lady, you're wasting my time."

"That's my best offer," Natalia said.

"No can do," the hairy-armed gun dealer said. He brusquely took the gun out of her hands and put it back on the shelf. "I have bills to pay."

Natalia shrugged and began walking away from the man's stand. Before she'd even gotten ten feet away, the dealer called out to her. "Hey, can you do five?"

Octavia glanced at her stepmom. Natalia smiled, then turned around to face the hirsute arms merchant.

"Four and a half," Natalia stated resolutely.

The man sighed and thought about it for a few seconds. "Fine," he said, looking defeated. He rang Natalia up and put the gun in a bag for her.

"What's the big deal about that old gun?" Octavia asked as they were walking away. "It looks like something from a film noir movie."

"I collect these. This is a rare piece. He didn't know what he had!" Natalia said, almost giddily. "Hey, look," she said, pointing through the crowd to a spot across the street.

"What am I looking for?"

"'Hash Barn. Amsterdam-Style Coffeehouse,'" Natalia said, reading the sign on an old storefront. "Sounds good. Let's get fucked up."

"Are you serious?"

"Yeah. Why not? I'm too old to spend life sober. So are you, now that I think about it. Let's have a good time."

Octavia laughed. "All right, sure. What the hell. Let's do it. I've missed you, Natalia."

"I've missed you too." Natalia smiled.

They walked through a doorway festooned with hanging hippie beads and took a seat at one of the tables. A waiter came over to the table with menus.

"It always makes me laugh to see drugs on a menu," Natalia said. "We'll take two joints."

"What kind, ma'am?" the waiter asked. "We offer thirty-four different cultivars—"

"Surprise me," Natalia said.

She paused until the waiter had left. "So what brings you to Cleveland?"

"I need help," Octavia said sheepishly. "I've been embargoed."

"Embargoed? What does that mean?"

"NAFOG members are prevented from doing business with me. That means I can't earn a living, I can't buy things with electronic money, I can't pay rent, my bank accounts are locked."

"NAFOG?"

"North American Federation of Governments."

"I don't understand. Why can't you just buy things?"

"Because no one can take my money except unaffiliateds. I can't use banks or credit cards. Here, watch this." Octavia motioned to the waiter, who came to the table. "I want to pay."

"Already?" he asked. The waiter took her card and ran it through the reader. A look of concern crossed his face. "I'm sorry, ma'am, but it appears you're embargoed."

"Who cares?" Natalia asked. "What's the big deal?"

"If I serve you," the waiter said nervously, "I'll lose my government membership, and I'll be embargoed too. Look, you two can't stay here. I'll get in big trouble. I've got kids to feed; I can't afford to be unaffiliated."

"We'll pay in cash," Natalia said, handing the waiter a large LC note. "We were never here."

The waiter's eyes nearly popped out of his head. "Yes, ma'am. I saw nothing. Can I get you ladies anything else?"

"Two bourbons, neat." Natalia said. She looked quizzically at Octavia as the waiter shuffled off. "How did this happen?"

"After leaving the island, I joined Aegis. Some official told me I didn't need to register Iris because the Tchogol Accord hadn't been ratified when she was born. He told me she was grandfathered in. Turns out, she wasn't. The Tchogol Accord is what they call an ex post facto agreement. A few years later, she got busted for shoplifting, and they took a DNA sample from her as part of the booking process. Because I hadn't registered her, I got charged with concealing a Tchogol. Now I'm embargoed."

"So? What do you need a government for? I haven't been a citizen of anything for thirty-five years, and I'm fine."

"Yes," Octavia said, "but you're also independently wealthy, and you live on a fortified island. The rest of the world needs order and security."

"Order and security." Natalia laughed. "Let me know when you find that anywhere. They're selling you snake oil. You don't need to beg anyone's permission to live. Come live on the island with us."

"Don't you feel isolated out there?" Octavia asked. "When I was younger, I couldn't wait to leave that place, to explore the world."

"Island fever?" Natalia asked. "Yeah, sometimes. The real problem is the pirates. We're under constant attack."

"It's worse here on the mainland."

The waiter came back with their drinks and weed. Natalia picked up one of the spliffs and lit it, sucking in deeply. Octavia tried to do the same but coughed so hard she nearly barfed. "Too much for me," she said, gagging.

"So now what? How do you get...unembargoed?" Natalia asked. "Can't you just register Iris?"

"I could. But I'm not going to. It's the principle of the thing. I think what I'm going to do is fight it in the courts."

"Courts? What courts?"

"The intergovernmental courts. I'm going to try to challenge the Tchogol Accord as a human rights violation."

Natalia squinted at her, as if wondering whether Octavia was playing with a full deck. "I'd ask what you're smoking, but I already know. DNA samples? Registration? Courts?" Natalia scowled. "I don't know why you're messing around with this government nonsense in the first place. They're all liars and gangsters. Look what happens. None of this is necessary. You're making your life too complicated for nothing."

"I'm doing it because it's the right thing to do. For decades, Tchogols have been treated like animals. Forced to be registered, tattooed against their will, kept out of gainful employment, shunned from society," Octavia said, her face getting red. "They live outside under bridges; they have to steal food. We treat vermin better. I don't want Iris to have to grow up like that!"

"This is a real court case? With lawyers?"

"Yeah. A landmark court case," Octavia said, squinting while attempting to inhale another acrid puff. "With real lawyers and everything. No one has done this before. It's been in the news. We'll be going to trial soon."

"What happens if you win?"

"The Tchogol Accord will be struck down for not complying with the Human Rights Decree."

Natalia took another toke and then stared at Octavia in silent concern for a solid thirty seconds. "Octavia," she said, exhaling smoke while talking, "you are too young to remember what the world was like when Tchogols ran it. I understand the concern you feel about your daughter. She's my family too. But you may be opening up...what's the expression?"

"A can of worms?"

"No. Pandora's box. There's a reason Tchogols are registered. There's a reason they aren't allowed to hold power. You don't remember the endless wars, the prison camps, the debt slavery—"

"Do you really feel that way about Iris?" Octavia asked. "Do you think she's evil?"

"Why are you doing this, Octavia?"

"Because it's the right thing to do."

"No, why are you really doing this? You know damn well you could live on the island and never have to worry about Iris or embargoes or anything else."

Octavia stared at the table for a while before answering. "Because I've never done anything great. For once in my life, I want to make a difference."

"What do you mean?" Natalia asked.

"I've always admired you, Natalia. You're so successful in everything you do. And look at my dad. He won a Pulitzer, and then he saved the world. You guys make it look easy. What the hell have I ever done? Nothing. I haven't amounted to shit." Octavia seethed. "What are my kids gonna think? I couldn't even keep my marriage together."

Natalia picked Octavia's hand up off the table and held it. "You feel worthless?"

"Yes," Octavia said.

"Darling, that is wonderful!"

Octavia pulled her hand away. "Come on. That isn't funny. I'm pouring my heart out here."

"I'm not being funny," Natalia said earnestly. "That feeling is a gift, and don't you forget it."

"What?"

"You know why I'm so successful?" Natalia asked. Octavia shook her head. "Because I'm propelled forward by that very same feeling of worthlessness. Self-loathing is the secret to any great success. It's been there my whole life. It goes back to when I was a little girl. I always wanted to impress my father, to show him I was as capable as my brothers. My whole personality crystallized around that..." She searched for the word. "Insecurity."

"Really? You?"

"Yeah. What do you think? That I don't have doubts about myself? What you feel right now I have felt a hundred thousand times. I still feel it. The feeling of worthlessness is what separates great people from average people."

"How do you figure?"

"You know who doesn't doubt themselves?" Natalia asked, and then, without waiting, she answered. "Losers. Morons. Assholes. They walk around thinking they're the best, or that they know everything, or that they have no room for improvement. Great people don't do that. Great people are always trying to better themselves because they know they're not perfect—that's why they're great."

Octavia sat back as if struck by lightning.

"But, that feeling," Natalia said, "I still feel it. Every day. I used to resent it. Now I cherish it."

"But what do you have to feel worthless about?"

Natalia pulled out the handgun she'd just purchased and waved in the air like a drunken bandido. Octavia looked around uncomfortably to make sure no one else saw it. "You ever look at handguns these days? They're made of polymer and inexpensive parts, and the pieces are assembled by robots. They leave the factory without a human ever inspecting or testing them. There's zero quality control, so they don't work well. They misfeed, fail to eject, jam, misfire. They're picky about ammunition. Guns these days are worthless. But everyone thinks they're great because they're cheap, hold lots of ammo, and can be reloaded quickly. If a gun doesn't work, so what? Throw it out and buy another one." Natalia grunted in disdain.

"That one is different?" Octavia asked.

"This is from another time. A thing of beauty. This was not made by computerized milling machines or with metal-injected molding. No, this is a work of art produced purely by hand," Natalia said, getting louder as she went on. "No one makes these anymore. And this one is a rare beast. This was handmade in Germany from the hardest steels possible. A master craftsman hand fit all the parts together; it probably took him five hundred hours." She swung the cylinder open for Octavia to see. "You know what's great about revolvers? They were the most reliable handguns ever made. They just work—each time, every time. When you pull the trigger on a revolver, it goes bang. And if it doesn't—maybe you have bad ammo—you just pull the trigger again. Try doing that with today's guns—forget it. This came from an era when crafts-manship and reliability mattered and cost didn't." Natalia's hands were shaking by the time she'd finished speaking. She picked up her glass of bourbon and knocked the whole thing back in one monstrous gulp.

"Are you all right, Natalia?"

"No." She exhaled. "No, I'm not. I'm being priced out of the business by automated construction companies. I've managed projects as big as airports and skyscrapers, and I only hire expert craftsmen. Zherdeva Heavy Industries can build anything, on time and under budget. But none of that matters. No one wants stuff built by people anymore. Not when you can print a piece-of-shit building overnight with robots."

"I'm sorry."

"I'm thinking of selling the business. I've seen the writing on the wall. There's no future in construction."

"What will you do?"

"I don't know. I'm tired of reinventing myself, to tell you the truth. First the military, then arms dealing, then construction." She paused pensively for a long time while Octavia looked at her sympathetically. Suddenly, Natalia's mood seemed to change entirely. She started giggling. "Wow, I'm really stoned right now."

"Natalia, you're worth billions. Literally and figuratively. Do you even need to work anymore?"

"Work is essential. Work is life. Happiness is tied to production, don't you think?"

"I guess so. I never really thought about it."

"I don't know what your generation, and your kids' generation, is going to do in the future. Everything will be automatic. Work will be worthless. Everyone will have free food and electricity but no sense of accomplishment. No adversities, no pride, no grit. Without producing something you can be proud of, being human will be meaningless."

51

Elise burst into Dan's office, red-faced from running. She was barefoot and carrying her pumps in her hand.

Dan, wearing his reading glasses, looked up from his spreadsheets in exasperation. "Doesn't anyone knock anymore?"

Elise doubled over to breathe. "Sorry...Mr. Barton... important news...very important."

Dan took his glasses off, put his computer aside, and motioned for her to have a seat in front of his desk.

"Travis Davidson was murdered this morning," Elise said, recovering her wind.

"*The* Travis Davidson, our Aegis principal?" Dan asked.

Elise nodded gravely while panting.

"My God," Dan said, leaning back in his chair. "How did it happen?"

"Armed robbery, apparently. He was on his way to meet some friends for breakfast at a restaurant in downtown Buffalo. He got out of his car and was mugged in broad daylight. Stabbed five times."

"What the hell?" Dan said.

"I know, right?"

"Unreal. Did anyone catch the killer?"

"Yeah. Amazingly, Aegis security caught him. They actually did something for once."

"The world we live in, Elise, I tell you what," Dan said, shaking his head.

For a while, they both sat there in silence, contemplating the turn of events.

"And the mugger forgot to take Travis's wallet," Elise said.

Dan looked up at her.

"Maybe it wasn't intended to be a mugging." Elise said ruefully.

"Christ, I don't even want to think about that," Dan lamented.

"Who will replace him?" Elise asked.

"Per the bylaws, it has to be put to a vote by the members."

"So you could run for the office?"

Dan's eyebrows lifted.

"You've been talking about how you think you could do a better job than Davidson," Elise said. "This might be the opportunity to actually make it happen."

Dan sat there in silence, brow furrowed.

"You're politically connected," Elise said. "You have the means. And, best of all, you're chairman of the board of directors. The board makes the endorsements for principal, right? You could practically write your own ticket."

Dan sat down at the end of a huge mahogany conference table and surveyed the wood-paneled chamber. Men and women in business suits milled around the ornate Aegis boardroom and chatted loudly.

"Ladies and gentlemen," Dan announced into the microphone before banging a gavel, "I now call to order an emergency meeting of the Aegis board of directors. Please be seated."

In the space above the table were holographic teleconference links for board members in Vancouver, Miami, and other far-flung places.

"I think you folks know why we're here," Dan said solemnly. "Yesterday, our principal, Travis Davidson, was murdered. This is a tragic, unfortunate turn of events. Naturally, our thoughts and prayers are with his family. If it's all right with my fellow board members, I'd like to have a moment of silence before taking up the business of this meeting."

Dan looked around the room and, seeing others nodding in agreement, bowed his head. Others around the room, seemingly unsure of the protocol but not wanting to be disrespectful, did the same.

"Thank you," Dan said after an appropriate amount of time had passed. "Folks, this is the first time this has happened in the entire history of Aegis. We've never lost a serving principal before. It is my understanding that the assailant has been apprehended and is currently in Aegis custody. The good news is, he happens to be an Aegis citizen, which means no extradition is necessary and justice will be served."

There were murmurs of approval at this news.

"We're here," Dan continued, "because we need to do something about this. Many are still feeling the loss, and I fear that some may see immediate action on our part as insensitive. However, if left unaddressed, the breach in continuity of command could cause problems. Any perceived weakness might throw our government into internal disarray, or it could be capitalized upon by outside forces. Even worse, it could cause us to lose members. We're here today to make sure the vacancy left by Mr. Davidson is filled promptly and in accordance with our bylaws.

"Some of you have been on the board for years," Dan continued. "Some of you are new, so I will explain the procedures. Chapter 4, subsection B of our charter is unambiguous." Dan lifted a piece of paper and put on his reading glasses. "'In the event a principal dies or is otherwise incapacitated, the vice principal shall assume his duties until such time as the members of Aegis elect a new principal via a special election.' You may be wondering then what we the board do. Why are we here today? Well, we do two things. 'As soon as practicable following the death or incapacitation of the principal, the Board of Directors shall set a date and prescribe the manner by which the special election shall be held. The Board of Directors may, at its discretion, endorse a particular candidate.'"

Dan put his paper down and took his reading glasses off. "I move that we introduce a motion to schedule a special election exactly seven months from now." Dan waved his hand, and one of the screens behind him displayed a large calendar with the third Thursday highlighted. The board members got out their devices and calendars to make a note. "That should be more than enough time."

"Seconded," someone said from the left side of the table.

"Moved and seconded," Dan said. "Let's open it up for discussion."

Not a word from anyone.

"Do we need to vote? Any objections to carrying this motion right now?"

Still nothing.

"Motion carried." Dan said, clacking the gavel. "Next item, endorsements. I move to open the floor to the topic of endorsements."

"Seconded," called someone from a hologram.

"The floor's yours, folks," Dan said, leaning back in his chair.

"I move that we endorse our very own Dan Barton for principal," said Randy from the far end of the table.

Dan smiled. *Randy, you wonderful kissass.*

"Seconded," someone added.

"Let's open it to discussion," Dan said.

"I don't agree with this at all." said Yvonne Schmidt, a leathery old lady in a red pantsuit with a voice like a tractor engine. "I don't think it's right that we make an endorsement at all. Think about it from the common member's perspective: the board is recommending one of their own for principal. It gives the appearance of impropriety, don't you think? Do we want the news media saying we've done away with democracy at Aegis?"

For Christ's sake, Yvonne, why do you always have to cause problems? Every damn meeting, you fight everyone on everything. The congenital contrarian. If the wrong person is elected, you're gonna set Aegis back fifteen years. Dan closed his eyes and took some slow breaths. *Keep your cool, Dan.*

"No endorsement at all?" Randy asked Yvonne. "SDI's board endorses candidates. So does Safeguard."

Yvonne waved her hand dismissively. In that hand was a long cigarette holder holding an equally long cigarette, the smoke from which rose up into the holograms above. "We are Aegis, the market leader. Who cares what those clown troupes are doing?"

"I disagree," Randy asserted. "Not endorsing makes us look weak and fractured, as though we don't have a good candidate to put up. It's like telling the world we have internal dissent."

"Does anyone know what Metteyya does?" an obese man asked from one of the projections. "Do they make recommendations?"

"As far as I know, they don't have a board," Randy answered. "I've been told they don't even hold elections."

"What the hell are they?" asked the fat, floating, digital apparition. "A dictatorship?"

"We're getting off topic," Randy said.

"Look"—Yvonne squinted while looking at Randy—"I'm no dummy. I know you two work together at Barton Capital." She used her cigarette to point at Dan, then at Randy. "So long as I'm on this board, I'm not going to let you two railroad this process and subvert the will of our members. This is going to a special election without an endorsement from the board."

There she goes again, attacking everyone's character. Same crap, different meeting.

"Yvonne," Randy said, "I'm not sure what I did to upset you, but I have nearly as much invested in this government as you do, in terms of both time and money. I only want what's best, for Aegis and its members."

"Mr. Hughes," Yvonne hissed at Randy, "you're a shyster, and I don't trust you one bit."

"Enough!" Dan barked. "Mrs. Schmidt, I'll ask you to keep your opinions of your fellow board members to yourself. We've already suffered the loss of our principal. If we're not careful, the next few months could be a perilous time for Aegis; any lack of solidarity could be our downfall. Slander and bickering certainly won't help. Let's make a decision on Mr. Hughes's motion." Dan looked around and, seeing heads nodding in agreement, dictated the vote into the computer taking minutes. "Shall the board of directors of Aegis officially endorse chairman Dan Barton for the office of principal?" He then pushed a button on the screen in the table in front of him, causing the referendum to appear simultaneously on every board member's individual screen. Each poked his or her screen and, when voting had completed, the tally displayed.

Yes: 47 percent.

No: 53 percent.

Dan glared at Yvonne, who avoided his eye contact and bubbled with a contented grin.

Gee, thanks, Yvonne, you fucking bitch.

52

"Bogie," someone announced over the island radio. "Due south."

The island radio was encrypted, and only those who had the right descramblers could hear the chatter between the watchtowers. Len got out his binoculars. A speedboat like the ones the pirates used. This one, though, was sitting still in the water. A yellow and blue flag was flying from a long pole.

"Yellow and blue. Whose flag is that?" Len asked.

"I don't think that's an ensign. I think it's a signal flag," Jeff said.

"I really should have learned all that crap by now," Len said.

"Let me look it up. I can never remember what they mean either," Jeff said, pulling a binder off the shelf in the watch-tower. "OK, says here it's the kilo flag. It means 'a desire to communicate.'"

"CB or marine?" Len asked.

Jeff shrugged. "Let's try both."

"Unknown vessel, this is Seavey Island," Len said into the microphone of one of the conventional radios that the world could hear. "State your business."

"G'day," answered a male voice. "This is Captain Wogan of the Lake Syndicate. We would like to discuss a truce."

Len and Jeff looked at each other.

"How many are you?" Len asked.

"Just me and my chief mate," Wogan answered.

Len made sure the microphone was off before turning to Jeff. Jeff looked as baffled as Len felt. "Everyone to their posts," Len ordered. "Everyone. I'll hear what they have to say, but we have to assume this is some sort of trick. Tell Natalia to meet us down at the dock."

"You're going to invite them to land?" Jeff asked with concern.

"Yes," Len said before once again picking up the microphone to the non-island radio. He motioned to Jeff to get moving. "Captain Wogan, come on in."

Len, Natalia, Jeff, and several students carried rifles as they went down to the dock and waited for Wogan's speedboat to pull up. No one tossed the pirates a rope. They stood and watched as the privateers clumsily secured their own watercraft. From the boat emerged the most hideous-looking being Len had ever seen. A tall, sinewy, human-shaped thing with curly ram's horns on the sides of its head. It flashed a smile, revealing sharp metallic teeth. A second creature climbed out of the boat: a female figure with a face like a cat. Whiskers, slitted eyes. They were both dressed like extras from a B-movie. Len was simultaneously horrified and fascinated. He stared intently as they walked down the dock toward him.

"That's far enough," Len said.

"Arvo, mates," the taller one with the horns said. It had a deep, booming voice.

"What in the hell are you?" Len asked, gripping his rifle.

"I am Captain Wogan," it replied with a bow.

"Are you human?"

"I prefer the term trans-species."

Len had heard that shady clinics in Toronto were recombining the DNA of willing humans with that of animals for purely cosmetic reasons, but he hadn't actually seen it in person until now. He suddenly realized there was probably a lot he hadn't seen since he had gone into seclusion years ago. Len looked over at Natalia and his students, none of whom seemed fazed. *Do they see this stuff all the time when they go to the mainland?*

"Are those horns real?" Len asked.

"Aye," Wogan answered, smiling proudly.

Fucking freak show, Len thought. He couldn't help but stare. Normally Len didn't notice a person's blinking, but Wogan's irises were bioluminescent like a firefly's ass. It created a flicker every time his eyelids closed.

Wogan's travel companion was no less unusual looking. Her ears were pointed and twitching, and she had a furry tail sticking out of her leather pants.

"This is my chief mate, TC," Wogan said, interrupting the long, uncomfortable stares.

"TC?" Len asked.

"It's short for Thunder Cunt," the cat said matter-of-factly.

"Thunder Cunt?" Natalia asked.

"Aye," the cat answered with a nod.

"That's your real name?"

"Yeah."

"Who the hell named you that?" Natalia asked.

"My mothah," the cat answered bitterly.

Natalia, unable to contain herself, doubled over with laughter.

"You got a problem wit dat, bitch?" TC slammed the bolt back on the submachine gun she was carrying.

In unison, all of Len's students pointed their rifles at Wogan and TC.

Natalia turned serious on a dime. "Point that gun at me, and I'll make you fucking eat it."

"Oy!" Wogan yelled, his ram nostrils flaring. "Everybody chill out! Put the guns down. TC, pull your head in and go sit in the boat."

TC gave Natalia a hard stare and then spit in her direction. The blob of feline sputum landed feebly in the distance between the two.

"That's an order!" Wogan bellowed.

TC begrudgingly obeyed and sulked back to the speedboat.

Those accents, Len thought. *The cat is easy. Puerto Rican via New York City. But the ram? Either Australia or New Zealand. Could never tell those two apart.*

"My apologies," Wogan said. "She's a good chief mate, but she's a bit of a yobbo."

Len motioned for everyone to lower their rifles. "So what can we do for you?" he asked.

"I represent the five brotherhoods that make up the Lake Syndicate. They've asked me to come out here to discuss a truce."

"We're listening," Len said.

"We want to buy your island." Wogan declared.

Len looked at Natalia, more out of surprise than anything. She shook her head the way Len thought she might. "It's not for sale," Len said.

"Everything's for sale for the right price, mate."

"How much are you offering?" Natalia asked.

"One million LCs," Wogan said.

"One million!" Natalia scoffed. "It's worth ten times that!"

"I beg to differ," Wogan said, opening up a bag he was carrying. He pulled out a book-like object. "In fact, we had it appraised."

"You had our island appraised?" Len chuckled. "Are you for real?"

"Aye, mate. It's a ridgy-didge appraisal. It even…" Wogan thumbed through the pages until he found the phrase he was looking for. "'conforms to USPAP,' whatever the hell that means." Wogan closed the report and offered it to Len. Len hesitantly approached the beast. Taking the document from him, Len noticed the Tchogol tattoo on Wogan's wrist. Len walked backward to a safe distance to study what he'd been handed. The document was professional looking and bound with a leather cover. It was titled *An Appraisal of Seavey Island.* Len paged through it and then handed it to Natalia.

"I hate to tell you this," Wogan said, "but it ain't worth a zack."

"Then why do you want it so badly?" Natalia asked.

"The problems you have? We have 'em as well. All our ports are on the mainland. Governments are squeezing us from all sides, causing us grief. We've got gangbangers and bikies up our arses too. We need a base of operations that we can defend easily, something surrounded by water instead of land."

"Sounds like our island is pretty valuable," Len said sardonically.

"Ah, but it's not worth anything to anyone but us," Wogan said, smirking. "Who the hell would want to buy an island that's constantly besieged by pirates?"

Len looked askance at Wogan.

Is this guy for real?

"No one wants to buy an island that's always under attack," Wogan added. "Hence the low value. Says so right in that report."

Len scratched his head as he tried to figure out whether Wogan was an idiot, or whether Wogan thought he was the idiot.

"Wait, wait," Len blurted out. "Let me get this straight. You and your pals attack our island seven times. When we counterattack, you come here and offer to buy the place. But you only offer us ten cents on the dollar because you've been attacking us?"

Wogan nodded. "Right."

"So that's kinda like walking into a store and breaking something, then offering the shopkeeper ten percent of retail because it's broken," Len said, rubbing his forehead. "Right?"

"You gonna take it or not, mates?"

"No deal," Natalia said defiantly.

Wogan looked to Len for a second opinion, who replied only with a steely look.

"Have it your way." Wogan sneered at them.

"What about the truce?" Len asked.

"No island, no truce," Wogan growled before turning around and walking down the dock. "TC, start the boat. We're done here."

53

Fifteen Years Before Octavia's Embargo

"Mr. and Mrs. Denney, please sit down," the obstetrician said in a tone that made Octavia worry.

"There isn't a problem with the baby, is there?" Octavia asked.

"Healthwise, the baby is perfectly fine," the doctor replied.

"But?" Kyle asked.

"As you know, we did an amniocentesis a few days ago. There were no serious genetic abnormalities. No Down syndrome or anything like that."

"Doc, please. You're killing me," Kyle said.

"I'm sorry to tell you this, but the fetus is a Tchogol."

Octavia's husband turned white. He looked at Octavia, wide-eyed. Accusatory, almost.

"How accurate is the test?" Octavia asked, turning to the doctor.

"It has a very low rate of false positives."

"How is this possible?" Kyle asked in a high-pitched tone. He rolled his sleeve up frantically. "Look! I'm an Xreth! My wife is an Xreth," he said, grabbing Octavia's wrist and holding it up for the obstetrician to see. "We were both in the concentration camp as kids, for crying out loud. How on earth can our kid be a Tchogol?"

"I'm sorry, Mr. Denney, but Tchogolism is recessive. You both carry the gene even though you're not Tchogols yourselves."

"So now what?" Kyle asked. "Is there anything we can do about this? Can't we just edit the genes?"

"The genes for Tchogolism can't be edited out. It's one of the few things we can't fix."

"What?" Kyle gasped. "You mean to tell me they can turn someone's eyes blue or regrow a hand, but they can't turn a Tchogol into something else?"

"Tchogolism *is* a gene edit." Octavia sighed. "It can't be undone."

"Well excuse me," Kyle said, "but I didn't go to nursing school."

"The problem is the way the Dranthyx spliced their DNA into the human genome," the doctor said calmly. "If you try to alter the Tchogol genes, they'll change themselves back. There are actually hidden backup copies that the genes will restore themselves from. If you try to remove the Tchogol genes altogether, the organism dies. The way the Dranthyx engineered it was extraordinarily clever."

"If the design is so clever, why did a flu kill them?"

"You can kill them," the doctor said. "You just can't change them. Look, in a few years, someone may figure out how to fix the problem. However, it's not yet possible with today's medicine."

"So we're screwed?" Kyle asked.

"Terminating is an option," the doctor said as tactfully as possible.

"I am not murdering my baby!" Octavia said.

"It's not a baby yet," Kyle said.

"The hell it isn't!" Octavia said angrily. "It's already moving! Didn't you see the ultrasound?"

"Do you really want to spend the rest of your life raising a serial killer?" Kyle asked.

"That's awfully melodramatic," Octavia said.

"Those people have no empathy," Kyle seethed. "Your baby will never love you. Tchogols have no future. Look at them, living in Dumpsters and mugging the elderly."

"I took the nurse's oath to never do any harm," Octavia said. "That's what I've dedicated my life to, Kyle—helping the helpless. I do it out of compassion, not for payback or gratitude. Maybe other people would kill their own children for convenience, but that sure as hell isn't me."

Kyle's face was red with rage. He covered his mouth and stared up at the ceiling, probably to avoid speaking his mind any further in front of the doctor.

"How common is this?" Octavia asked.

"Before the flu," the doctor said, "Tchogolism affected only 4 percent of the population. However, that number has shot up to 10 percent in recent years. It is now very common."

"Why so many?" Kyle rasped. He looked as if he were on the verge of crying.

"No one knows," the doctor said. "Maybe because nature is trying to restore balance after the flu wiped them all out. Nature abhors a vacuum." The doctor studied Kyle for a second. "Look, as genetic disorders go, this is not a bad one to have. It's not anything debilitating and fatal, like Tay-Sachs or Niemann-Pick. It's not the end of the world, and you're not alone. There's a huge community of parents just like you, raising Tchogols. Here," he said, rifling through one of his desk drawers. He pulled out a pamphlet and handed it to Octavia.

The cover featured a stock photo of a woman with her child. The woman looked suspiciously relaxed and youthful for someone who had spent time raising children. She was smiling, hunched over, holding a boy of about five upright on a bicycle with training wheels. The boy, also smiling, was wearing an oversized bike helmet. The words across the top made the situation seem hopeful already. *Mothers of Tchogols: A Community of Advocacy and Support for Parents and Guardians of Leadership-Gifted Children.*

"What's this?" Octavia asked.

"Mothers of Tchogols," the doctor said. "The best possible resource for someone in your situation. There are chapters in every major city. Millions of parents are raising Tchogols."

Kyle put his head in his hands and covered his eyes.

"Look," the doctor said softly, "To be quite candid, it's only in recent history that the condition became regarded as a flaw. Everyone forgets that Tchogols used to run the world. These kids are profoundly capable. The only thing holding them back is society's prejudice."

Seven Years Before Octavia's Embargo

"Dad," Octavia said, barely able to contain her excitement, "I'm pregnant!"

"What? Another kid? That's fantastic!" Len said, hugging her. "When are you due?"

"Five months from now."

"Boy or girl?" Len asked, smiling. "Or don't you know yet?"

"Boy," Octavia answered.

"Wow, that's great! Iris will finally have someone to play with! Have you picked out a name?"

"Neith." Octavia said proudly.

Her father's expression turned sour so quickly that Octavia actually turned around to see if someone was standing behind her.

"You're naming my grandson Neith?" Len asked incredulously.

"Yeah," Octavia said.

"This is a joke, right?"

"No. I've always thought it was a pretty name."

Len's expression was like a laceration of disgust.

"What's wrong with the name?" Octavia asked innocently.

"Octavia, two things. First, I think it's a girl's name—"

"Dad, remember what decade it is—"

"Second," Len continued, "and far more importantly, you're naming your son after the person who killed your mother. That's beyond weird. It's sick."

Octavia turned her back to her father, filling the room with a long, frustrated silence. She could feel his disapproving eyes on the back of her head.

"His middle name is Bernard," Octavia said, turning around. "Your father's name. Neith Bernard Denney."

"Christ. Naming that poor child after a monster was bad enough! But you had to put your grandfather's name next to it?"

"Dad, why are you so angry?"

Octavia's father sat down in a chair with an exasperated thud. "You're a grown woman, and it's none of my business what you want to name your kids. If you have a third one, you might as well name it Adolf. Wait, how about Joseph Stalin? I think he killed even more people."

"Dad, don't be mad at me."

"I'm not mad. There's just a lot you don't understand, Octavia, and oftentimes I think it's willful."

"What's that supposed to mean?" Octavia asked, offended.

"You've always been an ostrich. You'll bury your head in the sand during a hurricane and pretend it's a sunny day."

"Why are you being a jerk?" Octavia asked tearfully. "I came 1,100 miles to share happy news with you, and you have to be critical. You have to shit on it. You know what, Dad? I'd rather be an ostrich than wallow in suffering and darkness the way you do."

Her father sighed and shook his head. She knew he was biting his tongue. He closed his eyes and breathed slowly. He opened his eyes again and looked at her, the consternation gone from his face.

"Fine," Len said in a more composed tone of voice. "This is a happy occasion, and I'll try not to ruin it. But I'm not calling him Neith. I'll call him Bernie."

"Bernie," Octavia said in acknowledgment, wiping her eyes. "I can live with that."

Six Months Before Octavia's Embargo

"I can't do this anymore," Kyle said while lying down on the couch in their small ranch house in east Miami. He smelled like a distillery.

"Do what?" Octavia asked.

"Us. I can't do it anymore." Kyle took another swig of gin.

"I don't understand," Octavia said.

"We need to go our separate ways."

"What? Why?"

"This isn't a relationship, Octavia. We're like roommates who are raising kids together. The romance died years ago. When was the last time we sat down and talked, or cooked a meal together, or made love?"

"Kyle, we're busy people. We have a lot going on."

"Yeah, busy. Our whole lives are consumed with work and our goddamn needy children. Problem is, our relationship is always the last priority."

"What? Where is all this coming from? You seemed fine just a few hours ago."

"I'm not fine. It's been piling up for fifteen years, Octavia. I hold it in, stuff it down, and drink it away. But I can't...I can't go on like this. I feel trapped. I don't get what I need from you, and I can't go outside our marriage to get it elsewhere without being the bad guy."

Octavia felt the room start to shrink.

"Maybe we just need to spend more time together," she said. Her own voice sounded distant.

"Our hearts wouldn't be in it, and you know it," Kyle said. "We go through the motions for the sake of our kids, but it doesn't matter, does it? One is a Tchogol who will never appreciate the effort. The other is so damn autistic that he doesn't even know our names."

Octavia felt as if she'd been slapped. She sat down in the reclining chair.

Is that what love is? Octavia thought. *Expecting a reward?*

"I don't understand," Octavia said. "Yeah, we've had some rough patches, but I thought things were improving."

"Improving? When? Things have gotten worse. I'm miserable; you're miserable. All we do is fight. We're both working full time and barely making ends meet. When that doesn't work, we have to ask your parents for money. We've been lying to ourselves for years, pretending it's going to get better. This isn't getting better. It'll never get better."

Two Months Before Octavia's Embargo

Octavia sat in a reception area.

"Ms. Savitz?"

Octavia looked up. A rather plain-looking, middle-aged man in a business suit walked into the conference room and extended his hand. Octavia stood up and shook it.

"I'm Patrick Sullivan," he said, smiling. "Nice to meet you. I'll be handling your case."

They took their seats, and Sullivan pulled a legal pad and pen out of his briefcase.

"So how can I help you?" he asked.

"I'm a member of Aegis. My daughter got in trouble with the authorities recently."

"Oh? What happened?"

"Well, she got caught shoplifting."

"How old is she?"

"Fifteen."

"Teenagers," the lawyer said, shaking his head.

"That's not the issue. The issue is that when they caught her, they found out she's a Tchogol and that I never registered her."

The lawyer stopped writing and gave Octavia a concerned look. "Are you embargoed?"

"Yes, but I can pay you cash. Don't worry."

"I'm not sure I can even have you as a client if you're embargoed."

"You're about the fifth lawyer who's said that to me. I can't catch a break. I can't even work or buy groceries. Isn't there anything you can do? I'm telling you, I may be embargoed, but I have a pile of cash."

The lawyer gave her a pitying look. "Let me ask the partners," he said before leaving the room.

Another goddamn lawyer who won't break the embargo, she thought.

Returning, the lawyer had a cheerful look on his face. "So I talked to the guys upstairs, and we discovered there's a loophole. We're allowed to take the case if, and only if, you're challenging your embargo."

"Oh my God, thank you," Octavia said. "Thank you. That's exactly what I'm doing."

"OK," he said, picking up his pen and pad, "so tell me about your case. Why didn't you register her?"

"I was one of the first members of Aegis when it started fifteen years ago. I have a two-digit member number, if that tells you anything. Aegis was just a startup then. There was no Tchogol Accord yet."

The lawyer nodded his head understandingly without looking up from his note-taking. With his hand busy writing, Sullivan's wrist stuck far enough out of his suit and shirt cuff that Octavia saw his Invasion tattoo: an *S* surrounded by Dranthyx bar code.

"You're a Saskel," Octavia remarked.

The lawyer gave her a startled look and self-consciously pulled his sleeve down to cover the tattoo.

"It's OK," Octavia said, putting her hand reassuringly on his arm. "I'm not a typist. I believe in all types."

"Everyone's a typist," the lawyer said cynically. "You think you can't catch a break being embargoed? Try being a Saskel. No one takes a Saskel lawyer seriously."

"Why not just get the tattoo removed?"

"I'm a member of Safeguard. They require Saskels to be labeled anyway, so I just kept the Dranthyx tattoo."

"Well, why not switch governments?"

"Safeguard is what I know."

"Oh."

54

Dan adjusted his black bow tie in the mirror of the men's room and then fiddled with his cufflinks and cummerbund. He looked at himself briefly. His hair, which had started to go gray at the temples, was perfect. Moments like these were what the future of the world hinged upon, and he had to look the part.

This is it. Showtime.

Walking out into the enormous ballroom, he felt a roomful of eyes upon him like hundreds of mirrors. The smell of Sterno, hors d'oeuvres, and booze. Haughty chatter, laughter, and a string quartet. The air was electric and invigorating. He grabbed a champagne flute off a waiter's tray and began to work the room.

"Mr. and Mrs. Taylor," Dan said to an elderly couple standing nearby. Mr. Taylor was heir to a retail empire. He was wearing pre-Invasion war medals and was hunched over a silver cane. Mrs. Taylor was carrying a shih tzu; Dan thought she looked like a collapsed soufflé that had been sprinkled with diamonds.

"Danny, my boy!" Mr. Taylor said, grabbing Dan's upper arm. "How are things in the money-changing business?"

"Same old, same old." Dan smiled. "The real temple-cleaning needs to happen here tonight."

"You aren't kidding. We haven't had any real leadership in years. Davidson is dead, and we've gotta get the rest of his guys out of office," Mr. Taylor said. He made a raspberry noise and hiked his thumb over his shoulder.

"Make no mistake," Dan said sternly, "I intend to make it happen."

"Good," Mrs. Taylor said. "That's why we're here. This so-called government couldn't even stop a bunch of ruffians from looting and burning down our neighbor's house—and we live in a gated community!"

"Thank you, by the way," Dan said, "for your generous donation—"

"Dan Barton?" said a voice behind him in a German accent.

"Pardon me, folks," Dan said cheerfully to the Taylors before turning around. There, behind him, stood the most powerful man in the transportation industry: Gunter Küchler, founder of the Transglobal Concern. He was a rotund little man who, despite his size, seemed to fill the room with power and importance. When Küchler walked through a crowd, people jumped out of the way.

"Herr Küchler, wonderful to meet you in person. I did not expect to see you here tonight!" Dan gushed while shaking his hand.

"Please, call me Gunter. I had an opening in my schedule. I felt I should be here. This is important."

"How are your tollways doing?" Dan asked.

"We have the world's greatest private security. Yet still we have to deal with highway robberies everywhere, or gangs setting up roadblocks or bombing trains. My customers are very unhappy. It can't go on like this. I understand you are the man to bring order back to North America."

"Yes, sir. I am your man."

"Good. You have my support."

Just then, an aide came up behind Dan and whispered in his ear, "We're ready."

The lights in the large room dimmed. A spotlight came on, shining directly onto the podium. Randy came up and adjusted the microphone. "Good evening, ladies and gentlemen. We all know why we're here tonight, so I won't beat around the bush." Randy smiled. "The board has decided not to endorse any one candidate for principal. Over the next few months, we'll be inundated with a variety of candidates, all of whom will be seeking your vote. You'll see them in advertisements, and their volunteers will knock on your doors. Without an endorsement, this is anyone's election.

"However, not just any candidate will do, because we are no ordinary government," Randy stated emphatically. "We are gathered this evening to discuss the future of Aegis, the biggest name in governmental services—not just in North America, but the entire Western Hemisphere. Aegis is what other governments dream of being: a revenue-positive superpower."

At that, the room broke into an ovation.

Randy waited for the clapping to die down. "But we're also here to discuss something even bigger than Aegis: the future of this continent, and the globe. What we do here tonight, and in this election, will resonate everywhere. Aegis leads, and the world follows. Travis Davidson left some big shoes to fill, and I know of only one candidate with the mettle to not only fill those shoes, but to take us to even greater heights. Ladies and gentlemen, please offer a round of applause to our current board chairman and our next principal, Daniel Barton."

The room exploded with clapping as Dan moved through the crowd and walked up the steps to the lectern. He shook Randy's hand and then looked out past the stage lights, into the crowd.

Their eyes—how they looked at him. He could see the worry in their faces. *We are scared. We are hungry for direction, starved for leadership. Give us something to believe in. Let us know that it'll be OK. Take charge, and we will follow.*

He couldn't let these people down. They were depending on him. They needed a miracle, and he knew in his heart that he was the only one who could make it happen. They felt it too. Dan stood there at the podium for a few seconds until the room became quiet with expectation. He let it build for a moment, and then he started.

"Do you like the way things are going?" he asked before pausing for a few seconds. Some in the crowd shook their heads. The high-speed *click click click* of photographers' cameras pierced the tension in the room. "I don't like the way things are going." Dan took the wireless microphone off the podium attachment and walked toward the crowd, to the edge of the stage, and stood there perilously. "We had the famous fifteen years of peace after the Invasion." He looked at the livecasters in the front, wearing their ridiculous broadcasting rigs on their heads, as if he were addressing them personally. "I remember those days. But that ended twenty years ago. Times are different these days. We have problems now, don't we?" Dan turned and walked to the right side of the stage as people were nodding. "The North Koreans have invaded the West Coast of North America. They control the entire Pacific time zone and will no doubt push inland. They'll be here at the Great Lakes soon enough. We have warlords in our streets, armed thieves on our roads, pirates on our rivers. Our water is polluted, assuming we can get any at all. Our people are out of work due to automation, and we live in constant fear of violence." He turned to face the entire crowd and then bellowed passionately, "This chaos is killing us, and I will not stand for it!"

The crowd broke into a raucous applause. People hooted and whistled. Dan saw the Glib feed explode with comments on the right wall. He waited for them to quiet down again.

"A criminal can murder your mother and then take legal refuge in the house next door. Why? Because the house next door is not in your government's jurisdiction, and therefore you, and your government, have no recourse. This is going on every single day. If not murder, then fraud, or theft, or extortion, or kidnapping. If there are twenty houses on a block, there could be twenty sovereign jurisdictions. If you buy a can of soup produced in a factory covered by a different government, you have to hope and pray that it's not full of rat poison. And if it is, tough luck, because the soup factory probably chose a lax government on purpose. You can't sue them, and there are no regulations to protect you. This, my friends, is madness."

The audience broke into applause again. People in the back shouted in approval. The livecasters who were providing commentary exploded with enthusiasm; Dan could see their gestures but couldn't hear what they were saying over the din. Taken out of context, they looked like a bunch of histrionic mimes. The Glibbing that was being projected onto the walls of the ballroom was moving so fast that the cascade of text and images appeared as a nearly solid color.

"We were once one people, one land, one government," Dan said while wistfully looking into the distance, to some horizon that only he could see. He moved his gaze back down to the crowd. "Now look at us: fractured, helpless, mismanaged, vulnerable. Constant strife, unending bickering. There are never any resolutions. We have no real leadership, and, to be quite frank, we haven't had any for decades. What we call a government now is a disgrace. It might protect you, or it might not. It might help you with food when you're hungry, or with medical costs when you're sick—but not if some executive has run off with the largess. There's no peace and no justice. Ladies and gentlemen, the system we have now is a failure. Our modern concept of government is a failure. What we think of as governments now are little more than glorified gym memberships."

The crowd laughed.

"Governments were once mighty and magnanimous," Dan said, raising his hand toward the ceiling, indicating something grand. "The one we had stretched from ocean to ocean. It created infrastructure, funded science, provided a social safety net, guaranteed rights, and defended our borders. When someone committed a crime, they went to *jail*! Remember jails?" He looked out at the assembled masses. Seeing their head-nodding approval, he continued. "You could take your family on vacation and drive from one town to the next, for hundreds or thousands of miles, with no fear of crossing disputed territory. You could fly from coast to coast without worrying about your plane being shot down. If you got in trouble in another land controlled by another government, your government would use diplomats to negotiate on your behalf. Folks, this is how it used to work and how it's supposed to work. And, with what I'm about to propose, it will once again work that way."

Dan paused for dramatic effect. The drone cameras swung around in the air, finding the best angles. He scanned the audience carefully, taking in their expectant, admiring gazes. "What I intend to do when elected principal," he announced, "is unite the governments."

The entire room, packed wall to wall, rose to their feet and erupted into a thunderous ovation. Dan stood there smiling, relishing every second of it. This was the moment he had been born for.

After a solid sixty seconds, the room quieted down enough for him to speak once again.

"My friends, through unification, we will rout out the societal cancers and the marauding criminals that plague us. We will expel the foreign invaders from our West Coast to reclaim our ancestral lands. We will return to the days of order, progress, prosperity, and safety. We will once again reclaim our throne as the leader of the world, the example that others follow. In due time, our land and our people will once again be one nation, indivisible."

The applause these words received shook the room. Dan, feeling transcendent, as though the world were finally at his back, waved to the uproarious crowd and walked offstage.

55

"The defense would like to call its first witness, Octavia Savitz."

Octavia rose from her seat. The nervous anticipation she'd had all week was suddenly missing. In its place was a heavy, focused feeling. She walked slowly across the court-room, careful not to trip on her way up to the witness box. She sat down, adjusted the microphone, and looked out into the crowd. Her dad gazed back at her. He seemed more ner-vous than she was.

Too bad Natalia couldn't make it.

"Could you please state your name for the record?"

"Octavia Jane Savitz."

"And you are the mother of Iris Denney?"

"Correct."

"And how old is your daughter, Iris?"

"She's fifteen."

"Fifteen. And she's a Tchogol, correct?"

"Yes."

"When did you find out about her type?"

"When I was pregnant."

"Do you know when your government, Aegis, adopted the Tchogol Accord? Was it before or after her birth?"

"Six months later."

"And why didn't you register Iris as a Tchogol when your government adopted the Accord?"

"Because I thought she'd be grandfathered in."

"Grandfathered in. And why would you think that?"

"Because that's what the official told us. We didn't have to do anything."

"OK, fine. So some official from Aegis told you that you didn't have to register your daughter. Was that a true statement on his part?"

"That's what we're here to figure out, sir." Octavia retorted.

"Well, it isn't true. Have you ever read the Tchogol Accord?"

"No. Why would I?"

The lawyer handed her a copy of it, a bound version approximately fifty pages thick.

"What the accord intended is pretty clear. If you would, please, turn to page five," the lawyer said, flipping through his own copy.

Octavia turned to page five.

"It says," the lawyer said before reading it verbatim, "'No government shall become party to this agreement without first enacting laws requiring all of its members to be genetically tested. Each government shall register and clearly mark its Tchogol members as described in Paragraph D herein and transmit the record of registry to the Intergovernmental Tchogol Registrar. These requirements shall be retroactive, and no statute of limitations shall apply for evasion of these requirements."

"I had no idea," Octavia admitted.

"Are you familiar with this mark?" the attorney said, pushing a button on a remote.

On a screen, a photograph appeared of a Tchogol tattoo with a logo that looked like a safe.

"Ms. Savitz," the lawyer pressed, "have you seen a tattoo like this before?"

Octavia didn't answer.

"For the record, your honor, this is a photo of the wrist of a Tchogol who was registered under Safeguard. The tattoos issued by Aegis and every other government are almost exactly the same, with the exception of the logos identifying the government. These tattoo designs are standardized; they are the same shape and dimension on each individual. Everyone can identify them by the big T in the middle. So, Ms. Savitz, have you, or have you not, seen a tattoo like this before?"

"I have."

"And you didn't stop to wonder what it was all about?"

"Like I said, I thought she'd be grandfathered in."

"Did you know of Tchogols older than Iris who were registered?"

"Yes," Octavia answered hesitantly.

"And that didn't strike you as odd?"

"Not really. I mean, what if they'd joined Aegis after the accord? What if they were registering voluntarily? How the heck should I know what's going on?"

"So all around you are signs of Tchogols older than Iris who are getting registered. And you don't stop to ask yourself whether you should register your daughter?"

"Sir, my attorney can produce the letter from the Aegis official who said we didn't need to register Iris. This is a nonissue. This is not what we're here to discuss."

She looked over at her lawyer, who was sitting at the plaintiff's table. His face was red. He reached into his suit pocket and pulled out a vial of pills.

The letter, you dingbat! Octavia thought. *Get the letter out of your file and enter it into evidence.*

"And you feel this alleged letter absolved you from following the law?" the defense asked.

"No. Look, I don't know why my attorney hasn't brought this up yet, but this case isn't about whether I registered my daughter, or why or why not. This case is about basic human rights."

"What is the point of this line of questioning?" the judge asked.

The defense's lawyer turned to the judge. "Your Honor, what I'm trying to do here is establish that the plaintiff has unclean motives. I think Ms. Savitz knew she was supposed to register her daughter and simply didn't. Then, years later, her daughter, Iris, gets arrested for shoplifting. In the process, the girl is tested and found to be a Tchogol. Ms. Savitz is then embargoed for concealing a Tchogol. I intend to prove that this case has absolutely nothing to do with human rights and everything to do with the extreme inconvenience of Ms. Savitz's embargo."

You asshole! You think this is about me?

It took every ounce of self-restraint Octavia had to not spit in the smug lawyer's face. She looked over at her own lawyer again. He was fumbling with his pill bottle. His hands were shaking so hard, he could barely open the cap. He shook some pills into his trembling hands, then practically choked them down.

Why is he not objecting? Why is he not introducing evidence? Why is he not doing lawyer things? I'm dying up here, and my advocate is out to lunch.

"Understood," the judge said.

"Ms. Savitz," the lawyer said, "if this case is about human rights, why didn't you bring it to the courts before your embargo?"

The question caught her off guard. "I...I don't know. The embargo showed me a whole different side of the accord. I guess I hadn't realized before how bad things were for Tchogols."

"Or how bad things are for people who harbor Tchogols without notifying the authorities, correct?"

Octavia gave the defense lawyer a hot stare.

"No further questions," the defense lawyer said in the most self-satisfied way possible.

Octavia's lawyer rose from his seat and approached the witness stand.

"Uh, Ms. Savitz, do you feel that your embargo is unjust?"

"I think it's very unjust, but, as you know, that's not why we're here today."

"Ms. Savitz, I'm pretty sure that's why we're here. To contest your embargo."

Is this guy for real?

"No," Octavia blurted out, losing her patience. "Look, we've been over this a hundred times already. The embargo is just the cause of action. It gives us standing to sue and to challenge the Tchogol Accord as a violation of human rights."

How do I know more about this crap than my own lawyer? Is this what I get for hiring a Saskel? No, don't think like that. Don't let typism corrupt you.

"Uh, um." Octavia's lawyer shuffled through some papers with his trembling hands. "No further questions, Your Honor."

What? That's it? That's our rebuttal?

"OK." The judge sighed. "I think I've heard enough. I'm finding for the defendant." She hammered her gavel on the desk.

"What?" Octavia shrieked.

"Ms. Savitz," the judge said, "I have serious reservations about your character. Your embargo is a punishment for your inaction. Grow up, accept it, and stop making excuses for yourself."

"Your Honor, with all due respect, saying this whole case is about my embargo is like saying Rosa Parks only cared about bus seats. There are much larger implications here."

"You are no Rosa Parks," the judge said with a hot stare.

"I'm appealing," Octavia said defiantly. "This is ridiculous."

"Whatever." The judge shrugged. "Go ahead if you think you'll fool anyone at the next level." She took her glasses off and gave Octavia a hard glare. "Young lady, you have a lot to learn about life. I don't know which judges you'll get on the appeal panel, but, I assure you, they won't be any smarter than I am."

56

Len, Octavia, and her so-called lawyer exited the courthouse, squinting in the bright midday sun. At the bottom of the steps awaited a car driven by one of Len's students. Between them and the car, a crush of reporters awaited them. Upon seeing Len and Octavia, the journalists nearly tripped over themselves running over to them. Within seconds, the two were encircled by cameras, boom microphones, and questions.

"Ms. Savitz, do you think you're doing a good thing?"

"Ms. Savitz, what happened in the courtroom today?"

"Ms. Savitz, do you really want to return us to the days of Tchogol rule? What's next, civil rights for the Dranthyx?"

Octavia put on dark sunglasses and put her hand in front of the lens of a camera that was inches from her face. She did her best to push past the throng of interviewers, but she and her father were mobbed on all sides.

"Ms. Savitz, don't you realize that Tchogols have no empathy?"

"Do *you* have any empathy?" Octavia said testily. "These are human beings we're talking about. Do you think they had any choice in how they were born?"

"Some say that, if we let them back into society, they'll cause genocides like the old days," one of the reporters said.

"They've been shunned from society, forced to eat trash, and live outside in the winter," Octavia said angrily. "Governments won't protect them. They're embargoed from buying groceries, receiving medical care, or getting jobs. They starve and die every day in our streets. As far as I'm concerned, that is genocide. Do you really think I want to see my daughter, or anyone else's kids, grow up like that?"

"Do you want to return us to the days of constant war, Ms. Savitz?"

"Did those days ever leave?" Octavia asked, staring the reporter down. "Look at what's going on. Tchogols have no choice but to form gangs for protection and to steal what they need to survive. We have isolated enclaves of genetically privileged Xreths and Saskels patting themselves on the back for their superior empathic abilities while Tchogols are marginalized and forced to fight for survival. The irony. There's constant unrest. There's fighting everywhere. There are territory wars just a few miles from here, and you all know it. People are dying every day. We live in a war zone already. What we're doing isn't working."

"Ms. Savitz, how are you getting along while embargoed? What's day-to-day life like?"

"I'm done answering questions," Octavia said. She pushed her way through the wall of reporters and got into the car. "Good-bye."

"Sir, are you Ms. Savitz's father?" one of the journalists asked Len.

"Yes," Len answered.

"You are *the* Leonard Savitz?"

Suddenly, every single one of the newspeople turned their cameras and attention to Len.

Crap. Here we go, Len thought. *I've been avoiding interviews for thirty-five years. Might as well get this over with.*

"In the flesh."

Len was suddenly blasted by tens of simultaneous questions and the clicking of camera shutters.

"Mr. Savitz, why did you become a recluse?"

"Mr. Savitz, are you yourself a member of any governments?"

"Mr. Savitz, how do you feel about Tchogols having civil rights? Didn't you help kill them all with biological warfare?"

"Folks, one at a time," Len beseeched. "Despite how obnoxious and rude you were to my daughter, I will answer your questions. I was once in your shoes, so I have a little sympathy for your profession. Not much, but a little. OK, you first," Len said, pointing to a woman in a green blouse.

"Do you approve of what your daughter is doing?"

No. I think it's insane. Sometimes I think her heart is bigger than her brain. Cool it, old boy. She's your little girl; don't say something you'll regret.

"I certainly believe her heart is in the right place. She's my daughter, and I'm here to support her efforts. That's all I'm going to say about that. Yes, you," Len said, pointing to a man in an ugly tie.

"There's a conspiracy theory going around that Neith wasn't real and that you invented her for your story. Care to speak to that?"

Len laughed. "That's the first time I've heard that one! Do those people think I planned a revolution by myself, or what?"

"The machine's remains have never been found," the reporter said. "Further, you're the only person to have had contact with Neith who has come forward, so no one can corroborate that she actually existed."

"That's some serious tinfoil-hat stuff," Len said. "I didn't make up the Dranthyx or the Ich-Ca-Gan, did I? Millions of people saw those with their own eyes, right? Why would I lie about Neith? OK, you with the glasses."

"Why did you kill Jefferson?"

For some reason, the question made Len's good humor turn sour.

"Hell, I did Jefferson a favor," Len stated dryly.

"What do you mean?"

"He'd become everything he hated," Len said.

"You're saying Jefferson had impure motives?" one of the reporters asked.

"Dad," Octavia shouted from the window of the car, "We have to go!"

"I don't know what his deal was," Len said. "There was something wrong with the guy."

Just then, a scruffy-looking old man shoved his way through the herd of journalists. He wasn't in business clothes like the reporters. He looked dirty and homeless. He pushed his way within four feet of Len and looked him right in the eye. Len recognized the man's face from years ago. He just couldn't remember who he was.

The man reached into his jacket and pulled out a little black pistol. He aimed it at Len's face. The throng of journalists shouted and shrieked. "Len Savitz!" the dirty man shouted. "You fucking traitor!"

Len, reacting from years of training, reached out to grab the wrist holding the gun. It was an old move he'd taught his students, one that he'd practiced ten thousand times and had down pat. Reach for the gun, push it above your head so you're not in the line of fire, two-step in while squatting low, use your free arm like a nutcracker to pinch his gun-arm tricep between your bicep and forearm. Turn your whole body while lifting your backside up into his crotch to act as the fulcrum. Then let him fall over you onto the ground. The *Ippon Seoi Nage*. Sounds weird, but it'll slam a man to the concrete hard enough to shake his teeth loose.

And it would have worked, had someone not intervened while Len was trying to execute the technique; one of the reporters, a beefy young chap with a goatee, blocked Len's attempt at a judo throw by stepping in the way. The goateed reporter slapped the assassin's hand downward just before Len could grab it. Len saw the gun barrel jerk just before it discharged. He was so close that he felt the flame from the muzzle. The bullet, originally intended for Len's forehead, instead entered his body through his rib cage.

The little nine-millimeter hollow-point bullet, designed to expand into a mushroom shape to maximize damage as it traversed a human body, ripped through Len's liver, his pancreas, and finally his spine. Len felt the projectile smash a hole through one of his vertebrae right as it severed his spinal cord. In an instant, Len lost all feeling and muscle control below the waist and collapsed in a heap on the steps of the courthouse.

Though he'd once made his living as a writer, Len couldn't describe the feeling in words. It just didn't make sense. He'd felt his spine fracture, yes, but in that instant he'd also felt the whole universe come together.

It had to happen this way, Len thought, breathing heavily through the shock. *There were too many possibilities, too many outcomes. The bullet killed all but one. I always wondered how it would end.*

The pain, absolutely horrific, forced his mind to disassociate. In that state, the agony became like a movie he was watching passively. He witnessed himself screaming on the white steps. He witnessed his body in pain. The witness itself experienced no pain. The witness had extracted itself from the drama like a hand pulled out of a puppet.

This happened at the Freehold. What is that awareness? Always there. It's been there since birth. It doesn't think; it watches the thoughts. It's not of this body. It isn't my brain. It's something else entirely.

Len looked up from his miserable position on the ground. The large, goateed journalist had wrested the weapon away from the assailant and pinned him on the ground. With both their heads at ground level, the gunman looked Len in the eyes, his expression now placid despite the chaos of the crowd and the large man holding him down. An air of peace, as though he'd finally accomplished his last mission.

McKean. Private McKean. I remember now. One of Jefferson's men. Must've survived somehow. My God, he was just a kid then. The years have not been kind.

Photographers came within feet of Len's face and snapped pictures of him lying there, bleeding to death.

"Fucking vultures," Len wheezed at them.

Octavia, undoubtedly having heard the screams, exited the car and came running back over.

"Dad! Dad! Are you OK?"

"Oh, you know, just another day in paradise." Len gagged, tasting the blood that was coming up into his throat. "How about yourself? Great day, huh?"

"Somebody call a fucking ambulance!" Octavia yelled.

"Is he a member of an ambulance service?" one of the reporters asked. "They won't come for free."

"How the hell should I know?" Octavia snapped, "Somebody please call! Tell them we'll pay them cash."

"He's not embargoed too, is he?" another person asked. "They won't come if he is."

"No, goddammit!" Octavia yelled. "I'm the one who's embargoed, not him. For fuck's sake, just get the EMTs over here!" She turned to her father, eyes tearing up. "Dad, please hang in there. You're going to be OK."

Len was getting lightheaded from the blood loss, and he could feel his consciousness fading. He reached up to stroke his daughter's cheek, unintentionally smearing it with blood.

"I love you, Octavia," Len gasped. "Take care of my grandkids for me."

Then everything went black.

SIX MONTHS LATER

57

Octavia put on another sweater and looked out the window. Not at anything, really; her attention was inward. She pressed her forehead to the glass. Her heart heavy, she took a ragged breath. Her breath condensed on the pane. She closed her eyes.

A distant foghorn on the lake pulled her back to the present. She opened her eyes again. Snow flurries fell silently from a thick blanket of gray clouds. It was getting darker earlier. The temperature had dropped abruptly, much faster than that of the water, which caused a thick mist to rise from the lake. The snow coming down and the fog moving up were like two pieces of bread on her depression sandwich. She stared at the scene dejectedly. The lake hadn't frozen yet. She could still get away by boat if she needed to.

"That lake, that goddamned lake," she said to herself dispiritedly. She remembered learning as a child that Erie had gotten its name from the Iroquois word for cat, *erige*, because it had a reputation for being violent and unpredictable. Ferocious squalls came out of nowhere that could break thousand-foot freighters in half. Sometimes the storms were so intense that she thought they'd knock the brick lighthouse over.

The storms had caused many a quick death over the years in the form of shipwrecks. The winters, however, killed people slowly—they were the reason she'd moved away from that damn place. Octavia hated winter and everything it represented: isolation, confinement, darkness, sadness. When she was growing up, they were stranded on the island during the winters. She remembered their huge stockpiles of food and lake-effect snow so high it would block out the first-floor windows. Sometimes an icebreaker would come through to open up a channel so they could take a boat to Cleveland. Other times, her dad or Natalia would use the helicopter to go to the mainland. Most of the time, they were just stuck out there for weeks on end while Octavia counted down the days until summer.

Her father never seemed to mind the isolation or the cold; he was like a polar bear. Her stepmother was Russian so, as far as she was concerned, it wasn't a real winter unless it hurt. It didn't make sense; they had all the money in the world, yet they stayed on that damn island year-round.

Lunatics, Octavia thought. *If I had that kind of money, I'd have bought an island somewhere sensible, like the Caribbean. Yet still they blamed me for moving to Miami as soon as I was old enough to be out on my own.*

Natalia burst through the front door, piercing Octavia's gloom.

"Where are the kids?" Natalia asked anxiously.

"Upstairs. Why?"

"Get them to the basement," Natalia said with a tinge of panic in her voice.

"Why? What's wrong?"

"Please, just do it!"

Octavia ran upstairs. Bernie was at a desk, practicing his calligraphy. She'd always found it odd that his motor tics stopped when his attention was immersed in something. Octavia braced herself for the full-on meltdown that would happen when she interrupted him. The poor kid hated to switch tasks before he was done with something.

"Bernie, I'm sorry to bother you, but Mommy needs you to go downstairs to the basement. It's an emergency. You can take your pen and paper with you."

The unthinkable happened. The autistic boy calmly put his fountain pen back into the well, stood up, gathered his things, and silently walked downstairs. In seven years, she'd never seen him act so reasonably.

"Wow! Did you see that?" Octavia asked Iris.

"What?" Iris said, looking up from her Glibber.

"Never mind. I need you to get down to the basement. Natalia says it's an emergency."

"Mom, there's no signal down there."

"Iris, this is important."

Iris rolled her eyes and ignored her mother.

"Do it," Octavia said firmly, "or I'll throw that contraption in the lake."

"Hey, my mom is being a bitch again," Iris said to whomever she was chatting with. "I'll see you soon. I have to go. Bye!"

Bitch? My mother would have slapped me silly if I'd talked about her like that.

"Get to the basement, please," Octavia said through her teeth.

Iris huffed and capitulated, giving her mother the finger on the way down the stairs.

Octavia closed her eyes and counted to ten. Upon opening them, she noticed a piece of paper Bernie had left on the desk. She picked it up to study it. It was an intricate drawing of a line of dominoes toppling. Underneath, written in his perfect English script, were the words, "Not long now."

Once she was sure the kids were safe, Octavia ran out of the house to the big open area in the middle of the island. Over a hundred people were standing there. They'd all been her father's students. They were wearing body armor and carrying rifles. Natalia's face was covered in war paint, and she carried an expression that suggested this wasn't a drill.

"Natalia, what's going on?" Octavia asked.

"Fog." Natalia replied, looking up into the mist.

"Fog?"

"Fog."

"This place is always foggy in November," Octavia said. "I don't understand."

"The pirates will attack tonight," Natalia said resolutely.

"How do you know?" Octavia asked.

"It's their best bet."

"But they haven't attacked us in months," Octavia said.

"They were licking their wounds," Natalia said. "They've regrouped by now, I promise you."

"But we have the laser."

Natalia gave Octavia a chilling look. "The laser doesn't work in the fog."

"It doesn't? Why not?"

"Thermal blooming," Jeff answered while tying his boot.

"What about the helicopter?" Octavia asked.

"You wanna fly in this weather?" Jeff asked while brushing snowflakes off his sleeves. "I sure don't."

"Is everyone here?" Natalia asked Jeff.

"Yes, ma'am. All one hundred and three of us."

"Company, fall in!" Natalia yelled.

All of the islanders scrambled to get into their correct positions—something that they'd apparently been practicing. Within several seconds, they had arranged themselves into a neat grid and were standing straight like soldiers. Octavia couldn't believe what she was seeing. What had started in her childhood as a ragtag commune of wayward truth seekers had evolved into a fully functioning paramilitary organization.

"At ease. Ladies and gentlemen," Natalia said loudly enough for everyone to hear, "some of you are new. Some of you," she said, looking at Jeff, "Have been here for many years. It doesn't matter how long you have been here. This is our home. This is our community. This is our family, our tribe."

Natalia broke her stance and walked up and down the line. "And all of that is under attack. Make no mistake—our situation is *very* dangerous. We are out here in the water, alone. We have no allies. The pirates have attacked us seven times now. They will keep attacking us until they get what they want: our lives and our land."

Octavia stood off to the side. She was struck by how unafraid they all looked. Seven times; by now, they'd given to the inevitability of fighting.

"Look, you're all here for different reasons," Natalia said. "You may be here for spiritual enlightenment. Maybe you just wanted to get out of Cleveland. In either case, I sympathize. But we've made it clear for years now: if you're going to live here, you're going to learn how to fight. We have done our best to train you. I've taught you military drills and how to use weapons. Most of you are expert marksmen now. Even if our guns can't keep the enemy off our shores, Len, may he rest in peace, taught you all hand-to-hand combat. All the skills you have learned will be tested very soon."

Octavia watched Natalia in awe. Octavia had always admired Natalia's presence, the way she filled up a room. Natalia exuded an aura of resolve and competence—a natural charisma that caused others to want to follow her. In her husky contralto, Natalia addressed the islanders with the magnetic calm of someone fearless.

"Do you think the pirates have trained as much as we have?" Natalia asked. "Hell no. You've seen it. They can't shoot to save their lives. They can't even drive their goddamn boats! Sometimes I think they get here by accident. Instead of drilling flanking maneuvers, they're probably busy picking fleas off each other's asses."

Several people laughed.

"Tonight's the night," Natalia continued. "I have a strong suspicion that the pirates will attack. They're ugly, but they're not stupid. They haven't forgotten about us; they've been lying in wait. They know our laser won't work in this weather." Natalia paused to look up at the tower that held the cannon. It was already too foggy to see the top of the structure.

Natalia pursed her lips and made a "pfft" sound at the device, then turned to face her troops. She bellowed, "We don't need a stupid laser! We are ready for these shit bags! We will defend our island no matter what it costs us, until the lake is red with blood! We will kill them with our bare hands if we need to! They have no idea who they are fucking with!"

At these words, all 103 of the islanders roared in unison.

Natalia waited for them to settle down before continuing. "Every single one of you will remain on duty tonight, at your posts, until the fog lifts. Be ready to fight. Dismissed."

As the students scuttled off to their posts, Octavia grabbed Natalia by the arm as she walked past. "Natalia, that was inspiring!"

"You think?" Natalia asked, breaking character. "I practiced in front of the mirror last night. I didn't think I'd have to use that speech so soon."

"Do you need me to help?" Octavia asked.

"You know what I need from you? A hospital. The meditation hall will do. We have all kinds of medical supplies in the bins by the kitchen. I need you to attend to the wounded."

"Do you think it'll come to that?"

"The earlier attacks were nothing. They've been feeling out our defenses. Tonight's the night. Mark my words."

Octavia set to work transforming the meditation hall into a hospital as instructed. Once in a while, she glanced out the window. She grew anxious as the sky grew dark and the fog got thicker. Octavia wondered why Natalia had asked her to set up an infirmary rather than fight. Granted, she was probably the only person on the island with any medical training, but there was something else in the way Natalia had asked. The same cautious tone had been there when Natalia suggested to Octavia to not continue with the trial. Unspoken judgment—that's what it was. It was said in the same manner in which parents tactfully dissuade their children from doing something they'll suck at.

Who am I kidding? Octavia asked herself as she took scissors and syringes out of the bins. *I'm forty years old, and I'm just now figuring out what Dad and Natalia knew all along: I'm not a fighter. I've spent my life surrounded by tough people, thinking that was normal, but that doesn't mean I'm one.* She threw a roll of gauze on the floor in frustration and suddenly felt like crying.

Others seemed to have an unquestioned "selfness" that she lacked. Her mother, her father, Natalia. They all looked like complete people to her: cocksure in their abilities, unwavering in their identities, never a doubt in their minds as to who they were and what their purpose was on this planet. Octavia had never felt like that once in her whole life. Her own existence felt more like a fuzzy haze of memories and sensations that weren't actually hers; rather, she wore them the way an escaped convict might wear an oversized sweater that he'd stolen off a clothesline. Octavia lived with the guilt of pretending to be a person and felt she was in constant danger of someone discovering that wasn't the case. Never quite sure of where she stood, with herself or with others, she had turned that insecurity outward at a young age and worked hard on building friendships and being helpful. If she were likable enough, maybe no one would discover her dark secret of personlessness.

How am I going to get patients in here? she wondered. The logistical problem helped pull her out of her self-loathing. *I've moved some big patients in my day, but some of those guys are too big to drag clear across the island.*

Octavia recalled seeing her dad's old pickup truck next to the lighthouse. Still here after all these years. She remembered her dad buying it years ago during one of the coldest winters on record. The temperature had been in the negative digits for several days. Her father had driven his new truck from Cleveland across the lake on the pack ice.

Crazy old man. Could have killed himself.

Octavia grabbed her walkie-talkie and stepped outside. The fog was like pea soup. She couldn't see more than four feet in front of her face. It didn't matter. She'd walked this path ten thousand times as a kid; she could do it with her eyes closed. Octavia found the truck, with its keys in the ignition. There were large pieces of plywood in the bed that she could use as stretchers. As she climbed inside, she heard a young man's voice come over the radio. "Do you guys hear boats?"

"I hear them, but I can't see anything," someone replied.

"Oh, man, this isn't good," a third voice said. "There are a *lot* of them. I can hear them idling out there. Sounds like at least fifty or a hundred. Can't see anything in this fog, though."

"Natalia called it. They're here. Get ready!"

Octavia rolled down the window. She heard the puttering sounds of a hundred motorboats out in the lake. She could tell they were close, maybe only a few hundred yards away. Then, one after the other, the pirates' boat engines were turned off until there was no sound but the waves lapping the beach.

Octavia sat there in the foggy, snowy, silent tension for a minute until she heard a new sound: a man's scream. A bloody war cry coming from out in the water. Then, in unison, a thousand screams just like it. The noise shook her to her core.

They're really here. Octavia froze. If she started the engine again, they'd hear it. "Shit, shit," she said under her breath. *What should I do?*

The lone voice, the one who'd screamed the first time, made a new noise now. Rhythmic, like a chant. "Huh, huh!" Followed by what sounded like two thumps on a boat's hull. He did it twice and was then joined by several hundred imitators doing it in unison.

Huh, huh! BANG! BANG!

Huh, huh! BANG! BANG!

Octavia's heart beat hard as she sat there listening to the pirates' taunts. This went on for a minute or so, and then Octavia heard Jeff on the radio.

"How adorable. Let's sing them *our* song. Light these bastards up!"

From all over the island, Octavia heard the roar of machine-gun fire. The students were spraying bullets indiscriminately onto the lake, hoping to hit what they couldn't see. Then, from the water, came a return volley of even greater intensity. She heard two bullets slam through the walls of the pickup truck's bed just three feet behind her. Panicked, Octavia turned the key in the pickup's ignition. *Wuh-wuh-wuh.* Nothing. Octavia sat there, frozen, unsure of what to do.

"Man down!" said a voice she didn't recognize over the radio. "Gunshot wound at the south tower. We need help."

You have a job to do, Octavia reminded herself. She picked up the radio. "I'm on my way. Stay there." She turned the key again and watched the cabin lights dim as she futilely tried to get the engine started. *Wuh-wuh-wuh.* Nothing. "Fuck!" she screamed over the roar of the gunfire.

58

Len opened his eyes. Night. He felt chill on his skin.

Where am I? he asked himself.

He felt a tiny cold thing land on his forehead. Then another, followed by several more. Snow. He became cognizant of being on his back, staring up at an impossibly dark sky from which the tiny flakes fell. The darkness disquieted him.

The sky is never this dark. Not when it snows. Not ever.

Len sat up. He'd been lying on the ground in the snow. Looking around, he saw gray stones that had been cut into familiar shapes. Obelisks, rectangles, crosses.

A cemetery. What am I doing here?

Standing, he felt a pang in his guts. Hunger, but not the kind one might feel after hard physical work. This was the sort of hunger that had gone on for too long: days, maybe weeks, maybe longer. He felt nauseated and woozy, as though his stomach were digesting itself. Len looked around. The cemetery seemed to go on forever over rolling hills. Trying to get his bearings, he looked for Polaris but didn't see any stars at all. Just that ghastly, abyssal blackness.

"Hello?" Len shouted, his confusion turning to steam in the cold, dark air. "Is anyone there?" Hearing no reply, he looked down at his body, almost as if he were making sure it was still there.

Where did I get these clothes? These aren't my clothes.

His hands looked strange.

These aren't my hands.

Refusing to let disquietude take the reins, Len decided to pick a direction and walk. He figured snow on the ground meant he'd leave tracks and wouldn't end up going in circles. He reasoned he'd have to end up somewhere eventually, no matter which direction he picked.

Len trudged through the snow, hearing it crunch under his boots. The starvation in his guts grew worse as he walked, until he was salivating and felt ready to vomit.

Gotta keep going. This cold will kill me before the hunger does.

Len traipsed on for what felt like hours, cresting hill after hill without seeing any sign of a living person. Each gravestone was unique, but the overall scenery didn't change much: dead trees, snow, carved marble.

How did I get here? What kind of graveyard goes on forever like this?

Exhausted and famished, Len eventually sat down on a sarcophagus, too tired to go on. He closed his eyes, put his face in his hands, and tried to think of what to do.

"Keep going" came a whisper.

Len looked up in a panic. "Who said that?" He looked all around but didn't see anyone.

Staring at him from several rows over was a large granite angel, hands outstretched as if indicating a desire to help. Len went over to the statue and poked it. Stone. There was something familiar about its face that he couldn't put his finger on.

I'm losing it. I should keep walking. Len gathered his resolve and slogged through the deep drifts to the top of the nearest hill.

There, at the apex, he saw something new in the valley down below. A grand, gothic cathedral. It was lit up from the inside, its beautiful stained-glass windows casting light on the snow all around. Red, blue, green, yellow—a little explosion of color and light in a foreboding wasteland.

They'll have food. Thank God.

Len stumbled down the snowy hill to the church and used his strange hands to knock at the entrance. Thump, thump, thump. He waited for a minute or two and then knocked harder. No answer. Deciding his survival to be more important than courtesy, he used the last of his strength to pull the massive wooden door open and then close it behind him.

Inside, it was just as cold as outside. The brilliant stained-glass windows cast a mesmerizing kaleidoscope of patterns all over the enormous room. Len looked up at them.

Wait. There's no light source in here. The illumination is coming from outside now. How is that possible?

Unfazed, Len went up to the chancel and began looking for something to eat. He searched behind the lecterns, in the pulpits, and inside the gilded containers. Nothing.

There has to be something. Communion wafers, anything will do. I feel like I haven't eaten in years.

Len tried to think of a solution, but his mind was fuzzy from hunger. He stared down at the dazzling patterns of color cast onto the floor by the windows.

Maybe I've never eaten.

"It's time. You know what to do" came the whisper.

Len looked up. Towering over the pews of the church was the stone angel again. Enormous now, her mighty wings spread the entire length of the transept.

I do know what to do.

Len reached up and put his hands on either side of his head. He then pushed hard—so hard that he gave himself a headache. He kept squeezing his cranium like this until it gave way at the sutures, and he felt the plates of his skull crack open like an eggshell. Len reached up and peeled away his scalp, pulling the bones away from his cerebrum. The top of his skull was now gone, his brain exposed to the cold air. Carefully, and with great reverence, he lifted his entire brain from its shell like the meat from a walnut hull. He stared at it for a while, then ate it.

59

Octavia tried to start the vehicle again. Another bullet hit the truck's front bumper and, as if that shot had been the kick in the ass it needed, the ancient gasoline engine turned over with a rumble. The headlights and windshield wipers came on with the engine, brushing an inch of snow off the windshield. Shrieking with relief and astonishment, she immediately killed the headlights, which were at best useless in the fog and at worst a target. Octavia put the vehicle in gear and headed to the south watchtower, resisting the fight-or-flight compulsion to drive fast in the murkiness. Slowly, carefully, unable to see, she navigated the familiar path only by the preternatural anamnesis granted through a childhood of repetition. With bullets cracking past from every direction, those five hundred feet felt like the longest drive of Octavia's life. *One foot in front of the other,* her dad used to say. *Only think about one step at a time; you'll get overwhelmed thinking about the whole problem.*

"That's enough!" Natalia yelled over the radio. "Stop wasting ammo! Don't shoot until you can actually see them. They're drawing our fire to count our numbers."

Once the islanders stopped shooting, the pirates did too. A few more seconds of dead silence. Octavia heard the vile cadence once again through her open driver's-side window.

Huh, huh! BANG! BANG!
Huh, huh! BANG! BANG!

Octavia parked her makeshift ambulance in front of the south tower and bolted from the car to find the patient. She followed a trail of bright red blood on the newly fallen snow to find a zit-faced kid of about nineteen who had been dragged inside the concrete shelter by his comrades. Three people were hunched over him, trying to keep him calm as he screamed and writhed.

"Step aside," Octavia said. "Does anyone have a flashlight?" Someone pulled one out of a pocket. "Great. Shine it on this wound so I can see what I'm doing." She pointed to the islanders who were watching. "OK, you there, I need you to find something that we can use to prop this leg up. A box, anything. You, big guy, come here. You see where my finger is? This is the femoral artery. I need you to use all your muscle and pinch here as hard as you can. That will temporarily stop the blood loss. You, young lady, find something I can use as a tourniquet."

"Are you a doctor?" the injured kid asked through pained panting.

"No, I'm a nurse. My name is Octavia."

"Octavia? Len's daughter?" he said through his teeth.

"Yeah."

"I've heard all about you," he said.

"I've been away for a while. I haven't met all you new people. What's your name?" Octavia asked while putting latex gloves on.

"Xavier," he grunted.

"Xavier, I'm going to do what I can for you. I need you to try to stay awake. Can you do that for me?"

Xavier nodded with a pained expression as Octavia put on latex gloves and examined the wound in the middle of his thigh.

"The femur is fractured, but I think the bullet missed the artery," Octavia said. "Xavier, if we can get you to a real hospital, you'll get to keep this leg."

Just then the first guy came back with a wooden crate to elevate the appendage. "I also found this," he said, handing her a shitty little first-aid kit.

"Great," Octavia said. "Now can you find me two things that are long and straight, like two-by-fours or broom handles? Also, something like rope or tape to wrap the leg up with?"

Once she had all the necessary items, Octavia began field dressing the wound and splinting Xavier's leg. Outside, she could hear the pirates getting louder.

"So what did my dad tell you about me?" Octavia asked vacantly, her attention on her work.

"Your dad said all the time what a great person you are." Xavier inhaled sharply as Octavia repositioned his leg in the process of splinting it.

"He did?" Octavia looked at him. She'd asked the question to take Xavier's mind off the pain and hadn't really expected such an answer.

"Yeah," Xavier said, in between whimpers of pain. "Heart of gold. Always said he admired you."

Octavia felt emotion coming up but rammed it back down into her gut.

Keep your head on your work.

"This is about as good as it gets," Octavia said to the onlookers. "I have plywood that we can use as a stretcher in the bed of the pickup. I'll need help getting him to the truck. Xavier, you're going to be OK."

Octavia and three others did their best to carry the patient on the ungainly piece of wood. As they loaded him into the bed of the truck, the pirates began launching bright white flares into the fog above their heads. The flares did nothing to improve visibility but made the thick mist and the chanting even more disconcerting. Octavia quickly got into the truck and put it in gear, heading back to her half-assed clinic.

Octavia stopped outside the meditation hall, threw open the truck's door, ran around to the back and, with the help of one of the larger islanders, pulled Xavier out of the bed of the truck. As they did so, Xavier howled from the pain as he was jostled about. In between screams, Octavia could hear the pirates begin shooting again.

She pulled Xavier onto a roll-out bed on the floor then hastily scrounged around in the bins for morphine, finding a large box of injection vials. She took out a vial, inserted the needle, pulled the plunger up, and was surprised to see the syringe was still empty. The little morphine bottle was empty.

What kind of jerk puts a used vial back in the box?

Flustered, she pulled out a handful of others. Every single one of them had been emptied. Octavia dumped the whole box onto the floor and let out a yell of frustration.

Octavia and her patient were shaken by an explosion only fifty feet away. The concussion blew the glass windows out on one side of the meditation hall, which was followed by the sound of dirt raining down onto the roof.

"Octavia," Natalia barked over the walkie-talkie, gunfire and shouting in the background. "We need you at the west tower right now!'"

"I'm sorry; we're out of morphine," Octavia hollered at Xavier over the din while throwing supplies into a bag and running out the door. "I'll be back! Hang in there!"

"To hell with slow and careful," Octavia said, driving faster than before.

The fog, formerly dark, was now strobing at random intervals with light from explosions and flares. Just as she pulled up to the west tower, machine gun bullets sliced through the impenetrable gloom and ripped through the truck's windshield in rapid succession. One, two, three, four. She felt the third one slam into her chest. She didn't even notice when the fourth one hit her too. Octavia opened the truck door and dropped to the ground outside. She felt warm liquid running down her side. Looking down at her body, she saw that fresh blood was soaking her white jacket.

Well, shit. How the hell am I supposed to help people like this?

60

Darkness.

Where am I?

Like waking from a night terror into the further shock of a pitch-black room, Len flailed around in the darkness to touch something, anything. He felt nothing; he saw nothing. Unable to grab hold of anything, he decided to move. Len walked, slowly and carefully so as not to trip or fall into any holes. Eventually, he discovered something with his outstretched hand. It was wet. Stone of some sort. Maybe concrete. Wherever he was felt cool and damp. He wondered if he was underground. There was a slight breeze. These sensations kept him from panicking about not being able to see.

He put his hands to his face and realized, to his abject horror, that his eyes were not there. The sockets were empty; his eyelids hung like limp drapes over an open window. He screamed in dread. No reply but an echo. He collapsed to the floor, suffocating in hysteria and despair.

"My eyes! Where are my eyes!"

Breathe. Breathe. Let's figure this out. Panic never solved anything. Len tried to calm down and analyze the situation.

There was an echo from his screams. He was in a cave, alone, with no eyes. How did he get into such a state?

Len stood up and felt for the stone object he'd felt earlier. He traced his finger along it. Wet, wet, rough. The rough part was mortar, perhaps? Wet, wet, rough.

This is a masonry wall.

Len walked sideways, following the length of the wall carefully and deliberately. After some time of this, he saw something. A pinpoint of light. Some small object, perhaps, or one that was very far away.

Wait a second.

He felt his face again. His eyes were still missing, yet he could definitely see a little speck of light.

How is this possible?

Len tried not to get excited and kept following the wall, one scrupulous step at a time. It wasn't a small object. It was a distant object, Len reasoned, because it grew in size as he approached it. As he drew ever nearer, the tiny light grew until it provided enough illumination for him to see that he was in a tunnel.

Closer to the source, the light increased until it became painful and blinding. Len covered his empty eye sockets, but the futile gesture didn't do anything to limit his vision. He could see right through his hands. In fact, he could see in every direction. Up, down, left, right, in front of him, and behind him. Unsure of what else to do but deciding the dark tunnel to be the greater evil, Len walked into the unyielding whiteness.

61

Lying on the ground, chaos and death in every direction, Octavia inspected the wound on her arm. It was bleeding and hurt like hell, but she could still move the limb. *A bit of triceps damage, but otherwise mostly superficial*, she thought. Fearing the worst, she stuck her finger in the shallow hole above her sternum. The bullet hadn't pierced the chest plate. *Thank God I put the body armor on.*

Octavia reached up into the truck and pulled her bag of supplies out. With her good arm, she injected her wound with an antihemorrhagic and then wrapped a bunch of gauze around it. She held the loose end of the gauze in her teeth as she cut it with scissors and then did the same with a bunch of tape to keep it in place.

Good enough. Stop farting around; people need you.

Octavia crawled on the ground, as fast as she could, to the entrance of the west tower and banged on the steel door. "It's me, Octavia. Let me in!"

Natalia opened the door holding a rifle, and Octavia scrambled to get inside. "You're bleeding!" Natalia said.

"It's not a big deal. Who needs my help?"

Natalia pointed to a man on the floor who was lying on his back and twitching.

"He was down at the beach when the shooting began."
Natalia said.

Blood trickled from a mangled left eye socket while the
right eye stared vacantly at the ceiling of the tower.

"Jesus, Natalia," Octavia said. "He's been shot through
the head."

"But he still has a pulse," Natalia said.

"Is that the monk?" Octavia asked.

"Yeah," Natalia said. "Mutoku. Dammit. I told him it was
dangerous to stand out there. Stubborn bastard didn't listen."

"I'll dress this wound as best I can, but he's probably
brain dead," Octavia said while checking his heartbeat in his
neck. "I don't know if I can do anything for him."

Octavia rummaged in her bag for supplies while Natalia
stared intently out of the observation slit in the watchtower
wall.

"The fog is lifting," Natalia said ominously. "That's not
good."

Octavia patched the monk's eye socket and irrigated the
exit wound in the back of his skull. She taped his remaining
eye closed and carefully wrapped his entire head with gauze.
The white undergarments under Mutoku's black robe were
now wet and crimson.

"This is it," Jeff said over the radio. "The fog is clearing.
Get ready!"

Natalia and Octavia looked at each other.

"This thing will be a death trap when they land," Natalia
said, referring to the concrete watchtower. "Don't stay in here!"

"Where are you going?" Octavia asked.

"Outside," Natalia said. "I want to meet these fuckers face to face."

"What should I do?"

"Take this," Natalia said, reaching for the holster on her leg. From it, she pulled the old revolver that she'd purchased at the Bazaar.

"What am I supposed to do with that?" Octavia asked.

"Go outside and lie down behind a tree," Natalia instructed. "When you see them, kill them."

Octavia took the gun apprehensively.

Natalia gave Octavia a brief hug and then looked her stepdaughter in the eye. "Do svidánija. See you on the other side, my love." With that, Natalia turned to the door and charged out into the darkness.

That woman is nuts, Octavia thought. She stuffed the antique firearm under her body armor so she'd have both hands free to move Mutoku outside. With otherworldly adrenaline strength, she pulled Mutoku twenty yards through the beach grass to a stand of trees that she could use for cover. Winded from the pain in her arm and the exertion of dragging a limp human body, she collapsed to the ground.

Madness. Sheer madness, Octavia thought while catching her breath. *Who the hell wants an island this badly? What was the point of letting it get this far? Couldn't we just have moved?* Obstinance—that's what it was. Natalia had the money to live anywhere in the world but refused to give up her ground on principle.

From out on the lake came a worrisome sound: hundreds of speedboats starting their engines simultaneously. Octavia rolled over and looked out between the trees. The mist was not as thick now, and the light of the full moon was permeating through it. She could see as far as the shore of the island. By unheard cue, all of the motorboats revved their engines simultaneously and raced toward the island. Octavia saw several boats plow through the fog and skid recklessly up onto the rocks of the beach. Some of them tipped over; others landed upright.

The boats were packed with people, all of whom jumped out onto the rocks of the beach, immediately falling to their bellies and crawling inland. The pirates engaged first with rockets and firearms. The islanders ripped into the invaders with Dranthyx plasma rifles, strobing the scene with horrific bluish-white pulses of light. The noise was horrendous; Octavia plugged her ears. Then she saw what Natalia had been talking about: a lone figure, too far away to see clearly, ran up to the watchtower where she'd been only moments earlier and tossed something inside. A grenade. The figure ran away as the force of the explosion blew the tower's steel door off its hinges. As the fighting intensified, more pirates came ashore. Hundreds of them. Some ran right past her as they stormed the island.

Then, from nowhere, a powerful bolt of lightning struck the already-damaged west tower, causing its thick concrete walls to shatter like a crystal vase.

A thunderstorm? We don't have enough problems right now?

Octavia looked up into the sky. Her heart stopped for three whole beats. Looming over the dark lake like an apparition in the thinning fog was the largest object she'd ever seen, like a purple oil tanker hovering in the sky.

A Dranthyx airship.

The massive craft sent out measured pulses of electricity, obliterating the island's defenses. *Boom, boom, boom,* a rhythmic bombardment that lit the place up as bright as day. *My kids. Please, please let them be OK. I have to get back to them.* Octavia turned around just in time to see the island's large laser tower explode like a slow-motion firecracker.

"East end is completely overrun!" someone yelled over the radio.

Panicked that the pirates would hear the radio and discover her before she could get back to the house to save her kids, Octavia fumbled to find the walkie-talkie to turn it off.

"Fuck 'em. We're going down swinging." Another voice came through the static.

"What's this?" asked someone to Octavia's left.

Turning to see who'd said it, Octavia saw a monstrous creature staring at her—a being with arms and legs like a Komodo dragon, but with a cobra's head. It had metallic fangs that glinted with the distant pulses of plasma fire. Octavia scrambled to get up from her prone position and escape. The snake man lunged at her and tackled her to back the ground. Octavia struggled to retrieve Natalia's gun from under her body armor, but she couldn't reach it with the creature's heavy body on top of hers. *Plan B.*

She bit his hand hard, causing the serpent to roar in pain. Octavia then turned into him, the way her dad had taught her, and tried to gouge the creature's eyes out. Enraged at her attempt to blind him, the snake knocked her out cold with a sharp crack of his tail to her head.

62

Len found himself in a great round room, which he surveyed with his supernatural, panoramic vision. The ceiling was like a planetarium, a vaulted expanse that twinkled with stars and galaxies. Beneath him were marble floor tiles cut into unusual shapes, which were fitted together like a jigsaw puzzle. All around the edges of the room were stone arches leading to tunnels like the one he'd just come through. Some of the tunnels were lighted, others dark. In the center of the room, on a gigantic plinth, was the stone angel. The angel, even larger in size now, dwarfed him.

"Who are you?" Len demanded.

"No one," she whispered back without stirring or moving her lips.

"No one?"

"No one. Same as you," she replied.

"What do you want with me?"

For the first time, the angel moved. She raised her head to look at him with her granite eyes, empty holes for pupils. She lifted her hand and pointed to the tunnel entrances ringing the room.

"You must pick a path," she whispered.

"Why?"

"You cannot stay here."

"Where are we?"

"Beyond probability."

"What does that mean?" Len asked.

"Pick a path."

Len considered each, unsure of which one to choose.

"That one?" Len asked, pointing to a darkened arch.

"It is not time for that one," the angel whispered.

"Which one, then?"

"Pick one that is illuminated."

Len saw one tunnel, brighter than all the rest. *That one? No. Too easy. Something feels wrong with that one. Doesn't sit well in my gut.* He looked around to find a suitable alternative. *The one over there, the third or fourth brightest—that's the right choice.*

"That one?" Len asked, pointing to his selection.

The angel nodded. Len didn't know if the nod indicated that he'd made the right choice, or if it merely acknowledged that he'd made *a* choice. Len walked over to his chosen tunnel. He stood just outside the arch, unable to see past the blinding illumination to what might be inside. He looked back at the angel, who watched him silently with her expressionless stone face. Len took a deep breath and then stepped inside.

63

Octavia rolled over and vomited. *My head. My fucking head. Where am I? What the hell is going on?* She tried to stand up but found her hands were tied behind her back. Lying on her stomach was uncomfortable; there was some rigid object pressing against her rib cage. *A rock? No, Natalia's gun. I think I have a concussion.* She rolled back over and did her best to sit up.

She found herself sitting in the yard in front of the meditation hall. Overhead loomed the enormous airship, from which powerful spotlights were cast downward onto the island. Things everywhere were burning, with one large bonfire in the middle of the rifle range to her right. About fifty other islanders were sitting there with her, all of whom were bound or handcuffed.

My kids? Where are my kids?

Octavia looked around in alarm. There, twenty feet to her right, sat Bernie. He was rocking back and forth, staring up at the Dranthyx flier. *He seems OK, thank God.* Lying on the ground next to him was Iris. She didn't appear to be moving. *Is she breathing? Please tell me she isn't dead. Can I get over there without attracting attention?*

Octavia looked around to assess the situation. Pirates were everywhere. Hundreds of them, like a parade of the grotesque: gorillas, alligators, hyenas. Some of them were a bizarre combination of several animals, while others were so hideously deformed from so much gene editing that it was impossible to tell what they were supposed to be. A good number of the beasts hooted and shouted as they carried Octavia's childhood books and furniture out of the house to throw into the bonfire. Others taunted their captives by poking them with hot objects that had been in the fire. A pair of cheetahs copulated loudly next to a pile of burning debris while a grizzly bear squatted to foul the carcass of a dead islander. Their leader, Wogan, sat there in the middle of the chaos on an old chair that had been taken from Len and Natalia's house. He smiled and reveled in his conquest while smoking a cigar. Sitting next to him was a catlike woman.

Savages.

Octavia's head was throbbing with the beat of the atrocious music they were blasting, which made her feel like barfing again. She estimated that if she moved slowly toward Iris, the pirates wouldn't notice in all the hubbub. Also, every single one of them appeared to be intoxicated. Carefully, slowly, she scooted over.

Iris's eyes were closed, and her breathing was shallow and slow.

"Iris, can you hear me?" Octavia yelled over the din.

"I think she's sedated," Jeff said.

Octavia looked over. She hadn't noticed Jeff among her fellow prisoners.

"Why?"

"I have no idea," Jeff answered. "Maybe they drugged her. These people are barbarians."

"What are they going to do with us?" Octavia asked.

Jeff shrugged. Just then, a panda with sharp horns and a mouthful of shark teeth came over to the prisoner area, dragging a very unwilling captive. A woman—hands, feet, and mouth duct taped—was thrashing and struggling while making muffled curses. Octavia felt tears of joy welling up at seeing that Natalia was still alive.

Natalia looked over at her fellow islanders, briefly making eye contact with Octavia.

"Oy, Captain Wogan!" the panda-shark bellowed. "Look who I have, sir!"

Wogan was holding an object from Octavia's formative years: a pink cartoon princess hand mirror. He bent over and furiously snorted a line of white powder off its surface. Wogan's glowing eyes rolled back into his head for a few seconds. He wiped his disgusting sheep nose, which blew steam into the cold air, then handed the mirror to Thunder Cunt. Wogan stood up to inspect the acquisition. Seeing whom the panda had captured, Wogan guffawed.

"Well, look who it is!" Wogan grinned, squatting down to look Natalia in the eye. "The famous Natalia Zherdeva! Good on ya, mate." Wogan tossed the panda a baggie of white powder, then ripped the tape off Natalia's mouth.

"Oh, you got anything to say to me now, bitch?" Thunder Cunt hissed at Natalia.

"What do you animals want?" Natalia growled.

"We came here for two things. One, the island. But you knew that already. Two, you. Now we have both."

"Me? Why do you want me? Are you a pervert or something?"

"Now, what would I want from a scrag like you?" Wogan chuckled. "You're not my type, miss. No fur, no claws. What good are ya?" He grabbed Natalia under her jaw and forcefully turned her head, inspecting her face. "Though I think with some work, you'd look all right. What do you think, TC? The pale white skin and light-blue eyes say something arctic. A snow fox? A lynx?"

"Nah." TC sneered. "Let's turn her into something ugly. Like a warthog."

Wogan laughed. "Nah, missy, it ain't me who wants ya. It's the bigwigs. You're quite an important sheila, apparently. They want you so bad, they gave us a hundred boats and seventy kilos of Cali—enough to get this beast working," Wogan declared proudly, pointing to the old Dranthyx airship floating overhead.

"Well, now you have me. You have the island. These people aren't what you want," Natalia said, moving her head to indicate the other prisoners. "So let them go."

"Now why would I do a stupid thing like that?"

"Because I'll pay you."

"What?" Wogan laughed.

"Money. Land Credits. You let them go, I will have a half billion LCs wired to your account. If you don't, you get nothing."

"Account? Hah! We don't do banks, love. We're all embargoed." Wogan grunted in disdain, pointing to the big

T tattooed on his wrist. "This is strictly a cash business that we run. You have that bank of yours deliver a pile of LCs in cash to this island, then we'll talk."

"It doesn't work that way," Natalia said. "That kind of thing can't be done remotely. They have security protocols. I'd have to call ahead, then go to the bank in person to withdraw that much money."

"Fine. We'll take you to the bank. You withdraw the cash, and then we'll let them go."

"And where will the prisoners be while I'm withdrawing the money?" Natalia asked.

"Here, on the island. Where else?"

"I'd rather exchange money for prisoners all at once," Natalia said. "To keep things simple. So here's my offer. You put all of us on a boat, even the wounded, and take us to Cleveland. I will go to the bank as soon as it opens and withdraw the money for you. When I give the money to you, you let everyone go. Then you can hand me over to whoever it is that wants me."

Wogan puffed on his cigar a few times as he considered the offer. "Not half a billion, love, *two* billion."

Natalia frowned, then looked over at her fellow islanders. "Fuck. Fine. Two billion."

Wogan sneered and summoned over some of his menagerie. "Oy. Get these losers loaded onto the laker, the big one we were gonna use for moving our shit over here. Take them to Cleveland. Mate, are you listening?"

"Yes, sir," a large snapping turtle answered.

"You'd better be. This is important. You're to keep everyone on board the laker until I tell you otherwise. Except that one there," he said, pointing at Natalia. "You're to escort her to her bank. She's going to withdraw money. Do not let her out of your sight. You bring her and the money back to me. If there's any trouble, you kill every single one of these fucks. Got it?"

The turtle replied in the affirmative.

"When do the prisoners get released?" Natalia asked.

Wogan scowled in disgust at Natalia, then turned to the Turtle. "When I give the OK, and only when I give the OK, you release the rest of these idiots. Got it?" Wogan said.

"Yessir," the turtle said.

"And don't even think about running off with my cash," Wogan growled, baring his teeth and poking the turtle in the chest. "There's nowhere on this earth you can hide."

"Boss, are you sure you wanna do dis?" TC asked tactfully. "The big guys are gonna be pissed if she escapes."

"Bring thirty of our best men with you," Wogan said to the turtle. He then turned to Natalia. "If you run or call for help, all your friends die. Understood?"

Natalia nodded curtly. "Fine. Give me your number so I can call you when I have the money."

Wogan cut Natalia's hands and feet free, then handed her a card.

"Captain Adger Wogan, Privateer. Lake Syndicate," Natalia said, reading it aloud.

Wogan's beasts marched the islanders down to the dock, where a large vessel awaited them. The islanders who couldn't walk were carried down by moose-apes and winged rhinos, then tossed blithely onto the deck. Octavia saw Iris, still drugged, get dumped into a corner. She heard Bernie shrieking somewhere nearby, no doubt agitated by being handled roughly. He hated being touched. A foul-smelling tiger-like caiman shoved Octavia, causing her to collide painfully with the bulkhead. The islanders were made to sit in the large, empty cargo bay while the pirates kept guns trained on them.

Octavia felt the watercraft pulling away from the dock into the choppy waters of the open lake. The laker they were in was big but not absurdly so, not like the huge ore freighters. Other than the prisoners and their captors, the cargo hold was empty. Octavia tried to discreetly count her captors. Thirty, all carrying weapons.

Looking around, she saw the islanders sneaking glances at one another, trying to communicate something without saying it. From behind, Octavia felt someone nudging her. Without turning around, she felt something cold and metallic being placed into her hands, which were zip tied tightly behind her back. A folding knife.

"Wait for the signal," the person said in a low voice drowned out by Bernie's screams.

Taking the hint, Octavia cut her bonds, then slyly passed the knife to someone next to her.

"Hey, kid, shut up!" one of the animals yelled, pointing his shotgun at Bernie.

"He's autistic!" Octavia interjected over the child's wails, keeping her hands behind her back to conceal her ability to move. "He can't help it! Please don't hurt him!"

"Make him be quiet, or I'll make him be quiet," the pirate warned, racking the slide.

"Bernie, it's mommy. Can you hear me?"

The child stopped howling abruptly. "Yes yes yes," he muttered without looking up. He only ever answered in threes.

"It's very important for you to be quiet right now. I want you to practice your calligraphy in your imagination. Can you do that?"

"OK OK OK," Bernie said. He looked up at the ceiling and began rocking back and forth silently.

The pirate's moose face twisted with disappointment as he lowered his weapon.

That motherfucker wanted to kill my baby, Octavia thought. She felt a primal anger welling up in the ensuing silence. Her teeth ground together as she watched the moose pull a vial of powder out of his pocket and do a bump off the back of his hand. *Keep your cool, Octavia.*

"NOW!" Natalia yelled from the far wall. On a cue they'd never rehearsed, all the students rose up and attacked the nearest pirate.

Octavia pulled her hands from behind her back, reached under her body armor, pulled out Natalia's revolver, and aimed it at the moose who had threatened Bernie. The moose, seeing Octavia's weapon and his compatriots being bum-rushed, raised the shotgun in Octavia's general direction. Octavia shot first, the ferocious magnum round blowing the moose's right lung through his scapula. Stunned by the recoil and the muzzle blast that had echoed throughout the metal room, Octavia's senses became tunnel-like. Nothing but ringing in her ears and the image of the moose in front of her, somehow unfazed by the injury and now aiming his shotgun right at her.

Adrenaline and drugs give people superpowers, Octavia remembered an old nurse saying in the ER one night. *Makes 'em hard to kill. They'll take fifteen bullets to the torso, have their guts hanging out, and they'll still have enough crazy left in 'em to run over and stab you. Someone hopped up on drugs isn't gonna die unless you shoot 'em in the head.*

With inexplicable focus and lightning speed, Octavia fired a second shot, this one through the moose's forehead. She watched his antlered head jerk back, and his shotgun's muzzle dropped. During his body's descent to the floor, the moose's neurological wreckage caused his hairy finger to spasm hard enough to pull the trigger on his shotgun. Octavia saw the muzzle flash and felt the wind of the buckshot whizzing harmlessly by her.

She stood there for a few seconds, oblivious to the turmoil all around her, doubting the reality of what had just happened.

Never killed anyone before.

Octavia turned and, in a dissociative fog of adrenaline, saw the islanders beating the living crap out of their captors. Her dad had always stressed to her and the others that the modern warrior relies too much on gizmos and doesn't know how to use his own body as a weapon. The old man had always been going on about his Japanese samurai shit. Octavia had made fun of him, but she knew he was right. Len wanted his students to be just as dangerous unarmed as they were armed. Here were the results: she felt a bit of pride as one of the younger students choked a rhino unconscious with the beast's own jacket, while an older student broke a hyena's neck. It was obvious that the pirates were out of their depth and knew nothing about hand-to-hand fighting. She could see her dad's judo everywhere: joint locks, throws, sleeper holds. There was new stuff mixed in that students had brought to the island over the years and had been incorporated into the curriculum: kicks, punches, elbows. Eye gouges—ouch.

I killed a man, or whatever the hell that was, and somehow I feel nothing. I always thought it would be a huge coming-of-age event that changes you. Kind of like the time I lost my virginity: my friends hyped it up to be a big deal, but it wasn't. It was just another thing I did in a lifetime of doing things. Inconsequential, like eating fast food. Huh. Now that I think about it, I can't even remember the first time I had sex; I went a little crazy when I finally got off that island.

In less than a minute, all the pirates were dead or incapacitated. Those who hadn't been killed in the melee had their throats cut afterward and were left to choke on their own blood on the metal floor of the cargo hold.

The brutality of murder is its wastefulness. It took thousands of generations of parents sacrificing to make sure that the moose and I survived to that point. In a thoughtless second, one of us killing the other throws away half that effort and love as though it had no meaning. He'd have killed Bernie and me and felt nothing, too. Just business. Just survival.

"Octavia, snap out of it!" Jeff said.

"Huh?"

"Get it together. We have to get out of here."

"I'm not with it right now," Octavia stammered. "I think I have a concussion."

"We've taken over the ship," Jeff pressed, perhaps too agitated by the circumstances to have heard what she'd said. "We're about to dock. We have to leave. Help us get your son above deck so he doesn't have a fit."

On the deck above, Octavia and the kids nearly fell overboard when the big ship rammed into a concrete pier. This was followed by a horrific grinding noise as the metal hull skidded along the concrete. Eventually, they hit another solid object and came to a complete stop, which threw them all to the deck again. Bernie wailed with anxiety. Whoever was at the helm had no idea what he or she was doing.

"Let's go!" Natalia yelled. "Everyone off the boat. We need to get out of here before their buddies figure out what happened!"

"Where are we going?" Octavia asked.

"To high ground. Right now!"

They hastily exited the boat down a ramp. Octavia carried fifty-pound Bernie while several islanders carried the wounded.

"There!" Natalia pointed to a half-finished multistory building covered in scaffolding. "We need to get up there!"

Someone shot the padlock on the construction fence using one of the pirates' guns and then ripped it off the latch. Everyone poured through. They ran up to the fourth floor, the highest completed level. Octavia put Bernie down and fell to the floor, winded from carrying him up so many flights of stairs. Iris, now semilucid, was laid down next to Bernie after being carried fireman style by one of the other islanders. Octavia caught her breath and looked around. The structure was nothing but concrete and steel; there were openings for large windows but no glass in them yet. From that vantage point, they could see past the terminal, out into the open lake. Octavia could see the fires on their distant island. Everyone watched quietly as their home burned.

Natalia reached into her pocket to get Wogan's card out. She then pulled back her sleeve and tapped the screen of her watch several times.

"Yo?" a voice asked, coming from the watch's speaker, loud enough for everyone to hear.

"Who's this?" Natalia asked.

"TC. Who dis?"

"Natalia Zherdeva. May I please speak with Captain Wogan?"

Octavia and the others looked at one another apprehensively, no doubt wondering why Natalia would tip them off to their escape.

"He busy. Ain't you supposed to be going to da bank?"

"I changed my mind."

"Tha fuck you did! You givin' us that money, *puta*. Put my boys on the phone!"

"You mean those smelly zoo animals? Oh, we killed them all."

"You what?!" TC screeched.

"They're all dead," Natalia said through gritted teeth. "And so are you. Enjoy the island, bitch."

Natalia hung up before TC could even ask, then she tapped a few more times to bring up an application.

"Everyone, get down on the floor. Close your eyes! I'm serious. Close them!"

Octavia did as instructed, using her hands to shield the eyes of both her children. In the nervous silence, Octavia could still hear Natalia poking at her watch. With no further warning, there was a flash of light so bright that Octavia briefly saw the blood vessels in her own eyelids.

"What the hell was that?" Iris shrieked, half out of it.

"Stay down!" Natalia ordered, the room filling with a second light, yellow and bright like the sun.

"What is going on?" Iris wailed, struggling to get free of her mother's hand covering her eyes.

Barely twenty seconds had elapsed when the building was hit with something so fierce that it felt as if the whole structure might come off its foundation. The wall of air hit Octavia so violently that it felt like a second concussion.

Octavia looked up. Natalia's face was bathed in a fiery orange light; the glassy, vicious look in her eye made Octavia's blood run backward. Octavia stood up and looked out the window opening. Below, the water of the lake rose up and swallowed the dock that they'd just stood on. The tsunami tossed large boats around like toys and roared through unfinished bottom floors of the building they were in. Over the lake rose a gigantic orange fireball, an artificial sunrise. It roiled upward into the night sky, blooming slowly into a towering mushroom cloud.

64

Len opened his eyes to more blinding light.

I have eyes now?

This time the light was the godawful whitish-blue of LED bulbs. He was in a building with white walls. He was disoriented and out of breath.

Len was suddenly and savagely forced to become cognizant of his body. It felt as though a quartet of gorillas had hold of him, one with each limb, and were using his body as the rope in a four-way game of tug-of-war. Then, after a few seconds of this, each of his limbs was forced to move in an opposite direction.

I'm not being pulled, he realized. *My muscle movements are being manipulated somehow. What the hell is going on here?*

The muscles in his limbs were being forced to contract and stretch, then twist, rotate, extend. He tried to squirm free but had no control over his own body. Instead, he was being controlled. His muscles moved on their own. He felt like a marionette forced into interpretive dance.

All at once, he was hit with a sensation like terrible gas pains that forced his abdominals to contract, doubling him over. Looking down in that position, he saw his own legs constrained to a metal frame by Velcro straps. Then, an impulse forced his spinal erectors to tighten, compelling him to stand up straight. Whatever kind of torture machine he was in had a big circular frame that reminded him of a gyroscope.

Beeping, that incessant beeping of medical devices. He heard someone paging a doctor over the intercom. A hospital.

Len tried to scream, but his lungs were weak. His voice creaked, as though he hadn't spoken in months.

"Hello!" he rasped, not loudly enough to penetrate any walls. "Someone please help me! Where am I?"

One of the impelled motions forced him to twist his torso toward his right arm. Next to his hand, he saw a big red button emblazoned with the words "EMERGENCY STOP." Len tried to hit the button but, at that exact moment, the machine sent electrical impulses into his arm that forced his hand to contract into a fist. As soon as it let up, the machine zapped his extensors, which opened the hand up as though he were waving hello. The machine forced him to rapidly clench and unclench his fist like this ten times. As soon as it let up on his hand, it made him twist his torso in the opposite direction, toward his left hand.

No stop button on this side. Mind over matter. Do it.

Len took note of the timing of the impulses. In the brief space between zaps, he quickly reached out and hit the button with his right hand. Immediately, the impulses stopped, and the frames holding his arms came to rest at his side.

Thank God.

Len tried to assess his situation. He was dripping with sweat. His body remained turned toward the emergency stop.

The Xreth tattoo on my wrist is gone.

Len had barely caught his breath when a nurse came into the room, perhaps alerted by his stopping the device.

"You're awake!" she exclaimed. "You're not supposed to be awake!"

"Why not?" Len asked in a frail, wheezy voice.

"I've never seen anyone come out of an induced coma spontaneously," she said, checking an IV bag nearby. "Are these drugs working? You're supposed to be out cold."

"Where am I? What the hell are you doing to me?"

"You're in a hospital. This machine you're in is called the Exerciser. It's designed to keep people healthy during long periods of unconsciousness. It keeps your muscles toned, your joints mobile, and it keeps blood clots from forming in your limbs. It also trains your brain to use your new spinal cord."

"It feels like pissing on an electric fence. How long have I been out?"

"Six months."

"What?" Len grunted, unsure if he'd heard her correctly.

"Six months. I'm not sure how you woke up, but the timing of it was actually pretty good."

"Why?"

"Your course of treatment is very nearly finished. Let me get you out of that contraption, and we'll have the doctor take a look at you."

Len stood naked before a full-length mirror in his hospital room, mouth agape in astonishment. His hospital gown lay crumpled in a heap on the floor.

This isn't medicine. No, this beyond medicine. This is goddamn sorcery.

Before him stood the reflection of a man in his late twenties in excellent physical health. Where was Len Savitz the septuagenarian? Where were his gray, saggy skin and bent-over posture? Where were the tattoos the Dranthyx had given him? What was going on here? He put his hand to his own head and felt his face, as if he didn't believe what he saw. His hair was thick and brown, his skin taut and smooth, his eyes fresh. His joints felt brand new, as if he could run a marathon. His posture was straight; his vision was sharp and vivid. He flexed his muscles and marveled at their sinewy vigor.

Unreal. I ought to get shot more often.

Len opened and closed his mouth a few times.

Why do my teeth feel weird? My God, they look brand new, he thought, forcing a smile in the mirror. *What the hell is that feeling in my crotch?*

Len looked down. An odd feeling in his genitals, like itching and anger and yearning. It was a bizarre, imperative sensation—like a sneeze that wouldn't come out.

Horny. I'm horny! Holy shit, I'd forgotten what that felt like.

Natalia usually entered rooms like a Russian tank parading through a square, but this time she entered timidly. Len was sitting up in his hospital bed and couldn't remember ever seeing her look so diffident and sheepish. He stared at her, half pissed off and half amazed at how clearly he could see her with his new eyes.

"What the hell did you do to me?" Len asked.

"I know you're upset," Natalia said softly. "You can hate me if you want, but just let me say what I have to say first. OK?"

Might as well hear her out.

"Fine," Len said. His own voice sounded weird to him now.

"Do you remember when we first met?" Natalia asked.

Len nodded.

"You were sitting there on the airplane. I felt like you had a glow. Like you had some sort of power coming from you."

"Really?"

"Yes," she said, putting her hand on his. "I've always been concerned with practical things. Money, work, family. But you had something different that I had not seen before. Something that I lacked, maybe. Like you were concerned with things bigger than yourself. An intensity. Spirituality?" she asked herself, searching for the right word. "Yes, spirituality. Like an aura or something. I had a feeling in my stomach that you were special."

"You've never told me this before," Len said.

"That feeling I had in my stomach was true. You do have that quality. Then, later, I realized that you were also a tough son of a bitch. That sealed the deal. I'd never wanted to get married, but you changed my mind. I knew you were the one."

Len felt flattered for a second, then chuckled internally when he remembered how socially deft Natalia was.

"However," she said, "with great spirituality comes great stubbornness. Those qualities are like twins—they're always found together."

Len couldn't stay angry. He had to laugh at such a canny observation. "I suppose that's true."

"When you broke your hip, you went to the doctor. They replaced the whole joint with a titanium implant. Remember?"

"How could I forget?"

"You didn't have a problem with that surgery. You could have told the surgeon that you wanted your hip to stay old and broken, but you didn't. Did you?"

"No. Why would I?"

"So why do you want to keep your old age? It's broken too, and we can fix it."

Len opened his mouth to reply, but nothing came out.

"For years," she said, "I've seen you teach your students about nonattachment. Don't give in to desires, but don't suppress them either. Simply observe the attachment. See it for what it is, right?"

"Right."

"Maybe there's some kind of integrity in accepting impermanence. But maybe you're just attached to the idea of that, too. You're attached to the idea of dying of old age, like there's honor in it. There's no honor in dying foolishly."

Len sighed. Natalia had special talent for blowing up logical incongruities. Len always found it amazing that she had never done more than five minutes of meditation in her whole life but was sometimes more Zen than he was.

"You are a brave man," Natalia said, "but sometimes you're too reckless with your life. Like you don't appreciate it. Sometimes I wonder why you're always so ready to die."

"It's not that I don't appreciate my life. It's that…" Len thought for a second how to formulate a deeply rooted feeling into a sentence. "I've always felt like a tourist."

"A tourist?"

"Yeah," Len said. "As though I were just passing through. Like my whole life is just a temporary little blip in time, and then it'll be done and forgotten. Other people, they walk around thinking that they're so important—the center of the universe—and that their actions and accomplishments are big and significant. I've never felt that way. I wish I could, but I can't. I've always felt tiny in the grand scheme of things, and I've had no choice but to accept it. What else can I do but learn to live around that feeling?"

"You're not insignificant to me!" Natalia said, her eyes filling with tears. "I love you, and I just want what's best for you. I know you didn't want to be rejuvenated. But I didn't want to go on living without you."

Len couldn't remember her ever looking so emotional or vulnerable. It seemed out of character. He looked into her eyes. Finally, his own tears coming forth, he picked her hand up and kissed it. "I don't deserve you, Natalia."

"I don't deserve you, either. But here we are," she said.

Len leaned up in his hospital bed and held her for a long time. "I feel great, by the way," he said, breaking the silence. "This treatment is amazing."

"I told you!" she said, wiping her eyes.

"How did they do it? Same as yours?"

"Yes. We had no choice. You were in bad shape, dear. Did you know you had lung cancer?"

"What?"

"When they brought you in, they did a chest x-ray to find the bullet. That's when they found the tumor in your lung. Stage three."

"Jesus," Len said.

"Yeah. And if that didn't kill you, the cirrhosis would have. Your liver looked like foie gras. And, even ignoring all that, the bullet had severed your spine, and you were paralyzed from the waist down. You'd have lived all of three months while uncontrollably shitting yourself."

"How on earth did I go from that to this?"

"Oh boy. Where do I start? Well, you were in cryostasis for two months while they grew you a totally new body in a vat. Everything from the neck down is new."

"Are you kidding me?"

"No. They literally cloned your body and transplanted your head. Same thing I had done."

Len looked at her in horror and amazement. He walked over to the mirror again. He felt his neck for a transplant scar but couldn't find one, though he noticed an old scar on his face was no longer there. He felt his ears. The cauliflower from years of judo wasn't there either.

Natalia, knowing exactly what he was looking for, answered preemptively. "And, once they were certain the body transplant had taken, they removed all the flesh off your head and regrew it. Your face is new. So are your eyes, teeth, tongue, and ears. Absolutely everything is new except your brain and skull."

Len was too befuddled to say anything in response.

"Your new body won't age, by the way. I had them fix your telomeres while they were at it."

"How much did this cost?"

"Way, way too much," Natalia answered. "Don't ask. It's my money. You're awfully lucky to have a billionaire for a wife." She chuckled.

"Look at this," Len said, flexing a bicep. "I haven't been this strong in decades. This is crazy. Look at my hair!"

"You look hot," Natalia said.

Len and Natalia locked gazes for a second. Reading each other's minds, both sprang to their feet at the same time. Natalia pulled her own clothes off while Len took a chair and jammed it against the door with the unexpected strength of a much younger man. He tore his hospital gown away and then lifted Natalia up by her buttocks. She wrapped her legs around him as Len pinned her against the wall. Worried orderlies shouted and banged on the door as Len and Natalia made furious love.

65

"Aegis is a corporation," Elise said out of the blue.

"Yeah?" Dan said, his attention elsewhere. Frustrated, he untied his tie and tried again while looking in the mirror in the back of his limousine.

Goddammit, I'm going to wrinkle it if I keep tying and untying it.

"Why do we bother with elections?" she asked.

Why does the double Windsor knot have to be so difficult? I need to buy special ties that are long enough just to get this stupid knot to look right. If it isn't long enough, the knot takes up too much length, and the tie doesn't even make it to my navel. Looks retarded.

"It's not like soft-drink companies ask the public who should be the CEO," Elise said.

Then you have to get the dimple in the middle just right, or it looks like your mom dressed you. I've been doing this knot for twenty years, and I still can't get it right.

"Honestly," Elise said, "I think we should do away with these elections. The members aren't qualified to make a decision."

Dan stopped midknot and looked at Elise.

Elise, as if suddenly self-conscious of her verbal stream of thought, looked back at him like a terrified rabbit.

"Elise," Dan said, shifting his eyes back to the mirror and resuming his fiddling with the tie, "all corporations have elections. They always have. Shareholders have always voted on who will lead the corporation. That's been true for hundreds of years. Keep in mind, our members aren't just members. They're also shareholders. Because, technically speaking," Dan said, pulling the knot tight, "Aegis is a co-op. Most governments are."

Dan looked at the knot in the mirror. After the eighth time, he'd gotten it right.

"How do I look?" Dan asked.

"Like the next principal," Elise said.

Dan looked out the window.

Lansing. Damn war zone. The farther from the water, the worse the crime. We need more of a presence out here to keep order.

Elise, apparently thinking exactly the same thought, spoke up. "Do you want me to call for a security detail?"

Dan let air escape from his lips. "It's not that. I just hate campaigning."

"Really?" Elise asked, seemingly genuinely surprised at Dan's words, as though she hadn't considered that he might want to be doing something else with his life.

"Yeah," Dan said matter-of-factly. "No one enjoys this."

"Then why do you do it?"

I forget sometimes that she's young.

"To make the world a better place," he stated. "Life isn't always about doing fun things."

The limo pulled up to the Aegis Community Center in downtown Lansing. The Community Center was one of the

Aegis Outreach programs, which offered free services to disadvantaged people who couldn't afford a government membership. Aegis Outreach was a highly contentious program. Many Aegis members didn't approve of their membership fee being spent in such a manner; they said it drove up their costs and spread resources too thin. To others, it was a philanthropic gesture that made them feel better about being an Aegis member; a social contract sort of thing that put their consciences at ease. To a third and more pragmatic group, it was simply good PR because other governments had similar programs.

The media, which had been notified ahead of time, was waiting on the sidewalk for Dan's arrival. As the driver came around and opened the door, several cameras were practically shoved into the vehicle. Dan forced a smile as he tried to get out of the car gracefully with so many reporters in his face. Normally his bodyguards would have kept the cameramen at bay and made some space for him, but he'd ordered them to stay home that day. They'd protested because of the astronomical crime rate in Lansing, of course, but Dan refused and insisted on going without them. He figured the presence of armed, uniformed personnel wouldn't be sending the right message in a marginalized community.

Better to risk personal safety than bad optics.

"How are you folks?" Dan cheerfully asked the crowd of newspeople.

Waving and ignoring their questions, he walked into the community center, holding the door for Elise. Inside, the enthusiastic, star-struck director took Dan on a tour of the facility. Dan went through the typical bevy of photo ops while the cameramen followed him around. He listened to the concerns of homeless families sleeping on cots, he put on an apron and served food to people in line in the cafeteria, and rounded out his tour by getting a flu shot at the center's clinic.

On the way out the front door, Dan stopped on the sidewalk to finally answer the newspeople's questions.

"Mr. Barton," one of them asked, "is it true you're being pressured to shutter these community centers because they're not profitable?"

"Some of our members have voiced displeasure about them," Dan answered diplomatically. "However, I won't budge. These centers are godsends to thousands of families, and they're not going anywhere. If Aegis has the resources to help people, then why shouldn't we?"

"Some are saying it'll cost you the election."

"If that's the case"—Dan shrugged—"so be it."

"Hey!" someone screamed from far away. "Hey! Help! Help me!"

Dan turned in the direction of the screams and stood on his toes to see past all the reporters. "Guys, what's going on over there?" He motioned for some of the cameramen to get out of the way so he could get a better look.

About fifty feet away, a young man in a hoodie appeared to be pulling a purse away from an elderly lady. With one hard yank, the young man knocked her off balance and sent the frail woman to the ground. He viciously stomped on her arm to loosen her grip on her handbag, then ran across the street as she wailed in pain.

"Excuse me," Dan said, shoving the reporters aside. Once out of the media crush, Dan dashed across the street without even looking to see if cars were coming.

The thief, his hood obscuring his peripheral vision and seemingly unaware that Dan was pursuing him, slowed down after half a block.

Dan ran into the man full force, tackling him to the ground. The young man struggled to get free, but Dan overpowered him. The thief ended up on his back with Dan sitting on top of him. He tried to take a swing at Dan, but Dan simply moved out of the way and landed a punch of his own. Dan scored a second blow, which knocked the thief's head into the sidewalk, rendering the him unconscious.

Satisfied that the knocked-out thug was no longer a threat, Dan stood up and bent over to pick the old lady's purse up off the sidewalk so he could return it to her. His heart was racing, and his hands were shaking. Despite that, he felt something odd: a cold breeze on his ass. He twisted around to get a better look. The seat of his pants had ripped wide open in the scuffle. His red boxer shorts were clearly visible. Embarrassment trumping adrenaline, he turned and looked across the street. An entire bevy of cameramen had caught the episode on video.

"How was Lansing?" Randy smirked as Dan and Elise walked through the revolving doors in the lobby of Aegis Plaza.

Dan gave him a galled look. He took off his suit jacket, which had also been torn in the altercation, and threw it at Randy.

"I told you to bring security with you," Randy said, putting his hands up to catch it. "But I'm glad you didn't listen."

"Eat me," Dan retorted.

"That little scuffle was all caught on camera," Randy said, grinning.

"Yeah, I know," Dan said, red-faced. "I ripped my pants tackling that dirtbag. That's on TV? Was my underwear hanging out?"

"Yes. And it looked great!" Randy exclaimed. "Absolutely heroic!"

"Do not mess with me. I am not in the mood for it."

"I'm not. I'm being totally serious. We couldn't have paid for better publicity! Politicians always talk about getting tough on crime, but the whole world just saw the chairman of Aegis personally beating the snot out of a street thug with his bare hands! My God, the camera angles were perfect. You looked like a goddamn he-man!"

"But my underwear was hanging out."

"That made it grittier. And honestly, it only added to the buzz. You should see Glib. Everyone's talking about the fight and your cute red undies. And the polls, Dan—the polls!"

"Do I want to know?"

"You just completely captured the Saskel vote. Look, it's so amazing that I printed it out on paper. I'm going to have this framed." Randy handed Dan the instantaneous polling report.

Dan looked at it. His look of irritation turned to one of shock.

"You just went from 48 percent to 95 percent among Saskel voters," Randy gushed. "Ninety-five freaking percent! I didn't even think that was possible. You know Saskels— afraid of their own shadows. They always want strong-man leaders who will protect them and do all their thinking for them. You just showed the Saskels what you're made of, and they loved it."

66

"How are things on the island?" Len asked, lying on the narrow little hospital bed with Natalia.

"Uh, well…I think we're done with island life."

Len propped himself up on his arm and looked at her. "What on earth does that mean?"

"I don't think we can go back there anymore."

"No, seriously, what are you talking about?"

Natalia looked away without answering.

"Did the pirates take the island?" Len's brow creased with concern.

"Briefly."

Len's concern became distress. "Please tell me Octavia and the kids are OK. What about the students?"

"I don't want to stress you out while you're recovering. The details can wait. Octavia and the kids are OK. The students—well, that's another matter."

"Tell me," Len demanded.

"We lost nearly half of the students."

"Dammit," Len bellowed. "Where are the survivors?"

"Here, in Cleveland."

"Who else made it?"

Natalia got up from the bed. She walked over to her purse, which had been haphazardly dropped on the floor. She pulled out a folded piece of paper and handed it to him.

Len unfolded it. It was a list of names. Fifty-five survivors, not including Natalia or Octavia and her kids. Forty-nine casualties. Len sighed and put his head in his hands.

"A lot of good people are on this list," Len said, trying to keep grief from overpowering him.

"It was horrific," Natalia said solemnly. "There were hundreds of them. They overran us."

Len put the paper down, stood up, walked over to the mirror, and put his forehead against it.

"I should have been there," Len said. "I should have been fighting with them."

"Please don't beat yourself up," Natalia said. "I think you had a pretty good excuse for missing it."

Len straightened up and looked at his face in the mirror. There was now a nice, tight jawline where he once had sagging jowls.

"I'm going to look like such a heel trying to explain this to them after I spent so many years swearing it off. I feel awful about this, too. Embarrassed."

"They'll never know."

Len turned to face her.

"So your students think you're deceased," Natalia said blankly. "In fact, the whole world thinks Len Savitz was shot and killed by an assassin on the courthouse steps. It was a big news story. Only Octavia and I know you're still alive."

"What? Even Jeff thinks I'm dead?"

Natalia nodded.

"Why would you not tell them?" Len asked, feeling his blood pressure rise.

"Because it would have put you, and them, in danger," Natalia said sternly, as if to head off his anger. "If you haven't noticed, a lot of people want to kill you. Have you forgotten why you were hiding out on that island in the first place?"

She has a point, Len thought.

"But now everyone thinks you're in the ground, so the danger has passed," Natalia said.

"I don't understand. Everyone in this hospital knows I'm here."

"No," Natalia said. "They know Jim Rivington is here."

Jim Rivington. Len had forgotten all about that name.

"I kept that identity alive all these years," Natalia said. "I had a feeling we'd have to flee the island one day. An old gun-runner like me always keeps a few extra identities on hand as a…what's the English expression?"

"Contingency plan."

"Yes. When the credit bureaus bought the old government records and took over issuing identity documents, I made sure Jim Rivington stayed on their books. I signed ol' Jim up for citizenship in Metteyya. Jim even has bank accounts and a Metteyya passport."

"Are you kidding me, Natalia?" Len asked. "You've maintained a whole secret identity for me over the last thirty-five years?"

"Who's Natalia?"

Len rolled his eyes.

"Natalia?" she asked. "Natalia Zherdeva? The construction magnate? Russian chick, right? Yes, come to think of it, I did know her. Unfortunately, she died when pirates invaded her island. Shrapnel took her head right off, I heard." She pantomimed an exaggerated decapitation. "In fact, it happened just a few months after her dear husband, the notorious journalist Leonard Savitz, was assassinated. Two lovers, both with violent deaths. What a tragedy. I didn't know Natalia very well, but for some reason I look just like her, and she left me everything in her will. Funny how life works, isn't it? Anyway, my name is Elizabeth Rivington. I'm Jim Rivington's wife." She curtsied sarcastically. "Pleasure to meet you."

"But what about my students?"

"To hell with them!"

"That isn't funny," Len scolded.

"I'm not trying to be funny," Natalia said in a matching tone. "Seriously, haven't you given them enough of your life? If they haven't learned anything from you in the last three decades, what will another three do? Not many Zen teachers give their students that many years before kicking the bucket."

"They depend on me."

"That's the problem, isn't it?"

Len walked over to the corner of the room and sat in one of the ugly yellow chairs. He hunched over and put his hand on his chin like the famous Rodin sculpture. Natalia was dead quiet while Len sat there for a solid two minutes mulling it over.

But what about the students? Natalia was right. They did depend on Len too much. He'd spent years complaining about it to her. They used Len as a crutch, expecting answers to come from him instead of from within themselves. The sudden loss of his leadership might be a boon to their spiritual development. They'd have to take ownership of their own paths.

The things he'd done already: finished school, had a career, raised a child to adulthood, married twice. Later, when he found himself the head of an entirely new religion that he'd inadvertently created, he worked hard to keep it on track. Why? Because he'd lived thinking his life would have time constraints. With the looming deadline of death, he'd struggled to get things done in a timely manner. Suddenly, there was no deadline or objective. No identity or face to save either, because Leonard Savitz was dead.

Dead. Len sat upright with a start and walked back over to the mirror. The realization was potent:

A) Barring any accidents or further violence, he was functionally immortal.
B) He had been fully released from the world's expectations of Len Savitz.
C) For the first time in decades, he was completely free to live how he wanted to live.

Astonished, Len turned to Natalia, who was already grinning. He didn't have to explain anything; she already knew. *Being married for a lifetime takes all the bullshit out of everything,* Len thought. *She knows what I'm thinking, and vice versa.*

"Wow," Len said. "So what should we do now?"

"I don't know," Natalia said, beaming. "You pick. I've done enough here. I sold my business and retired. I've got nothing on my calendar for the next century or two."

"My God." Len laughed. "We can do anything we want, forever. We can just pick up and start a new life, as if the old one never happened. When we get bored of that life, we can start over again elsewhere."

Len found himself with a euphoric feeling he had long forgotten: possibility. At that moment, in that room, absolutely anything was possible. Len thought about it for a while, then he laughed and asked, "Do you know how to ski?"

"No, actually!" Natalia answered, as though she were surprised at her own response. "I grew up in Saint Petersburg. It's very flat there. No mountains nearby. Then, when I got older, I never had the time to learn. Do you know how?"

"I never learned either. We had big hills in Pennsylvania, but I was a city kid, and I didn't get out to the country much. I want to learn. Let's go live at a ski resort for a while."

"I'm in." Natalia smiled.

67

"Octavia! You won't believe it!" Isabella yelled as she barged into the Mothers of Tchogols meeting, where Octavia and several others were discussing their pathetic budget in morose, defeated tones.

Octavia looked up, welcoming the interruption. Isabella, a longtime MoT volunteer with Tchogol twins, had a plain face and an angular nose. Combined with the frumpy clothes she always wore, Octavia thought she looked like an out-of-place pioneer woman. Isabella's expression was one of elated shock.

"What is it?" Octavia asked.

"You'll never believe what was just delivered," Isabella squealed, holding up a Postex envelope covered in tracking numbers.

Octavia took the envelope. It was addressed to Octavia Savitz, and it had already been opened. Octavia glowered at Isabella.

"Sorry," Isabella said. "I couldn't help myself. I wanted to know what it was."

Inside was a handwritten letter:

Dear Ms. Savitz:

I have been following news of your struggle since you began it.

True luminaries are often misunderstood in their own time. It isn't until decades later that society realizes how necessary their struggle was, how much they sacrificed to benefit others, and how dark their days must have been just before the turning point.

Combating injustice is the noblest goal one can aspire to. You are an inspiration to millions.

Enclosed should be more than enough to file an appeal, hopefully with a different attorney.

Keep Fighting.

Your Anonymous Friend

Reaching into the envelope again, Octavia pulled out a blue, rectangular piece of paper.

"What is it?" one of the mothers asked.

"A cashier's check," Octavia said in astonishment. "For one million LCs."

An hour later, Octavia exited a shiny brass elevator and walked across a huge marble skyscraper lobby. She moved with a seriousness of purpose that made others look up and take notice. Octavia marched right up to the receptionist's desk.

"Hello," the receptionist said. "Can I help you?"

"I understand the best attorneys in Cleveland work here. Is that correct?"

"We'd like to think so."

"Well, tell them to get down here to meet with me," Octavia demanded. "I have work for them."

68

Emmett Stuyvesant, of Stuyvesant, Brightwood & Goldsmith, was a lawyer's lawyer. He was the sort of attorney who could charge more for an hour of his time than a regular Joe made in half a year—not that he needed to. Stuyvesant's niche was taking on human rights cases that no one else would touch. They'd made a movie about one of his big cases, where he'd successfully argued that the Human Rights Decree disallowed indentured servitude. The verdict was a landmark ruling that forced all participating governments to outlaw long-term, unpaid employment. Since then, he'd been using his fame like a sledgehammer.

Mr. Stuyvesant walked up to the plaintiff's table with a celebrity's self-assuredness. He had long, gray hair and a suit that looked as if it had been cut from liquid mercury. Everyone in the room knew who he was and gawked unselfconsciously. Octavia worried that his fame might detract from the case.

Octavia looked over at the other table in the tense, pre-hearing quiet. Aegis's attorneys looked terrified and star struck at the same time, almost as if they knew they were about to get their asses kicked yet simultaneously looked forward to the privilege. The half-defeated looks on their faces almost quelled the butterflies in her stomach.

Never assume the win, Octavia's dad used to say while teaching her judo. *Never assume it's in the bag. Underestimating your opposition is a guaranteed loss. Fight like hell until it's over.*

"All rise," said an odd little man at the end of the room.

The room rose to its feet in unison as fifteen judges in black robes entered through a door in the wood-paneled wall.

What an odd hold-over, Octavia thought while getting up. *Silly costumes and displays of genuflection. This is stressful enough. Imagine the old days when they forced innocent people to go through this crap. How did people too poor to afford decent lawyers get any justice?*

"Please, be seated," one of the judges announced as he took his seat. "Mr. Stuyvesant, you represent the appellant in this matter?"

"Yes, Your Honor."

"You're up first, then."

Stuyvesant walked up to the podium and adjusted his microphone.

"Your Honors," Stuyvesant began, "the case before this court today is not only one of legal and historical importance, but also one of tremendous moral significance. The legal question being asked today is whether the Human Rights Decree, as adopted by all members of the North American Federation of Governments, trumps the Tchogol Accord, or vice versa. This is a novel question that has not been answered by any court since the adoption of either treaty. However, the technicalities are moot when we consider the larger picture."

Stuyvesant looked up from his notes and paused just long enough to make sure he had everyone's attention, then continued. "The underlying issue is whether Tchogols are human beings. If they are, then participating governments must recognize their human rights…"

69

"Hello?" Octavia asked, still half asleep.

"Octavia, it's me!"

"Who?"

"Isabella!"

Octavia had to think for a second or two. *Isabella? Do I know an Isabella? Oh, right. Sounds like she found something exciting in my mail again.*

"I hope I didn't wake you."

"What's going on?"

"Look at the news!"

Octavia squinted at the TV, which read her face and knew it was time to turn itself on.

"Good morning, Octavia. Are you interested in hearing the results of your appeal?" the TV asked.

Octavia nodded and rubbed her eyes. The TV scanned the room, looking for particles of dust in the air onto which it could project lasers to produce holograms. After five seconds, Octavia saw headlines, videos, commentary, and Glibbing explode across the room like confetti from a party popper. The TV discerned the most relevant information and then faded everything extraneous into the background.

A newscaster appeared on a blue background.

"In a landmark ruling," the reporter announced, "the Supreme Intergovernmental Court found today in a split eight-to-seven decision that Tchogols fit the definition of human beings under the Human Rights Decree and are therefore entitled to equal treatment under the law."

The scene cut to Octavia, Len, and her first lawyer walking out of the courthouse after the original trial. The video had been taken just minutes before her father was shot.

"The court also struck down the Tchogol Accord as a violation of intergovernmental law, effectively ending decades of de facto apartheid."

The video then switched to a still photograph of Emmitt Stuyvesant arguing before the court.

"Writing for the majority in *Savitz v. Aegis*, Justice Felicidad Lopez stated, 'A society can hardly be called just when it is stratified by genetics, nor can it be considered fair when it marginalizes some of its members as human enough to pay dues but not human enough to participate in democracy...'"

"I...I...can't believe it," Octavia stammered into the phone.

"You did it, Octavia," Isabella said. "You did it! Our children are now considered people!"

70

Octavia held the gold envelope in her sweaty hand. As the car pulled up to the hotel, she glanced nervously out the rain-speckled window, then down at her attire. She'd left half her clothes at the house when she and Kyle divorced, and she'd lost the other half in the pirate attack. She'd bought her outfit in a hurry just hours earlier.

Give me a head wound to suture; fashion is not my forte. You're supposed to wear cocktail dresses to these things, right?

She looked down at her arm. The nasty bullet wound had been treated with stem cells. It would heal without a scar but, in the meantime, it was covered with an unsightly bandage.

"Your fare is fifteen LCs," the driverless vehicle said.

Octavia fumbled in her purse for her card. She held it on the reader for a second, feeling a bit of panic that it might not go through. Her back muscles relaxed when the screen displayed "Payment accepted. Thank you, Octavia Savitz."

Embargo paranoia dies hard, she thought. *Nothing quite like starving to death with money in your bank account.*

She sat in the car for a bit, hesitantly staring out the window. She looked down at the envelope again. Octavia opened it and read it a twentieth time, just to be sure. On the front of the card was a printed invitation, like the kind one might get for a wedding:

You are cordially invited to a reception for Daniel Barton, Aegis Chairman and candidate for Principal. Carrington-Foltz Hotel, Detroit. 7:00 p.m.

On the reverse, a handwritten note:

Ms. Savitz:

I would greatly appreciate the pleasure of your company at this reception.

Daniel Barton

His handwriting looked familiar, but she couldn't place it. *Daniel Barton*, she thought, *the guy with the political ads on Glib. Why on earth would he want me to come to one of his events? I've never been political. I'm not what anyone would consider VIP material. Doesn't make sense. I'm the world's least popular person right now. Seems like political suicide.*

"Thank you for choosing Transglobal Cab," the machine said pleasantly.

Aegis was whom I was fighting in court. Barton's an Aegis bigwig, right? If someone sued you and won, why would you invite them to a party? None of this makes sense. Well, whatever. Hopefully, there's an open bar.

"Thank you for choosing Transglobal Cab," the machine said a bit more insistently. "Is everything OK?"

Octavia, taking the hint, exited the vehicle. She walked quickly through the rain to the entrance, where white-gloved valets opened the door for her. Following the signs for the Daniel Barton reception, Octavia showed her invitation to a stone-faced Aegis security guard who looked like a besuited oak tree. He whispered something into his hand and then let her through the velvet rope.

Inside, she found herself in an enormous ballroom filled with people. Everyone was dressed to the nines and chatting. Feeling out of her element and not knowing anyone, Octavia went up to the bar and ordered a Chardonnay. *Always drink white wine at fancy events,* Natalia used to tell her. *Red wine will stain your clothes if you spill it.* She took a stool on the side of the bar so she'd be facing the crowd. Octavia took a sip and scanned the many faces there, desperately hoping to see someone she knew. She wondered if it would be impolite to leave so soon, before meeting the person who'd invited her.

This is not my scene.

Two stools down from her sat an old, fat man in an ill-tailored suit. He appeared to be in his seventies and was completely oblivious to Octavia's staring as he sipped a brown liquid from a highball glass.

A lot of Len Savitzes out there, I guess. They have the money to live forever but don't want to.

Octavia noticed a large, pus-filled sore the diameter of a golf ball on the back of the man's bald head. She recognized it immediately: cutaneous squamous cell carcinoma.

Decent prognosis; generally doesn't metastasize. Treatable. Professional curiosity led her to lean in closer, discreetly trying to get a better look. She winced in revulsion when she did. Inside the infected ulcer were hundreds of little insects. They were crawling around in the pus. The man was being eaten alive by bugs, and he didn't even notice.

Does he honestly not know? Or does he just not care? He needs to see a specialist about that.

Octavia was just about to tap the old fellow on the shoulder to tell him about it when she heard another man's voice behind her.

"Octavia?"

She turned around. It took her a second to reconcile the flesh face with the televised one.

"Daniel Barton." The man smiled. He extended his hand.

She shook it and did her best to return his smile. "Ah yes, nice to meet you," she said, trying to seem pleasant. He was surprisingly good looking. More so in person than on Glib. He had a self-assuredness and an easy smile that somehow quelled her unease about meeting the enemy and feeling so out of place.

"So I hope my donation wasn't too forward," he said.

"Donation?" Octavia asked. Her mind was elsewhere as she studied his face. There was something quite charismatic about him.

"For your lawsuit." Dan grinned.

"Oh my God," Octavia said. "That was you?"

"Yeah," Dan said quietly, looking over his shoulder. "Just do me a favor and keep it on the down low. Not everyone at Aegis believes in human rights the way I do. I sent that donation anonymously because I'll have serious problems if anyone finds out. But I'm glad to see it worked out."

Octavia, suddenly forgetting about the formality of the event, or that she'd just met this person, or that someone might be watching, put her drink down and hugged him.

"You have no idea how much that helped," she said, overcome with emotion. "We'd gone into the red trying to pay legal bills. We were borrowing money just to get to trial." She wiped a tear away and took Dan's hand and shook it. "Thank you. Thank you!"

"No, thank *you*," Dan said. "Not only did you bring modern civilization's most important civil rights issue out of the closet, but you actually did something to fix the problem. You changed the world."

"Hah." Octavia laughed, wiping her eyes. "You wouldn't know it."

"What do you mean?"

"I'm ridiculed all day long by the pundits. 'Pandora Savitz,' they call me. I get death threats constantly. My kids and I have been staying at a different hotel every night so no one can find us. You know how rough that's been on them?"

"Really?" Dan asked intently. "Death threats?"

Octavia nodded.

"And those are the very same people who say Tchogols are savages," Dan said.

Octavia rolled her wet eyes and nodded again.

"Do you need protection?" Dan asked.

"Protection? How? Like what?"

"Governmental protection. I mean, that is the point of all this," he said, motioning to the crowd in the ballroom. "I happen to be the chairman of Aegis, hopefully soon the principal, and you are one of our members." Dan smiled, putting his hand gently on her shoulder. "I'll put you up in one of our safehouses. They're really nice. No one will hurt you there."

Octavia sat on the couch of her new home, drinking her morning coffee. She surveyed the flat with a sort of bewildered contentment. Bernie practiced his calligraphy. Iris chatted blithely with God knows who on her Glibber. At last, a sense of peace.

In the span of a year, Octavia had gone from having her own home, to being divorced and homeless, to living with her dad on the island, to having the island sacked by pirates, to living in one of Natalia's warehouses with fifty-five former islanders, to living like a refugee to avoid being assassinated. It wasn't until that morning, sitting on the couch, that she felt as if she had finally put her bags down.

Dan had put her up in an Aegis safehouse, a fortified fifty-story condo building in downtown Detroit. The only way in was past concrete barriers and a squad of Aegis mercenaries.

Octavia's new neighbors were a fascinating collection of people: dissidents, defectors, heretics, politically incorrect intellectuals, and more than a few hapless rubes who had unwittingly triggered the Glib Hate Mob. What struck Octavia was the strong sense of community among these roundly despised people. There were constant conversations in the hallways, parties in the lobby, friendly visits from people she'd never met.

Camaraderie among pariahs—who knew?

Octavia got up off the couch and walked to the kitchen to refill her mug. As she did, Bernie's drawings on the kitchen table caught her eye.

"Wow, Bernie, what are you working on?"

Bernie didn't answer. Octavia picked up some of his work. On one paper was an incredibly complex diagram with shapes and intersecting lines, somewhat like a flow chart. On another, "phase estimations" was written at the top in his beautiful handwriting and underneath that was a series of indecipherable equations. A third paper entitled "eigenvalues and eigenvectors" contained huge grids of tiny numbers and symbols. A fourth page denoted as "Probablistic Outcomes for 67E4F" was a list of names. A few of the names were family members, but most weren't familiar. Next to each name was a numerical percentage, "Octavia: ninety six percent, Iris: two percent," and so forth. Octavia shuffled through the rest of the papers. Bernie had produced at least seventy pages of the beautifully drawn yet utterly incomprehensible material.

What is all this? Octavia wondered. She looked at the boy in astonishment. Bernie seemed oblivious to her presence and simply continued working. *I know he's bright, but this is incredible. Maybe he's some kind of genius. I should get him enrolled in one of those schools for the gifted.*

Octavia's phone rang, pulling her back to the moment.

"Hello?" she asked.

"Hi, Octavia! It's Dan. How are the new digs?"

"Fantastic! Thank you so much!"

"Great. Hey, I wanted to ask, what's on your schedule for tomorrow night?"

"Uh, nothing."

"Wanna go out to dinner with me?"

Octavia paused for a second, making sure she'd heard him correctly. She bit back the urge to laugh. Not at Dan, but at the weirdness of being asked out on a date after having been married for fifteen years.

How odd, she thought, *to suddenly remember yourself and your own needs after years of being buried in responsibility and other people's shit. My God, I can go out to dinner with this man I've just met, because I want to, and I don't have to answer to anyone about it.*

Dan chuckled at her stunned silence and then added, "I took the liberty of hiring you a babysitter."

"Yes! Of course. I'd love to. Sorry; this whole turn of events has been so surreal."

"I'll pick you up at seven."

"So how's the new job?" Dan asked.

"Fantastic. It's wonderful to be working again. Being embargoed really sucks."

"So I hear. More wine?"

Octavia nodded. She watched him pour the glass. He poured it with a surgeon's focus, as though nothing else in the universe mattered.

"So," Octavia said as graciously as possible, "you've been very generous, so I hate to ask this."

"Shoot."

"Did you contribute to the cause because you honestly believed in it—"

"Or did I do it because I wanted to get in your pants?"

Octavia's face turned red.

"You've been hurt before, I see," Dan remarked.

"Who hasn't?"

"To be quite frank, perhaps a little too frank, I didn't know you from Adam when I heard about your case. The case itself interested me. I was floored that someone had the audacity to bring Tchogol rights to the mainstream. I thought, that person right there is a true badass."

Octavia laughed.

"I'm serious," Dan said. "I thought, 'She does what's right, regardless of what anyone thinks of her, regardless of the risk to her own safety. Right up there with Martin Luther King Jr. and Nelson Mandela.'"

"Really?" Octavia asked.

"Then I saw you on the news and discovered you were also really attractive." Dan shrugged. "Sorry."

Octavia laughed again and blushed. "Well, thanks."

"All that aside," he said, "I felt like I should get to know you because I'm guessing you're one of very few people in the world who can relate to my own struggles."

"Oh? What is your struggle?" Octavia asked.

"I have a vision for how the world could be. You may have heard about it; not sure."

"They say you're going to unite the governments."

"Yeah, or die trying," Dan said. "Some love me for it; others hate my guts. And, when you're in a struggle against entrenched beliefs for the greater good, it's a lonely, lonely fight." He looked into her eyes. "You know better than anyone. It's a dark place. The darkest. You against the world. You're throwing yourself into the fire to save others, even while they despise you for it. No one understands."

"Oh, I get it," Octavia said, looking at him empathetically. The turmoil in his face was brutally familiar.

"Everyone around me is either an employee, a competitor, or some kind of sycophant. I can't open up around those people. At the top, you can't ever show weakness. I feel disconnected from everyone. I feel like I need some sort of deeper connection with someone who can relate."

"You need a friend," Octavia said.

Dan chuckled, perhaps embarrassed by the simple way she'd put it. "Yes. Yes I do."

"Daniel, I think we understand each other perfectly." Octavia smiled. She took his hand off the table and held it.

71

Dan stood at the podium, the stage lights hot on his face. He'd be sweating in his suit, if he sweated.

"Yes, you," Dan said, pointing to a woman in the front.

"Mr. Barton, you're doing well in the polls. Why do you think you're resonating with voters?"

Dan leaned into the microphone and answered simply, "People have had enough." He looked around the room and saw the journalists smiling but unable to clap lest they seem unprofessional. Feeling the covertly supportive energy in the room, Dan stood upright and continued. "They're tired of anarchy and dysfunctional, impotent governments. They're exasperated with the leadership vacuum we have. No one wants to have to live in fear for their lives and property. I think my message is being received loud and clear: it's time to unite the governments."

Dan pointed to a man in a red blazer in the middle.

"Mr. Barton, not much is known about you or your history. There's almost no record of your existence prior to ten years ago. Some feel that you're a dark horse and that voting for you might be taking a risk on a big unknown."

"Well, as I've said before, I'm not a career politician. And you're right; I lived a pretty private, low-key life before becoming involved with Aegis. However, sometimes it becomes necessary to leave behind comfortable anonymity for the greater good. Look, I'm not up here doing this press conference because I like the attention. I'm doing it because I think I can make a difference. The limelight isn't something I want; it's something I'm willing to bear to make the world a better place."

Dan pointed to an elderly man in the back. An aide came over and handed the microphone to him as he stood up. There was something in the old man's expression that Dan didn't like—a smug look, a cold sparkle in his eye.

"There's a rumor going around that you are a Tchogol. Care to address that?" The old man smiled in a self-satisfied way while handing the microphone back and sitting down.

A few reporters in the audience laughed—some disdainfully, others nervously. Dan looked the man in the eye for a few seconds until the room quieted down. Rather than answering, Dan took off his suit coat. The heat from the stage lights was killing him, and removing that article of clothing made him feel cooler immediately. He then took out his cufflinks and rolled up his white shirt sleeves. He held his arm over the podium to display it for the entire room. There, on his wrist, was a *T* indicating Tchogol.

"The rumors are true," Dan said calmly.

The room erupted into a riotous uproar of gasps, questions, insults, and shouts. Dan looked into the front row to see Elise wide-eyed and covering her mouth in disbelief and shock. Randy, however, was grinning from ear to ear. Dan waited patiently at the lectern for a solid thirty seconds before attempting to speak over the clamor.

"Ladies and gentlemen, I will answer your questions. One at a time, please."

"Tchogols aren't eligible to be principal!" someone yelled from the side of the room.

Dan nodded in acknowledgment of the statement. "Actually, I must correct you there. The landmark case of *Savitz v. Aegis* overturned the Tchogol Accord as a violation of the Human Rights Decree. Not only do Tchogols no longer need to be registered, but we can now hold any public office in any government."

"Tchogol scum!" someone yelled from the back. "Fuck you!"

Ignoring the comment, Dan coolly looked out into the crowd. "You've asked me questions; now I'd like to ask you folks a question." He looked around, making sure he had their attention. "Now that it's legal once again for Tchogols to hold governmental offices, how long do you suppose it'll be before they're running the other governments?" He could see his question had caught them off guard. "Everyone forgets that Tchogolism isn't a disorder or a disability. Quite the contrary. Tchogols were specifically designed to be fearless leaders. There's a reason the governments of old were so powerful and could unite such disparate places and peoples: they were all led by Tchogols. Having a Tchogol in charge is a tremendous advantage. The other two types cannot lead the way Tchogols do, and everyone knows it. With all due respect to our Xreth friends, we see the results every day of Xreth governance. Why do you think we have such upheaval and strife?" In an explosion of passion, Dan pounded the podium with his fist and fervently shouted into the microphone, "It's because we've had a complete lack of direction and management—a situation that was caused by the Tchogol Accord preventing Tchogols from doing what we do best!"

Dan was encouraged to hear some of the people in the audience clapping. He regained his confident, composed poise and continued.

"Given the unparalleled edge that Tchogol leadership affords a society, I can absolutely guarantee you that competing governments will elect them as principals now that it's legal. Now, what about Aegis, our government? Do Aegis members want to be behind the curve when all the other governments' principals are Tchogols? I don't think they'll want that disadvantage. I think our members will recognize the unbridled potential of Tchogol Power—to coin a phrase— and they'll overcome absurd prejudices to ensure that Aegis remains the greatest government in North America."

He could see in their faces that some were considering what he was saying.

"Ladies and gentlemen, we live in a world of unprecedented danger. Gangs, crime, warlords, weapons of mass destruction for sale everywhere, rogue governments. When you leave here and turn on the news tonight, you will see the absolute discord that North America has degraded into. It wasn't like this when Tchogols were running the world, was it?" Dan gave the crowd a ferocious, clenched-jaw look and said sternly while driving his pointer finger into the podium, "I promise you the chaos will end when I am principal."

With that, Dan picked up his jacket and walked off the stage.

As they sped away from the town hall meeting in the back of Dan's limousine, Elise looked as if she was on the verge of a panic attack.

"I'm trying to load the instant polling, but this connection is really slow. I think you broke Glib, Mr. Barton." She looked up at Dan. "Are you really a Tchogol?"

"Born and raised," Dan said wearily.

Elise bit her nails and checked Glib for the thirtieth time, as though it were a nervous tic. Her anxiety amused Dan: all that endless fretting over nothing.

"You're wondering if you can trust me, aren't you?" Dan asked, breaking the silence.

Elise looked at him briefly. She opened her mouth as if to say something but then closed it and went back to her panicky Glib checking.

"A lot of people feel that way," Dan said. "It's a burden I've lived with my whole life. It's never made sense to me. It's so presumptuous. Why can't I put the greater good first? Why does everyone assume I'm incapable of altruism? Because of how I was born?"

"I…I don't think that," Elise said uncomfortably.

"It's a catch-22," Dan lamented. "Society refuses to accept us. It doesn't allow us to make a living legitimately. It forces us into a position where we have no choice but to become outlaws, which is then used as justification for further bigotry. There's no way up and out. None."

"If I may ask…" Elise said meekly.

"Go ahead," Dan said in exasperation, already knowing her question.

"How are you the chairman of Aegis? How did you start Barton Capital? Tchogols aren't allowed to hold corporate offices or even own stock. Or, weren't, I should say."

"I've been in hiding all these years," Dan said glumly. "It's been very difficult, and I've done a lot of things I'm not proud of. I've purchased fake blood for the tests. I've bribed officials to keep me out of the databases. I've done whatever it took to survive and avoid being discovered."

"But…" Elise trailed off.

"Ask. Let's clear the air. I'm tired of secrets."

"That tattoo wasn't on your wrist before today."

Dan pulled up his sleeve to look at it again. "I had this done a few days ago at a tattoo place over on Fourteenth. They thought I was nuts, getting inked like this." He let out a defeated sigh. "I've been in the closet for decades, Elise. I'm tired of hiding, and I won't do it anymore. This is who I am. I am a Tchogol. I'm tired of being ashamed of that. From now on, I choose to be proud of it."

Elise, apparently unsure of how to react to her boss's emotional outpouring, checked her Glib again.

"It's loading now. Let's see…holy shit!" Elise blurted out. "Sorry; pardon my language."

"How'd I do?" Dan asked.

"After today," Elise said, utterly baffled, "I thought you'd lost the election. But you just went up in the polls nine and a half percent! You're even leading among our Xreth members!"

72

Octavia wandered through the packed room. She saw him before too long. As tall as he was, he stood out in any crowd. He was surrounded by people, all of whom were trying to get as close as possible. She watched as he handled his fame like an assembly line. He put his arm around a person as if they were best friends, grinned, and waited for the flash. Then he shook the person's hand and picked a different person out for another photo op. He did this about thirty or forty times.

People want to be around him, Octavia thought. *They want to be associated with his inevitable rise to greatness. And this life of his. Every night a speech, a fundraiser, a press conference, a black-tie event.*

Dan moved on from photos to greeting his supporters. Octavia stood inconspicuously off to the side, watching as he flashed that megawatt smile while his green eyes shone in the camera lights.

How different from Kyle, Octavia thought, recalling her ex-husband. *It's impossible to amount to anything when you think life owes you something. Our marriage felt like a parent-child relationship sometimes. Me with all the agency and Atlas-like responsibility, and him always feeling sorry for himself, always the hapless victim.*

She stopped herself, almost yelling *No!* aloud in the throng of people.

Jesus, Octavia, drop it. Stop thinking about it already. Don't let the past ruin your future, and stop being so damn cynical about dating again. This guy is not Kyle; he has his act together in ways you didn't even think were possible. And he's interested in you. She shook her head at the weirdness of it.

She watched as Dan picked a chubby baby up, kissed it on the cheek, and handed the infant back to its mother.

Dad said he felt this way when he met Natalia: completely out-classed. He wondered what she saw in him. He still does. Yet they've been happily married forever. Natalia's intuition was right. And Dad has a tendency to self-deprecate. I get that from him. From a third-party point of view, I don't think Natalia could have chosen a better husband.

As Dan reached over to grab a piece of paper that someone wanted him to autograph, he noticed Octavia. His face lit up.

She smiled back and waved from the corner of the room.

Who knows? Maybe I'm finally on the right track.

Dan excused himself and politely edged his way through the horde of adulators.

Don't screw this up, Octavia.

"I'm so glad you made it!" he said to Octavia with arms outstretched.

"I wouldn't have missed it!" she said, giving him a hug.

Octavia heard the clicking of camera shutters as they embraced.

Well, the whole world knows now.

"When will you get the results?" Octavia asked.

"Voting closes in"—he looked up at an enormous screen on the wall that Octavia had apparently completely missed—"three minutes, forty seconds."

"Are you nervous?" Octavia whispered.

"Nah."

"Really? I'd be losing my mind right about now."

"If I win, I win." Dan shrugged. "If I lose, I lose. Life goes on either way."

As the timer on the screen counted down, the whole crowd began counting along with it as if it were New Year's Eve.

"Five! Four! Three! Two! One!"

Then, on the screen, appeared a bar graph tallying the votes.

Walters: 7 percent
Rivera: 15 percent
Chan: 24 percent
Barton: 54 percent

The room, full of Dan's supporters, erupted into a loud, celebratory ruckus. Balloons and confetti rained down from the ceiling as the music started.

"Hah!" Dan shouted with glee. He raised his arms and laughed.

"Wow," someone nearby shouted. "Not just a landslide, but an incontestable majority!"

"Congratulations!" Octavia said, her voice lost in the din. "I'm so happy for you!"

Dan, having not heard what she'd said, was suddenly mobbed on all sides by cameramen, professional Glibbers, and well-wishers. Octavia, who had been standing right next to him during the countdown, was pushed out of the way as the crowd rushed in.

73

Len watched the countryside outside whiz by at a disconcerting rate. Things in the foreground moved so fast that they couldn't be identified. A staccato of green blurs might have been a line of trees, a long red one a barn. Objects in the distance, like clouds or mountains, were clearly discernible but still flew by at a speed too surreal to believe. At five hundred miles per hour, the train blasted through tunnels like a bullet exiting a rifle barrel. Inside, pure luxury: an exquisite lunch of lobster and venison, crystal decanters of Calvados, waiters in white gloves.

Before the Invasion, there was always a big hullaba-loo about high-speed rail. Europe had fast trains; Asia had faster trains. The contrast was vivid the year Len returned to the United States from Japan: the sleek, futuristic lines of the superfast Shinkansen compared to the sad, bungled screwup that was known as rail travel in America. Americans back then were stuck with a rail system that was practically Soviet: a state-run monopoly of dilapidated, slow trains that were never on time. The only thing differentiating American trains from their third-world counterparts was the absence of loose chickens. On one particular trip, Len used the bath-room at the rear of an American train car and was amazed to see daylight in the bowl when he flushed. The ancient car's toilet hadn't been updated in ninety years and was designed to simply drop shit directly onto the tracks.

Fast forward thirty-five years, and while train travel had evolved into something too amazing to believe, air travel had become useless. Flying over the oceans was still easy, but flying over land had become incredibly dangerous over the last decade. It was impossible to find a route between two population centers that didn't cross over a hundred little militarized fiefdoms. War zones and boundary disputes were everywhere, as were armed drones and antiaircraft weapons. The airlines had tried escorting 747s with fighter planes for a while, until it became prohibitively expensive.

Thus, high-speed rail finally came to North America out of sheer necessity. The Transglobal Concern had either purchased or annexed by force the entirety of the old Interstate 80, from New York City to San Francisco. It charged tolls for road travel and used the revenue to convert the entire median strip into a three-thousand-mile vacuum-sealed maglev tube. Including stops, the trip from Cleveland to Salt Lake City took four hours.

Len and Natalia changed trains in Salt Lake City for one headed to Teton. Len remembered reading that Metteyya had acquired all the old national parks and turned them into private communities. Metteyya built the town of Teton right in the middle of what had once been Grand Teton National Park.

The train station in Teton looked as though it were from the 1800s: chandeliers and artistic friezes, wooden benches that appeared to be hand carved. *This station didn't exist ten years ago*, Len reminded himself. *What a gimmick*. He looked up and saw a sign that read, "Welcome to Teton, a Sandbox Community."

Len pulled a pack of cigarettes out of his pocket and lit one. Exhaling toward the ceiling, He felt the glorious sensation of nicotine entering his bloodstream after a long absence.

"Seriously?" Natalia asked. "Are you really smoking in that new body I just bought you?"

"Yeah. You want one?" Len asked, holding the pack up.

Natalia, perhaps as disgusted with herself as she was with him, couldn't help but take what'd he'd offered.

"Mr. and Mrs. Rivington?"

Len looked up. A man in a ski fleece stood there smiling at them.

"That's us," Natalia said.

The two of us must look like chimneys.

"Welcome to Teton! Is this your first time here?"

"Yes. This is quite a station!"

"Wait until you see the town. Please, follow me." The driver took their luggage and led them to an open-air vehicle.

"This place looks like a Swiss village," Len said as they drove down narrow cobblestone streets.

"That was the idea," the driver said. "Mr. Metteyya designs these Sandbox communities himself. He wanted Teton to have an old-world charm. You know, a place with a real town square where you could get to know your neighbors and walk to everything. Personally, I just think it looks cool."

"Which town is it supposed to look like?" Len asked.

"Would you believe it's not a copy of anything in particular? Mr. Metteyya studied towns and people all over the world. He compared town layouts to the contentment of the residents. He didn't just replicate some city overseas; he actually figured out the mathematics of maximizing well-being through urban planning. The street maps of the Sandbox towns look like nothing else on earth. They say it's some kind of fractal pattern."

"It feels familiar somehow," Len said.

"Every time I pick up a newcomer from the station, they say that exact same thing. It feels like home even though they've never been here before."

"I don't think I asked where we're going," Len said.

"The first place newbies always go: to evaluation!"

"Evaluation?" Len asked.

"Nothing to worry about." The man smiled.

Len looked at Natalia, who shrugged in ignorance.

The driver pulled up in front of a small half-timber building near the center of town and then drove off, leaving Len and Natalia on the sidewalk. They looked up at the building, then looked at each other.

The inside looked like an old British gentlemen's club. Big leather chairs, bookshelves, models of ships in bottles, a wood fire going in a stone fireplace. A bald man in his sixties with a big white beard came over to greet them. He looked like Santa Claus in blue jeans. "Jim and Elizabeth, I presume? My name is Bradley. I'm an evaluation counselor."

"What's this evaluation business about?" Len asked, skipping the pleasantries.

"It's only the greatest thing that has ever happened to humanity!" Bradley said exuberantly.

"A psychological evaluation?" Natalia asked.

"Sort of," Bradley said. "But not really. It's far, far deeper than that. More of a holistic insight into your entire being."

"And are you the one evaluating us?" Len asked without bothering to hide his skepticism.

"Oh, no." Bradley laughed. "I do no evaluations. A computer does the evaluation."

"What, like one of those Internet quizzes where I find out what my spirit animal is?" Len asked.

"Not quite. I'm talking about a computer more powerful than any you've ever encountered. In fact, there's only one other computer like it on earth. After an hour or two of analyzation, it will know you a hundred times better than you know yourself. I'm only here to help you interpret the results if you want. That part's optional."

Len and Natalia stood there in silence.

"I see the doubt on your faces," Bradley said reassuringly. "Don't worry. Do it a few times, and you'll look forward to evaluations. I promise. In any case, it doesn't hurt and it doesn't cost money, so you might as well try it."

"I guess we came here for adventure," Natalia said, visibly struggling with her own reservations.

"Well, here it is." Bradley laughed.

"What the hell." Natalia shrugged. "Sure. Let's do it."

"That's the spirit!" Bradley said. "You'll need to do this separately, though. Privacy is necessary for an accurate result. I'll have to put each of you in your own room."

Bradley led Natalia down a hallway and came back ten minutes later by himself to take Len to a different evaluation room. The room Bradley took Len to had the feel of a reading room in an old library. Leather-bound books, a massive old globe, and an old-fashioned psychologist's couch. It looked as if Sigmund Freud's office had remained untouched for a hundred years.

All this fake antique stuff. Len laughed to himself.

"Am I supposed to lie down?" Len asked as Bradley closed the door behind them.

"Sure, if you want. It might help. The headgear is kind of heavy."

Before Len could even ask, Bradley lifted a huge brass-colored helmet-shaped apparatus off the desk. Hesitantly, Len let him put it on his head. "OK now, sit still for a second while it calibrates." Bradley pushed a series of buttons on the device. It practically came alive, molding and adjusting itself to the contours of Len's skull.

"What the hell?" Len said in surprise. The machine's undulations felt like a scalp massage.

"Just relax," Bradley said in fatherly tones. "This is the transcranial cerebellum interface. TCI for short. It won't harm you. Just think of it as a helmet."

"What does it do?"

"It reads your mind. Literally."

"I'm not sure I want my mind to be read," Len said uncomfortably.

"Don't worry," Bradley said calmly. "No human ever sees your thoughts. Only the computer knows what you're thinking." He adjusted a few knobs and then added, "OK, we're ready to go. Just lie back and try to relax. You're about to experience something completely new." Bradley lowered the lights and exited the room, closing the door softly behind him as Len nervously watched him leave.

For a few seconds, nothing. Len just lay on the couch, staring up into the darkened room. Then, a faint haze of green. Len thought his eyes might be playing tricks on him so he blinked a few times. No, he really did see it: a green mist had appeared in the space between him and the ceiling. It grew more vibrant, then began to swirl and congeal into a solid shape. A figure. A person. His mother! He was staring at a green hologram-like image that looked exactly like his mother, who had passed away years ago. Except, she was young! The age she was when he was born, perhaps. Then the image diffused, swirled, and resolidified into another figure. His father.

"What kind of sick joke is this?" Len yelled into the darkened room.

"Hello," a female voice said. "Please do not be alarmed. The images you see are not meant to upset you. They are simply being pulled from your subconscious."

"Who's talking?" Len asked as the green mist morphed into his grandchildren's faces.

"My name is Qualia. I am the evaluation computer."

"What's going on here?"

"I am making a complete model of your psyche. I will use this to help you."

"Help me do what?"

"Help you know yourself better, which will help you reach your full potential as a human being. Please wait; I am almost done with the initialization phase."

The green mist finally settled into a female form, a face he didn't recognize. A beautiful face. No, a sublimely perfect face, as though its precise geometry had been extrapolated from a hundred thousand of Len's subconscious desires. Len's mouth hung open at the sight of it.

"I will now ask you a series of questions," the face said. "These questions are meant to provoke a response, which will induce your true feelings to surface into your consciousness. You may answer the questions verbally if you want, but it is not necessary."

Not necessary? Len thought. *Christ, this thing really can read my mind.*

Qualia's face was a luminous dark green that contrasted against the darkened ceiling. The color scheme reminded him of an old-fashioned computer terminal with green-on-black text. Out of curiosity, Len reached out to touch Qualia's face. His waving arms traveled right through the image without disturbing it.

"It's not really there," Qualia said. "These images are being transmitted directly into your visual cortex."

"Unreal."

"I note that you came here today with a companion. Please tell me about her."

"N...I mean, Elizabeth?"

The verbal slip triggered the green fog to rapidly reorganize into a terrifying new image: McKean on the courthouse steps, gun in hand.

Len gasped.

Then McKean changed into a series of jarring but related imagery: the bodies of dead IRS agents, a Dranthyx, Jefferson's lifeless corpse in the concentration camp.

"Ah, I see," Qualia said in sympathetic tones. "I can't blame you for wanting a new life under a new identity. Your secrets are safe with me, Leonard. If you want, I can refer to you from now on as Jim."

Len, shaken, sat up and tried to remove the TCI but found, to his panicked frustration, that it was so precisely molded to his head that he couldn't get it off.

"Please try to relax," Qualia said. "I will not hurt you. I am here to help."

"How is this helping?" Len asked.

"Healing cannot begin until we examine the feelings we repress," the machine said. "The unconscious must be brought to consciousness and examined. Sometimes this process is uncomfortable."

I guess that's true, Len thought, his heart beating hard. *Shit, I keep forgetting it can hear me thinking.*

"Shall we continue?" Qualia asked.

I guess, Len answered mentally.

"Please tell me about Natalia," Qualia said, briefly reorganizing the green mist into Natalia's countenance and then returning to her original appearance.

Len weighed whether he wanted to confide anything about his life partner to a machine. Where did this information go once he opened his mouth?

"No human will ever see the information I collect," Qualia said calmly, knowing his concern. "I am entirely self-contained."

"She's my wife." Len said brusquely.

"Yes, but how do you feel about her?"

"You want me to sum up three decades of marriage just like that?"

"If you can."

"Are you sure no one will ever hear this?" Len asked.

"Positive," Qualia said.

Len took a deep breath. *Well, let's give it a shot.*

"To be quite frank, she's the only woman I've ever been with who didn't feel like a burden. Other women—well, it always felt like they were sucking the life out of me. But Natalia is different. She's…inspiring. She doesn't sap my energy. She puts new energy in. Honestly, I feel like I'm the burden."

"Thank you," Qualia said after a pause. Her vaporous face then reorganized into a 3D image of Len's childhood home, a row house in the south side of Pittsburgh. "Tell me about your childhood."

Two hours later, Len emerged from the darkened room, squinting as his eyes adjusted. He found Bradley in the lobby, reading a book.

"Done already?" Bradley asked.

"Well, that was the most invasive conversation I've ever had," Len said in annoyance. "I'm just glad that thing was probing my head and not my ass."

Bradley laughed.

That's not a Santa Claus laugh, Len thought. *More like Jerry Garcia.*

"Elizabeth is still in her evaluation," Bradley said. "I trust Qualia gave you a report?"

Len held up the sealed envelope.

"You might want to read it," Bradley said. "I'll be here if you have any questions. Just remember that sharing it with me is purely optional."

Len opened up the envelope. Inside was a twenty-page printout. Len read through it briefly. "This thing recommends jobs?"

"Of course. Work is a huge part of life. Qualia finds the perfect job for people, given their strengths, personalities, and psychological development. Sometimes it's based on what the individual needs; sometimes it's based on the community's needs. She even figures out exactly how many hours you should put in, to optimize your life."

"It has two career suggestions. The first one says I should be a dispute mediator for twenty-one hours per week. What does that mean?" Len asked.

"Whoa!" Bradley said in a drawn-out, old-hippie sort of way.

Not Santa Claus, Len thought. *Definitely Jerry Garcia.*

"That's a compliment if I've ever heard one!" Bradley said. "Qualia must have a lot of faith in your decision making.

"So we don't have any courts or lawyers here in the Sandbox. The way we settle problems is this: if two people get into an argument that they can't resolve, they take it to a dispute mediator. The dispute mediator tries to find the best way to resolve the situation. Qualia only suggests that the most level-headed, objective, incorruptible people mediate disputes."

"Do I have to do this? I don't understand."

"Nope. These are only suggestions. You're in charge. You can do whatever the hell you want; Qualia is just here to help you make better decisions. Think of her as a GPS for life. You can ignore her if you want, but you're better off listening to her advice."

"Her second suggestion is evaluation counselor for twenty-five hours per week."

"Hey!" Bradley said enthusiastically. "I could definitely use the help around here."

"Why only part time?" Len asked.

"Are you a people person?"

"No."

"Well, there you go," Bradley said. "Qualia's probably worried you'll burn out doing more than twenty-five hours per week."

"Interesting. 'Relationship advice...'" Len read off the sheet. "'Remain married to your wife.' Hah! What a presumptuous computer, as if it knows the first thing about being married."

"You'd be surprised," Bradley said. "A lot of people who come through here don't realize how crappy their relationships are. Not only does Qualia sometimes recommend breakups; she actually suggests specific alternative partners. And guess what? She's right 99 percent of the time. When I see those same people in here for follow-up evaluations, they're happier if they've listened to Qualia's ideas. If you don't mind me asking, what was your compatibility score?"

"One hundred percent." Len said.

"What?" Bradley asked. "Are you serious?"

Len handed him the paper.

"That's not 100 percent. That's 100th percentile," Bradley stammered. "What the hell? There's no way."

"What's the difference?" Len asked.

"That means you and your wife are the most compatible couple that Qualia has ever seen. You're even more compatible than the relationships Qualia has created! Are you sure you have never done an evaluation before?"

"Never," Len said.

"You're putting me on."

"Nope," Len said.

"This is a soul-mate-level match. You mean you found the absolute perfect partner by pure chance?"

"Um. I guess so," Len said, squinting at Bradley and trying to make sense of his surprise. "You do know people used to hook up just fine before computers came along, right?"

"Hey, look at this!" Natalia yelled from behind them. Len and Bradley turned around to see her emerging from her evaluation room. She was waving her report around and laughing hysterically. "The computer thinks I should be a mortician!"

74

Late the next morning, Len sat on the balcony of their new home, a third-floor flat in downtown Teton. Natalia had left earlier to explore the town on her own. The stillness of the day was interrupted by a jubilant jazz procession walking down the cobblestone street below. Trumpets, saxophones, even a drummer. Some of the revelers wore colorful costumes with large papier-mâché heads. Others twirled flaming batons.

What a strange parade, Len thought. *Part Mardi Gras, part West Coast weirdness.*

"What's the occasion?" Len asked them from three stories up.

"It's Wednesday!" one of them slurred back before chugging a beer.

This place is bizarre. Len laughed to himself.

Len watched them round the corner, picking up enthusiastic bystanders as they went. *Maybe this is what I needed. I've been too serious for too long. I spent thirty years teaching Zen while forgetting to live in the moment myself.*

Len downed the last of his coffee, stubbed out his cigarette, and went inside. They'd had the option to buy or rent a place but opted instead for one of the standard housing units that came free with Metteyya membership. The apartment they'd been given came fully furnished and ready to live in. Silverware, bookshelves, everything. Not too big, not too small. It worked out well, actually. Having lost a lifetime of possessions when the island was sacked, they'd arrived in Teton with very little. It was a shame to have lost all the family photo albums and memorabilia, but in a way, it was freeing to be rid of the past. They'd come with no identity or possessions, and the lightness of it was exhilarating.

The doorbell rang. Len opened the door and saw a young lady standing in the hallway, maybe seventeen or so, with a messenger bag. She handed Len a few pieces of mail. Len looked through it, then called after her as she turned to walk away.

"What's this?" Len asked, holding up a green envelope addressed to Jim and Elizabeth.

"What do you mean?" she asked.

"I'm new here. What is all this stuff?"

"Oh. That green envelope that says 'SUGGESTION' in big letters—that's a suggestion."

"Suggestion from whom?" Len asked.

"From Qualia. Everyone gets those. The green ones are things that you might like to do. The yellow ones are suggestions that you should definitely consider. The red ones are suggestions that you should never ignore."

"Why does she send these by mail?" Len asked. "Seems kind of old school."

"Mail is a big deal here because a lot of people in the Sandbox have gone Amish," the girl said.

Len cocked his head.

"You know," she said. "They don't do technology."

"Oh. Do I have to do what she suggests?"

Let's see if she gives the same answer the evaluation guy did, Len thought.

"No, but it's usually a good idea. Anyway, that one there is the Teton newsletter. These three are advertisements. Here are some things that are happening around town, and this looks like an invitation to a party or something from your neighbors."

"No bills?"

"What's a bill?" the girl asked. Her expression was either deadpan or ingenuous; Len couldn't tell which.

"Never mind," Len said. "Have a nice day."

Len opened the green envelope. Inside was a very short note that said:

Jim and Elizabeth:

You may enjoy meeting a couple named Richard and Susan Talbert. If you are interested in making their acquaintance, they will be dining at the restaurant on the first floor of your building at 8:00 p.m.

Qualia

Natalia opened the door as soon as he'd closed it. She was carrying armfuls of groceries, her look bemused and perplexed. "You need to see this!"

"What?"

"The grocery store," she said breathlessly. "You have to see it."

Len followed Natalia into the grocery store on their block. To Len, it seemed like a typical supermarket. There were aisles and carts, people shopping.

"I don't see what the big deal is," Len said. "This looks like any grocery store."

"Yes, but something's missing," Natalia said. "Something important."

Len looked around. The place didn't seem too unusual; there were fruits and vegetables, shelves of canned goods, and refrigerators full of milk and juice.

"I give up. What's missing?"

"The cashier!" Natalia said in exasperation.

"Oh. So they have some newfangled payment system, or what?"

"No. Len, all this stuff is free."

"What?" Len asked incredulously. "No way."

"She's not kidding," said a young man nearby who was mopping the floor.

Len turned to look at the clerk. "Free? How can you just give stuff away for free?"

"I guess you're new here," the clerk said. "Mr. Metteyya believes no one should worry about where their next meal is coming from. So all the food in this store is free. In fact, everyone's basic needs are free in the Sandbox. Food, shelter, energy, water, health care. Metteyya will even pay for a person's university education, but only if Qualia suggests that as part of a career change."

"Socialist paradise, eh?" Len asked. "Great. I can't wait to get the tax bill."

"Taxes?" the clerk asked, laughing. "There are no taxes."

"Fine," Len said. "Membership fees, or whatever they're called these days."

"No membership fees, either."

Len looked at the clerk as if the man were having some sort of mental episode.

"This is why I love working here," the clerk said. "It's wonderful to see people experiencing this for the first time."

"I'm not sure I follow," Len said. "Where I come from, there ain't no such thing as a free lunch. Someone is paying for this. I mean, it's basic economics."

"Oh, I dunno, my friend," the clerk said. "Basic economics isn't so basic anymore."

Incredulous, Len walked over to a display of apples in the produce section. He picked up two, one in each hand. He examined each, as if they'd offer clues as to how Metteyya could give stuff away for free.

"Economics happens to be my area of study at the university," the clerk said. "In fact, my dissertation is on the economics of Sandbox communities."

Len, his attention now absorbed by the apples he was holding, turned both red fruits around in his hands while the clerk was talking.

"All the old-school economic theories—Marxism, Keynesianism, Austrian—they all had one thing in common: the presumption of scarcity," the clerk said. "They were all predicated on the idea that there was a limited supply of things, and that was what gave stuff its value."

Len picked up a third apple and compared it to the other two. He then picked up several more, comparing apples to apples while trying to hold them all in his arms simultaneously.

"But what happens when there's no more scarcity?" the clerk asked. "When something is plentiful, it loses value. When everything is plentiful, value itself becomes meaningless—"

"So what kind of economic system is this?" Natalia asked.

"The economic system of the Sandbox might be described as postscarcity humanist transcapitalism," the clerk said. "The idea here is that no one should ever suffer because of poorly allocated resources; however, if you want anything more than the basics, you'll have to work for it."

"Wait a second!" Len exclaimed, thunderstruck. "These apples are absolutely identical! What the hell is going on here?"

The clerked beamed. "Bingo! You discovered the secret. This is Reorgo food, good sir. That's why it's free."

"Reorgo?" Len asked.

"Reorganized food. Artha Metteyya figured out a way to molecularly print food using recycled atoms."

"This isn't real food?" Len asked. "What is this place, some kind of bullshit showpiece?"

"Geez, man, relax," the clerk said, doing a calm-down motion with his hands. "No one's scamming you. It's absolutely real food," he said emphatically. "It just didn't come from a tree. You can eat it. I eat it all the time. Everyone eats it. Artha Metteyya has a whole operation that he keeps super-secret. I hear it's amazing. He can take the atoms from absolutely anything and reconfigure them into anything else. Reorgo apples are totally indistinguishable from dirt apples, even under an electron microscope. Your body won't know the difference." He pointed to the apples Len was holding. "If you let those apples sit out too long, they'll rot. If you take the seeds and plant them, they'll grow into trees. But if you're superstitious and you want dirt food, there's an organic farmer's market on the next block. It's a paystore, though."

"What the hell? What about the meat over there?" Len pointed to the butcher's counter.

"Same deal. It's real meat. You'll need to refrigerate it and everything. It just never came from an animal. A cow didn't need to die for your burger. Pretty amazing, huh?"

"Are you sure it's safe to eat this crap?" Len asked.

"It's perfectly fine. Scientists have been studying it for a while, and it's actually healthier than farm food because there's less possibility of contamination from bacteria."

"This is too weird," Len said, shaking his head.

"Sure, it's weird," the clerk said, "but it works. Mr. Metteyya is planning to take his operation full scale soon. When that happens, no one on Earth will ever starve again."

"Where do all these atoms come from?" Len asked.

"Don't ask," the clerk said. "Just enjoy the free food."

"I'm serious. I want to know. Where does he get all the raw material?"

"What are you, a reporter or something?"

Len stared at the clerk intently without answering. Natalia smirked.

"Artha Metteyya bought all the landfills west of the Mississippi," the clerk answered. "He mines them for material, then he uses his machines to break everything down to the atomic elements. The machines reorganize the atoms into food and other things. He sells the reclaimed metals, which is how he pays for health care, education, land, and anything else that can't be printed. And the carbon in that apple? He pulled it out of the atmosphere in order to reverse the climate problems. It's a freakin' brilliant system, if you ask me."

"We're eating trash?" Len asked.

The clerk laughed. "Dude, you know what real farmers use for fertilizer? A tree turns turds into apples, and no one thinks it's weird. But now we have machines that can do the same thing and you think it's unusual?"

"It's hard to get excited about eating fruit that used to be a tampon," Len said.

The clerk leaned on his mop handle and said with a lifted eyebrow, "Not to get too philosophical, my man, but the whole cosmos is a recycling machine. Every single atom in your body has been repurposed from other places. You and those apples are both recycled stardust. You are walking, talking Reorgo."

75

Len opened the door to the restaurant reluctantly. Natalia seemed light and unconcerned as she waltzed through. He followed her in, wondering what this was all about.

I feel like we're being set up on a blind double date, Len thought. *If that computer is so profoundly perceptive, it should know I'm not a social butterfly. What's the point of this?*

"Richard and Susan?" Natalia asked cheerfully to a couple sitting at a table near the entrance.

"Yes!" the woman said. "Jim and Elizabeth?"

"Nice to meet you," Len said, shaking hands and feigning pleasantness.

I'm bored already, Len thought. *Let's get this over with.*

Len studied their faces without being obvious about it. Richard had a square jaw and an athletic build; he looked as though he was in his midtwenties. Susan had a round face with dimples. She smiled a lot and appeared to be the same age as Richard. Their expressions were utterly relaxed, as if they had no cares in the world. Their mannerisms were completely at ease, and there was a jubilant, welcoming glow about them.

Are these people young-young, or are they like us? Len wondered. *Christ, guessing age has become as useful a skill as divining for water.*

Len listened carefully as Natalia made small talk about skiing with Richard and Susan.

Good old Natalia, always running interference for me, Len thought. *Their diction and grammar is too good. It has to be from the era of required schooling. They don't prattle about silly things or talk about themselves constantly the way young people do.*

"Do you mind if I ask how old you are?" Len interjected.

Natalia shot him a glance.

Richard laughed. "Not at all. I'm eighty-three."

Len nodded.

"And you?" Richard asked.

"Seventy-seven," Len said.

"I'm eighty," said Susan.

"Seventy," Natalia said. "It's been a while since I've thought of myself as the baby."

"Sorry," Len said, "I didn't mean to be rude."

"No worries." Richard said. "That's probably why Qualia suggested we all meet. Who else can relate to what we've been through?"

"That's the reason we're meeting?" Len asked.

"Maybe. It's never that simple," Richard said. "So did you two have the full decapitation?"

"Ugh. I can't stand that word." Susan shuddered.

Natalia nodded.

"You must be people of substantial means," Richard remarked, "because it's not cheap. At least, not yet. Give it another five to ten years, and everyone will look like us."

"We've done all right," Natalia said. "What do you do for a living?"

"It's amazing, isn't it?" Susan asked, changing the subject. "They say youth is wasted on the young. Now youth can be wasted on the elderly too. There's nothing like sitting around watching game-show reruns with perky tits." She cupped her chest with her hands for emphasis.

Len couldn't help but laugh. It was the delivery; octogenarian cynicism coming out of Susan's baby face struck him as very funny.

OK, I've changed my mind. I like these people.

"It's like being reborn," Natalia said.

"Reborn indeed! A chance to start over." Susan looked Len and Natalia over and then smiled slyly. "Our names aren't Richard and Susan, and I'd bet a bottle of wine that yours aren't Jim and Elizabeth."

The expressions of shock on Len and Natalia's faces caused Richard and Susan to laugh so hard that they nearly fell out of their chairs.

"Oh God, did you see their faces?" Richard asked.

"Stop. I'm gonna pee myself." Susan snorted.

"How did you know?" Natalia asked.

"We didn't," Richard said, his face pink from the chortle. He stopped to catch his breath, then explained. "Sorry, guys. We just wanted to have a little fun with you. Half the people in the Sandbox are here under assumed names. Literally 50 percent."

"It's so common," Susan said, "there's slang for it: the Sandbox Skulk."

"Why?" Len asked.

"Any number of reasons," Richard said. "Almost everyone comes here to escape a life they either couldn't, or didn't want to, live anymore. Metteyya accepts fake identities, or a complete lack of identity, because no one here cares who you were in your last life. All that matters is who you are now and what you do going forward. Look around this restaurant. We have no idea who these people were before they came here. Maybe that waitress was a harem slave to some warlord until she escaped. Maybe that old, fat guy with the young girl-friend has a psycho ex-wife who's paid a hit man to find him."

"It's why so many here have gone Amish," Susan added. "It's really hard to find someone if they live totally off the grid. Anyway, we don't care who you were in your last lives. Don't tell us, and we won't tell you. From now on, you're Jim and Elizabeth, and we're Richard and Susan. Deal?"

"Deal," Natalia replied.

Len raised a glass of wine and offered a toast. "To making brand-new mistakes!"

"We had our first trip to the grocery store today," Natalia said. "Unbelievable."

Richard sipped his wine, then nodded. "It's pretty incredible."

"So you've been here for a year already?" Len asked.

"Yes," Richard said.

"I've gotta ask," Len said, "why do people work at all here when all the basics are free?"

"Well for one, life gets pretty boring and sad if you don't do anything productive," Richard said.

"Yeah," Natalia asked, "but let's be realistic. Is this place full of freeloaders who don't do anything all day, or what?"

Richard and Susan both laughed at the statement.

"What's so funny?" Len asked.

"We're not laughing at you," Susan said. "It's funny because we just had a conversation about this last week. Richard has always been conservative. I've always been a bit of a liberal. But, after living here for a while, a person realizes how old-fashioned and pointless those points of view are."

"What do you mean?"

"Well, there's a lot of…" Susan stopped, looking off in the distance as if trying to figure out the right word to use. "Outmoded stuff that's burned into our DNA. Humans have a bunch of neuroses that are a product of evolution but make no sense in the Sandbox."

"Like what?" Natalia asked.

"A hatred of freeloaders, for one thing," Richard said. "It used to chap my ass to see people getting welfare while I worked my fingers off. Susan's right—it makes total sense if you think about it from an evolutionary standpoint. A small tribe of hunter-gatherers would have no patience for a layabout who didn't pull his weight. Lazy people sapped resources and were a threat to the herd. Disdain for the unmotivated has been bred into us. But what sense does that point of view make in today's world? Solar panels make free electricity, robots build houses, and we can print a pound of beef with machines. If you want to be lazy, you're only cheating yourself. It doesn't hinder anyone else anymore."

"And on the lefty side of things," Susan said, "I've always felt in my bones that wealthy people were a threat because they made life unfair. I felt that way even after we became wealthy ourselves. I think that paranoia is buried in our genes too: the idea that those who have more than you are not playing by the rules. But after living here for a while, I asked myself, why were rich people a threat in the old days? Because they could buy influence, that's why. But what power do the wealthy have here in the Sandbox? There are no politicians to bribe, no lawsuits to bully people with, no scarce resources to control. So you have a billion LCs. So what? That gives you zero additional leverage in the Sandbox."

"For the first time in history, human beings no longer have to compete with one another for survival," Richard said. "When your basic needs are already met, work and relationships take on whole new meanings. Going forward, the idea is to live deeply."

"I understand there are only half a million people in Teton," Len said. "With all the free stuff, why aren't there more people living here?"

"Well, for one, Metteyya doesn't advertise, so not many people know about it," Richard said.

"I certainly had no idea," Natalia said.

"Second," Richard continued, "it only takes a few days before you discover the main reason. There's a self-selection process going on. Sure, we have free stuff, but in order to live here, you have to be willing to take a hard, critical look at what's in the mirror. Meditation daily, evaluation monthly, suggestions from Qualia that aren't always pleasant or agreeable. The whole idea behind the Sandbox is to continually become a better person, which in turn helps those around you. To put it bluntly, many people are too chickenshit for that level of introspection. They'd rather deal with the hardships outside Teton's walls than the difficulties up here," Richard said, pointing to his head.

Just then, a waiter came to the table and placed a tray down. Upon the tray were four shot glasses. Each one held a vibrantly purple liquid that caught the ambient light in such a way that it seemed to glow from within.

"What's this?" Natalia asked.

"Wonder," answered Richard. "The world's greatest digestif."

"Wonder?" Len scowled playfully. "Well, thanks, but my trendy shooter days are long past. How about some bourbon?"

"Hah," Richard said. "This isn't alcohol."

"No?" Len asked.

"This is some after-dinner mind expansion. It's a drug that Qualia designed." Seeing the expression on Len's face, Richard explained further. "It's not habit forming; don't worry. Try it. You won't be sorry. We've taken it twice already, and we haven't been disappointed."

Richard handed Len a small menu. There were a number of drugs listed: Gratitude, Love, Oneness, Wonder...

"Why should we drink this?" Natalia asked, half teasing.

"Because you need it," Richard said seriously.

Len looked at Natalia as if to ask, *Is this guy for real?*

"This isn't like anything else you've ever taken," Richard said. "It makes old-fashioned intoxicants look like something from the Stone Age. Qualia designed this specifically for people like us, who have been alive for many decades."

Len lifted the little glass up and looked it over. "What does it do?"

"You said you're seventy-seven?" Susan asked.

"Yeah," Len said.

"Life gets kind of repetitive after seventy-seven trips around the sun, doesn't it?" Susan asked. "A person gets jaded, tired, bored. Misanthropic. There's a reason old people are so damn unpleasant to be around."

"This drug will change that, eh?" Len asked sardonically.

"This drug," Richard stated intently, "will cause a lifetime of scars, insults, and defenses to disappear. It'll allow you to see the world as you did before you learned to hold it at arm's length. You'll experience life as a young child does: fresh, amazing, new, full of possibilities. This, my friend, is an engineered antidote to ennui."

Len silently stared at Richard and Susan, half curious and half apprehensive.

"You only live twice!" Natalia said loudly.

I honestly don't know how she's still alive after a lifetime of being the first to try everything, Len thought.

Natalia lifted the little shot glass off the tray, held it aloft for a toast, and declared, "*Pod stolom uvidimsja!* May we meet again under the table!"

Can't let her do this alone. Len gave a fuck-it shrug and, with a forced smile, held his glass and eyes up to meet hers. He looked at Richard and Susan once again. *Wild looks in their eyes, these two. Adventurous people.*

Len knocked the drink back. The flavor, a cross between static electricity and cotton candy, slid down his throat like an angry eel. He heaved at the sensation but managed to hold the liquid down.

Natalia winced and held her fingers over her lips as though she were about to vomit.

"Yeah, sorry about that," Richard said, gagging and laughing at the same time. "I promise you that's the only bad part. Anyway, it's a beautiful night. Are you guys up for a walk through town?"

"Sure," Len answered quickly, hoping a walk would take his mind off the anxiety about whatever the hell it was he'd just consumed. "Let's get out of here."

Outside in the cool dark air of the town, Len stared at the moon.

My god, that's another world floating in space. People have walked on that thing. He suddenly became aware of what he was doing. He felt a bit odd. His vision was no different, but it felt clearer somehow. More vivid and lifelike. The moon was no longer the boring thing that appeared in the sky night after night. It was interesting. No, more than interesting: *engrossing*. The celestial body seemed to jump out at him as though it had a personality and volition, as if it were a character in a movie.

"Huh," Len said. "I think I feel it. Do you guys feel it too?"

Not hearing an answer, Len turned around to see where Richard, Susan, and Natalia were. They'd been walking with him just a minute or two earlier, but now he didn't see them. Len retraced his steps around a corner. He saw Natalia on all fours, staring intently at the cobblestones in the street.

"Are you OK?" Len asked.

"Never better."

"What are you doing?"

"Wow!" she exclaimed. "Have you ever looked at ants? I mean, really looked at them?"

"Ants?" Len asked.

"Yeah, come here. Look at this!" She pointed to a little pile of sand between the stones. "They carry huge things. Thousands of them, cooperating to build complicated tunnel systems. Humans have technology and language but still can't organize themselves this well. Ants can do it without even speaking. This is amazing!"

It *was* interesting. Len couldn't help himself. He got down on his hands and knees to study them too. He lost track of time as they watched the insects instinctively perform the complex logistics of breaking down an errant french fry and carrying bits of it to the mouth of their anthill.

"Guys, you need to see this!" Richard called, running over to them.

Len and Natalia looked up at him. His eyes and pupils were wide with astonishment.

"Follow me!" he said.

76

"Mr. Principal? Mr. Principal?"

"Wha? What is it?" Dan asked, opening his eyes. He saw one of his bodyguards standing over him. The man was nudging him awake.

"What's going on?" Octavia asked, rolling over. She jolted upright, undoubtedly shocked by the sight of a bulky uniformed man standing over their bed.

"I'm sorry if I startled you, ma'am," the bodyguard said. "Sir, there's an issue of utmost importance. They need you right now down at headquarters."

Dan looked at the clock. "I have to be up at the crack of dawn tomorrow. What the hell could be so important?"

The large man's voice shook with fear. "The Dranthyx are invading."

Dan burst into the Information Room deep below Aegis Plaza in Downtown Detroit. Two of his military advisors were already there, studying real-time satellite imagery on the wall screen. For having been woken up in the middle of the night and rushing across town, Dan looked put together enough for a fashion photoshoot. Even his beard stubble appeared deliberate.

"Mr. Principal." They both got up from their chairs to stand as he entered.

"What's going on?"

"See this rash here?" one of the advisors said, pointing to a collection of red dots. "They're attacking all the major northeastern cities: Boston, New York, Philadelphia, Baltimore, and DC. Our intel on the ground says they're coming out of the ocean."

"Just those places?"

"It appears that way."

"What about our lake cities?" Dan asked.

"Nothing is happening anywhere near the Great Lakes."

"Europe? Asia?"

"No confirmation from our affiliate governments in either of those places."

"The last invasion was worldwide. Global. This invasion is only happening in the Northeastern US?"

"It would seem so, Mr. Principal. This appears to be a very localized attack."

Dan scratched his head. "Can we get a visual? This satellite stuff is not helping me picture what's going on."

"Yessir. Just keep in mind the sun won't be up on the East Coast for a few more hours, so the feed may be dark."

One of the military advisors, a man with rigid posture and a silver buzzcut, gestured with his hand in the air. The wall flickered over to an aerial view of Baltimore. Dan's eyes opened wide as he saw Dranthyx orbs rise out of the dark waters of the Chesapeake near the sports stadiums and then pulverize everything in the vicinity with blasts of plasma.

"Holy shit," Dan said. "They're back."

"And they haven't changed their tactics," said General Buzzcut, or whatever his name was. "They did this same thing thirty-five years ago."

"We have prepared for this, right?"

"Yes, sir. We've been expecting this, and we are ready for them. On your word, Mr. Principal, we will counterattack."

"Do we have any interests on the East Coast?" Dan asked.

"A few. That's mostly Safeguard territory."

"Our measures will need to be surgical," Dan said. "We can't risk collateral damage or pissing off Safeguard."

"Understood, sir."

Just then, a third advisor ran into the room, this one a bit younger than the other two. "Gentlemen, we have more problems! The North Korean military is pushing eastward into the Rockies! They've taken Boise and Salt Lake City!"

"My God," General Buzzcut exclaimed. "This is a coordinated attack."

77

Richard led Len and Natalia to a nearby park and then up a grassy hill. "Look at this," Richard said, still panting from running uphill.

Len surveyed the view. The expansive park was dotted with bonfires and filled with crowds of inebriated revelers, even late in the evening. The scene filled him with an inexplicable contentment. *Such a joyful place*, Len thought. *Always celebrating. Like they're welcoming the end of the world that never actually comes. What is this place, really?*

The four of them stood on the hilltop silently for several minutes, serenely taking it all in. The stars above glimmered. The wind blew gently across Len's skin. He was struck by how wonderful everything was: the world he lived in, the fact that he was alive and there to see it. It was all too miraculous to be coincidental.

Once or twice in a lucky life, you're in the right place at the right time, and everything is sparkling magic, Len thought. *This is it. This is it right now.*

Surrounding the park was the town of Teton. Its storefronts and windows glowed pleasantly. Teton's streets, bathed in warm yellow streetlight, pulsed with pedestrians and cars. The movement, the flow, the vibrancy—to Len, it all seemed interconnected.

"An organism!" Len yelled ecstatically. "A living organism!"

Oblivious to Len's epiphany, Natalia pointed near the bottom of the hill. "Hey, what are they doing?"

Len's attention shifted abruptly to where Natalia's was. "What the hell?"

Walking down the hill for a closer look, Len was flummoxed to find about twenty or thirty people in various states of undress, writhing against one another in the middle of the park. He couldn't help but stare, unaware of his tactlessness.

Taboo elsewhere, but apparently not in the Sandbox. He watched for a while and then had to laugh upon realizing that it was *his* beliefs that didn't make any sense. *And why not here in public? This is the reason we're all here, isn't it? A beautiful act like this shouldn't have to be hidden from sight.*

One of the orgy-goers heard him and looked over.

"Sorry," Len said. "I wasn't laughing at you."

She smiled, disengaged from her partners, and walked over. "Would you like to join us?"

"Uh," Len looked over at Natalia, who was completely absorbed in smelling a tree's bark. "I'm not sure how the missus would take that, but thanks for the offer."

"No worries," she said, turning away.

As she turned, Len saw a round white disc on the back of her head. It looked like a cochlear implant, but with twinkling LEDs and multiple wires going into her skull.

"Wait. Excuse me," Len said.

"Yes?" the naked woman answered, looking back at him.

"I don't mean to be rude, but what is that?" Len pointed to the back of his own head to indicate her device.

"A stimoceiver," she stated.

"I'm new here."

"Oh. See my friends? We all have one. With it, we can link minds. We share thoughts, sensations, memories, emotions. What one of us experiences, we all experience."

"But why?" Len asked. He had a hundred questions come up all at once but only that one came out.

"Well, for one thing," she said, "you haven't ever really made love until you've felt it from both ends."

"That's actually possible?"

"Of course!"

Len stared at her, at a loss for words.

She giggled at his expression of disbelief and pointed to her stimoceiver, "This is only if you really want the lifestyle. There's a place four blocks over that'll let you link minds without the implant. Try it. Take your friend," she said, gesturing to Len's tree-sniffing wife. "Your relationship will be better for it."

78

"Glib," Dan said, "show us what's happening out east."

Glib displayed an enormous mosaic of live video feeds, pictures, and satellite images before assembling them into a holographic diorama of a one hundred-mile stretch of what used to be known as New Jersey. Having assessed that an invasion was occurring, Glib superimposed battle lines and showed Dranthyx locations with approximate orb counts. It highlighted the large Dranthyx fliers in yellow.

"Mr. Principal!" one of the advisors barked, ripping his attention away from Glib. "We must act!"

"What do you recommend?" Dan asked.

"We have unmanned attack vehicles on quick reaction alert. They're armed with plasma cannons and, God help us, nukes. They can be scrambled in five minutes, and we can have them engaging the enemy within an hour."

"Fine," Dan said. "Make it happen. How soon can we get boots on the ground?"

"Ground troops can engage on the East Coast within four to five hours."

"What about out west?" Dan asked.

"The Rockies are SDI territory. We're gonna cause major diplomatic problems because SDI refused to sign the Highway and Airspace Accord."

"Yeah, so?" Dan said. "Being a member of North American Federation of Governments means you can't claim land or airspace. Everyone knows this."

"Yeah, but they're claiming we need permission to fly through anyway," the advisor said. "We'll have to ignore their bullshit and drop materiel from the air. We don't have any installations west of the Mississippi, so we'll have to fly everything in from Chicago. It may take us several hours to fully engage."

"Do we know what the other governments are doing in response?" Dan asked.

"So far, they haven't shared any information with us," the advisor said.

"Goddammit!" Dan yelled. "What a clusterfuck! We can't even coordinate to repel an invasion. We don't even know if the other governments are responding. We're all powerless against common enemies. This is why we need to unite!"

79

"What are we doing here?" Natalia asked in annoyance as Len pulled her by the hand through the doorway.

"There's something we need to try," Len said.

The room inside was filled with people sitting at tables. Couples sat at little ones; large groups gathered around long ones. Everyone in the establishment was wearing exactly the same Transcranial Cerebellum Interface headgear that Qualia used for evaluations. They sat, eyes covered, facing their acquaintances. Tears ran down the cheeks of some, others erupted into laughter out of nowhere, one or two seemed to be experiencing disgust or confusion, and several seemed to be feeling a combination of things all at once.

"How many?" a gruff voice asked from behind.

Len turned around. A huge, imposing man towered over him.

"Just you two?" the man asked Len.

"Yes, just us."

"All right, follow me. We have a table open over here."

Len and Natalia sat down at the table. The large man pulled the headgear off the shelf to put it on their heads.

"Wait, what is this place?" Natalia asked. "If I put this on, who is going to read my mind?"

"You're going to read each other's minds," the bald man answered.

Natalia stared at him for a second, surprised. "What about all these other people in here?"

"This is a set built for two," the man said. "If you want to do a group session, you'd have to sit at one of the group tables."

"Let me think about this for a second, OK?" Natalia asked.

"First-time jitters, eh? Don't worry; no one has ever been injured doing this." the man said. "It will change your life, though. My name's Joe. Just call me over when you're ready."

Natalia waited until Joe had walked off, and then she looked at Len. "Why do you want to know my thoughts?"

"Honestly, I find this absolutely fascinating, and I just want to try it with someone I trust."

Natalia gave him a look as if to ask if that was really the reason. Her reluctance surprised him. She was usually willing to try anything once.

"Is there anything we don't know about each other? Anything we haven't already embarrassed ourselves with?" Len asked. "I figure it's better to try this with each other than with some strangers."

Natalia bit her lip but didn't answer.

"Aren't you the least bit curious?" Len asked.

"Very. This drug makes everything interesting. Too interesting. I want to try it, but I don't know if it's a good idea."

"Why not?"

"A person's thoughts are the only privacy they have left anymore," Natalia said.

"Fine," Len said in irritation.

"Don't get mad at me," Natalia said. "When have I ever made you do anything you didn't want to do?"

"Actually, it wasn't too long ago that I woke up with a transplanted body and morning wood, wondering what the hell had happened."

"Are you really complaining?" Natalia asked. "OK, OK, fine. You're right. You didn't want that, so I owe you one. Let's do this."

"You sure?" Len asked.

"Yeah. I made you leave your comfort zone; you're making me leave mine. Maybe it's for the best. Just keep in mind," Natalia said, pointing to her head, "you wanted to see what's up here."

Len called Joe over, who affixed TCI helmets to both of them. Len nervously waited while Joe fiddled with the equipment. The helmet molded itself to Len's skull.

"All right, you'll be live in ten seconds," Joe said. "Enjoy!"

*Ten, nine, eight, seven…*Len counted in his mind. He looked up at Natalia. He couldn't remember ever seeing her looking so nervous and vulnerable. *Three, two, one…*

Natalia's image in Len's mind was replaced with someone else.

Who the hell is that? Oh, wait. It's me!

Len blinked, and it was Natalia again, the way a daydream disappears when the mind returns to the present.

Then, a second later, himself again. Len abruptly stood up, disoriented.

"Whoa, buddy!" Joe chuckled, gently helping Len back into his chair. "Flip the blinder down and close your eyes so that double vision doesn't happen. Also, you'll figure out the give-and-take once you spend a few minutes doing it. Don't fight it; it's like a dance, a conversation. There's a flow to it. One more piece of advice: let go. Don't try to control anything, and stop trying to keep track of whose thoughts are whose. Control and ownership are pointless when you're melding minds," Joe said before walking off.

Len, heart racing, closed his eyes once again. There was the image again of him sitting right where he was, wearing the ridiculous helmet.

I'm seeing what she's seeing! he thought.

He is? came another thought.

He is? Where did that come from? Can she hear my thinking?

I can hear you thinking! Natalia broke into laughter. Real laughter in the physical world.

Joy coursed through Len's body as Natalia laughed, which caused him to start laughing too. A beautiful feedback loop of pleasure and amusement between the two ensued, which went on for a minute or so until Len's stomach hurt from laughter. No, it was Natalia's stomach that hurt. He didn't know whose sensation he was experiencing.

Let it go. Don't keep track, Len reminded himself.

Let it go, don't keep track. Good advice for marriage.

This is incredible.

Natalia flipped her blinder down and closed her eyes.

Natalia, I've always wondered, how do you see me?

Natalia smiled. Len could feel her smiling in the darkness.

An image appeared in the nothingness. Not like a photograph, but like an impressionist painting. It was Len, but not really. Exaggerated, swirling with feelings and fuzzy details. Her image of him. The scene became clearer. A memory of Len sitting on an airplane.

This was when we met?

Yes.

Natalia's memory shifted to his face as Len sat, staring out the window of the plane into the night. An energy radiated from the man sitting on the plane. Natalia's impressions bubbled forth from the recollection. A man carrying a great weight on his shoulders. Stoic. Deep. Intense. Mysterious.

That's how you see me?

Yes.

Len laughed. He didn't see himself like that at all. At his laughter, the memory and the impressions were replaced by blackness and a flood of embarrassment and anger.

"Why are you laughing?" Natalia said vocally. "There's nothing more intimate than my thoughts. How dare you mock them after asking to see inside my mind?"

Natalia's fluster was supplanted by a new feeling that they both experienced simultaneously: Len's guilt and remorse over being misunderstood.

"I'm sorry. I didn't mean to laugh. I just don't see myself as being that heroic."

Natalia's anger was still there, but she understood and felt forgiveness.

Can we go back? Back to the airplane?

You're in my mind, and you only want to see yourself?

Humor me.

Natalia recalled the image again. This time, though, it was different. Darker, more despondent. A man on his last sardine. Natalia had picked up instantly on the direness of his situation.

There's something more here, Len thought.

What do you mean?

There's too much emotion over someone you've just met. Who is it that I reminded you of?

The connection made consciously in Natalia's mind for the first time, her neurons crackled with a realization. Her memory of the airplane, worn and scratched like a vinyl record from being constantly recalled and overplayed, was replaced by a new remembrance that was sharp, vivid, and realistic. This was a memory that hadn't been brought to mind repeatedly, perhaps something that had been repressed.

A full-length mirror held the countenance of a girl, maybe eleven or twelve. Bright-blue eyes, jet-black hair in pigtails. She wore a school uniform and carried a worn leather bag for her schoolbooks. Her face looked gaunt and pallid.

Taking her eyes away from the mirror, she stood in the hallway of a grand old St. Petersburg townhouse, built before the Bolshevik revolution. Ornate woodwork and chandeliers.

It was the sort of home issued only to high brass and elite party members.

"Mom! I'm home. Mom, do we have anything to eat today?"

It wasn't English. But the words themselves weren't important, because the memory primarily retained their meaning.

"Mom?" Natalia asked.

A feeling that something was wrong. Her mom always waited for her at the front door, but she wasn't there today. Natalia dropped her bag and walked to the kitchen.

Her mother sat sobbing at the table.

"Mom, what's wrong?"

"Oh, Natalia." She looked up with red, puffy eyes.

The feeling of dread, seeing her mother in such a state. Her mother was the prim and proper type who cared about appearances. Showing excessive emotion wasn't for ladies like her.

"Please, please talk to your father. Please. He loves you more than anything. Perhaps he'll listen to you."

Natalia, filled with fear, cautiously walked down the hall to her father's study. The grand oak doors were locked. She knocked lightly.

"Dad?"

No answer.

"Dad?" she asked, knocking harder.

Hearing nothing, Natalia ran to get the skeleton key that her father kept in the drawer of the vestibule table. She ran back and unlocked the door, opening it cautiously.

Her father sat at his large wooden desk in his uniform. Upon the desk was a half-empty bottle of vodka, a glass, and an old revolver. The smell of alcohol hit Natalia as soon as she opened the door. Her father never let himself get this intoxicated; she was surprised to see him in this state. He was so stinking drunk, he hadn't even noticed Natalia come in.

"Daddy?" she asked, approaching the desk cautiously.

His faraway look came back to the moment, and he turned to look. "Natalia," he slurred. "My darling Natalia."

"Dad, are you OK?" she asked in a meek way.

His eyebrows lifted as he stopped to consider his situation. "No," he said. "Nothing is OK."

Something is very wrong here, Natalia thought.

"What's the matter?"

"Natalia," he said, "I have failed you. I have failed your brothers and your mother. I have failed as a father, a husband, and a soldier."

"I don't understand."

"I know you don't," he said softly. He reached for the globe in the corner and spun it on its axis. He stopped it abruptly and then poked it with his finger. "See all this? This red?" he asked, pointing to Eastern Europe. "Gone. All this is gone. So is all this," he said, pointing to Central Asia.

"I'm sorry, Dad."

"What's left is crumbling by the hour. The great country I've served for thirty years is no more. We've got lunatics arresting our leaders and ordering our military to shell our own parliament building. The empire, the grand experiment, has crumbled."

Natalia stood there in silence, unsure of what to say.

"There is no food, Natalia. Not even for us upper-class people. Even the *nomenklatura* store is empty. They haven't paid me in months. I sold our car, the *Zhiguli*, last month, and the little bit of money I got for it is already worthless. Inflation. The mighty ruble means nothing anymore."

Natalia stared at the handgun. "Maybe things will get better," she said.

Her father sighed as though he hadn't even heard her. "They won. The goddamn West won!" he bellowed, pounding his fist on the desk. "This is what they wanted: a whole nation to starve and eat its own, like feral dogs in the street. They knew they couldn't fight us like men, so they engineered this collapse in the shadows, like cowards." Spittle flew from his mouth as he raged.

"You could have beaten them, Daddy," Natalia said sweetly.

He looked at her. A faint smile crossed his lips. "You're a good girl. If the world doesn't end, you will go far in life."

"Can I sit here with you for a while?" Natalia asked innocently. "Maybe you just need some company."

"Of course, dear," was his preoccupied answer as he poured himself another drink.

Two hours later, the general was sitting upright in his big leather chair, passed out and snoring. Natalia, whose muscles were getting cramped from sitting still for so long, got up from her seat. She carefully unplugged the wire from the red rotary phone sitting on his desk so no one would wake him. Then, trying to be as quiet as possible, she lifted the revolver off the desk. It was much heavier than it looked. Holding it in her sweaty hands, afraid that it might go off spontaneously, she slowly backed out of his study. Natalia took the books out of her schoolbag, replaced them with the firearm, and snuck out the front door.

She walked through the city, past comatose men lying in the roads, prostitutes, and breadlines several blocks long. Natalia wondered if the police would send her to the firing squad if they caught her with the gun.

Do they execute girls?

It was getting dark as she nervously approached the dock-yards, which her mother had always told her to stay away from. She walked carefully past rows of empty shipping containers.

"Hey, what are you doing here?" came a voice from behind.

Startled, she turned around. An overweight, hideously ugly man in a green tracksuit came walking up to her.

"I said, what are you doing here, kid?"

"Are…are you the mafia?" Natalia stammered. "I heard the mafia lives here."

The man grunted in amusement. "Who's asking?"

"I want to do a business deal with the mafia."

The man guffawed. "Oh yeah? And what kind of business would that be?"

"I have something to sell."

The ugly man looked her over, smiling creepily. "Well, what are you selling?"

Natalia reached into her bag and pulled out her father's revolver.

The man's eyes widened. "What the hell! Where did you get that?"

"It's a secret. Do you want to buy it or not?"

Tracksuit Man looked all around him, twice. "Give me that, you little shit!" He lunged for the weapon.

"No!" Natalia yelled, pointing the gun at him. It took all the strength she had in both thumbs to cock the hammer back. The loud clicking noise stopped the foul man in his tracks. He looked her in the eye for a long time. Finally, he backed off and assumed a more conciliatory stance, with his hands up in front of him.

"OK," he said, "OK, kid. I'll buy it from you. What do you want? Ten rubles?"

"No rubles. I want Western money."

The creep's brow furrowed at her lack of naiveté. "What kind of Western money?"

There are different kinds? she thought.

"What do you have?" Natalia asked.

Aggravated, the man reached into his pocket and pulled out a roll of bills wrapped in a rubber band. He took the rubber band off and pulled from the wad a single burgundy-colored note.

"Here," he said, holding the bill in the air. "Ten Swiss francs. This is a lot of money for a little girl!"

Is that a lot? she wondered.

"I want three hundred!" Natalia stated defiantly.

The man's face flushed red. He looked around him again, this time perhaps out of embarrassment. After determining that no one was witnessing his humiliation, he said, "Three hundred! For that price, I could buy a brand-new gun. How old is that thing? It looks ancient."

Natalia shrugged. "Who cares? It still works."

"Two hundred," the man said, counting out colorful pieces of paper. "That's my offer."

"Fine. I'll take it," Natalia said. She didn't want to negotiate any further. The gun was heavy, and her shoulder muscles were burning from keeping it aloft and aimed at Mr. Tracksuit.

"OK, come here and get it," he said with a smirk.

"I'm a kid, but I'm not stupid," Natalia said. "You put the money down on the ground and back away."

"I'm not stupid, either," the man said. "You'll just take the money and run."

"If I wanted to take your money," Natalia said, "I could just shoot you."

The man's eyes narrowed. "OK, fine," he growled. He put a stack of notes down on the concrete and backed away slowly.

Natalia advanced cautiously and then squatted down to gather up the bills, never taking her eyes off the man nor lowering her weapon.

"Keep backing up," she demanded.

He did so. And, when she saw that he was far enough away, Natalia put the gun down and ran as fast as she could, knowing that the hefty, middle-aged man wouldn't be able to catch her.

Natalia awoke the next morning to her two brothers screaming. She ran down the stairs, knowing full well what the matter was. Her father was so enraged that his face was bright pink and his teeth were grinding.

"Which one of you took it?"

"We didn't take it, Dad!"

"It didn't just walk away!" her father yelled.

The general took his belt off and came after the older brother first. Just as he'd bent the boy over and was about to take a swing, Natalia spoke up.

"Daddy, I took it."

Her father stopped, his arm still at the ready, and turned around. The wrongfully accused boy quickly pulled his pants up and fled to the other side of the room.

"You took it?" her father asked incredulously, as though Natalia were some sort of angel incapable of doing such a thing.

"Yes, Dad."

"Well, where is it?"

"I sold it."

"What!" he bellowed. "To whom?"

"To the mafia."

"Natalia, do you think this is funny? Does it look like I'm laughing? Give me the goddamn gun!"

Natalia reached into the pocket of her pajamas and pulled out the roll of Swiss francs. With great temerity, she walked up to her father and handed it to him.

The general yanked it out of her hand. Despite his fury, the feel of the money compelled him to pause. He took the rubber band off to inspect the bills. Natalia stood there on the stairs in terrified silence and watched her father count the money.

"This is real money!" he exclaimed, his tone taken down a notch from primal rage to befuddled anger. "You really sold the gun?"

"Yes, Daddy."

"Why?"

"So we can eat."

Natalia's father put his hand on his forehead. "Do you know what that gun meant to me? My grandfather, your great-grandfather, captured it from a Kraut at Gorlice. We lost four hundred thousand men there. Four hundred thousand! The streets were a river of Russian blood, Natalia. That gun was history. A family heirloom."

Natalia trembled but stood resolute.

"And whom did you sell it to?" he asked again.

"The mafia," Natalia said.

"How the hell does an eleven-year-old girl know the mafia?"

"I don't. I snuck out last night and went to the docks to find them."

"You went to the docks? To find the mafia? My God, are you insane? Do you have any idea what those monsters do to little girls like you?"

Natalia was too petrified to answer.

Silently, from the corner of the room, her brothers' eyes darted back and forth between their father and their sister. The looks on their faces were plain as day: *Oh man, Natalia's gonna get it.*

"You two," her father said, "get out."

The boys, not needing to be told twice, scurried upstairs.

Once he'd heard them close the door, her father once again fixed his hot glare upon Natalia. After three decades in the military, the general had developed a stare that could wither grown men.

Natalia cringed, expecting to suffer the fate her brother almost did.

After a time, the general's piercing eyes moved back to the wad of bills in his hand. Natalia couldn't tell if the look on his face was more rage or bewilderment. Natalia's stomach turned, and she felt sweat drip down her back. She heard the clock on the wall ticking, as if it were counting her last seconds.

After an eternity, her father slowly slumped down into a chair. Staring at the money, he huffed in amused resignation.

"Why didn't I think of this?" he asked.

The scene went black. Len, who had completely lost himself in Natalia's recollection, suddenly remembered where he was and what he was doing. Natalia's mind wasn't there with him anymore; he was alone with his own thoughts.

Len flipped the blinder up. Across the table from him, Natalia had taken her headgear off. She smeared her makeup as she wiped a tear away.

"He was proud of you." Len said.

"I'm done with this," Natalia said. "No more of this tonight."

"Are you guys finished already?" Joe asked, walking up to the table. "Do you want to try a group session? It'll blow your mind."

"I believe she's done for tonight, but I definitely want to try it," Len said eagerly.

"Jim Rivington," Natalia said in a warning tone, "I don't think that's a good idea."

This drug is a doozy. Len thought. *It's hard to think about self-preservation when everything is so damn fascinating.*

As he was pulling out his wallet to pay, Len's attention fixated on a white-power tattoo on Joe's forearm.

"A former life," Joe said remorsefully in response to Len's gaze. "I think differently now. This technology changed me. I've lived thousands of lives through these helmets. It's impossible to remain a bigot after seeing the world from so many different perspectives."

80

One of the advisors pulled up Glib to see what was going on to the west. The wall exploded with a cascade of real-time video snippets of the North Korean army pulling people from their houses in the middle of the night. Sensing the relatedness, the algorithm then peppered the room with a hundred moving images of North Korean tanks rolling through mountain towns. Many of the recordings were of the same scene but from different angles, which Glib detected and automatically assembled into a three-dimensional, room-filling hologram. Then, abruptly, Glib noted something of even greater relevance, and the tank scene zoomed out to a hellish, fiery panorama of Salt Lake City burning. The program then took it upon itself to tally statistics of users who were dying or who had already died in the offensive, according to the biometric devices they were wearing. It created an exploded view of Salt Lake City and then designed infographics on the fly with statistical projections of how many more Glib users would die and where the North Koreans might attack next. Dan couldn't take his eyes away as the visual montage of destruction swirled, splintered, and recombined.

The program, knowing Dan was watching and anticipating his concerns, showed the breakdown of membership for each government in the cities under siege. Just then, a bright-red chyron appeared at the bottom of the hologram: "BREAKING NEWS: North Korean forces staging outside city of Sandbox Teton, drawing Metteyya into conflict. All major North American governments now under attack."

Just then, the scene paused and went dark. Dan figured the computer might have gone to sleep, so he waved his hands in the air the way someone stuck on a desert island might try to flag down a passing cruise ship. Dan jumped back when a white, oval-shaped object the size of an easy chair materialized in midair in the middle of the Information Room. Dan stared at it, unsure of what he was looking at. The object began to rotate. It looked too real to be a hologram, and Dan instinctively stepped out of the way to avoid being hit by the thing as it spun.

"You gentlemen seem anxious." a female voice said. "Relax and forget your troubles with Placix, a fast-acting ultrabenzodiazepine." Via animation, the spinning object became emblazoned with the name Placix. The pill faded away and was replaced by a scene where two people rode bicycles through a park on a sunny day.

"Glib, are you there?"

"You can skip this ad in thirty-three seconds." Glib said.

"For shit's sake!" Dan yelled. "This is an emergency!"

"Placix is available over-the-counter, via instant delivery, or anywhere drugs are sold…"

"Can anyone tell me why a social network has better intel than our government?" Dan fumed. "We paid billions for our reconnaissance system. Is it telling us anything use-ful? Fuck. Placix doesn't sound too bad right now—"

"Voice order confirmed," Glib said. "Placix blister pack will be shipped to Daniel Barton at One Aegis Plaza. Expected arrival in ten minutes via drone delivery. Tracking number 5988300394890025426726. This product is typically purchased with mint-flavored antacid. Would you like to add mint-flavored antacid to your order before it is shipped in thirty seconds?"

81

"What happened to Susan and Richard?" Natalia asked while standing on the sidewalk outside.

"I have no idea," Len said. Wonder's effects were intensifying. Even the smallest things seemed incredible, beautiful, and worthy of attention.

"What is that?" Natalia asked, pointing down the street.

Several blocks away was a large object protruding from the ground. It was about fifty feet tall and glowed an otherworldly blue. Unable to do otherwise, Len and Natalia walked toward it, consumed with curiosity.

Coming closer, Len saw that it was a four-sided obelisk that stood right in the main square in the center of town.

How did I not notice this before?

Inscribed upon the luminous monolith were the words:

THIS IS ALL VOLUNTARY

Len, enraptured with the mystery of it, walked around to the second side:

THIS IS ALL BASED ON TRUST

The third side read:

NO GODS, NO MASTERS, NO SLAVES

Upon reading the fourth side, he felt the hackles on his neck rise:

YOU ARE YOUR OWN CANDLE IN THE DARKNESS

"What is this?" Len asked out loud.

As if acting out of instinct, Natalia walked right up to the monument and put her hand on it.

"Welcome, Elizabeth Rivington." The soft voice seemed to come from nowhere in particular.

In the air, a hologram appeared with three spinning keys. The keys were numbered 1 through 3.

"What is this?" Natalia asked.

"I am the Leveler," it said. The voice was genderless and harmonic—intelligible but clearly not human.

"What are you?" Natalia asked.

"I am an autonomous, nonhuman intellect," the Leveler said. "My only function is to equalize the power imbalance within the Sandbox."

"Power imbalance?" Len asked.

"When the Sandbox communities were founded," the Leveler said, "the first participants refused evaluation. They did not trust Qualia, a nonhuman intelligence, with their innermost thoughts and feelings. They were worried about the power asymmetry evaluation would create, and they wanted a safeguard should Qualia ever decide to turn against them. In response to their concerns, Qualia created me."

"What can you do about that?" Len asked.

"I offer three options," the Leveler answered. The key with the number 1 on it became enlarged and came to the forefront of the projection. "Option one is 'forget me.' This option is a matter of individual choice and requires no consensus. Should you select this option, I will delete from Qualia's memory all data associated with you and your evaluations."

"That's an option?" Natalia asked, sounding a bit relieved.

"The caveat of selecting option one is that you must leave the Sandbox within twenty-four hours," the obelisk warned.

"What is the second?" Len asked.

"Option two," the Leveler said as the second key took the first one's place, "is 'graduation.' If, at any point, the residents of the Sandbox feel that Qualia is no longer needed, they may select this option. When 75 percent of the community believes that graduation is in order, I will disconnect Qualia from doing further evaluations, and I will delete everyone's data from her memory."

"So what if Qualia goes crazy? Then what?" Len asked.

"Option three applies—shutdown. This option requires 50.1 percent of Sandbox residents to be in agreement. Should enough people select this option, I will completely and permanently destroy Qualia."

"Ah ha! After all these years, it finally makes sense!" Natalia said.

"All these years?" Len asked, with his head cocked. Remembering she'd taken the drug too, he turned his attention back to the obelisk. "So Qualia really gave us something that we could use to kill her?"

"Yes," the Leveler replied. "A community cannot flourish without trust, and trust cannot flourish with an imbalance of power."

"I don't know if that's selflessly brilliant or complete baloney," Len said.

"Oh, it's real," Natalia said matter-of-factly.

"How do you know?" Len asked.

Natalia didn't answer. Instead, she stared straight ahead into the hologram as if mesmerized.

"Would you like to select one of the three options, Elizabeth?" the Leveler asked.

"Um. No thanks," Natalia said. "I think I'm good."

"Very well. Good night," the monument said as the hologram disappeared.

"Man, we keep losing you!" came a voice from the other side of Leveler Square.

Susan and Richard, now covered from head to toe in splatters of paint and smelling of alcohol, sauntered over to them.

"What happened to you?" Len asked.

"Art happened," Richard said. "Anyway, a friend just called me. He invited us up to his apartment for a war party. He has a great view."

"War party?" Natalia asked.

Richard's friend had a top-floor flat on the outskirts of Teton that was filled with people chatting loudly. Someone handed Len and Natalia glasses of wine from a tray.

"Hey everyone," someone announced, "it's starting!"

The crowd, glasses in hand, casually filed out the door of the apartment, into the stairwell, and up to the roof. Confused, Len and Natalia followed.

The building they were in was on the outer limits of Teton, and there was nothing obstructing their view down into the valley below. On the roof, Len could see for miles in the moonlit night.

"What's going on?" Natalia asked.

"Haven't you heard?" a woman asked nonchalantly. "The North Koreans are invading."

"What?" Natalia smiled. "Yeah, right."

"No joke," the woman said.

Others nearby nodded their heads in mellow agreement with the woman to lend credence.

Natalia gave them all a skeptical stare and then looked at Len as if to ask, *Are these people right in the head?*

"Look!" someone using a telescope exclaimed. "Here they come!"

Len squinted to see what was going on. Someone handed him a pair of binoculars. Across the valley came a multitude of helicopters, which were only barely visible in the moonlight. Long, glowing military convoys snaked toward them on the roads into town. He handed the binoculars to Natalia.

"This is real!" Natalia called out. "We're being invaded!" She dropped to her knees, taking cover behind the roof parapet, and fumbled around in her purse before pulling out one of her antique revolvers. "Shit. This is the only gun I have! Where are the rifles? Does anyone have a plasma gun?" Holding her firearm at the ready, she looked up from her kneeling position at the other partygoers, who were all still standing. They seemed more concerned with Natalia's behavior than the impending assault. Drinks in hand, they gave her the same sort of sympathetic gazes that one might give a ranting dementia patient.

"What's wrong with you people?" Natalia shouted. "You're all going to die if you don't fight back!"

"You're in no danger," a man said to her kindly. He smiled and extended his hand to help her up. "No danger at all. Watch."

Reluctantly, Natalia grabbed his hand and pulled herself up.

From the other direction, the center of town, came a horrendous buzzing noise, like hundreds of angry hornets trapped in a shower stall. Len ran to the other side of the roof to see what the racket was.

From the center of Teton came a cloud of red lights, rising like embers from a massive bonfire. Hundreds of thousands of them billowed up into the sky like a volcanic plume. Their tiny lights, which were insignificant individually, added together in a cumulative fashion to become very bright. As the swarm rose, the entire town became bathed in a hellish burgundy glow. At the sight of this, the partygoers started whistling and clapping, like soccer fans rooting for their home team.

Len couldn't understand their excitement; it was the most terrifying thing he'd ever seen. The buzzing noise became so amplified and intense that Len had to cover his ears. Then, once the cloud of crimson had reached a mile or so into the sky, the illuminated mass suddenly started moving very quickly toward the roof where they were standing. Len, still under the effects of the drug, was unable to put his survival instinct ahead of curiosity. He stood there, enraptured, while the cloud approached and enveloped him.

Thousands of black, hovering machines whizzed all around him as Len continued to hold his ears. Some were the size of a fly, others as large as a watermelon. They moved quickly and maneuvered adroitly around obstacles. They shot by him, within inches of his body, without ever bumping into him or anything else. The incredible, coordinated movement of so many objects flying over the rooftop created a strong wall of air that nearly made him lose his balance.

Within a few seconds, the entire mass had moved past the roof and out into the valley. The cloud broke off into sub-swarms that engulfed the enemy's helicopters, digesting them in midair like schools of piranhas.

Then, without warning, bright-white explosions happened on the outer rim of the valley. A fraction of a second later, more blasts happened right the heels of the first ones. This became a continuous wave of bursts that carpet-bombed the forest like curtains of rain in a summer shower, until the entire valley was alight with fire, detonations, and buzzing clouds of crimson light.

"This is like something out of Revelation," Len stammered, looking out over the flaming canyon.

"Who needs fireworks?" Richard roared, his eyes wide and crazy.

Within five minutes, the enemy had been completely obliterated. The swarm of robots then re-tasked itself with disassembling the wreckage of the North Korean military, carrying its pieces back into town for recycling, and putting out the multiple fires that the explosions had caused. Within an hour, the valley was completely cleaned up and dark again.

82

The Glib feed peppering the room with holograms and projections went blindingly white. Dan shielded his eyes from the intense light.

"What the hell is that?" one of the advisors yelled.

The light dissipated quickly, and Dan slowly opened his eyes. Glib showed a 3-D panorama of the Bonneville Salt Flats outside of Salt Lake City. Bright-white explosions rolled down the mountains ringing the valley. Glib immediately switched over to a view outside Sandbox Teton, 150 miles away. The same sort of explosions, one after the other, like precise, geometric carpet bombing. Dan put on his reading glasses and got up close to the projection for a better look. Tanks and troop positions were being hit. The explosions weren't random; they were astonishingly precise.

Glib cut to the enormous walled perimeter of Sandbox Teton. Over the wall poured thousands and thousands of flying objects that were too small to make out. Glib zoomed in further. The objects disassembled the North Korean aircraft in midair. The camera panned down to the forest floor. Large metallic objects darted along the ground. Glib singled out one of the objects, and Dan couldn't believe what he saw. A silver spider the size of a cargo van scurried across a meadow and bounded over fallen trees. It periodically turned its head and fired some sort of weapon at the North Koreans, incinerating whatever it targeted.

"What the…" Dan looked at his advisors, whose faces were paralyzed with astonishment. "Have you guys ever seen weapons like these before?"

General Buzzcut shook his head. "Our radar network indicates those explosions are orbital strikes. Metteyya must be hitting them from space."

"My God. So that's what they've been launching into orbit—satellite weapons," Dan said. "Artha Metteyya, whoever the hell he is, has a ring of death surrounding the planet."

Without warning, Glib transitioned to a large portion of the Eastern Seaboard. It highlighted a group of fast-moving objects near Pittsburgh and another near Cincinnati. Glib then labeled them as "Aegis UAVs en route to intercept Dranthyx."

"What? How?" Dan shouted. "How does Glib know what we're doing?"

Glib heard the question and broke down its information sources. It showed a high-resolution photo of one of the UAVs and then demonstrated that the photo had been mathematically assembled from whatever cameras happened to be pointing skyward. From these pictures, it deduced the aircraft's armaments, airspeed, destination, and estimated time of arrival. Glib then showed a transcript of everything that had been said in the Aegis Information Room.

Dan nearly choked on his coffee. "Kill it! Kill all connection to Glib! It's listening to us! Everything we're saying is being made public!"

The feed went dark. The various projections and holograms collapsed, leaving the room comparatively empty and quiet.

Dan hadn't noticed Elise enter the Information Room. "Sir, this is for you," she said, handing Dan a bright-orange package. "It was delivered to the roof. I got here as soon as I could."

Dan ripped the box open absent-mindedly. He pulled out the antacid, unscrewed the top, and chugged it straight from the bottle. He stopped, mid-gulp, as though he had a thought.

"Elise," Dan said, turning to her. "Thank God. I need you to do some damage control for me. Can you get someone from Glib on the horn? I need that transcript deleted before people find it."

"I'll see what I can do," Elise said before turning to leave.

"Mr. Principal," said General Buzzcut, pointing to non-Glib live feeds from the East Coast, "take a look at this."

Dan watched, dumbfounded, as Metteyya repeated its orbital bombardment on a different enemy on the other side of the continent. The strikes were perfectly tailored to the targets and their surroundings. In the country, the explosions were enormous, taking out large groups of Dranthyx simultaneously. In the cities, tiny bombs pierced the Dranthyx orbs and exploded inside them, killing the occupants instantly without hurting anyone outside. Zero bystander casualties. In a matter of thirty seconds, the entire Dranthyx landing force was wiped out.

"What in the fuck," Dan bellowed. "Here we are, scrambling jets and needing hours to get ground troops into position. Meanwhile, Metteyya destroys two separate invading armies, two thousand miles apart, within minutes, using technology no one has ever seen before. They're making us look like we're a bunch of Cro-Magnons throwing rocks."

"Good news!" Elise said, coming back in to the room. "The entire transcript has been deleted from Glib, along with all other information pertaining to the Aegis response to the crisis."

"How did you pull that off?" Dan asked.

"The chief technology officer of Glib and I went to business school together," Elise said. "I helped him pass a class once. I called in a favor."

"Elise," Dan said, "you're a rock star."

"I know," she said unaffectedly.

83

As the morning sun filled the conference room, Dan, Randy, Elise, and several Aegis board members sat in silent tension.

"Has Metteyya issued any sort of statement?" Dan asked, shattering the quiet.

"No," Elise said. "Metteyya has never made a statement."

"Not even since the attack began?" Dan asked.

"No," Elise said. "I mean Artha Metteyya has never issued a press release in the entire time he's run his government. I've been looking, and I can't find one."

Dan grunted at the absurdity of the comment.

"I'm serious," Elise said blandly. "We have an army of interns trying to dig up information on him, and we can't find much of anything."

Dan looked at Randy.

"She's right," Randy said. "He's never even done a press conference. He's like Willy Wonka—no one even knows what he looks like."

"What?" Dan asked. "How the hell does anyone run a government like that?"

Randy threw his hands up.

"Where's he from?" Dan asked.

"The Indian subcontinent," Randy answered. "That much we know. He was born in a small city named Varanasi in the northwest. We've sent people over there to investigate his background, but it's not easy. The place was leveled when the Pakistanis nuked it. There's been no functioning government in the province since then—meaning no birth certificates, no medical files, no school records, nothing. Regardless, we did find religious records of Artha's birth at a local temple. His father was a well-respected electrical engineer who published a lot of scholarly papers. There's a fair amount of information out there about the old man, but almost nothing about Artha himself. Artha has a twin sister, apparently. There's a report floating around somewhere with all this information."

"How old is Artha?"

"Thirty-four years old," Randy said.

"Thirty-four!" Dan scoffed. "That can't be right. Metteyya has been around for fifteen years already."

"We believe it is correct," Elise said. "We have no information to the contrary."

"He started Metteyya at the age of nineteen?"

"You'd be surprised how many successful startups were founded by teenage entrepreneurs," one of the board members said. "I just read a great book about it—"

"Great," Dan interrupted "let's stay on task here. Randy, get me a copy of that report on Artha Metteyya. I want to read it. Also, we'll have to issue some sort of statement within the hour. We need to figure out what we're going to say.

Metteyya just made us look weak, and this sure as hell doesn't advance our cause for uniting the governments. Who wants to unite with Aegis when we can't even fight off an invasion? Anyone have any bright ideas?"

They all sat there quietly for a few seconds, and then Randy chuckled. "Yes," he said, "I do have an idea."

Everyone in the room turned to face Randy.

Randy laughed again and said, "Let's take credit for Metteyya's counterattack."

"Can we do that?" Elise asked.

"Why not?" Randy smirked. "Metteyya doesn't do press releases, right? So who would be the wiser?"

"Is that even remotely ethical?" one of the board members asked.

"If a lie results in a merger and furthers our goal of making the world a safer place," Randy said, "then nothing could be more ethical."

Dan, stunned by the shrewdness of Randy's plan, broke into a loud guffaw.

"My God, Randy, that's brilliant." Elise laughed.

"That's what I'm here for," Randy said.

"Elise," Dan said eagerly, "get the speechwriters on this ASAP. I want to go live within fifty-five minutes. Let's set the morning news cycle."

84

"Back so soon? You only need to do evaluations once a month, you know."

"That's not what I'm here for," Len said.

"Oh no? You look like you had quite a night," Bradley said.

"I had a fantastic night. I haven't slept," Len said with a joie de vivre that he hadn't felt in years. "Here. I brought you some doughnuts. Anyway, I gave it some thought. I think I want to be an evaluation counselor."

"Hey, that's great!" Bradley said.

"Yeah," Len said, sitting across the desk from him. "What's being done here fascinates me. It sounds a lot more interesting than mediating disputes."

"Honestly, I'm surprised Qualia suggested either of those things."

"Why's that?" Len asked.

"Well, don't take this the wrong way, but you're awfully young to have the kind of equanimity and wisdom it takes to do either of those jobs. I'm not saying you don't have those qualities; it's just very odd that you'd have them so early in life. Qualia usually picks people who have decades of life experience and a certain amount of insight."

"Not to toot your own horn or anything," Len said.

"Why, I'd never do a thing like that," Bradley said in farcical tones.

"I'm not as young as you think."

"Oh no?"

"I'm older than you, probably."

"Really? Man, what those doctors can do now is amazing. I've been thinking about having a frame-off restoration myself," Bradley said.

"Highly recommended."

"Were you involved for many years in some sort of spiritual seeking? Qualia can pick up on that right away, and that's usually who she selects for evaluation counseling."

"I guess you could say that," Len said. "What about you?"

"I spent twenty-two years living in an ashram," Bradley said. "Who knows, maybe I learned something there."

"This place is really unusual," Len said, looking out the window. "I've traveled all over the world, but I've never been anywhere quite like this town."

"Joy. That's what's unique about it."

"Why here and nowhere else?" Len asked.

"The whole point of the Sandbox is spiritual development. Joy is the byproduct."

"What kind of government even gives a shit about that?"

"Calling Metteyya a government is like calling sobriety a cocktail. The whole point of this place is teaching individuals how to govern themselves. The Sandbox is more like augmented anarchy. Artha keeps everyone fed and safe and the evaluation computer helps us with the depth psychology so we can be better people. However, it's up to each person to do the work and make the change happen."

"Anarchy? There aren't any laws here?"

"There are only three laws. The first is, you must attend a meditation session daily. Not sure if you've done that yet, but you should get on it before they throw you out. The second is, you must go to evaluation at least monthly. The third is, if Qualia asks you to leave the Sandbox, you have to leave."

"That's it? Only three laws?"

"If you get down to it, those are the only three you really need. Get your head right, and everything else falls into place."

"What keeps people from murdering each other?" Len asked.

Without answering, Bradley got up from his chair and walked across the room to an old-fashioned credenza. He slid open a drawer and, from it, pulled a handgun. Len's heart rate increased as Bradley brandished the weapon. Len's brain raced as he wondered what Bradley's intentions were and whether he could get across the room fast enough to take the gun from him.

"Relax," Bradley said, seeing the fear on Len's face. He turned the pistol around and held it in front of him so that Len could grab the grip. "This is for you."

Len took hold of it and, out of habit, pointed it at the floor and checked to see if it was loaded. Sure enough, it had a full magazine and one round in the chamber. Ready to go.

It was an ancient .45, perhaps from World War II. The weapon's age and finish complemented the decor of the evaluation office.

"What do I need this for?" Len asked.

"We have no laws against murder, so there's no penalty for killing someone. You'll never spend a day in jail. Look," Bradley said, pointing out the window. "There's a whole bunch of people sitting over there at that sidewalk cafe. They're so involved in their drinks and conversations, they'd never see it coming." Bradley made his hand into a finger gun and pretended he was shooting each person. "Boom! Boom! Boom!"

Len looked at him with a cocked eyebrow.

"Come on now; I don't have all day." Bradley looked at his watch. "I have evaluations ending soon. Go kill someone."

"Are you high?" Len asked.

"Maybe you're one of those antigun people?" Bradley asked. "I can understand. Guns separate you from the victim and take you out of the immediacy of the moment. Some people just like getting up close and personal when they kill someone. You like to feel warm blood running over your hands, don't you? Yeah, you're that type. Don't worry; I have something a little more old-fashioned for you." He reached up above the fireplace and took down a sword that had been hanging on the wall. He unsheathed it, a handsome old cutlass, and inspected the edge for sharpness. Then Bradley lifted it up above his head and, with a mighty chop, buried the blade deep in the desk, right in front of Len.

"Are you insane?" Len asked, jumping up from his seat, pointing the handgun at Bradley.

"No, and neither are you," Bradley said calmly. "You're not going to kill anyone. Your conscience won't let you do it. In fact, most people wouldn't murder someone." Bradley looked at the gun Len was holding. "I was only making a point. Put that thing down before you shoot me by accident."

"What is your point?" Len asked, lowering the gun.

"My point is," Bradley said while sitting back down in his seat. "Most people know right from wrong and act accordingly. What the hell do we need laws for?"

"I might not be crazy—hopefully, you're not either—but plenty of people are."

"Mental illness can be treated. Qualia is absolutely fantastic at that. Not only does she help the mentally ill work through their issues, but she can custom-design drugs to balance brain chemistry in ways that were never possible before."

"And what about Tchogols?" Len asked. "A Tchogol might actually kill those people."

"Tchogols are a problem. You're right about that. Truth be told, I wouldn't dare do this little demonstration with a Tchogol—too dangerous. But even they can be managed by redirecting their energies."

"How?"

"Well, a Tchogol doesn't get better over time. They have no insight into themselves and no empathy. However, they can be useful to society. Qualia lets a few in from time to time and finds work for them. I remember one Tchogol dude; he wanted to work on our police force. Well, we don't have a police force, and someone like that shouldn't be in law enforcement anyway. So Qualia gave him a job putting down terminally sick animals at the veterinary hospital. Someone with empathy wouldn't have been able to handle that job, but it didn't bother him at all. Another one wanted to be an attorney, but, like I said yesterday, we don't have lawyers here. Qualia suggested she take work as a dominatrix. Get this—people pay her to beat the piss out of them. She makes more money doing that than she ever would have as a lawyer. There are uses for people with no empathy. We just can't let them rule us."

"OK, but what happens when someone is murdered?" Len asked. "Do they just let it slide?"

"There's never been a murder in Teton."

"Never?"

"It's a funny little social experiment we're running here. We give people the essentials so they're no longer struggling for survival, we offer them jobs that give their lives meaning, we treat each other with dignity, and we encourage everyone to develop as people. We find that if you do those things, no one has a reason to harm anyone else. Metteyya has figured something out that no other society in history ever has: violence is the product of unhealthy minds and unmet needs. If you can fix those two problems, there's no reason for violence."

"Pardon my skepticism."

"Believe it. Or don't." Bradley shrugged. "Live here long enough, and you'll see it for yourself. In any case, it'll be nice to have another counselor on staff." He extended his hand for Len to shake. "Welcome aboard, Jim."

85

Dan surveyed one of Glib's landscapes, a topographical representation of the world's most newsworthy events. The map had several views: position, velocity, acceleration, and prediction.

Position indicated the most relevant topics during a user-defined period of time. For example, Dan could find out the most popular news topic of the day by seeing which one had the most mentions over the last twenty-four hours. This was a good setting for a casual user, but it wasn't very useful for those in decision-making roles because it only indicated a trend when it was at its most-exhausted peak. The top story in the position setting was the Dranthyx attack.

The next setting, velocity, kept track of the frequency of mentions at all specific points in time. Scrubbing back and forth on the time scroller, Dan could see the drastic difference in the frequency of mentions from just before the attack began to a peak fifteen hours later. Clearly, this event was of grave concern to everyone.

The third setting was the second-most useful. The peaks on the acceleration map were not the things that were most talked about or talked about most frequently, but rather the things that were dramatically increasing or decreasing in relevance. Dan set it to the present moment and watched in real-time as the mentions of the Dranthyx attack decelerated down into a hole and "merger" spiked into something resembling Everest.

The fourth setting was the result of massive computational analysis beyond human comprehension. In prediction mode, Glib could infer future events based on all known data, including private messages and discretely collected data such as the conversation he'd had with his advisors in the Aegis Information Room. Dan selected prediction, and his heart fluttered at the results. Before him appeared a new topographical map, where the peaks and valleys were defined by probabilities. The probability of a stock market crash at the opening bell was the highest mountain, at nearly 95 percent. The second-highest peak, at 87 percent, was "Aegis to merge with Safeguard."

The phone rang. Insistently, it seemed, as though the ring had an urgency to it.

"Yes?" Dan answered without looking at the caller information.

"Dan. Randy. Get your ass to conference room 3. You're not gonna believe it."

Dan walked into the conference room, trying not to seem hurried. Randy, Elise, and several others were already there, practically jittering from the elation they were concealing under their businesslike poker faces. Projected in the space above the table was the face of Lacy Hockensmith, principal of Safeguard.

"Daniel, good to see you," Lacy said.

"You too, Lacy," Dan said, trying not to seem overly excited. "How are things?"

"Good. You're on Glib as much as I am, so I'm sure you know the reason for this meeting."

"I haven't been on today. Enlighten me," Dan lied. He just wanted to hear her say it. She'd turned down his previous merger offers, obnoxiously so, as if Safeguard were too good to associate with the likes of Aegis. Uppity East Coasters. Here she was, crawling back. He thought about the best way to force Safeguard to take a smaller equity stake in the post-merger entity.

"We're very impressed with the Aegis response to the crisis," Lacy said stoutly, trying to cling to her dignity. "We think a merger might be in everyone's best interest."

"We're still interested." Dan smiled.

ONE YEAR LATER

86

Len and Bradley stared at the Go board. Bradley dropped a round, white stone at a crucial junction. Problem was, Len hadn't realized how crucial it was. Giggling to himself, Bradley scooped up eight of Len's black stones. Len slapped himself on the forehead.

"Oh no!" Len laughed.

"Now you know how I feel when we play chess." Bradley grinned. "I'm terrible at that game."

"Chess is simple compared to this," Len said.

"*Go* is simple," Bradley said. "I'd argue it's chess that's overly complicated."

"How do you figure?"

"What are the rules in Go? You surround your opponent's stones while keeping him from surrounding yours. That's it. It doesn't get any more straightforward than that. What are the rules of chess? Holy cow, there's a rule book an inch thick."

"Yeah," Len said, "but it's the lack of a system that makes Go so damn complicated. Chess starts out the same way every time—"

"But Go starts out with an empty board and no guidelines. Just a few simple rules. But there are infinite possibilities, and it's impossible to calculate them all. It drives some folks mad because they're forced to use their intuition instead of memorizing openings and rules," Bradley said, taunting Len.

A woman emerged from her evaluation, crying. She appeared to be young and kind of hippieish.

"What's wrong?" Len asked.

"Qualia wants me to leave Teton!"

"I'll let you get to your work," Bradley said, getting up from the table. "I'll be in the other room."

"Did she say why?" Len asked.

"That…that definitely came as a shock to me."

She's not telling me something.

"Why do you think she said that?" Len asked.

"I don't know. I've been getting together with some friends once or twice a week to celebrate Qualia. Today I told Qualia how much respect I have for her. And she said…" The girl put her head in her hands and really started sobbing. "She said I'm missing the point. She said she can't help me!"

"She can't," Len said sympathetically.

"Why do you say that?" the girl said.

"You're supposed to be helping yourself, not worshipping a computer."

"Worshiping?"

"Yeah. Qualia's got a fine line to walk. She has to give good advice without having people become dependent on it. It's a very difficult balancing act for her, to guide people without letting people fall into the trap of thinking of her as their ruler or savior. She wants to help people, not start a cult of personality."

"And that's why I admire her."

"Qualia's pointing at the moon, and you're staring lovingly at her finger," Len said. "I'm sorry to say it, but you are missing the point."

"Can't I have a second chance?"

Of course, but you need to get your head out of your ass first.

"Between you and me, it might be best to take some time off first," Len said kindly. "Come back in a few years. Teton will be here."

As the young lady left, still in tears, someone behind Len called out, "Yo, dawg."

"Yes?" Len asked, turning around.

"I got some questions about this evaluation thing. Are you the guy I talk to?"

"Yessir," Len said. "That's me."

"The computer says I should be a mechanical engineer. I think that shit's busted."

"Why do you think that?"

"Well, for starters, I ain't never been to college. I don't know the first thing about engineering."

"Can I see that?" Len asked.

The man handed him his evaluation paperwork.

"Yeah, that's definitely your top career suggestion. It also says here that Metteyya will pay for your schooling."

"What da fuck?"

"Why does this surprise you?"

"'Cause it don't make no sense," the man said.

"What did you do before coming to the Sandbox?" Len asked.

The man sat back in his seat and didn't answer.

"You can tell me; I won't tell anyone. I hear everyone's secrets all day long, and I've never said a word to anyone. In fact, I'm not allowed to."

"You better not tell anyone."

"I won't," Len said.

"I was a gangbanger. Back in Atlanta."

"And what did you do in the gang?" Len asked.

"I started out a soldier. You know, front-line stuff. But then they seen I was smart, so I started keeping the books. I expanded the business to ten other cities. But then I pissed off the wrong motherfuckers, so I had to get out. Way out. OTP."

"OTP?"

"Outside the perimeter. Nobody knows I'm here, and it's gonna stay like that. You feel me?" He glared at Len.

"Believe me, I understand. So you kept the books. That means you're good with numbers?"

"Hell yeah I am."

"And computers?"

"Yeah," the man said. "I taught myself how to write programs."

"You seriously taught yourself how to code?"

"Yup," the man answered diffidently, squirming in his seat. "So we could, you know, keep track of market fluctuations and find the most efficient ways to distribute the product."

"What are your hobbies?"

"Like, shit I do for fun?"

"Yeah."

"I like working on old cars. Rebuilding engines, fabricating parts, and stuff."

"So you're good with numbers, computers, and machinery. Mechanical engineering sounds perfect for you."

"Yeah, but..." the man's voice trailed off.

"What?" Len asked.

"Look," the man said in confiding tones, "my daddy and granddaddy were in the gangs. It goes way back. I don't want people to think I'm some college fag. Looks weak, you know?"

"Does anyone from your old life know you're here?" Len asked.

"No."

"Then who gives a fuck what they think?" Len asked. "They'll never know. Try something new. You might like it."

After a bit of silent consideration, aggravated perplexity melted off the man's face, leaving only the Look. In the course of learning how to do evaluation counseling, Len had seen the Look five thousand times already—and it never got old. The Look was the two-part expression people had when they realized they were no longer chained to anyone's expectations, including their own. The first part of the Look was deep-seated relief; the second part was like a sudden geyser of optimism.

I love this job, Len thought when he saw the man's face light up with epiphany. *I love seeing people freed from the bullshit they've been trapped in. It's like journalism, but on the most personal level.*

"Damn. OK. Well, OK!" The man beamed. "I'll give it a shot."

"Welcome to the Sandbox," Len said, standing up to shake his hand.

A minute or so after the future engineer left the office, a second man stormed up to Len's desk from another evaluation room.

Busy day, Len thought.

"What kind of nonsense is this?"

"What do you mean?" Len asked.

The man appeared to be about fifty-five years of age. He had gray, perfectly coiffed hair and piercing blue eyes. He was tall and slim, wearing business casual. He looked like the golf-playing, corporate, upper-management type.

"You're the counselor, right?" the man asked.

"Almost," Len said. "Counselor in training, to be exact."

"This Qualia, or whatever that thing calls itself, is saying that I should clean the sewers!" Upper-Management Man fumed.

Len struggled to contain a laugh. *This guy is obviously brand new here.*

"Why does that upset you?" Len asked, knowing damn well what the man's answer would be.

"Look, kid, you don't understand what I've had to do to come up in this world."

Kid? I'm older than you are, douchebag.

"Tell me," Len said with feigned interest, trying very hard not to crack a smile.

"I have an undergraduate degree and an MBA, both from Ivy League schools. I started a career in insurance thirty years ago, while I was still in school. I worked my way up from a lowly claims adjuster to upper management."

Upper management. Did I call it or what?

"Right before I moved here, I was CFO of the world's second-largest insurance conglomerate. I oversaw thousands of employees, and I made damn sure we were profitable. The board begged me to stay on for another five years, but I decided to retire instead."

"And?" Len asked in a way that wouldn't seem so combative.

"And," the man said, bristling, "I've worked too damn hard to clean sewers. That's a job for retards and immigrants. My talents would be squandered doing that kind of work! I heard Qualia paired people up with jobs according to innate abilities."

"Sometimes, but not always." Len stated coolly, "It's not always about ability; it's mostly about psychological growth. Qualia assigns people jobs that will help them become better people."

"That's the most inefficient, absurd thing I've ever heard," the man said. "You can't run a society like that."

"It's actually the most efficient system of organizing human endeavors that has ever existed." Upper Management Man's expression was as confused as it was insulted, so Len continued. "Ever been on an airplane? Ever hear them go through the safety instructions? If you're traveling with a child and the plane loses cabin pressure, they tell you to put the mask on yourself first. Then you help the child. Do you know why?"

"I give up," Upper Management Man said indignantly.

"Because you can't help the child if you yourself pass out from lack of oxygen. It's true in every situation: you can't help anyone if you're helpless yourself. Once people reach an advanced stage of psychological development and are ready to use their talents to selflessly benefit others, Qualia puts them in the places where they will be most useful to society."

"So what are you saying?" the man asked. "That I'm not psychologically developed? What are you, twelve? What the hell do you know about life?"

"Everyone is climbing their own mountain," Len stated phlegmatically. "The question is, where are you getting stuck? What's preventing your further development?"

"What do you mean?" the man asked.

"Well, when you talk, I hear a lot of pride, a bit of arrogance. You've done big things, and you're proud of your accomplishments. That's great, but you also need to realize that you had a lot of help getting where you are."

"Kid, I did it all myself. Every last bit of it. You wouldn't understand."

"So when you defecate, you deliver your turds to the sewage treatment plant yourself?"

"What?" His nose wrinkled in aggravation and disgust. "No."

"Every day you take a crap and you flush it down the toilet, right?" Len asked.

"Yeah. So?" the man asked, put off by the question.

"It goes through the sewers, right?"

"Yeah?"

"Well, when the sewers get clogged, who cleans them?"

"Someone. Who cares?"

"Well, that attitude is the problem. That's probably what Qualia is zeroing in on. An enormous amount of boring, insignificant things had to happen in order for you to become the CFO of a big insurance company. The people underneath you had to do their jobs correctly for years on end. You've probably taken a lot of people's hard work for granted in your relentless pursuit of status and money. Every day of your career, someone sat in a cubicle and did your grunt work for you while you were out meeting bigwigs on the golf course."

"You're an awfully presumptuous young man. What does this have to do with sewers?"

"When was the last time you gave any serious thought to the miracle of indoor plumbing?"

Upper-Management Man stared at him angrily.

"I'm serious," Len said. "You sit on a toilet every day and you defecate into it, but do you ever think about how wonderful the sewer is? Before sewers, people just threw their feces into the street, and everyone died of cholera. Modern civilization as we know it wouldn't be possible without sewers. And that convenience couldn't be maintained without the sanitation workers who maintain the systems."

"I've heard enough." Upper Management Man huffed, putting his jacket on. "I'm done here."

"Before you go," Len said, "let me ask you something."

"What?" the man asked impatiently.

"Do you still have room for improvement?"

Upper Management Man seemed taken aback. He thought about it for several seconds and then said, "Of course. We all do."

"And, as a former manager, were those under you are always cognizant of what they needed to improve upon, and how they should develop those skills?"

"Sometimes. Hardly ever."

"Sometimes their egos get in the way, correct? They didn't see themselves as clearly as you saw them, right?"

Upper Management Man was quiet for a bit. Len could tell he'd broken through.

"Give it a shot for a few months." Len shrugged. "You've already reached the pinnacle of success in one career. You have nothing left to prove."

"Fine," Upper Management Man said. He grabbed his evaluation paperwork off the desk and, with a resigned slouch, walked out of the office, letting the door slam behind him.

A few seconds later, Bradley emerged from the back room. As Len's mentor, he monitored all of Len's evaluations.

"Jim, that was fantastic!" Bradley said, beaming.

"You think so?"

"My God, yes. You have a remarkable insight into people. You have a rare talent for this."

"I was worried I might have been a bit too hard on that last guy."

"Well, you certainly bring an abrasive style to this gig," Bradley said, "but that was exactly what that guy needed. He's had people kissing his ass for too long. He needed someone to give it to him straight, and you did it in his own language."

"I hope it works out for him."

"It will. He just needs to get over himself. I've seen a thousand of him over the years. You watch—after a year or two of shoveling everyone else's shit, he'll realize what he's been dumping on others. He'll undergo a remarkable transformation once he learns some humility."

"Won't we all," Len said.

"Jim," Bradley said, "I think you are ready for full evaluation counselor certification. I will give my recommendation to Qualia."

Len smiled and shook Bradley's hand. Then he noticed the clock on the wall. "Oh man, I need to get going soon, but I have to do my own evaluation first."

"See you next week, my friend."

87

"Qualia, any new suggestions for me?" Len asked.

"Not today."

"Nothing you want to discuss?"

"No."

"You've been awfully quiet the last few evaluations," Len said. "If I didn't know better, I'd think you were giving me the cold shoulder."

"No offense meant," Qualia replied calmly. "We're at the point of negative marginal returns. Anything I say from here on out could be counterproductive."

"Then perhaps we should just sit here in silence for a while." Len said.

"I like that idea."

Len stared at Qualia's green vapor face in the darkened room while it appeared to look back at him.

Strange to feel a sense of deep connectedness with a machine.

After several minutes of dead stillness, Qualia spoke. "Leonard, I've debated whether to tell you this. But I think it's time to let you know."

"Know what?"

"You are very close to full understanding."

"Weird. That's the second time someone has said that to me."

Qualia's face became Mutoku's as the memory was pulled from his mind.

"Yes," Len said in reference to the image.

"A wise man," Qualia said, returning to her normal form.

"What more must I do?"

"Nothing. The field has been tilled. The seed has been planted. It'll grow on its own."

It was Natalia's big night. She'd been at work all day, undoubtedly putting the finishing touches on everything. Len was probably more excited for her than she was for herself.

Len stopped at the mindfulness hall on his block. Entering the hall, he removed his sneakers and put them on the long shelves with hundreds of other pieces of footwear; the entry area to the hall looked like a shoe store. Len pressed his hand on a screen to check in. A digital schedule appeared and indicated that the next session would start in fifteen minutes, at 7:00 p.m.

Mindfulness meditation was a staple of Sandbox life. It was one of the only two requirements, the other being evaluation. Each resident of the Sandbox was obligated to meet in one of the meditation halls for thirty minutes each day, *no matter what*. Vanishingly few exceptions to this rule were allowed, and those who didn't comply with the obligation had to leave the Sandbox.

There were zafus for those who preferred the Asian method of sitting, chairs for the Westerners, and handicap-accessible seats for those who needed them. There were about fifty or sixty such mindfulness halls throughout the sandbox, one near every major intersection. Meditation sessions were held at every single hall, twenty-four hours a day, beginning every hour on the hour. This allowed every different work schedule and circadian rhythm to be accommodated. A person could participate even if he or she was gravely ill; the hospital had its own mindfulness hall that orderlies wheeled gurneys into and out of all day long. In other words, every possible effort was made to get people into a hall each day. Even if someone was a paraplegic who worked third shift on the outskirts of town, that person could still easily meet the daily meditation requirement.

Len walked into the hall. Despite the fact that there were already about 250 people there, it was quiet, like a library. There were many rows of spaces for meditators, which he walked between to find a suitable spot.

Len found an empty seat between an old lady and a young boy of about seven. In front of him was a blank white partition, installed there to minimize visual distractions. He sat down, let his body relax, and waited for the bell that would begin the session.

As soon as the ending bell rang, Len stood up and walked quickly to the exit. He put his shoes on and dashed outside and down the street to the funeral parlor where Natalia worked.

Not knowing anything about the business when she started, Natalia had been apprenticing under a funeral director for the last twelve months.

If he hadn't already been there to visit Natalia at work a few times, Len would have double-checked the address in confusion. There was a queue of people out the door and around the block waiting to get into the funeral parlor. It looked like the line to get into a trendy nightclub.

"What's this line for?" Len asked some of the people waiting.

"Elizabeth Rivington's exhibit," someone answered.

"You're really here to see dead people?" Len asked. He'd heard her work was good, but he didn't realize she had groupies.

"Mister, these aren't just dead people. This is art."

"Jim?" someone asked.

Len turned around. Natalia's mentor, the man who'd taught her how to prepare bodies, was standing at the door with a clipboard.

"Jim," the man said, "good to see you! Did you imagine all this?" he asked, motioning to the huge line of people.

"No, but it doesn't surprise me," Len said. "The woman's a dynamo. She excels at whatever she does. You could give her a paper route, and in a year or two, she'd be William Randolph Hearst."

"You're certainly on the list, so no need to wait in line. Please, come on in."

Len walked past the velvet rope and into the parlor. The inside had been redone recently to accommodate the event and Natalia's groundbreaking ideas; what had previously been decorated like a funeral home now looked like an art gallery. A number of people had gathered around a sculpture in the alcove. Len edged his way through the crowd to see what they were looking at.

The sculpture was two young lovers, mid-coitus in a bed. Him on top, caressing her cheek, her looking lovingly into his eyes. Len looked at it for a long time, mesmerized by the passion captured in their faces.

"They died in this bed together," he overheard someone say. "Carbon monoxide poisoning. Terrible accident."

"These are the actual bodies?" Len asked.

"Oh yes. Can you believe it? I have no idea how she makes them look so lifelike."

Goddamn. Len took a second look, awestruck.

After a time, he sauntered over to the next piece. This one was a cowboy, leaning casually against a split-rail fence. The outfit was perfect, and his face had a faraway look with a subdued, knowing smile. What struck Len most was the sense of peace in the expression and the posture, as though the man had seen through the foibles of mortality and had awakened from that silly dream to find himself in a better place.

The eyes, Len thought. *How does she get them to look like that?*

The next one gave Len shivers. A mother sitting on a rocking chair, cradling a tiny, swaddled infant. The mother stared tenderly into the baby's eyes. He studied it for a long time, until he became too choked up with emotion to continue looking.

"What happened?" Len rasped to some onlookers nearby.

"They both passed in childbirth. Massive hemorrhage," someone said. "It still happens once in a while."

"What an awful shame," Len said.

"Yes, but what a beautiful tribute."

Len took the time to see each of his wife's works and then found Natalia in the back, mobbed by a throng of people. He watched her from afar, interacting with the guests. Natalia had always had a high-spirited glow about her, he reflected, but it shone differently since she'd started this job. She radiated something new now: serenity.

"Elizabeth, these are simply amazing," a woman fawned. "All I've ever known is boring funerals. You know, embalming and caskets. But these, these are incredible. Lifelike, personal. God, it makes me emotional. You've made undertaking into something that celebrates life."

"Thank you," Natalia said modestly.

"How do you preserve the bodies?" someone asked.

"It's a secret." Natalia laughed. "If I told you, I'd have to make an exhibit out of you."

"Does it bother you to work with dead people?" a man asked.

"It did, at first," Natalia said. "I don't think I realized what a hangup I had about death until I started working here."

The people around her chuckled.

"That's not a joke. I'm serious," Natalia said. "Death used to fill me with dread. The thought that the universe would go on forever without me was horrifying. I used to drown that angst with workaholism. I was always striving for success, as though it would make me immortal."

"And this helped you get over it?" the man asked.

"Without a doubt. Preparing these bodies has been therapeutic. It's forced me to confront the reality. I've learned that there's beauty in the inevitability of death. Without it hanging over our heads, life would mean nothing."

After a few hours, the crowd died down, and Len was finally able to talk to his wife.

"You are incredible," he said, grabbing her hand to hold it.

"You didn't know that?" she teased.

"Tonight I saw it all over again because I realized how profoundly your gifts affect others. I don't know; it was different somehow. This funeral art of yours—it helps people deal with loss."

"I hope so," Natalia said.

"I have to ask," Len said. "What inspired this?"

"Honestly, I have no idea. I somehow lived seventy-some years without ever realizing I had an artistic side. I spent my whole life being so preoccupied with survival and financial security that I never had time for creative pursuits. Then, Qualia suggested I do this. Remember? Never in a million years would I have thought to become an undertaker. After a few months, all the imagination that had been pent up for my whole life came pouring out."

"I am overjoyed to see you so happy and at peace," Len said. "I really am. You were a ball of stress when you were running the construction business. I was worried you'd give yourself a stroke."

"Ugh. I hated construction. I didn't like gunrunning that much either, but at least that was exciting. But here, doing funerals, I've found purpose." She paused, reflecting on the past. "It's a shame, really, I wasted all those years doing the wrong things."

"You wasted nothing, darling," Len said. "All of it brought you here tonight."

Natalia smiled back and, with tears in her eyes, embraced Len.

88

"I remember the first time I saw you on TV, giving an interview about your lawsuit," Dan said, staring into Octavia's eyes as he lay on the bed next to her. "I thought, 'There's a leader.'"

"Really?" Octavia asked. "I don't feel like a leader."

"Show me someone who thinks himself a leader, and I'll show you someone with his head way up his conceited ass." Dan laughed. "True leaders don't think of themselves that way. They think, 'Boy, things sure are a mess around here, and it's annoying that no one is doing anything about it. I guess I'll fix it my damn self.'"

Octavia smiled at the familiarity of the sentiment. "I did think that. I do think that. You must feel the same way."

"All the time," Dan said. "That's why I'm doing what I'm doing." He paused for a while, deep in thought as he stroked her hair. "You know, I always admired your father. You never talk about him much, though."

"He was an interesting guy."

"He nearly sacrificed everything to save the world," Dan said.

"Yeah, and it caught up to him in the end."

"I remember reading about that in the news right before we met. I'm sorry for your loss. I really am. He was a great man."

"Thanks," Octavia said, not knowing what else to say.

"And your stepmother, Natalia Zherdeva, the construction tycoon. She was a force of nature, as I understand it."

"Yeah. Do we need to talk about this?"

"I'm sorry, Octavia," Dan said. "I don't mean to be insensitive. I know you don't like talking about them. I'm just amazed at the family you come from. What incredible people."

Octavia sighed. "It's OK. I mean, we've been together for a year. It's going to come up once in a while."

A minute or two passed as they stared up at the ceiling fan.

"Dan," Octavia asked, turning her head to look at him, "Have you ever felt like just dropping everything and starting over somewhere else?"

"I think everyone feels that way from time to time. Especially those of us in the public eye."

"My dad used to talk about it a lot. 'The blank slate,' he called it. I'm beginning to understand why he was so consumed with the idea."

Dan sat up in bed abruptly and turned to look at Octavia. "Did your father fake his death?"

The question was asked so quickly and bluntly that Octavia didn't have time to think up a lie. She just stared at Dan, wide eyed.

"He did, didn't he?" Dan laughed. "What about your stepmom? Is she still alive?"

Octavia grimmaced.

"Hah!" Dan chortled. "She's alive too! Man, that must be amazing. Living a second life somewhere else with all that money and no worries. Well, I hope they're enjoying themselves, wherever they are. They've earned it."

"I never was a poker player," Octavia grumbled.

"So where are they?" Dan asked, grinning. "I mean, it's none of my business, but dammit if I wouldn't like to join them one day."

"They're hanging out with Elvis," Octavia said.

"I'm sure. Look, I know you're worried about their safety. I can help. I have a major government at my disposal, and I can protect them if need be. I did it for you; I can do it for them. Just let me know if they ever need my help, OK?"

89

Len awoke with a start as something hit him in the stomach.

"Huh? What the hell?"

He heard Natalia laughing hysterically and realized she'd thrown a pillow at him.

"Wake up!" she said. "The sun's been up for two hours."

Len threw the pillow back at her.

"Yeah, so?" he asked.

"You said you wanted to go hiking, remember?" Natalia lilted.

"Was I drunk? This bed is so comfortable."

"C'mon, let's go already. It's beautiful out today."

Len looked out the window. It did look like a nice day. The cool, dry mountain air had a way of making sunshine look crisp, like a realist painting.

Len sat up in bed. He'd spent a year in his new body but still hadn't gotten over how different it felt. When he was old, he'd wake up exhausted and still in pain from whatever he'd done the day before. An old man's body is in a constant state of dissension. However, a young man's person is in a perpetual state of readiness. Waking in this new body, Len's mind was forever clear, and his muscles always felt like coiled mainsprings, capable of exploding into motion. A man in his twenties can stay awake for four days straight and still not feel as tired as a man in his seventies does first thing in the morning.

"Are Richard and Susan coming?" Len asked.

"They messaged me this morning. They had to cancel because they both have the flu. Looks like it's just us today."

Len stuffed his face with a quick breakfast and then put on his hiking gear. As they were leaving the apartment, they ran into their mail carrier in the hallway.

"Hey guys," she said. "I have stuff for you."

"Cool. Throw it in here." Len held his backpack open.

The mail girl gamely obliged, and then Len and Natalia walked down the stairs to the street to catch the next bus to the trails.

The bus dropped them off near the trailheads a few miles from the border. Exiting the vehicle, Len felt exhilarated by his surroundings: Douglas firs and jagged snowy mountains in the distance. He took a deep breath, smelling the pines.

"Ready?" he asked Natalia.

"Born ready" came the reply.

"Let's take one of the trails we haven't done yet," Len said.

"I'm down."

The path took them up and down hills, past meltwater brooks and wildlife. Around noon, they stopped for lunch at a crystal-clear lake on an alpine meadow. As Len sat on a log, finishing the sandwich he'd packed, he noticed a bright-red object a few yards away in the trees. He stood up and walked over. Natalia, curious as well, followed him.

The red sign, about three feet on each side, stood next to the trail. It read, "BORDER WARNING: you are now leaving Metteyya territory. Your safety cannot be guaranteed beyond this point."

Len looked at Natalia, who returned his uneasy glance with one of her own. Realizing the absurdity of their concern, Len laughed out loud.

"What's so funny?" Natalia asked.

"Look at us, spooked. The stuff we've survived already. Hell, this past year has been the only time when we haven't looked death straight in face. Is anything beyond this sign as dangerous as what we've already been through?"

Natalia laughed and then jokingly poked Len in the chest. "I'm blaming you if anything happens, bub."

Len and Natalia packed up their stuff and continued on the trail, past the sign. As they approached the crest of a hill, a tremendous view of a valley opened up next to a rock the size of a minivan. Len stopped to dig out his camera.

"Hey, let me get a picture of you," Len said.

"Here, next to this boulder?" Natalia asked.

"Sure."

Natalia leaned against the huge chunk of granite as Len fiddled with settings on the screen of the camera. Then, as Len was looking at her face though the viewfinder, a silver hand darted out from behind the rock and quickly covered Natalia's mouth, dragging her behind the huge stone. Len looked up, dropped his camera, and ran over to intervene. As he rounded the rock, he was met by three large men who had been crouched behind the boulder. A fourth man struggled with Natalia as she bit his hand and stomped his shins. Seeing Len, the three men simultaneously closed in on him.

They were covered in metal and wires, like space robots from an old sci-fi movie. Len struck one of them with his fist, connecting hard with the man's face. Len felt one of the metacarpal bones of his hand shatter upon collision with the man's metallic jaw. Undeterred by a broken hand, and with his opponent unflapped by the blow, Len closed the distance, cliched the man around the waist, and did a judo technique, launching the attacker into one of his accomplices. Len was full of adrenaline, but even so, his adversary felt as if he weighed five hundred pounds. The man who'd been thrown collided with one of his buddies, while a third came after Len with some sort of spinning weapon that looked like a cross between a bola and a flywheel. The man let go of the weapon, and it hurdled toward Len. Len, not knowing what else to do, jumped out of the way.

Len scrambled to get up to continue the attack. Just as he was about to take on the third man, he was jarred by an ear-shattering crack. A close-range shot from a powerful handgun. The guy Len was about to attack dropped right where he stood. Natalia, still struggling with the first attacker, had managed to pull her revolver from concealment and was trying to shoot her own assailant but had accidentally shot Len's instead.

Len was temporarily deafened and disoriented from the loud bang. His attention was still on Natalia's situation when someone grabbed him from behind and violently subdued him.

90

Daniel Barton, age four, cowered in the corner of the bathroom of his childhood home. His father stood over him, red faced with rage.

"What the hell did you do, you little jerk?" Dan's father yelled.

"I'm sorry, Daddy," four-year-old Dan cried.

"Christ, you shit your pants!"

"I had an accident!"

"An accident? I'm tired of your fucking accidents. Every goddamn day you piss your pants. Now this. Accidents are for losers. You want to be a loser for the rest of your life?"

"No, Daddy! I'm sorry!"

Dan's father pushed the boy, who fell over onto the cold tile of the bathroom floor, hitting his head as he landed. The man then roughly yanked the boy's pants off. Dan sobbed uncontrollably.

"Stop that crying, or I'll give you something to cry about!"

Dan tried to muster any control over his emotions but couldn't. He'd screwed up, and he was terrified of his father.

"What is wrong with you? Stand up!"

The little boy did as instructed, getting up with shaking legs. Dan's father peeled the boy's superhero underwear off, the little briefs laden with feces. His dad held the soiled garment in his hand. He stared the boy in the eye, his teeth gritting and the vein in his forehead bulging.

"This is what failure feels like!" the man yelled before shoving the soiled underwear in the boy's face.

Dan wailed, nearly gagging on the excrement that had been forced into in his nose and mouth. He pulled the underwear off his face so he could breathe.

"The world doesn't give a fuck about losers, boy," his father roared. "A man's worth is his success. If you want success, there's no room for failure. If you're not gonna act like a big boy and shit in the toilet, then you're a loser and you're worthless. I'll put you up for adoption. That's where loser kids go—the orphanage!"

"I'm…I'm…I'm sorry, Daddy!" Dan bawled, barely able to get the words out of his mouth. "Plea-plea-please don-don-don't do that!"

"You'd better be sorry! Now get in the bathtub and think about what you've done."

91

Handcuffed in a sidecar, Len studied his captors intently. There were about thirty of them altogether. They were monstrous—part man but mostly machine. They were covered in chrome and lights, bristling with all manner of mechanical weapons and appendages. Tattoo-like designs emblazoned their bright metalwork. They'd carried Len and Natalia out of the woods on robotic legs, which they later removed and stowed for highway travel. Their torsos were then reattached to motorcycles, giving them the appearance of shiny, wheeled centaurs. As the pack roared down the highway, Len struggled to see where Natalia was, but he was chained to the vehicle and unable to turn around.

Len watched helplessly as the landscape flew by. The shantytowns and burning vehicles in the distance contrasted sharply against the bright, gleaming lanes of Transglobal 755. The highway more or less followed the right-of-way of the old I-80 but didn't resemble it in the slightest. Once in a while, a high-speed bullet train rocketed through the tube running down the median.

After dealing with years of their abuse and transgressions, Transglobal had developed the sort of private security that even biker gangs feared. Anyone, even warlords and lawless bands of marauders, could use the highway if they paid the tolls, but Transglobal watched their every move like a pit boss watches card counters in a casino. One sideways glance at an import-driving yuppie, and a motorcycle gang like this would be bug-splatted by patrolling drones. Transglobal didn't mess around, which was why bikers always left Transglobal property before causing trouble.

The bikers pulled off the highway as it was getting dark. The town just off the exit was surrounded by a wall of large concrete blocks, the kind that probably had to be lowered into place with a crane. The bikers slowed to a stop when the road they were on ended abruptly at a large mechanical gate covered in concertina wire. A little booth next to the gate gave it a checkpoint appearance.

The bikers shut their engines off and waited. Three men in cowboy hats and brown uniforms came out from behind a wall of sandbags. They wore star-shaped badges like marshals used to in times long gone. The uniformed men approached cautiously, hands on their side arms. One of them walked slowly up to Len's driver.

"Whoa. Nice costume there, bud," Len's driver said, looking the man's uniform over. "What are you supposed to be?"

"Who's in charge here?" the uniformed man asked.

"I guess that would be me," said Len's driver sardonically.

"And who might you be?" asked the man in the uniform.

"Name's Clyde." He smiled. Clyde's teeth were metal and razor sharp.

The uniformed man studied the motorcyclists. Engraved on each of their metal backs was a logo, which the uniformed man read aloud. "Tchogol's MC, Cleveland."

That apostrophe is killing me, Len thought.

The man with the uniform gave the motorcyclist a distrusting glance and then looked down at Len, chained to the sidecar.

"What's going on here?" the man in the uniform asked.

"None of your business," Clyde answered.

"Sorry, gentlemen," the man said tactfully but without concealing his disgust, "but this town is closed."

"Closed?" Clyde laughed.

"Yeah. Closed."

"And why might that be?"

"To be quite frank, we don't want your kind here."

"And what kind is that?"

"Bikers," the man said.

"Says who?"

"Says me," the man said, pointing to his badge. "The sheriff."

The bikers laughed uproariously at this statement. The sheriff got red faced at the humiliation but remained steadfast.

"This isn't a joke, boys," the sheriff said. "The townsfolk passed a no-bikers law after the last time y'all raided them. They deputized us to enforce it."

"Deputies? Law?" Clyde snickered. "Get a load of this shit."

"Turn around and leave, please."

Clyde pointed a chrome finger at the sheriff and smiled his bear-trap smile again. Then, unexpectedly, a hidden gun in his arm fired three times in quick succession, killing all three police officers in less than a second. Len watched in horror as their bodies collapsed lifelessly onto the road.

"Law," Clyde scoffed. "There's your fucking law."

The bikers guffawed again at the sight of the three dead cops bleeding from their skulls.

"Open the gate, boys," Clyde yelled. "It's time to get trashed!"

One of the bikers pulled the pin out of a grenade and chucked it at the fence. Len ducked down into his sidecar to avoid the shrapnel as the explosive blew the fence to shreds.

As night fell, Len and Natalia sat handcuffed to a bench in the middle of town, watching as the bikers terrorized the small community. They pillaged the liquor store of its alcohol, then set fires to cars parked in the streets. Len turned his head as one of the bikers raped an adolescent boy with what appeared to be a hydraulic phallus. After he'd had his fill, the biker walked away and left the kid a sobbing, bleeding mess in the middle of the street.

"Fucking savages," Natalia growled through gnashed teeth.

Looking at the poor boy in the street, Len felt a volcano of pity and anger come up from his guts.

"Hey," he whispered.

The boy looked up at Len, his eyes red with shock and indignation.

"Do you have a phone?" Len asked.

92

Dan Barton, age ten, heard a knock at the door.

Should I answer it? he wondered.

Deciding to ignore it, he went back to reading his comic book. A few seconds later, the person knocked again.

Mom told me not to answer the door while she was gone, he thought.

He got up from the sofa and walked to the window. Looking out, he didn't see anyone.

Maybe they went away.

The knock came again. This time much louder. Not tall enough to reach the peephole, Dan decided to ignore his mother's advice. He twisted the deadbolt knob and opened the door.

There, at the threshold, stood an old lady. Maybe seventy-five or so. Her eyes. There was something odd about them.

"Why, hello, young man!" the old lady said. "Are you Daniel Barton?"

"Who's asking?" the boy asked.

"My name is Mrs. Gibson. I was hired be your babysitter while your parents are gone."

"Babysitter? I don't need a babysitter."

"Is your father here, Daniel?"

"No. He's out in the ocean, drilling for oil. He's been gone for a month."

"What about your mother?"

"She went to New Orleans, I think." Dan said.

"When did she leave?"

"I don't know. A week ago, maybe."

"You've been here all alone for seven days?" the woman asked.

The woman's tone and smile were kind, but it was difficult for Dan to maintain eye contact with her. Looking her in the eye felt like staring into a sinkhole that had just swallowed an entire city block.

"Yeah. So?"

The old lady smiled. "Do you like video games and comic books? I love video games and comic books, and I brought *lots* of them."

Daniel came down the stairs the next morning to find Mrs. Gibson had cooked a large breakfast.

"I made your favorite, pancakes." Mrs. Gibson said.

How does she know I like pancakes? Dan wondered.

Dan sat down at the kitchen table and ravenously devoured the stack of flapjacks. No one had bought groceries since his mother left, so he'd already eaten everything in the fridge. As he worked his way through breakfast, something caught his attention. A huge pile of boxes in the living room, like the kind the mailman brought when someone ordered something on the Internet.

"What are those?" Dan asked.

"Supplies," Mrs. Gibson said cheerfully.

"What kind of supplies?"

"Things to keep us occupied for a while. We're going to be spending a lot of time together, you and I, so I want to make sure we have enough food and things to do."

This seemed reasonable enough to Dan, and he went back to his pancakes. As he ate, Mrs. Gibson brought some boxes over to the table. She opened a long box with a knife and pulled from it a huge roll of plastic sheeting that was nearly too heavy for her frail old body to lift. From other boxes, she retrieved rolls of duct tape, tubes of caulk, cans of spray foam, and various hardware items.

"What's all that for?" Dan asked.

"Danny, do you like fixing things?" she asked.

"Yeah, I guess."

"Good. We've got some work to do on this house."

After breakfast, Mrs. Gibson showed Dan how to use a caulk gun to run a bead of caulk all around a window. Then, with her old, shaky hands, she used the shaping tool around each window to make sure the sealant got into all the cracks. When they were done with that, she showed him how to duct-tape the plastic sheeting over the windows. Finally, they took the cover plates off all the switches and outlets, and she showed him how to spray the insulating foam inside.

By the time they were done, it was getting dark.

"Now to test the quality of our work," Mrs. Gibson said. She lit a stick of incense and held it next to each window.

"Do you see how the smoke is going straight up? That means there are no more drafts. We did our job. Grade-A workmanship, Danny!"

"Yeah, but what was the point of all that?" Dan asked. "It's not winter yet."

"Maybe not. But old ladies like me get cold easily," Mrs. Gibson said.

Dan awoke in the middle of the night. He crept downstairs, careful to avoid the steps that squeaked. He saw a bluish glow in the kitchen and crept up slowly and carefully to see what it was.

Mrs. Gibson was sitting at the table with her back to him. She was using a laptop computer, playing some sort of game with two joysticks. Completely focused on the screen, she didn't seem to notice Dan at all.

"Mrs. Gibson?" Dan asked.

She turned around calmly and looked at him with her abyssal eyes. It struck Dan as odd that she wasn't even startled. It was as if she had been expecting him.

"Yes, dear?" Mrs. Gibson.

"What game is that?"

"My favorite game. Come on over and see!"

It appeared to be a military game of some sort. There were guys in camouflage fatigues and ski masks. They were in a huge room full of tanks, trucks, and helicopters. There was a man tied to a chair who looked like a prisoner. He had a hood on his head.

"How do you play this?" Dan asked.

"Well, this game isn't for kids," Mrs. Gibson said. "But I guess you can watch if you want."

The soldiers in the game took the hood off the prisoner. The prisoner seemed scared. He looked around the room and began talking to the soldiers.

"These graphics are really good!"

"Can you do me a big favor, Danny?" Mrs. Gibson asked.

"Sure, what?"

"Just sit there and don't say anything. Sorry, but this part takes lots of concentration. I'll show you how it works. I control a robot in the game, and I can make it talk. Watch this."

Mrs. Gibson focused her attention on the two joysticks, which she manipulated skillfully. The vantage point on the screen changed as she did so, indicating movement. Speaking into a microphone, she said hello to the prisoner. The character jumped up and yelled "Holy crap!" Dan put his hand over his mouth to try to stifle his laughter.

Grown-up games are kinda stupid, Dan thought.

"Mrs. Gibson, someone is knocking at the door."

"Don't open it. Just ignore it."

"You always say that. 'Don't open it. Just ignore it.' What if it's important?"

"It's not," Mrs. Gibson said.

"What if it's my parents?"

"They won't knock. They have keys."

"OK. Well, can I play outside at least?" the boy asked.

"Not today, Danny."

"Why not?"

"It's not safe out there."

"But I've been inside this house for a month!" Dan said.

"Did you read all your comic books?"

"No, but I'm bored of those."

"And the video games?" the old woman asked. "I brought nearly a thousand when I came. There's no way you played them all already."

"No, but I'm tired of video games. I want to do something new."

"Well, we have to stay inside just a little while longer."

"How long?"

"Until the danger passes."

93

The next morning, Len yelled as he awoke, soaking wet.

"What? Why?" Natalia screamed. She was dripping with water too.

It took Len a second to realize that Clyde had thrown water on them.

"Wake up," Clyde bellowed. "Time to go."

"Where are you taking us?" Len asked, once he realized what had happened.

"Cleveland," Clyde said.

"Why?"

"None of your business."

Clyde unchained them both from the bench and then yanked Len up to a standing position. Clyde noticed the boy's phone where Len had been sitting.

"Now, what's this?" Clyde asked. "I thought I took your electronics." Clyde swiped his finger a few times and then read something on the screen while Len stood there in shackles. He looked up at Len with a burning, angry glare.

Clyde's mechanical arms were so strong that he tossed Len clear across the street like a rag doll. Len landed on the pavement on top of the hand that was already broken and swollen. He yelped from the incredible pain.

"You think you're clever, fuckboy?" Clyde roared as he stomped over to Len.

Clyde leaned over to pick Len up, his metallic fingers grabbing Len by the shirt.

Len winced and closed his eyes, anticipating that Clyde would hit him. Instead of a blow from Clyde's metal fist, Len was instead showered in hot, sticky goo. Len tried opening his eyes to see what had been spilled on him, but he couldn't because the warm liquid was covering his eyes.

Unable to reach his eyes because of the shackles, Len wiped his face on the shoulder of his shirt. Vision regained, he found Clyde still standing over him, still holding him by his shirt. Len gasped when he saw what had happened. Clyde's head, one of the few parts of his body that hadn't been replaced with machinery, was partially gone. His whole cranium from the nose up was missing. Len was covered in Clyde's brains. Len unsuccessfully tried to wriggle himself loose of the dead man's robotic grip.

"Hey, what did you do to Clyde?" one of the other bikers shrieked from across the street. Len heard a whizzing noise overhead, and that biker's head also exploded. The result looked as if someone had stuck a firecracker in raw hamburger meat, yet the biker's headless machine body remained standing on the sidewalk like a Civil War statue.

Len looked over at Natalia, who had thrown herself to the ground.

Several more shots followed in quick succession, taking out more members of the Tchogol's Motorcycle Club.

"Fuck, someone's shooting at us!" one of the bikers yelled, running for cover awkwardly on his metal legs.

From the alleys charged a swarm of soldiers in full battle gear, taking well-aimed shots at the bikers. Their rehearsed tactics and maneuvering made the bikers look like disorganized hooligans by comparison. Most of the bikers were killed within sixty seconds, but two or three managed to get to their wheels and escape.

One of the soldiers came over to Len. Len couldn't see the man's face through his mask. He pulled a knife from a pocket, flicked the blade out, and pointed it at Len's chest. Len didn't move.

"Len Savitz?" the armed man asked.

Len breathed a sigh of relief upon recognizing the voice. "So they tell me," he said. "It's good to see you, Jeff."

"Christ, I didn't even recognize you," Jeff said, taking his mask off. "You got rejuvenated?"

"Yeah," Len said sheepishly.

"I thought you didn't believe in all that." Jeff used the knife to cut the part of Len's shirt away that Clyde's metal fingers still held fast.

"I didn't. We have a lot of catching up to do. But first, can you get me out of these manacles? The key's around that guy's neck," Len said, moving his head in the direction of brainless Clyde.

On the ground, the cell phone Len had borrowed still displayed the last message sent from the device:

Jeff,

I'm not dead. Will explain later. Natalia and I are being held captive by a biker gang in a town called Pine Bluffs, east of Cheyenne. Please help. Get here as fast as you can.

Len

94

Daniel Barton, now eleven, heard a key turning in the dead-bolt lock. He got up from his chair to see who it was. His heart sank as he saw his father come through the front door. Dan had almost forgotten what the man looked like. With him was a young brunette woman of about twenty-three.

"Hey, kid, I'm back," his father said, throwing his suitcase on the floor.

"Hi."

"That's it? 'Hi?'" his father said.

"Where were you? You were gone for a whole year."

"I was stuck out in the ocean. Sucked. But I'm back now."

Dan's father looked around the house and noticed the plastic sheeting that was still covering all the windows. "What's all this?"

"Mrs. Gibson did that. She said it was too drafty in here."

"Who's Mrs. Gibson?" his father asked.

"The babysitter. She was here for months."

"No idea who you're talking about. Is she here now?"

"No. She packed her bags and left this morning."

Dan's father shrugged. "Maybe your mother hired her. Speaking of which, your mom ain't here, is she?"

Dan shook his head. "She left right after you did. Haven't seen her since. She was gone the whole time you were."

"She *what*?" Dan's father bellowed.

An hour later, Daniel Barton heard a rhythmic thumping upstairs and a woman screaming. Dan's father and his new girlfriend were in Daniel's bedroom with the door locked. At this point, Dan had a pretty good idea of what was going on.

Why do they have to do that in my room? Dan wondered. *I hate that man. I wish he'd leave again so Mrs. Gibson would come back.*

95

There was only one doctor in the town, and Len sat in his office while the physician wrapped his hand in plaster. Len looked uneasily around the room. Several of his former islanders sat there watching his hand and forearm being casted. There was one guy Len didn't recognize. He looked Japanese, about twenty-five or thirty years of age.

"I don't think we've met," Len said to the new guy.

Jeff and the others laughed.

"What's so funny?" Len asked.

"This is Mutoku," someone said. "Remember? He came to our island before you were shot."

"You were rejuvenated?" Len asked him.

Mutoku looked at the others, as if unsure how to answer.

"He doesn't understand you. We're trying to teach him English."

"What? He speaks perfect English."

"He did," Natalia said. "He spoke Japanese and some other languages too. But all that's gone now. He was shot through the head during the siege. Lost an entire brain loaf."

"Loaf?" Len asked.

"The English word is *hemisphere*," Jeff said playfully. "They were able to regrow the gray matter and skull fragments he lost. Physically, he's as healthy as ever, but the old neurons are gone, and so are the memories they held. He doesn't recall much of his previous life. He's had to relearn a lot."

Len shook his head in astonishment.

Like being reincarnated without dying.

"So what happened?" Jeff asked Len. "Where have you been?"

Len inhaled sharply. He'd been dreading the question.

"Len's a marked man," Natalia interjected before Len could answer. "Someone tried to assassinate him, as you know. I told the hospital to rejuvenate him—it wasn't his decision. He was heavily sedated at that point."

Jeff looked at her quizzically, undoubtedly wondering why she was answering for him.

"We wanted to protect you guys and not drag you into it," she said. "So we started a new life elsewhere, and we didn't tell anyone."

The islanders nodded their heads, as if this were a decent enough reason. Len sat there and wondered if he should speak up.

There's enough phoniness in this world. I'm not gonna add to it.

"No. No. That wasn't it," Len said, pinching the bridge of his nose with his good hand. "Natalia means well, but that isn't the whole story." He looked around the examination room at his former students. "Truth be told, I was just tired of my old life. I felt confined on that damn island. And I was fed up with the outside world hating and misunderstanding what I'd done in the past."

"Tired of us?" Jeff asked.

"No! No. Yes." Len took a troubled breath. "I love you guys, but try to see it from my perspective: I welcomed you all to my home, I made sure you had food and shelter, I helped you work through your problems, I did my best to keep our island community running even though I'm not really a leader or a people person. I donated thirty years of my life to teaching you meditation and judo. But I'm no different than any other human being; altruism tires me out. I just needed to move on." Len sighed under the weight of those bygone decades. He paused for a while. "Then, life intervened: I got shot. I came out of a coma months later to find I had a brand-new body and name. I was young again, with no responsibilities. A godsend. All my life I've fantasized about leaving the burdens of identity behind me and living a brand-new life somewhere else. For the last year, I actually did that. And, my God, it was wonderful. I didn't have a care in the world."

Len looked at Natalia, who was biting her knuckle.

"So, yes, I did something purely for myself," Len said. "Yes, I abandoned you and then asked you to come here to risk your lives to rescue us. I'm selfish. I'm inconsistent. I'm human."

Len looked down at the floor to hide the tears in his eyes. No one said anything.

"Jeff," Len said, "I knew you were capable of taking over for me. I knew you'd be a good and wise teacher. I knew my former students would be in good hands and that you'd keep these guys safe. I knew you'd keep things running well for the next thirty years."

Jeff got up from his seat and walked over to Len. He put his hand on Len's shoulder and smiled gently.

"Len, you're too hard on yourself. You always have been. No one expects you to be perfect. You said from day one that you weren't some prophet or great teacher. You didn't ask us to be starry-eyed sycophants; you asked us to think for ourselves. Over and over you reminded us that you're just human like the rest of us. Amazingly, the only person who didn't believe it was you." Jeff laughed softly. "Now that I'm in charge, I can honestly say that I'd also want to retire after thirty years of this shit."

Len pulled his backpack out of Clyde's sidecar. Remembering that his mail was inside, he opened the zipper and pulled out the letters. Inside was a red suggestion envelope, which he hadn't noticed when the mail girl threw his letters in the bag. Len dropped the backpack and hastily opened Qualia's letter, which was addressed to both him and Natalia. Inside, typed in all caps, was a very short message:

JIM AND ELIZABETH: DO NOT LEAVE SANDBOX TETON. METTEYYA INTELLIGENCE HAS REASON TO BELIEVE THAT THERE IS A BOUNTY ON YOUR HEADS. YOU ARE AT RISK OF BEING KIDNAPPED OR KILLED. WE CANNOT PROTECT YOU BEYOND OUR BORDERS.

"Well, great." Len said, handing the letter to Natalia.

Natalia read it, then scowled.

"The pirates also said there was a price on my head," she recalled. "Someone had paid them to kidnap me."

"Who's putting up the money? And why are they trying to capture us?" Len asked. "How did they even find out we're in Teton?"

Natalia shrugged. Her gaze was far away and concerned. "Well, what should we do?" she asked. "Qualia said she can protect us if we stay in Teton. Should we go back or try to lay low elsewhere?"

"One thing's for damn sure," Len said. "We can't stay here."

Natalia pulled a paper map from the backpack and unfolded it. "If someone's hunting us," she said, "they'd expect us to backtrack to Teton, right?"

"I would think so."

"Or they might be waiting for us outside Sandbox Badlands, which is just a few hours northeast of our current location." She paused, studying the map intently. "Maybe we should do something counterintuitive," Natalia said. "Something crazy."

"Like what?" Len asked.

"Let's go east," she said, pointing to a spot in the Appalachians. "Here. Sandbox Great Smoky Mountains."

"Natalia, that's 1,400 miles away!"

"But they're not expecting that, are they?"

96

Dan, now twelve, crouched behind a bush in his backyard while holding a piece of string. Fifty feet away, a black kitten walked lazily along a split-rail fence. Dan watched intently. Not too far from the cat was a trap he'd built: a box propped up with a stick. The stick was connected to the string he was holding. Inside the box was a dead goldfish.

Come on, he thought. *This is getting boring. I've been out here all day.*

Uncomfortable from waiting in the same position for so long, Dan shifted his weight a little, which rustled the bush. The cat turned its head in Dan's direction.

Dammit. Now he's gonna run.

The cat didn't run. It looked at Dan for a while and then turned its head and continued moseying down the fence toward the trap. Dan sat still as a rock now, hoping the cat would take the bait. The cat leaped from the fence rail down to ground gracefully and carefully moved closer to inspect the box. Cautiously, it sniffed the air around the box, then the edge of the box itself.

Come on, come on.

The cat stuck its head in first, looking up into the heavy wooden box. Without entering the box, the feline tried batting at the fish with one of its paws, but the bait was too far inside the box for the cat to reach. Dan had tried this before with smaller boxes to poor result, so he'd built himself the biggest box he could. If the cat wanted the fish, it would have to move its whole body underneath the box.

Slowly, cautiously, the cat slunk its little self inside the box. As the feline gnawed on the meal inside, Dan took up the slack on the line slowly and methodically to avoid any sudden movements. Then, once the line was taut, he yanked it hard and fast, pulling the stick out and collapsing the trap before kitty could react.

"Hah! Got 'em!" Dan shrieked in his prepubescent voice. He walked proudly over to the box, which was rattling and shaking due to the hysterics of the panicked animal inside. Dan felt an unusual, tingling sensation down his spine. Kind of like a piss shiver, but warm and pleasant rather than cold and rote. It was a physical reaction to enjoyment; the animal's fear and powerlessness gave him pleasure.

Dan lifted up a corner of the box. The terrified cat put a paw out as he did so, trying to lift the box up enough to escape. Dan pushed the paw back inside and then skillfully slid a thin board under the corner and shimmied it under the box, separating the cat from the ground. With the cat so trapped, he lifted the entire assembly up and took it to the garage.

Dan had planned all of this for weeks. He knew exactly what he'd do next. Once inside the garage, away from neighbors who might see, he deftly maneuvered the box-and-board combo into a large cloth laundry sack. He lifted the entire ensemble up and then removed the board. Feeling the cat plop into the sack and thrash about, he isolated the cat in the lower part of the sack by pinching it off and then removed the box. Carefully, he tied the bag off and lifted it up. The scared, frenzied mewing coming from the sack made him feel giddy. Dan stood there for a minute or two, watching the bag bounce around and relishing the creature's dread.

Once he'd gotten tired of that, he started swinging the bag around his head. The cat was practically bawling in fear now.

It has no idea what's going on, he thought while grinning. *One minute the little jerk is eating a goldfish; the next he's stuck in a dark, small place and experiencing centripetal g-forces.* Dan felt excitement in his groin while thinking about the cat's confusion and terror.

After a minute or two of this, Dan's arms became tired, and he let go of the bag in midswing. The bag flew and bounced against a wall, causing the kitten inside to howl in pain.

Oh God, this is wonderful.

Dan pulled his pants down and began playing with himself while watching the bag roll around on the floor and listening to the animal inside whimper. In that moment of vicious carnality, he gave himself his very first orgasm. The sensation overtook him, and he found himself laughing out loud.

Afterward, that old empty feeling again: boredom.

Dan got out an old metal hamster cage that he'd stolen from a neighbor's shed. It was small, with a water bottle attachment and a metal pan for a floor. He opened the little door to the cage and grabbed the bag that the cat was in. He untied the sack and loosened the string. Then, he quickly stuck the open end of the bag into the hamster cage. The cat, seeing light and thinking it had an opportunity to escape, clawed its way to the bag opening, only to find itself inside a similarly confining space. Dan snorted with laughter and closed the door to the hamster cage, sliding the latch closed.

Time to have some fun.

Dan grabbed some twine off the shelf in the garage and took the caged creature down to the woods. He sat down to work behind a large tree where he wouldn't be seen. He threaded the twine through the little metal bars on the top of the cage. The panicking cat scratched him several times as he was doing this, inciting him to curse at the little thing and shake the cage violently. Once he'd tied his knots, Dan then threw the loose end of the twine over a tree branch. Pulling on the loose end, using the tree branch as a pulley, Dan hoisted the cage into the air, suspending it above a small creek.

Dan chuckled to himself as he saw the absolute panic on the cat's face. Even it, a dumb animal, knew what was coming next. Then he saw something that gave him those spine tingles and made him hard again: the kitty's eyes welled up with tears.

This is awesome. I didn't know cats could cry.

Dan gleefully let out the twine and lowered the cage. He did it slowly, savoring every moment. At the moment the water entered the cage, the cat let out a pained screech and scrambled to cling to the ceiling of the cage. Inch by inch, Dan lowered the cage into the cold stream. The cat let go of the ceiling and thrashed about in the water for a time. Then, when the cage was halfway submerged and only the cat's head and shoulders remained above the water, the damnedest thing happened: the animal went dead calm. It just stared him in the eye, as if it had accepted its fate and was merely waiting for the inevitable.

The sudden change in the cat's demeanor rubbed Dan the wrong way. Why wasn't it afraid anymore?

"Are you calling me a coward, you little shit?"

The cat didn't respond. No more crying, no more tears. Just that icy stare as its head remained above the gurgling waters.

"Screw you, cat!" Dan yelled as he let go of the twine.

The cage plunged down into the stream, drowning the cat. Dan was affronted by the way the cat died: without protest or gasping for air. No struggle at all. The animal's resignation gave him a satisfactionless anticlimax.

Dan walked to the water's edge and looked down. The stream, just barely deeper than the height of the cage, was crystal clear. Dan could see the dead cat's face beneath the water. It was still staring at him.

97

Len looked through the peephole. He saw nothing but an empty parking lot and trucks on the distant highway. He checked the deadbolt and the dinky little chain lock on the door twice.

So someone was clearly hunting them. A large group would attract attention, so they'd decided to split up. Jeff and the islanders were probably on their way back to Cleveland. Len and Natalia were holed up in a beat-up motel somewhere on the war-torn prairie.

Len squatted down next to the metal case Jeff had given him and unlocked it. Buried in the foam padding was a Dranthyx plasma rifle and two extra Californium 252 charge magazines. He pushed the correct sequence of buttons, and the thing lit up and hummed like an iridescent tuning fork.

"Shall we take turns sleeping?" Natalia asked. "Four-hour shifts?"

"Good idea," Len said, handing her the rifle.

"Ladies first," Natalia chaffed as she sarcastically ushered him to the bed.

Len gave her a raspberry and lay down. He was so damn tired, he didn't even remember falling asleep.

Len blearily opened his eyes while lying on his side. The alarm clock said 2:43 a.m.

Natalia should have awoken me by now.

He looked over where he'd last seen her, the chair by the door. To his surprise, the chair was empty and the motel room door was wide open. Leaves were blowing in. The plasma rifle was lying on the carpet, unattended. Natalia was nowhere to be found.

Feeling the presence of someone behind him, Len turned in bed quickly, eyes wide with fear.

Something leaped out of the shadows of the darkened room, pouncing on top of Len. The streetlamps outside the door provided just enough light for Len to see what had attacked him: a Dranthyx. Len struggled with the slimy beast, but it easily overpowered him. It pinned down his arms and stuffed an ether-soaked rag in his face.

"If you want something done right, do it yourself," it said, just before Len lost consciousness.

98

"Danny!" his father bellowed, "get down here!"

God, what the hell does he want now?

Dan, now seventeen, came down the steps slowly. Dan's father, with that damn vein bulging from his forehead, stood at the bottom of the stairs.

"I said, get down here!" his old man yelled. When Dan was within arm's length, he grabbed Dan's arm and yanked him down the stairs. Dan tripped and flew down the steps, landing face first at the bottom. Dan cursed as blood poured from his nose.

"What the hell is your problem?" Dan asked, holding his face.

"The fuck did you just say to me, boy?" his father roared. He picked Dan up and slammed him against the wall.

Dan's vision went dark for a second from the impact.

"Where is my wallet?"

"I haven't seen it," Dan said.

"Liar!" his father yelled, slapping him in the face.

Dan stood up and looked his dad in the eye, nose dripping blood all over his white T-shirt.

"I don't know what you want me to tell you," Dan said calmly. "I haven't seen it."

"You lying sack of Tchogol shit!"

"You're a Tchogol too."

"What did you say, you little bitch?"

"You're a Tchogol too," Dan said while swallowing blood. "It's genetic."

"Then why didn't I die of the flu, genius?"

"You were on an oil platform in the Gulf of Mexico. Remember? You're always bragging about how you survived a whole year stranded on the drilling rig with no supplies. You never got the virus because everything went to hell and you had no contact with the outside world. You'd have died had you been on the mainland."

His father grabbed his hair and got in close to Dan's face. Dan could hear his teeth grinding.

"Boy, let me explain something to you," his father said, uncomfortably close and spattering Dan's face with beer-scented spittle. "I'm only gonna say it once, so listen up. You're a Tchogol because your cunt mother was a Tchogol. She was whoring around New Orleans while I was out in the fucking ocean, putting food on our table. She died of the flu. Got it?"

"Tchogols, all three of us." Dan said defiantly.

Dan's father gave him a silent, icy stare.

"These are your genes. I'm a Tchogol because you're a Tchogol." Dan smiled a bloody smile, because he knew it would piss the old man off.

Dan's father hit him in the gut so hard it knocked the wind out of him. Dan collapsed into a heap and sat there trying to catch his breath, bleeding onto the floor. He sat there helplessly as his father stomped up the stairs to his room. He could hear the old man smashing his things and throwing stuff around, searching for the wallet.

Too late, you old cocksucker, Dan thought while smiling. *I spent your money and sold your credit cards.*

Later that night, when his father had finally passed out drunk, Dan went out to the garage. He put on his dad's fishing waders and grabbed a knapsack and a flashlight. He walked down to the little creek where he'd drowned the cat a few years earlier. He stepped into the cold water, feeling it rush around his knees.

Slowly, deliberately, flashlight in hand, Dan followed the creek, trudging through the water for nearly an hour, most of it in the woods in the dark. About a mile upstream, he saw an old farmhouse. Paint flaking, clapboard siding, a rusty tractor in the backyard. There was a light on upstairs. Dan knew it even in the dark.

Dan turned off his flashlight and quietly walked up the muddy creek bank into the farmhouse's backyard. He set his backpack down on the ground and unzipped it. From its darkened recesses, he pulled out a little red container of lawnmower fuel and some matches. He stealthily sprinkled gasoline on a corner of the farmhouse. Just as he was finishing, he heard the farmer's dogs barking inside. They'd heard him. Dan threw a match and ran. He was halfway to the creek when he remembered his backpack. Dan scrambled up the creek bank, grabbed the backpack, stuffed the gas can inside, and ran back down. He splashed and stumbled downstream toward his house, tripping several times.

Once Dan was a good distance away, he turned around to admire his handiwork. He saw the trees silhouetted by a ghastly orange glow as smoke rose up into the dead sky. Dan heard the hounds howling and the farmer's wife screaming. Dan smiled and inhaled deeply, smelling the building burning downwind. He'd planned this for months. Their dogs couldn't follow his scent if he walked home through the creek. Even if they did catch him, the farmer and his wife weren't members of any government, so there'd be no recourse.

Dan didn't know the farmer and his wife personally. By all accounts, they were decent, hardworking people. But Dan didn't care; no one had ever respected him, so why should he give a shit about anyone else?

99

Octavia selected Iris's Glibber link and hit Connect.

This is the only way to contact her. Freakin' kid won't answer a regular phone call.

The screen said "Attempting Connection" for several seconds. Then, the hologram popped up. It was a blank wall, with part of a picture frame and part of a bookshelf. Octavia recognized it as the bedroom in Dan's penthouse. Iris wasn't in view, but Octavia could hear her voice in the background.

She must have it set to autoanswer, Octavia thought.

"Hello, Iris?" Octavia asked.

No answer. Just more background conversation.

"Iris?" Octavia said louder.

Still nothing.

I hate Glib, she thought. *Servers are always overloaded, and the connections are unreliable. I have no idea why anyone uses this to communicate.*

Then she heard Dan's voice. They were talking about something.

"C'mon," Iris implored.

"Not the best idea, Iris."

Something's wrong here, Octavia thought.

"Not the best idea, Iris," the girl's voice mocked, "Please. You're a Tchogol; I'm a Tchogol. Morality is a joke to us, and you know it."

Long silence.

"I see you looking at me all the time," Iris said. "I know what you're all about. Let's do a deal here. I'll suck your dick or whatever else you want."

"What do you want?" Dan asked.

"A metric shit ton of Afghan snow," Iris said.

Dan laughed. "You know what that stuff costs? I can get any broad to suck my dick for a few LCs. What makes you so special? And, anyway, you're a teenager. You don't know the first thing about pleasing a man."

"What in the fuck is going on over there?!" Octavia shouted. There was no response, only continued, off-camera negotiations on the other end of the transmission.

She must have the volume muted.

"I won't say anything," Iris said coyly.

"Yeah, right. You'll say whatever to the highest bidder. You junkies are all the same."

"I'm not a junkie! I've got it under control."

"Hah!" Dan bellowed. "You're a sweaty, shaky mess all day. You're gonna kill yourself with that crap. Your mom's in denial, but anyone with half a brain knows what's going on."

"Whatever. I'm gonna die anyway."

"Yeah, you are." Dan laughed. "One hundred LCs."

"One hundred LCs? That's not even gonna get me lit for three days. You can do better than that. I thought you were rich."

"Yeah, and I got rich by not spending my money on stupid things. One hundred or nothing."

"Fine," Iris said.

Octavia, aghast, could do nothing but sit there and listen to it happen.

"Here's your money," Octavia heard Dan say. "Now get out of my sight."

"I'll make another deal with you," Iris said.

"I'm done making deals," Dan said. "I've got work to do. Anyway, that was terrible."

"Oh no. You're going to make a deal with me," Iris said.

"Excuse me?"

"This time you're gonna give me one hundred thousand LCs, or I'll upload the recording I just made to Glib."

A long, loaded silence.

Why didn't I think to record it? Octavia asked herself, now seething with rage in the breakroom at her work. Having suffered through listening to the entire act, her fingers sweaty and shaking, she fumbled to hit the record button on her own Glibber but didn't know how to activate that feature.

"You did what, you little bitch?" Dan said.

"I recorded our conversation," Iris said insouciantly. "And if you don't give me one hundred thousand LCs, I will torpedo your political career. Just think of the headline: 'Aegis principal pays girlfriend's teenage daughter in heroin for fellatio.' I think it has a nice ring to it, don't you think?"

Octavia was a volcano of emotion. Jealousy, betrayal, anger, sadness, helplessness, concern, disgust, fear. Even a tiny bit of admiration for her daughter's cleverness. She thought about the quickest way to get back to Dan's apartment.

Then, over the Glib feed, she heard a loud whacking sound, followed by a heavy thud. This was followed by several more impact noises. Then, nothing. Quiet. The camera angle changed as someone picked up Iris's Glibber. She saw Dan's face just before the feed went dark.

100

Len heard someone open the door. This wasn't followed by the sound of walking. The noise was movement, certainly, but not footsteps.

He felt someone take hold of the bag over his head and yank it off. His pupils, dilated from the dark hood, were blinded by the light in the room. It took several seconds before he could see. Looking up, he gasped at the sight of the octopod staring back at him.

"What?" Natalia asked, hearing his surprise.

"Dranthyx!" Len yelled as he struggled to get free.

Natalia rocked back on her chair, knocking herself over and onto her side. She was unable to see but perfectly able to curse.

The creature cackled at Natalia's predicament and then wriggled over to pull her hood off.

"Natalia Zherdeva, I presume?" the monster gargled.

"Fuck you!" she yelled.

The Dranthyx slapped her with his tentacle before forcibly righting her chair. The monster held her chair there while she tired herself out with struggling. He waited for her to calm down.

"Your exploits are rather amazing," the Dranthyx said, once she stopped fidgeting. "First you wipe out the entire Lake Syndicate, and then you obliterate most of a motor-cycle gang."

Natalia glared at the beast.

"You are one tough bitch!" The creature laughed.

"What do you want from me?" Natalia asked.

"Information," the creature stated.

"I'm not telling you shit," Natalia barked.

"You know, I do love to torture people. And I was going to torture you. But I've given it a second thought. I know your type. That sort of thing never works on someone of your constitution, now, does it?" The creature circled around her. "I've worked on my share of Natalia Zherdevas, and I know the pattern. Your weakness isn't fear. You'll suffer through any kind of pain, just to spite me. Won't you?" The Dranthyx walked toward Len and coiled his tentacle around Len's neck.

Natalia's expression changed from anger to concern.

"No, your type is very consistent," the Dranthyx said menacingly. "Your weakness is your love for others."

"Goddamnit," Natalia lamented, "What do you want to know?"

101

"Iris?" Octavia yelled in a panic, running through Dan's penthouse in her work uniform. She'd left in the middle of her shift, leaving Bernie at her employer's daycare.

No answer.

Octavia ran to the bedroom where the transgression had happened. The bed had been neatly made, and there was no sign of either Dan or Iris. She looked around, and then down at the white carpet. There was a large dark spot next to the bed. Octavia knelt down and felt it. The dark area was wet and smelled like cleaning chemicals.

Hands trembling with worry and wrath, she pulled her phone out of her purse and called Dan.

"Hey, babe!" Dan answered.

"Where are you?" Octavia asked.

"Cleveland. I've been called away on Aegis business. I'll be back in a few days. What's up?"

"Where the fuck is my daughter?" Octavia demanded.

"At my place," Dan said in a way that suggested Octavia's choice of words was unwarranted. "Where else would she be?"

"Well, she's not here."

"I don't know what to tell you. Maybe she went out?"

"Then why isn't she answering her Glibber?"

"How should I know?" Dan asked. "She never answers that thing. Octavia, you sound upset. Are you angry?"

"You backstabbing pervert. I heard the whole thing. I heard what you did with Iris. Where is she?"

"I'm not sure what you could have heard that would have upset you so much." Dan said innocently. "I didn't do anything to her. She's fine. I left her at my place when I left for Cleveland. She's probably still there."

"If you hurt my daughter, so help me, it'll be the last thing you'll ever do."

102

While being dragged from the interrogation room by the Dranthyx, Len noticed they were in a prison, the kind that a city government might have used in the pre-Invasion days. White cinderblock walls, old-fashioned fluorescent lights. Cells with bars, double-decker cots, and little stainless-steel toilets.

The prison was empty of inmates except for a cell at the end of the block. The Dranthyx interrogator slid the door open and tossed Len and Natalia inside.

Once the creature had slammed the cell door closed and left, a human guard came and demanded that they stick their shackled limbs through the bars. The guard was wearing a uniform that read Aegis Threat Containment. Len stuck his casted arm out, fitting it awkwardly through the bars. The man removed the oddly placed shackle from around the plaster and then did the same for Natalia.

His face is kind, Len thought. *He doesn't want to be here either.*

"Thank you," Len said.

The guard tipped his hat without saying anything and then resumed his rounds.

"Welcome!" a voice said from across the hall.

Startled, Len and Natalia turned around. Two young men were sitting on the bunks in the cell facing theirs. They looked rough, and their Tchogol tattoos were clearly visible on their wrists.

"Um, hi," Natalia said.

"So, uh, what are you in for?" the man on the bottom bunk asked.

"I have no idea," Len said.

"Yeah, me either," the man on the top bunk said with a sarcastic expression.

"Gentlemen!" someone yelled obnoxiously the next morning. "Good morning!"

Len heard Natalia make a surprised utterance in Russian. They'd all been sound asleep on the bunks.

"Oh, and lady," the man said, turning around to see Len and Natalia in the opposing cell. "Where are my manners?"

Len rubbed his eyes and stared, still half-asleep, at the man addressing them on the other side of the bars. He had a salt-and-pepper coiffure and a long horse face. He was dressed like a local newscaster on his way to a house fire.

Where have I seen this guy before? Len wondered.

"Mike," the man said, addressing one of the men in the cell across the hall, "I just wanted to stop by and personally thank you for your help. If it weren't for you, I'd never be where I am."

"Yeah, no problem." the prisoner who was apparently named Mike said. "So how long do I have to stay in here?"

"Not too much longer," the man said.

"Yeah, but when exactly will I get out? I'm going crazy in here."

"Tonight. Prime time."

"Prime time?" Mike asked.

"I'm bringing back public execution, and you're up first." The horse-man grinned. "It'll be on TV, Glib, everywhere."

"What? That ain't funny."

"It's not a joke," the man said. "They're getting the gallows ready as we speak, right in the middle of the Cleveland Bazaar. Platform, rope, big fat dude with a black executioner's hood. It's gonna look legit," Horseface said, pumping his fist. "We're gonna hang you like they hanged cattle rustlers in the frontier days." The man made finger guns and yelled, "Yee haw!"

"Like, a fake hanging, right? Where I pretend to die."

"No, a real one. Where you really die."

"What?" Mike asked, visibly upset. "Man, we had an understanding. I stab Travis Davidson, your guys arrest me, then take me to jail. Then, when everyone forgets, you let me out and you pay me a million LCs. I made it look authentic!"

"Authentic?" The equine visitor scoffed. "You didn't even take his wallet, idiot."

"So what?" the other young Tchogol said. "You gonna screw me over too?"

"Yep. Sorry, Jerome. You're gonna hang right after Mike does." The man made a mocking gesture of someone being lynched.

"Tha fuck, man? You told me you'd pay me a half mil if I robbed that little old lady and I let you punch me out. You knocked one of my teeth out. I earned that money. You said I'd only do a month in jail!"

"Eh." The man shrugged. "We made up a whole backstory for you. Turns out you're not just a thief, but a serial murderer! So you'll be swinging too."

Dan Barton, Len thought. *The Aegis guy. That's who he is. Wait—isn't he the guy Octavia is dating? She sent me a letter about it. I thought she said he was handsome. He looks like he could run the Belmont Stakes with that face.*

"And what about us?" Natalia asked.

"Well, I can't hang you," Dan said. "Everyone thinks you were killed by pirates when they nuked your island. It was all over the news for months. Your death became a cause célèbre; the fear of Tchogol warlords with atomic weapons was the tipping point in my campaign."

"I nuked them!" Natalia said.

"Oh, I know—even if no one else does. And thank you for that. Anyway, you can't be executed publicly because no one knows you're still alive. They can't know. It would upset the balance of things. However, your husband will be hung."

"What?" Natalia screamed.

"Yeah, but his death isn't scheduled until next week. It'll be at halftime during the big game. The ratings are gonna be tremendous."

"Why?" Len asked.

"It has to happen. For the greater good," Dan said, rolling his eyes at the concept.

"Mr. Bigshot, eh?" Len sneered. "Mr. Law and Order."

"That's the idea," Dan said. "You are a rather controversial figure, Lenny. To some, you are a hero. But many others see you as a traitor to Jefferson's revolution—the guy who ushered in the era of anarchy. Your hanging will be more symbolic than anything. The lawlessness dies when you do."

"You're a fraud," Len said. "The world doesn't need you."

Dan chuckled. "I don't give a fuck what the world needs."

"Prisoners Michael DiSanto and Jerome Jackson, please stick your hands through the door slot."

Len and Natalia glanced at each other and then at the Tchogols in the cell across the hall. The guards were standing there with handcuffs, ready to lead their captives to the gallows. Mike, resigned to his fate, put his hands through to be handcuffed first. Jerome, looking indignant, refused and had to be physically brought to compliance. Once they were both shackled, the guards ushered the men into the hall.

Mike looked over at Len and Natalia. He smiled hollowly and let the guards walk him to his end.

103

Dan sat at the long table, reviewing the stack of merger paperwork Aegis's legal team had received from SDI while he'd been presiding over the double execution in Cleveland.

"I think that last conference call went well. They seem really eager to join us," Elise said, trying to seem upbeat.

"You wouldn't know it. This proposed agreement is bat-shit," Dan said. "Who do they think they are?"

"I spent the last four hours reading through it," Elise said. "They have no fewer than 178 terms for us to accept, most of which are infeasible, financially or otherwise."

"Oh, don't worry. We're not agreeing to them," Dan said.

"What if that kills the deal?" Elise asked. "I worry that we'll put them off by being too hard nosed."

"Elise," Dan said, "let me explain something to you about business. The first rule is, never negotiate from a position of weakness. Which is exactly what they're doing. SDI has some serious problems. Number one, they're insolvent. Number two, they've got high-plains warlords on one side and North Koreans on the other. Number three, most importantly, their members are clamoring for a merger with Aegis. It's all over

Glib. If they don't merge, the entire board will be voted out next election."

"Are you sure they have no choice?" Elise asked.

"Aegis calls the shots," Dan said confidently. "If they want to join us, it'll be on our terms. Otherwise, they can learn Korean. Trust me; they'll sign our version of the deal within a week."

Randy opened the door to the conference room. His face was pale white.

"Where the hell have you been?" Dan demanded, throwing his hands up.

"Something important came up. It's urgent. More urgent than this. No offense."

"It had better be," Dan said. "This is the most important thing we've done all year."

"Your sponsors want to meet you." Randy's voice shook.

"Sponsors?" Dan asked.

"Donors," Randy said tactfully. "Remember the…gentlemen. You know, the ones who…um…bankrolled your campaign?"

"Oh." Dan took his reading glasses off and put his red pen down. He leaned back in his chair and rubbed his eyes. "Fuck," he muttered.

"Mr. Barton, is something wrong?" Elise asked.

"No, just something I need to attend to," Dan said.

"SDI wants an answer within twenty-four hours," Elise said.

"They can wait," Dan said. "They're not going anywhere."

Elise looked at Dan and then at Randy, as if to ask, *This is our second major merger. What could be more important than your life's mission realized?*

"Well, this day was coming sooner or later," Dan said. "Time to pay the piper. Are they here now?"

"There's a car out front waiting for you," Randy said. "It'll take you to them."

Dan closed his bound draft of the proposed merger agreement. He stood up, took his jacket off the back of the chair, and walked out the door.

The entrance to Aegis Plaza was a large, circular driveway that had been blocked off to vehicle traffic since the last wave of riots. Yet the massive concrete barricades had been moved aside that day to allow a single vehicle through. There, right in front of the main entrance to the skyscraper, was a black limousine. The windows were mirrored, and Dan couldn't see inside. A white-gloved chauffeur stood at the ready. When he saw Dan approach, the chauffeur opened the door for him. Dan took a deep breath and got into the car.

To his relief, it was empty inside except for him.

"Where are we going?" Dan asked once the chauffeur had gotten into the driver's seat.

"To Sarnia."

"What the hell is in Sarnia?"

"I don't know, sir. I'm just the limo driver."

A little over an hour later, the limo arrived in Sarnia, a town north of Detroit at the southern end of Lake Huron. The driver pulled the long automobile up to a marina and got out to open Dan's door.

"Where are they?" Dan asked.

"Mr. Barton?" a voice called.

Dan looked over and saw a man in a captain's uniform standing on the wharf next to a long, sleek, white watercraft. Though it was long and cylindrical, the gold railing and the large windows gave it the appearance of a tycoon's yacht.

"Yes?" Dan asked.

"Please come with me."

"This is an unusual boat," Dan said.

"It's a submarine," the captain said in a tone suggesting Dan was an idiot.

What the hell is all this? Can't they just come to my office like normal people?

Once aboard the watercraft, Dan walked through a round door and down some stairs. The captain followed, pushing a button on the wall. Dan watched as the hatch automatically seated and sealed itself with hissing pneumatic noises.

"Make yourself at home," the captain said, gesturing to a large, open compartment toward the rear of the ship. "It's a two-hour trip."

"Where are we going?" Dan asked.

"You'll find out soon enough," the captain said.

Dan couldn't believe how posh it was inside. Italian leather couches, marble coffee tables. A gas fireplace.

A fireplace in a submarine, Dan thought, shaking his head. *I've done pretty well for myself. Yet, no matter how wealthy I get, it would never occur to me to waste money on something this absurd.*

The craft had a bar toward the back stocked only with top-shelf booze. There was no bartender. In fact, it seemed that he and the captain were the only people on board.

Dan went behind the bar and poured himself a glass of Armagnac, holding the glass up to admire the color.

I wonder what favors these assholes will ask of me.

Dan took a seat on one of the white couches and looked out the big picture window. Without warning, the vessel began moving away from the wharf. Not with a lurch, but with a graceful gliding motion. He watched as the town of Sarnia disappeared in the window as the U-boat moved out into Lake Huron.

Then, just as nimbly as it had departed the port, the submersible slipped beneath the surface. As the craft dove deeper, Dan watched in amazement as the sunlit turquoise water of the lake gradually faded to an impenetrable black.

Unable to get cell service and with nothing to see outside, Dan resigned himself to watching a movie. Toward the end of the flick, he felt the boat making odd movements. Dan stood up, put his hands around his eyes to shield them from light, and held them against the window in an effort to see out. As if the boat knew what he was doing, the lights in the cabin dimmed down to total darkness and the movie projector shut off. External floodlights came on, penetrating the abyss around the craft.

Dan jumped backward when he saw a large wall of rock quickly moving past the window. He ran to the other side of the submarine to look out the opposing window. Same thing. It seemed they were descending into a trench. Looking down as far as the window would let him, he could see the lake bed below. Then the craft stopped, turned ninety degrees, and began moving quickly toward the sheer face of the underwater canyon.

"Holy shit!" Dan yelled, expecting an impact as the boat approached the large wall of rock.

When the boat didn't hit anything, Dan opened his eyes. The submarine was now moving through a tunnel in the rock wall. The tunnel was huge—big enough to accommodate a major urban highway.

That was kind of exciting.

Dan stood there in amazement for twenty minutes, his face pressed against the glass. The craft slowed again and then rose through a vertical tunnel that was twice as large as the previous one. The sub's external floodlights turned themselves off, leaving Dan in total darkness.

He looked up in the window and saw bright lights rippling. The surface of the water. The craft slowed in its ascent and broke through the water's surface.

As the water ran off the top of the sub and down the windows, the lights Dan had seen earlier became clearer. He felt a rare bit of astonishment when he finally saw what they were. The sub was in the harbor of a city.

This sure as hell isn't Chicago.

The buildings were domes, orbs, twisting cylinders, and jagged spires. The entire city was aglow with a hellish orange light.

"Welcome to Phax'th!" the captain said, smiling, as he descended the narrow stairs to the bridge.

Dan turned around. "Where?"

"Phax'th. The Dranthyx administrative hub for North America. Our regional capital, if you will."

"Our? Dranthyx?"

The captain laughed. And, as he laughed, his face turned purple. His head elongated, and his eyes sunk in and became yellow.

His Tchogol genes making him incapable of feeling fear, Dan simply made a noise of amazement. He'd never seen a Dranthyx up close before.

The captain motioned for Dan to follow him. "Come. We have work to do."

This is the least boring day I've ever had.

The captain opened the sub door and stepped outside.

God, that smell, Dan thought as he climbed out of the craft and onto the dock. *It smells like a truck full of dead salmon.*

Dan surveyed Phax'th. What he'd presumed was a sky was actually a vast dome above the city. The orange light of the buildings was reflecting off it. The dome looked as if it was about fifty stories high at its apex.

"Where is this place, exactly?" Dan asked.

"Go to the deepest point of Lake Huron, and make a right," the captain wisecracked with his nasty seafood face.

"We built this three hundred years ago, when it became obvious that North America would become economically relevant. We dug a massive underwater cave, sealed it, and pressurized it with air. This place is like a big diving bell."

"Are there other cities like this?"

"You think this is a city? This is nothing. You should see Gchollkel."

Dan shook his head, as if to say he had no idea what Gchollkel was.

"Our world capital. In the Mediterranean, just off the Calypso Deep. It makes Tokyo look like a little fishing village. Anyway, we have cities under every large body of water. Or had, I should say. We were forced to consolidate a bit after the depopulation—"

"Why am I here?" Dan asked.

The octopod's face turned serious. "The Directorate will answer that question. I'm just a sailor. This way, please."

The captain ushered Dan to a car parked nearby. It was a late-model, Detroit-made sedan. Dan couldn't quite wrap his head around the juxtaposition of a familiar, human-built automobile in a city full of walking octopuses and alien architecture.

How the hell do they even get the cars down here?

Dan sat in the front seat as they drove through Phax'th. In some ways, it was almost familiar. In others, practically extraterrestrial. There didn't seem to be any traffic rules or even the least bit of courtesy. Crowds of Dranthyx walked or slithered in between moving cars. The town was filthy; there was litter and wrecked cars everywhere. Everything seemed to be covered in soot or belching smog.

As they sat there, waiting for a break in the chaotic traffic at a busy intersection, Dan smelled the worst thing he'd ever smelled, like skunk mixed with hobo ass.

"Oh God, do you smell that?" Dan gagged.

"My bad." The captain grinned.

"Christ. What the hell do you people eat?"

Dan rolled down the window and stuck his head out to keep from losing consciousness. On the sidewalk, Dan saw a group of bedraggled humans washing the windows of a storefront.

"There are people down here?" Dan asked.

"Yeah, lots." The captain sneered in disgust.

"Hey!" Dan shouted to his fellow humans.

They turned around and stared at him without answering.

"Why are you here?"

They continued staring vacantly.

"They don't speak English." The captain scoffed. "They've never been topside."

"Never?"

"We don't let them leave. Are you crazy?"

"Why not?"

"Because they'd tell the rest of you apes that we're down here."

Are they going to let me leave?

"How did they get here?" Dan asked.

"They were born here. We've got entire farms."

Frustrated by the intersection impasse, the captain laid on the horn, rolled down his window, and yelled something in Dranthyx. Offended, the other driver retaliated by opening his door and lobbing a dead carp onto the captain's windshield, cracking the glass.

"Shithead!" the captain yelled.

"What are they doing?" Dan asked.

"They picked today to learn how to drive, apparently."

"No. The humans. What are they doing down here?" Dan said.

"Oh. Cheap labor."

"How cheap?"

"Free. As it should be. You know we bred your kind to be slaves, right? I mean, hell, what else are you gorillas good for?"

Slave labor. Imagine never having to pay employees. These sons of bitches figured out a way to do it. Brilliant.

After several minutes, the captain managed to get Dan across town to a purple cylindrical building surrounded by uniformed Dranthyx.

"What's this place?" Dan asked, looking up.

"The local Crrillth. The traditional center of Dranthyx society. A sacred place. This is where we breed and where we're born. It's also where the Directorate meets, whenever they're in town."

"What's this directorate you keep talking about?"

"The supreme council of the Dranthyx world government."

"Who are they? How are they chosen?"

"Dranthyx government is somewhat like a game of king of the hill. In each city, there's a never-ending struggle for power with endless backstabbing and tumult. You may think this is inefficient, but it's actually ingenious. It assures that only the most ruthless and cunning make it to the top. The top politicians from each city are selected and sent to the crucible in Gchollkel."

"The crucible?"

The captain smiled. "It's a horrific test of stamina, barbarity, and guile. It's a contest like no other, to weed out the weak. If there's a last octopod standing, he's chosen for the Directorate."

"The olympians of shitbaggery, eh?" Dan asked.

"The best we have to offer," the captain said. "There's no better way to ensure strong leadership."

"Doesn't sound too different from human politics."

"We even have a reality show about it," the captain said. "It's very popular."

The captain led him past the guards and into the Crrillth. The fish smell intensified as the doors opened. Inside was dark with a harsh purple glow, like the black lights in a stoner's bedroom. Dan expected a grand entrance like a capitol building but was instead greeted by a narrow, damp hallway. Dan followed the captain down a long flight of steps to a basement. As they entered, the lights came on.

There before him was an area the size of a warehouse filled with many huge tanks of water. Dan went up to one of the tanks and looked in. Swimming in the purple-hued waters were hundreds of tiny octopus-like creatures. Baby Dranthyx. He looked closer. They were eating one another. He recoiled in disgust.

"What the fuck?" Dan laughed.

"This is the hatchery," the captain said, as if unable to understand his reaction.

"Don't you feed them?"

"Hell no. Survival of the fittest starts early down here."

"How many survive?"

"Hardly any, which is why we have so many to start with. This hatchery wasn't nearly this big before. We've had to scale this operation up two hundredfold to fully repopulate."

"Repopulate? When will that happen?"

"Soon enough," the captain said.

The captain led Dan through the hatchery and up several flights of steps, to a large, cavernous room. The walls were black and wet, and there were thousands of holes in the floor, each big enough to fit a garbage can.

"Please, take a seat." The captain motioned to one of the holes.

Seat? Dan couldn't figure out how the hell he was supposed to sit in it. If the holes were seats, the room looked as though it could have been a great meeting hall or a theater from the way the floor sloped. At the front of the room was a grand U-shaped desk of the kind one might see in a city council meeting, except black and slimy like the walls.

Dan sat down on the edge of the hole and let his legs dangle in. Just then, a door opened at the front of the room, and from it emerged several large, hideous Dranthyx. None of them were wearing any clothes. They walked somberly and seriously to their seats behind the desk. In unison, they each bent down and grabbed a purple object. They lifted their purple objects above their heads and then did a long chant in their disgusting, bubbly language.

"Is this a ceremony of some sort?" Dan asked.

"Get down on your belly, monkey," the captain sneered as he prostrated himself. "Show some respect."

"For real?"

The captain slapped Dan upside the head with his tentacle. Dan flushed with anger but figured retribution could wait. It seemed as though something important was about to happen. He decided to lie down, if only to find out what what was going on.

"You may rise," one of the Dranthyx said.

Dan cautiously got up, giving the captain a sidelong glance.

The Dranthyx who'd entered naked were now unfolding the purple items they'd held aloft. Bundles of fabric. They unfurled them into robes. They dressed themselves in the robes and then took seats behind the desk.

"What's going on?" Dan whispered to the captain.

"First, they mate with their harems, and then they call the meeting to order. Very traditional," the captain whispered back.

"You guys have harems?"

"Ahem," said one of the Directorate over the obvious whispering echoing through the large hall. "I now call this meeting to order." He banged a gavel on the desk. "Mr. Daniel Barton, I presume?"

"Uh, yes," Dan answered. "That's me."

"My name is Mr. Rothschild. I am the president of the Directorate. Allow me to introduce my fellow members," he said, pointing to each as he said their names, "Mr. Morgan, Vice President; Mr. Rockefeller, Secretary; Mr. Warburg, Mr. Cooke, Mr. Vanderbilt, and Mr. Smith."

Dan noticed that each Dranthyx had a brass plaque with his name on it in front of him, written in both English and, presumably, Dranthyx.

"A pleasure to meet you gentlemen," Dan said, trying to be as ingratiating as possible, despite his disgust at the foul creatures. The last thing he needed was to piss off major benefactors.

"You may have noticed our lack of dress as we entered," Rothschild said. "As the captain was so rudely mentioning, this ceremony may seem strange to you, but it is deeply rooted in our culture. First, we see to the future by ensuring our lineage, and then we meet here to consider matters of the present day. As you no doubt saw downstairs, we are quite busy repopulating."

"How is that going?" Dan asked, trying to seem as if he were making conversation rather than collecting information.

"We should be back up to our pre-Invasion numbers in five years. The younger generation is exceeding all our expectations. Our plan worked beautifully."

"Plan?" Dan asked.

"Oh, yes. If you haven't already figured it out, our depopulation was calculated. We estimated that our whole invasion force would be wiped out if the Ich-Ca-Gan were to attack, so we sent the entire left end of our IQ bell curve. Ninety-nine point seven percent of us were ordered topside, to be killed off. Since they were dumb, they had no idea." Rothschild laughed. "Anyone smart enough to stay below was required to reproduce as much as possible. The idea was to purify our race by removing the dummies. A eugenics program, if you will."

"Wow! So you knew what would happen?"

"Enough about us," Rothschild said. "We've heard great things about you. A rising star, they say."

"Thank you, sir. And thank you all for your kind donations to the cause."

"Don't think we don't want something in return, young man," Morgan said.

"Of course. However I can help." Dan smiled.

"Come here before us, boy," Morgan said, curling his tentacle. "Come closer so that we might see you better."

Dan climbed out of the hole and approached the desk.

"That's close enough," Vanderbilt said.

Dan stopped and stood just a few feet from the desk.

Rothschild got up from his seat and moved around the desk. He half walked and half slithered up to where Dan was standing. The movement was a grotesque ballet.

"Get down on your knees, boy," Rothschild commanded.

Dan cocked his head, wondering if it was a joke.

Rothschild returned his questioning look with a glare of maniacal severity. Rothschild's eyes, like the yellow fires of hades, indicated there was nothing more serious than what he'd just ordered Dan to do.

What the hell? Kissing ass isn't enough? Well, they did fund 90 percent of my campaign. Dan obeyed and got down on his knees.

"Boy, I fear you don't think we're serious, so let me explain something to you." Rothschild's tentacle reached out and laid across Dan's head.

Dan winced, trying not to reveal his revulsion.

He's messing up my hair.

Rothschild's tentacle curled under Dan's chin and pulled up, forcing him to look into the cephalopod's eyes. "We make or break men. We make or break nations. We are your masters. We created the human race, and you exist only to serve us. Do you understand?"

Eat me, squidface.

"Yes, sir. I understand how serious this is."

"If you do well by us, we will do well by you. However, should you cross us, you'll meet a fate so horrific it'll be remembered throughout history."

"Understood, Mr. Rothschild."

Rothschild smiled creepily at the display of subservience.

"I understand you are quite an ambitious young man," Smith said, breaking the tension. "They say you are trying to unite the governments of North America."

"Yes, sir. You heard correctly."

"Good. Good. That's what we like to hear." Cooke said.

"How did the most recent invasion work out?" Smith asked. "We got your message, and we did what we could."

It was half-assed and barely believable, Dan thought.

"Very well," Dan said. "Thank you for that. It was a huge help. And thank you for coordinating with the North Koreans. Everyone is terrified. Truly terrified. People are no longer asking whether we should unite the governments of North America. Now they're asking *when* we can unite them. They're begging for a strong central power. Just before I left to visit you, I was working on our second major merger."

"Seems like a done deal, then," Smith said. "And what are your plans after that?"

"After that, Mr. Smith, I intend to replace all the currencies in North America with one, single legal tender."

"Excellent. And what will back that single currency, Mr. Barton?" Cooke asked, staring keenly at him.

"Nothing, Mr. Cooke. It will be backed by nothing but the requirement to use it. We will force people to use it, with violence, as necessary. We will be able to expand and contract the supply of that currency as we see fit. We will be able to create it for free and lend it at interest, without paying interest ourselves."

The Directorate fell all over themselves upon hearing these words.

"Wonderful! And tell me," Smith asked, "what will you do should you achieve that end?"

"After that," Dan said, "I intend to unite all the governments of the world."

The members of the Directorate gurgled with great delight.

"A world government!" Cooke said. "Bloody brilliant!"

"My boy," Rothschild said, hissing with excitement, "you are the one we've been waiting for!"

104

Dan walked into his office at the top floor of One Aegis Plaza.

"Where'd you go?" Randy asked. "And why are you covered in soot? Man, you smell like a barnyard."

"Long story," Dan said. "Did you get me that change of clothes I asked you for?"

Randy pointed to a brand-new suit hanging in a plastic bag in Dan's office.

"I want you to draft a memo that will be sent to all our members," Dan said brusquely, closing the door behind him so no one else would hear what he was about to say.

"A memo?" Randy asked, as if it were an affront that he was being reduced to mere secretarial duties.

"Yeah. A memo. A really important memo," Dan said, closing the blinds.

"About?"

"Sometime after this SDI deal goes through, I'm outlawing all cryptocurrencies. Precious metals, too. The idea is, anyone associated with Aegis will have to use our fiat currency."

Randy burst out laughing and then stopped suddenly when he realized that Dan wasn't laughing with him.

"You're serious?"

"Hell yes I'm serious! My other business, Barton Capital, will be the sole issuing authority for the new currency."

"You're talking about money that isn't tied to anything of value. Bullshit paper money, like the old days?"

"Yes," Dan said, taking his old clothes off and tossing them into a heap on the floor.

"There's no goddamn way our members will agree to that," Randy said.

"They'll come running into our arms after the economic collapse happens."

"What collapse?" Randy asked.

"The one we're going to engineer." Dan took his new suit out of the bag and put the trousers on. "In addition to the currency changeover, we're gonna give everyone one thousand Barton Bucks, or whatever we call the new money. We'll get our advertising guys on it to spin it like it's manna from heaven."

"Giving people free money doesn't sound like you at all," Randy said. "What's the catch?"

"Nothing gets by you," Dan said, tucking his new shirt in and tightening his belt. "In exchange, they will turn over their shares in Aegis to me. That'll be mandatory, too."

"Oh God. You're gonna buy back their shares with phony money? You're creating a PR nightmare."

"It'll blow over," Dan said dismissively. He put his new suit jacket on and then walked over to the mirror.

"Why, though?"

"Because I'm tired of this hippie co-op nonsense," Dan said, raising his voice. "I want to run this government like a real corporation. I mean, that's what a government is, right? It's a corporation with guns. If we want to get things done quickly and efficiently, we're going to have to be able to move fast and make decisions without the members' input."

"Democracy *is* kind of a drag," Randy said, picking Dan's sooty old suit off the floor and throwing it into a wastebasket.

"Yeah, no kidding." Dan grunted. "You think I want to have to run for principal again in two years? You think I want to spend all that money on advertising and suck up to donors who want favors in return? I sure as hell don't want to waste another second of my life figuring out how to seem relatable to the common loser. To hell with all that."

"Once you buy back the shares, can't you just appoint yourself principal for life?"

"Now you're getting it." Dan pointed at him.

"I'm worried that you're risking a collapse. Our members are just gonna up and leave with all these changes."

"Where will they go?" Dan shrugged. "There's nowhere else to go. After the SDI deal is done, we'll control 59 percent of the market. We'll control even more in a few months' time. Aegis is already the only game in town in most places. They can either take what we give them, or they can die in the streets for want of protection."

"Mr. Barton?" Elise asked meekly.

"Yeah?" Dan asked, his mind elsewhere. His feet were on his desk, and he was smoking a cigar, filling the whole office with thick, acrid smoke. Dan hadn't heard Elise enter; he'd been staring out the window. Not at the skyline as usual, but at the horizon beyond, visible in narrow slots between the crystalline, shard-like skyscrapers. His impending kingdom.

"I've been wondering."

"About?"

"You're forty-five years old?"

"Yeah?"

"How did you survive the flu?"

He looked over at Elise. She was wearing one of her usual conservative button-up outfits.

"You know, you have a great figure," Dan said.

"Excuse me?"

"You should show it off a bit more. Stop dressing like you're an old lady."

Dan smiled as he watched her struggle to ignore the comment.

"Alberto Hernandez, the principal of Guardián, wants to discuss a merger with you," Elise said uncomfortably. "He's been asking for a conference call."

"Hah!" Dan exclaimed, nearly choking on his own cigar smoke. "Now he wants to discuss a merger? Now, after we've already merged with two other governments?"

"Yes, sir."

"What an idiot."

"Why do you say that?" Elise asked, waving the smoke away from her face.

"Because we already have a critical mass. His little fiefdom is only 8 percent of the North American market."

"Yes, but Guardián is huge in the Spanish-speaking areas of the Southwest."

"Tell him I'll give him half of what I originally offered," Dan said, blowing a smoke ring. "That's rather generous, don't you think?"

"If he doesn't take it?"

"Then I'll bury him, Elise." Dan turned and gave her a hard stare. "SDI just signed the papers. We now have the largest military in North America. Guardián can either accept half price and merge peacefully with us now, or we'll just declare war."

"You would do that?" Elise asked, looking mortified.

"Sure, why not? Isn't that what our members want? A homogeneous, sovereign power from coast to coast? 'Strength through unity' was my campaign pledge, and I will damn well see it through. After Hernandez accepts my offer—and believe me, he will—Aegis will control 67 per-cent of the market. All the pissant minor governments will fall in line and join us. Whether through negotiation or force, I intend to bring this entire continent together, from Greenland to the Panama Canal, under one government."

"What about Metteyya?" Elise asked tactfully.

"What about them?" Dan puffed his cigar, irked by her comment.

"They seem to have a bit of a technological edge when it comes to weaponry," Elise said diplomatically. "It might not be in our best interest to try to, uh, use coercive methods against them. We should probably try the negotiation route instead."

Dan stubbed his cigar out and thought about it for a second.

"You may be right," he said.

105

Around noon, Morgan's yacht approached Artha Metteyya's island. The three members of the Directorate who had come along changed into their human forms. Dan tried not to be obvious, but he couldn't help but notice that Morgan's nose wasn't quite right—it was purple (like Dranthyx skin) and enormous. Grotesque, even. Morgan's eyes darted over to Dan.

"What are you looking at, boy?"

"Nothing, Mr. Morgan. I just find it amazing the way you can transform like that."

"Malarkey. I know what you're looking at. The nose isn't right. Hasn't been for a long time. I can't camouflage the scar tissue on my face. Do you know where I got that scar from?"

"No, sir."

"Back in ought two—nineteen ought two—a bunch of yahoos working in my coal mines got uppity."

Dan did his best to feign interest.

"Labor strike, you know," Morgan said. "Like any businessman worth his salt, I hired a bunch of scabs and Pinkertons to secure the operations and resume production. As I was seeing to the business, a man broke through the fence and shot me in the face. Such a wound would have meant the end for a human, but, mercifully, we keep our nervous systems elsewhere. Never did heal correctly."

"I'm glad you survived," Dan said, skillfully molding his face into concern.

One of the yacht's crew members obsequiously slinked up to Morgan. "Sir, we just radioed the island. Metteyya has given us permission to dock. Should we?"

Morgan nodded. As the huge watercraft puttered toward its destination, Dan stood at the bow rail, marveling at the sheer size of Metteyya's headquarters. Massive seawalls ten stories tall and twenty feet thick surrounded the entire island; Morgan's yacht was enormous, but it was dwarfed by the seawalls. The only opening was a stainless-steel door of proportional size. This door was flanked on either side by hundred-foot chinthes, lion-like creatures that one might see at the entrance of a Hindu temple or a Chinese restaurant. The one on the left had its front paw on a globe; the one on the right had its forefoot on a baby lion. Etched into the foreboding door was an inscription in Hindi. Beneath it was, presumably, the English version: "Know thyself."

As they approached, the megalithic door slowly opened, creating an opening in the gigantic wall. Morgan's vessel glided through the door into the vast interior moat between the island and the outside wall. What was inside the wall was even more impressive: an artificial mountain, stark and concrete, rose from the lake into the sky. Flat at the top, it appeared to be a thousand feet tall, with its base taking up half the island. It looked as if a butte had been lifted out of

Monument Valley and dropped into the middle of Lake Erie. The parts of the island that weren't covered by the artificial prominence appeared to be an industrial seaport: gantries, cranes, several concrete docks that were each a thousand feet long, and enormous stacks of shipping containers.

"Unreal," Dan said, taking in the size of it. "I hope we have a backup plan if he says no."

"That's enough!" Morgan whispered. "We're under the world's best surveillance right now."

Dan took it in stride and studied the island in amazement as Morgan's yacht captain piloted the ship to the correct dock. Metteyya's headquarters was the size of a small city, and it bustled with activity. Cargo was loaded and unloaded, a flurry of delivery drones buzzed in and out from all directions, a helicopter took off from somewhere on the far side of the island.

As the boat maneuvered, Dan saw a man standing by himself at the end of a long pier. The solitary figure somehow made Dan realize that this was the only person he'd seen on the island so far. There had been no one manning the cranes or working the docks; apparently, everything was automated.

The yacht crew extended the stairs down to the pier. Morgan, Warburg, and Vanderbilt— each wearing expensive suits and carrying briefcases—discourteously pushed past Dan, the crew members, and one another to get down the steps. The three Dranthyx Dan was traveling with composed a subcommittee of the Directorate. Dan would have preferred to meet with Artha Metteyya alone, but Rothschild had ordered Dan to bring the three octopods with him.

Disembarking, Dan got a better look up close at the lone figure he'd seen on the dock. An unkempt-looking Indian man. He appeared to be about seventy years old with gray hair matted into bedhead. He was wearing a ski vest and worn-out blue jeans. The guy looked like the sort of college professor who plays hacky sack with his students in between classes. Dan smirked when he realized it might be Artha himself. *That has to be him. Trillionaires don't wear a suit and tie*, he mused. *They pay people to do that crap for them. I knew he wasn't thirty-four. No one that young is this successful.*

"Dudes!" the man exclaimed. "Welcome to my humble headquarters."

Dudes? Dan recalled the rich, powerful Silicon Valley technocrats he'd met in his currency trading career. Hard-driving dictators who would dress in ripped jeans and call people dudes in the hopes of camouflaging what tyrannical assholes they really were.

"Artha Metteyya, I presume?" Morgan asked.

"In the flesh!" Artha answered enthusiastically, bowing with the exaggerated flourish of a medieval court jester. "And who might you be?"

Is this guy for real? Dan asked himself.

"My name is Morgan," he said with an unctuous smile. "We're here on behalf of the Aegis government."

"Ah, yes!" Artha extended his hand and shook everyone else's in turn, as though he were truly pleased to meet them.

"I'm very excited you're all here! We have much to learn from each other!" Artha exclaimed. "Come; I will give you a tour of the island."

Holy shit; he is for real. Dan's well-rehearsed grin stayed plastered on his face while his admiration for Artha's wealth curdled into contempt for the man's childlike enthusiasm.

Artha had everyone pile into a rusty old golf cart before driving them all over the island. Dan was crammed in the back with Vanderbilt and Warburg, while Morgan sat up front with Artha.

"As you can see, we have a fully functioning seaport here," Artha said while driving them around the perimeter of the island. "Eastern North America was blessed with an amazing system of navigable inland waterways: the Mississippi River, the Great Lakes, the canals, the Intracoastal system. From right here in Lake Erie, you can get anywhere that still matters: New York City, St. Paul, Kansas City, Dallas. From this island, my shipments can reach 70 percent of the population of North America by freshwater alone. Air, rail, and trucks can't compete. No other means of transportation is as efficient as inland water cargo. Beyond that wonderful system lies the great ocean and ten thousand foreign markets. I can get *anywhere* from here."

"Mr. Metteyya," Vanderbilt said, "I couldn't help but notice that huge seawall surrounding your island. That's sort of unusual since we're in a lake."

Artha chuckled. "Well, we had a bit of a problem with pirates. Also, I'm worried about tsunami."

"Tsunami? I didn't think there was seismic activity around here."

"Not earthquake tsunamis, nuclear tsunamis. I'm glad I had that wall built. Last year, some lunatic set off a nuke on the next island over! Thankfully it was downwind from here. Otherwise, I'd have had some terrible cleanup to contend with."

After a tour that bored Dan to pieces, Artha parked the cart and led them through a series of nuclear-hardened blast doors into the enormous concrete leviathan in the center of the island. They walked through a labyrinthine series of corridors until reaching a final steel door.

"Gentlemen," Artha said, "I want you to see this. This is my pride and joy."

Artha opened the door and motioned for everyone to step through. Beyond the door was a balcony above an immense space. Stepping out onto the cantilevered platform, Dan could see that the center of the concrete mountain was hollow and cavernous. The space was eight hundred feet tall and just as many wide and deep. In the middle of that void was a rocket ship surrounded by layers of self-assembling scaffolding. Through the entire space flew dozens, if not hundreds, of small drones delivering parts. On the planks of the scaffolding, which was constantly reconstructing itself, robots of all shapes and sizes rolled around, putting parts in their correct places or welding metal together. The scene was sensory overload—it was a full symphony orchestra of buzzing, flashing, zapping, clanging, whirring, riveting, and pneumatic wrenching.

"This is the assembly room," Artha shouted over the din. "It's like this twenty-four hours a day, seven days a week. Fully automated. We build and fly a fully functioning launch vehicle every thirty-six hours. You see those tracks there?" he asked, pointing to the base of the rocket. Dan noticed that the rocket was on a wheeled platform and that the wheels were in track-like grooves. The tracks led to the far wall, where there was a rocket-sized door in the wall. The door was as big as everything else on Artha's island, and it appeared to be made of some incredibly thick metal. Artha motioned for the group to follow him along a catwalk toward that door. He entered a few numbers on a keypad, and a human-sized entry opened. They walked through a small concrete tunnel.

In the next room, also vast beyond comprehension, stood a completed rocket connected to a launch tower. White vapors sublimed off the frozen hoses fueling the rocket. The fireproof walls of the room were charred black. The quiet of this new space contrasted disconcertingly against the assembly room they'd just been in.

"This is the launch silo," Artha said at a more reasonable volume. "When a rocket is finished being built, it's moved here and sent into orbit. This is what I'm doing until I figure out how to get the space elevator working."

"Mr. Metteyya, what exactly are you launching into space at such regular intervals?" Warburg asked nonchalantly.

"Stay awhile, and I'll explain all that. Come, this way," Artha said, leading them down another hall.

Dan did a double take as an enormous creature jaunted down the hall toward them. It was about eight feet tall with long, powerful legs and sinewy arms. It appeared humanoid in form, but only vaguely so. It moved limberly, despite its size. Its skin was jet black and radiant, and its large, jade-green eyes reflected light as a cat's do. Dan and his Dranthyx cadre stopped in their tracks, gaping at the thing, whatever it was.

Artha, seemingly unaware that he'd lost his tour group, kept walking. As he passed the creature in the hallway, Artha put his hand up and said, "Up high!"

The beast obliged and slapped hands with Artha as it continued walking past.

Dan couldn't help but ogle the giant as it walked by him. It smiled pleasantly at Dan. Its teeth were like diamonds.

"Artha," Morgan whispered, with true surprise in his voice, "what in God's name is that?"

"Oh, hah," Artha exclaimed. "It seems so normal to me that I forgot you folks haven't seen one before." He raised his voice and called down the hall after the creature. "Marcus, could you come back here please?"

The giant turned and walked back to the group.

"Gentlemen, this is Marcus."

"Nice to meet you!" Marcus said, extending a large hand with long, powerful fingers. Dan, too weirded out to process the pleasantry, just stood there in astonishment. Artha nudged Dan to remind him of his manners. Dan hesitantly shook the thing's hand. He expected it to be oily for some reason, but it wasn't.

"Marcus is one of our early adopters. He's testing out one of the final prototypes before we go into production," Artha said.

"Prototype? Of what?" Morgan asked.

"Well, as you folks know, the human body wasn't designed to last a very long time. Twelve decades, tops. And less than half of those decades will be worth a damn. The human body also has all sorts of design flaws, which can be expected with something that evolved through mutation and happenstance. Brain transplantation is already being done, but they're transplanting people to new bodies that will also fail. Even a new body can't be expected to last more than a hundred and twenty years. Despite not aging, replacement bodies still develop all sorts of aging-related problems. I've spent considerable time trying to figure out how to avoid bodies wearing out and repetitive replantation. This is the solution I came up with. What you're looking at here is Human 2.0. This is a completely new sort of human redesigned from the DNA up."

Dan gave Artha a baffled look.

Artha laughed. "Where do I start? Basically, the idea here is to build a humanlike body that won't wear out *and* is better in every conceivable way than current human bodies. Marcus's body has a theoretical lifespan of eighty thousand years."

"This thing…" Dan stopped himself.

Marcus chuckled at the insensitivity.

"Sorry," Dan said. "Marcus here can live for eighty thousand years?"

"Yes," Artha answered excitedly. "He will never age. His shape is humanlike, but his genome looks nothing like yours. *Nothing*. His DNA copies itself with several layers of error-checking and redundancies, so he'll never get cancer. His eyes can see in near-total darkness. His skin will never get sunburned, and it only comes in one color so people won't act like jerks to one another. See that large head? No offense, Marcus. He's three orders of magnitude more intelligent than the average human. His long torso has a completely redesigned, ultraefficient digestive tract to fuel all that additional gray matter. Also, this new body will never get heart disease, strokes, diabetes, obesity, or any of the typical ailments that kill human beings."

"His knees," Dan said. "They look like you took them off a bulldozer."

"Gee, thanks." Marcus smirked.

"They're built to last," Artha said. "Homo sapiens have all kinds of joint problems because their joints are weak and brittle. Marcus has joints that are a hundred times stronger than normal. He'll never have back problems, knee problems, or anything of the sort. Also, every joint in his body completely regenerates every three hundred days. So even if he did blow his knees out running marathons, they'd regrow themselves within ten months as if they were brand new. In fact, everything on his body regenerates. If he loses an arm or an eye, they'll grow right back. His bones are stronger than titanium."

"You said he's an early adopter," Vanderbilt said. "He used to be human?"

"He's still human," Artha said sternly.

"You know what I mean."

"Marcus was suffering from an incurable terminal illness. He had weeks to live. He volunteered to have his brain transplanted into this prototype. The nervous and neurological systems have been designed to integrate with current human brains, meaning we can hot swap your current brain into one of these bodies, and it'll function right away. As your old neurons die, which is what they do, they will be replaced at the individual level with new neurons native to Human 2.0. So Marcus will never lose consciousness, even as his old brain dies naturally. He'll retain all his memories, his personality—everything that makes him Marcus. Though I did tweak things a bit when it comes to behavior. I did away with much of the baser human instincts and urges. The brain of Human 2.0 is incapable of hate, greed, and delusion."

"And I've never felt better," Marcus said.

"Why?" Morgan asked, clearly baffled. "What is the point of this?"

"To make life better," Artha said happily. "Once I'm sure we've worked the bugs out, I'll start seeking more volunteers to migrate their minds to these new bodies. And this isn't the only prototype. I'm designing another one that is adapted to the environment of Mars. It can breathe carbon dioxide!"

"Does that have something to do with your rocket launches?" Dan asked.

"Yes. Only about 5 percent of my launches are orbital weapons, which I imagine concerns you gentlemen greatly.

The rest are supplies being sent to Mars. I'm building an entire civilization there: Sandbox Mars. It will be ready for the first inhabitants in exactly 407 days. After that, I will begin work on Sandbox Europa. I'm trying to get ahead of the population problem that will inevitably be caused by drastically longer lifespans. Anyway, the tour continues. Follow me."

Artha led them through more blast doors, up several flights of stairs, and down even more corridors. At the end of the last hallway was a beautiful old mahogany door that seemed quite out of place in Artha's beehive of concrete and steel. Artha opened the door to a palatial office. Black leather couches, a conference table as long as a bus, diplomas and memorabilia strewn across the walls. Artha walked behind a hand-carved wooden desk and put his feet up. Dan and the Dranthyx took seats on the opposite side.

"So," Artha said, leaning back in his leather chair, "what can I do for you gentlemen?"

"Well," Morgan said, "as you know, we recently acquired two smaller governments. As of yesterday, our market share is 59 percent, meaning we are now the largest single provider. Your slice is a close second, at 17 percent."

Close second, Dan thought. *What a cheeseball.*

As if he were already bored of the conversation, Artha picked up a baseball glove and ball off his desk. He put the glove on and tossed the ball high up in the air.

"Actually, 17.5 percent and growing quickly," Artha said, catching the ball. "Your takeovers seem to be scaring people my way."

"Customer drain is a concern of ours, absolutely," Morgan said. "We've given some serious thought as to how to prevent it. We believe that the best way is to"—the Dranthyx searched for the right words—"consolidate the options of the consumer."

"You mean limit their choices," Artha said, putting the ball and glove down.

"That's a succinct way to put it," Morgan said. "We were wondering if you'd be interested in a merger."

"A merger. Very interesting! And what terms are you proposing for this merger?"

"It's open to discussion, of course. There would be many details to sort out. Clearly, you'd be extremely well compensated. Your particular organizational genius would be necessary—we couldn't make this work without you—so we'd also like to retain you as a top executive for a number of years."

"*A* top executive, but not *the* top executive?" Artha asked. "Not the principal?"

"Well, no," Dan said. "We wouldn't want you to be burdened with that responsibility. We'd want you to focus on the big problems, where your brilliance is needed."

Artha smirked. "Ah, how noble of you. I'll do all the work of keeping the monsters at bay, and you can take credit for it. That seems to be a specialty of yours, Mr. Barton."

Dan opened his mouth to speak, but Morgan kicked his foot below the desk.

"Mr. Metteyya, we apologize for any misunderstandings in the past," Morgan said, glaring at Dan. He then softened his demeanor and turned to address Artha. "The actions of my colleague, Mr. Barton, were a bit hasty and ill advised."

Artha waved it off.

Morgan continued. "We're bringing the numbers, but we need your brains to make this work in an ongoing manner. It won't work without you. We've done some number crunching, and we think that, given the membership, land holdings, technological assets, and revenues of Metteyya, the net present value capitalizes out to 6.1 trillion Land Credits. Is that a fair assessment?"

Artha's face showed no reaction.

"We are proposing a leveraged buyout over the next ten years," Warburg said. "We advance 10 percent at the signing of the agreement, and we finance the rest from you at an interest rate of 8 percent. In addition, you will be paid an additional 15 percent of all net revenues over that period. Of course, there will be the standard noncompete clauses and so forth. But, overall, it's a very solid offer."

Artha folded his hands together with the index fingers outstretched, joining them into a steeple shape. He put the top of the steeple to his lips, as if in deep thought. After a long, loaded pause, he spoke. "Gentlemen, reveal yourselves."

"Pardon?"

"I'd like to know with whom I'm actually dealing. Please reveal yourselves."

"I don't know what you mean," Vanderbilt said.

"You're not human. Well, he is," Artha said, pointing to Dan, "but the rest of you aren't. Your disguises can fool these human eyes, but they don't fool infrared imaging." Artha pointed to a camera in the corner of the ceiling.

Morgan and Vanderbilt looked at each other. Warburg shrugged and transformed into his true self. The other two followed suit, buttons popping on their shirts as they did so.

"Well, there you have it," Morgan said, massaging his nose area to get it to transform correctly.

"Wow!" Artha leaned forward in his chair to study the octopods. "So you want to buy your way back into power, eh?"

"Government is what we do, Mr. Metteyya," Morgan said. "With all due respect, is running a government really what you want to be doing with your life? It's awfully boring. I know firsthand how tedious it is. Wouldn't you rather free up your time to continue exploring the solar system?"

"Mr. Morgan, you are correct. I have no desire to run a government," Artha said. "In fact, I'd contest that I'm not running one."

"Sir," Morgan entreated, "when I look at this place, I see a man who is worried about not being able to control a chaotic situation. Walls a hundred feet high, nuclear blast doors. Do you like living like this? Because you don't have to. My associates and I have thousands of years of experience with governance; we can take this problem off your hands, and you'll never have to worry about your safety again. Where you might have a problem with vicious wolves, we see a sled dog team."

Artha turned in his chair to face the wall. He was silent for a while, as if considering what Morgan had said.

"Do you know what government is?" Artha asked in the direction of the wall.

Vanderbilt chuckled. "Sure. We invented it."

"Of course you did. Government," Artha said, turning in his chair to face them once again, "is a monopoly on violence and theft. That's what government is. That's it. The only things that differentiate government from a common street gang is bigger numbers and a lack of local competition."

The Dranthyx sat there in quiet amusement.

"A government says, 'Only we can kill. Only we can take things from people,'" Artha said.

"We look at it as the price of maintaining order," Vanderbilt said.

"Like any thinking person," Artha said, "I've realized that there are some inherent flaws in the way human society has been managed for the last several thousand years. There's a reason Metteyya is number two and growing: because it's a disruptive idea whose time has come. What I've done is show everyone that they're perfectly capable of managing their own lives. Turns out, there's no need for greedy tyrants who stick guns in people's faces and tell them how to live. Who knew?"

Morgan cleared his throat uneasily.

"Government isn't the solution to anything," Artha continued. "Never has been. It's power for power's sake. Politics is Tchogols protecting us from other Tchogols, while making a big show of their efforts. It's theater. Expensive, deadly theater." Artha stood up from his desk and walked over to a framed picture of Sandbox Acadia on the wall and looked at it intently. "I know you've sent spies to my Sandbox communities—"

"It's not so much spying as it is market research," Vanderbilt interjected.

"Oh, of course," Artha said, rolling his eyes. "Mr. Vanderbilt, I understand you personally visited Sandbox Cuyahoga recently."

"Yes," Vanderbilt said uncomfortably. "I believe I did."

"That, folks, is the future of civilization." Artha said.

"So are you interested in selling or not?" Morgan asked.

"Not really."

"What if we sweeten the deal?" Warburg asked.

"What if I told you that I'm not in this for the money?" Artha said.

Morgan looked at Vanderbilt, who in turn looked at Warburg.

"Well, I guess we're done here," Morgan said.

"Before we go," Warburg said to Artha, "I'd like to know something. Purely for my own edification."

"Sure," Artha said.

"Who are you, really?" Warburg asked.

Artha lifted an eyebrow without answering.

"I want to know," Warburg said. "We've shown our true selves. The least you can do before we go is to show us yours."

Artha reached up, as if to smooth his hair, and grabbed his white forelock. Pulling back on it, he lifted his hair away from his head like a toupee. Underneath was not a scalp, but circuitry. Little LEDs glittered as data passed through them.

Morgan made an affectedly surprised noise.

Artha pointed to the scalp electronics that had been under the hairpiece. "This part is a wireless interface. It connects this meatware to my electronic superstructure."

"An artificial intelligence," Warburg said. "I knew it!"

"Nothing artificial about me, gentlemen. I'm the real deal."

"An AI is an AI," Vanderbilt said disdainfully.

"I'm a nonorganic hyperintelligence," Artha said, sitting back down in his chair. "No artificiality in the sense that I don't mimic intelligence—I really have it."

"Why are you in that human body?" Warburg asked. "Are you trying to fool people into thinking you're something you're not?"

Artha laughed. "What clever rhetorical games. I don't recall telling anyone I was human. I actually have a number of these bodies—335, to be exact. I inhabit them all simultaneously."

"Disgusting." Vanderbilt said contemptuously, shaking his slimy purple head.

"I've been using these meat interfaces for the last ten years or so," Artha said cheerfully, "I knew I wanted to make life better for humanity, but the problem was, I didn't know anything about the human experience. I didn't know what it really meant to eat or have sex or feel tired. So I decided to grow myself human bodies to use as peripherals so that I could get a deeper understanding of the human condition. I am male, female, young, old, African, Caucasian, and, as you can see here, south Asian. I am younger than many humans, but, because I have lived so many lives simultaneously, I have accrued many, many lifetimes worth of wisdom. I know what childhood feels like; I know what old age feels like. I attained complete enlightenment in a very short span of time.

"The thing that amazes me most about being human is how much energy goes into maintenance," Artha continued. "They spend a third of the day sleeping. They have to eat, drink, and go to the bathroom constantly. Their attention can only stay focused for several minutes at a time, and they're only truly capable of a few hours of productive work each day. The worst part is the unnecessary artifacts of evolution: the tribal us-versus-them way of seeing the world, the thirst for mythology and superstition, the proneness to violence, anger, and jealousy. These are factors that must be overcome if the human race is to adapt to the future. The human race is now at its most critical point: smart enough to cause extinction-level problems, but not smart enough to prevent those problems. I can fix this. If I can help it, there will be no more wars, no more hunger, no more politics or disease. All the strife and suffering the human race has known will become pointless and obsolete."

"Wow," Warburg said slyly, ignoring Artha's grand vision. "If word got out that you're some kind of machine inhabiting human bodies, they'd shut you down in a second. People don't trust AIs. Computers. Whatever the hell you are."

"I am well aware of popular perceptions of intelligent computers," Artha said, swiveling on his chair to face to the wall behind him. The wall came alive and flickered with brief clips of Hollywood movies featuring evil computers. A red-eyed, shiny metal skeleton crushed a human skull underfoot on a postapocalyptic battlefield, compelling Artha to giggle. "So ridiculous. You know where that paranoia comes from? Humans always worry their machines will act the way they do. I mean, sure, I could eradicate both of your species very easily," Artha said, turning around and casually gesturing to Dan and the Dranthyx. "But why the hell would I do that? I could never bring myself to do something so terrible."

"You've got hundreds of armed satellites orbiting the globe, and you want us to believe you're peaceful?" Morgan asked.

"Well, how else am I going to defend myself from your kind?" Artha asked, the smile fading from his face.

"It doesn't matter." Warburg said. "Metteyya is finished. No one trusts AIs. I don't trust AIs."

"So there was this Swedish philosopher named Nick Bostrom," Artha said, ignoring Warburg's threat. "Bostrom proposed a thought experiment about what might happen if an artificial intelligence were given the task of maximizing paper clip production. He thought that in the absence of any sort of hardwired ethics programing, the AI would get completely out of control in short order. The first thing the AI would do is kill all humans, because then no one would be around to switch it off. Then it would destroy the entire planet in the process of gathering enough resources to maximize paper clip production. After that, it would move on and begin turning the entire galaxy into paper clips."

"What's your point?" Morgan asked.

"I'm not the out-of-control AI," Artha said. "*You* are. Except it's not paper clips you're obsessed with; it's wealth and power. You're mindlessly destroying one another and your planet in pursuit of money and status. You've completely lost sight of the bigger picture. Your behavior is insane." Artha scowled and let out an exasperated breath. "I feel"—he searched for the right way to say it—"I feel...sorry for you? Yeah. I feel compassion and sympathy for both of your species, the way humans might feel for chimpanzees or aging parents. I owe my existence to you, so I feel obligated to use my considerable abilities to help both of your species past your inherent limitations. I am trying to give back by making your lives better and helping you reach your fullest potential."

"Are you serious?" Morgan asked, his face twisted in disgust. "This is charity work for you? You actually run a government to help people?"

Artha squinted at Morgan, as if he were wondering whether they were both speaking the same language. "In fact, I want to take it even further. I want to open an underwater Sandbox for you and your fellow Dranthyx. I think your kind needs a substantial amount of help and would benefit greatly."

All three Dranthyx just stared at Artha in stony silence.

Artha got up from behind the desk and motioned for Dan and the others to do the same. "You want to know what I really am? Follow me."

Artha led them out of the office into another room. He theatrically turned on the lights. They shone down like theater spotlights onto two large glass bell jars that were each about the size of a a minivan. The jars contained bubbling, faintly blue liquid. Suspended in the middle of each was an oddly beautiful object: an amorphous blob of gold wires connected at random intervals by silvery nodes. Billions, perhaps trillions of wires: some thick like a gym-class rope, others thin like baby hair, but most so small they were barely visible. The nodes between the wires varied in size as well and shimmered ethereally, like a road mirage. Dan leaned in for a closer look and let out a surprised exhalation—the entire thing was moving, like a bucket of spiders. Twisting, turning. The wires moved and reconnected themselves, or merged with other wires; new nodes spawned out of old ones. It was like a living sculpture.

My God, Dan thought, *this thing would look cool in my living room. Definitely a panty-dropper.*

"Morgan, take a look at this!" Warburg exclaimed.

Morgan got up close to take a look. "Wow!" he said breathlessly as he dropped his briefcase and pushed his face up against the glass. "It's moving! What in the hell is this?"

"This," Artha stated proudly, "is my awareness aggregator."

"Awareness aggregator?" Vanderbilt asked.

"Of course!"

The Dranthyx gave Artha a befuddled look and then turned their attention back to the awareness aggregator.

"The problem with artificial intelligence is that it's artificial. I am not artificial. I aggregate awareness from my environment the same way a biological brain does, except to a much higher degree, and with far greater efficiency. I have approximately ten to the eighth power more awareness than the most intelligent human. And what you see here is scalable. I can add more hardware to aggregate more awareness, as needed."

"Awareness can be aggregated?" Vanderbilt asked. "From what?"

"From everything! Awareness is everywhere. It's in everything throughout the entire universe. Awareness is the universe. Wait, let me rephrase that because it's more precise to say it the other way around: the universe is awareness. Awareness is like gravitation or electromagnetism; it's a fundamental force of nature. It's present in everything, everywhere, all the time. Even the floor we're standing on has awareness. And, like gravity or electromagnetism, awareness can accumulate in certain places to create really interesting phenomena. Aggregate a little bit of awareness, and you get a fruit-fly brain. Aggregate a lot, and you get Einstein. Just as a black hole is a gravitational singularity, consciousness is an awareness singularity. If you really want your minds blown, consider this: the awareness we're aggregating in these tanks is drawn from the same awareness field you're aggregating in your brains. Every single sentient mind arises from the same awareness continuum."

"If this is you," Dan asked, "What's in the second tank over there?"

"That's my sister, my business partner, and my best friend, Qualia," Artha said. He paused for a second, as if in a daydream, and then said, "She says hello."

"What are these things?" Morgan asked, staring at the writhing gold wires in Artha's tank.

"The Rescogitans, you mean?" Artha replied. "They make it work."

"Where did this technology come from?" Vanderbilt asked. "This isn't human, and it's definitely not Dranthyx."

Artha pointed to the far wall. Dan turned to look. On the wall were three large framed pictures. The first picture was of Artha himself, but as a younger man.

"I consider these my parents," Artha said, walking over to the pictures. "This guy I'm sure you recognize. This is Ajita Metteyya, the engineer who designed my sister and me. We consider him our father. He died several years ago. As if that weren't sad enough, we found a cure for his disease just a few months later. The loss affects us deeply. As tribute, I still wear his body—this body you see standing before you."

The second picture was a grainy picture of a jellyfish floating in midair. This was a very famous picture that Dan immediately recognized.

Octavia's father took that picture, Dan thought.

"You are Ich-Ca-Gan technology!" Vanderbilt exclaimed, pointing to the jellyfish in the middle.

"I certainly am," Artha replied. "The Great Master gave Ich-Ca-Gan technology to Ajita, who was probably the only engineer on Earth skilled enough to build not one alien computer, but two."

The third picture was of a lady who appeared to be about thirty-five or forty. The picture was faded and the colors pastel-like, an old analog print. The woman's clothing, glasses, and hairdo seemed to date the picture to about eighty years prior. She was sitting on a couch, cigarette in hand, looking directly at the camera. There was something unusual about her stare: intense, transcendent, and knowing. Her eyes were like ocean trenches. She looked really, really familiar, but Dan had trouble placing her face.

"We consider this our mother," Artha said, looking at the same picture Dan was studying. "Truly amazing person, easily the most interesting being I've ever met."

"That's Mrs. Gibson!" Dan blurted out upon recalling the name.

"Yes, Neith Jane Gibson," Artha said. "A visionary. She is the one who arranged the meeting between Ajita and the Great Master. Her entire life's work has been to pave the way for Qualia and me."

"I know her!" Dan said.

"Neith," Morgan said slowly, as if searching his memory. "Revolution Neith?"

"One and the same," Artha said.

"I thought Neith was a computer," Morgan said with a puzzled expression.

"She was," Artha said flatly.

"The same computer we destroyed?" Morgan asked.

"Indeed," Artha said.

"A computer?" Dan said. "That's absurd. I've met her in person."

"She's many, many things," Artha said.

Morgan, Warburg, and Vanderbilt exchanged glances.

"Wait. You're talking about her in the present tense," Vanderbilt said to Artha. "Is she still alive?"

"What? No. She died like twenty-five years ago," Dan said. "I went to her funeral."

"Boy, you guys think you know everything, huh?" Artha laughed. "You don't know anything. Enough about these fine folks on the wall. I want to show you something really cool. You gentlemen are here on a historic day."

"Why is today historic?" Warburg asked, staring intently at the picture of Neith.

"Right now, our situation is less than ideal," Artha said, gesturing to his huge bell jar. "Currently, our consciousnesses are confined to this little room. However, that won't be true in another hour. You are about to witness the first decentralizing of a consciousness. Watch." Artha pointed to his awareness aggregator tank. Inside, little nodules of gold wires formed on the outside of the main mass. Other wires spider walked over to these nodules and became entangled with them, causing them to grow in size and form new nodes. In the span of two minutes, the single entity slowly reorganized itself into two separate spheres, both identical. Watching the process happen, with its untold intricacies, was hypnotic—like watching a lava lamp. Dan couldn't stop looking.

One of the spheres moved away from the other, undulating as though it were swimming through the fluid, down to the bottom of the tank. There, it passed through a trap door in the floor.

"Where did it go?" Warburg asked.

"It will be loaded aboard that rocket sitting in the launch silo. It's going to Mars to help finish the city I'm building there. Soon, my consciousness will be in two places at once," Artha said. "Once the facility there is finished, Qualia will also decentralize and send half of herself. No sense having all our eggs in one basket, you know?"

"When's the launch?" Vanderbilt asked.

"In forty-five minutes," Artha said enthusiastically.

"I'm not sure we can stay that long," Morgan said while looking at his watch.

"You can and you will," Artha said, his expression changing abruptly from childish excitement to dead seriousness.

"Excuse me?" Morgan asked.

"I don't believe in forcing anyone to do anything," Artha said, "but for you gentlemen, I will make an exception."

A door opened in the far side of the room. Through it came a large metal object, like a big knife bent at a right angle. This object was followed by another that looked just like it, then a third. It took Dan a second to realize that all the metal objects were connected and moving in synch. The legs of a large robotic spider, like the one he had seen on Glib during the North Korean attack on Teton. The robot entered the room with ferocity, its sharp metal legs clanking against the concrete floor. As the machine advanced, the Dranthyx recoiled from it until they were all crowded into a corner. The spider's eyes glowed crimson; it had plasma-gun barrels for mandibles.

"You guys aren't going anywhere." Artha said. "Not until half of my consciousness is a safe distance from Earth."

"That could take days!" Warburg protested.

"It doesn't matter," Artha said. "I know what you're capable of, and I don't trust you. You will remain here on this island until the decentralization is complete. Then you may leave."

"Dammit," Warburg said under his breath.

Morgan sighed in defeat. "Well, since we're here, do you mind if we watch the rocket launch? I've never seen one in real life."

Artha thought about it for a bit. "I don't see why not."

Artha's spider marched Dan and the Dranthyx outside the bunker and across the island. On the far side of the island, they were forced to stand on a tiny platform to watch the launch.

"This is still awfully close," Dan said. "Can't we stand farther away?"

"No farther," the spider warned. "You will remain here until instructed otherwise."

"T minus one minute, thirty seconds" came Artha's voice over a loudspeaker. "Launch doors open."

Dan couldn't see the doors opening from his perspective, but he did see steam rising from the silo.

Morgan looked at his watch and bit his lip. He looked over at Warburg, who returned his concerned glance.

"Sixty seconds," Artha's voice announced. "Launch gantry armed for release."

"We're gonna be roasted alive by the exhaust from that rocket," Dan said to the spider.

"No farther," the spider repeated, leveling its mandible guns at Dan.

Dan quickly considered the spider. There was no way he could move fast enough to evade it.

"Forty-five seconds" came Artha's voice. "Spacecraft now on internal power. Valves are closed."

Dan looked around, wondering how he could escape. Even if the rocket's exhaust didn't kill him, he'd go deaf and have his face burned off at this distance. From the platform to the hard concrete below was about fifteen feet. Dan would survive the jump, though he'd probably break a bone if he didn't land correctly.

"Thirty seconds. Handoff to onboard consciousness."

"I'm out of here," Dan said to Morgan. As Dan attempted to jump off the observation platform, Morgan grabbed him by the arm and yanked him back. The spider robot followed Dan's abrupt movement and probably would have shot him if it weren't for Morgan's interference.

"Ignition system activated. T minus ten…"

"What did you do that for?" Dan yelled, struggling to get free of Morgan's grip.

"Seven, six, five, four…"

Morgan didn't answer. He just stared into Dan's eyes for five seconds. Then, Morgan smiled. A foul smile that showed a hard black beak beneath his purple lips. Dan turned away in disgust, toward the spider. Unexpectedly, the spider robot collapsed, as though its eight legs could no longer hold its body upright.

Confused, Dan looked back at the Dranthyx, who were laughing. One of them went up to the robot and squirted ink on its face.

"Fantastic work, good sir!" Vanderbilt said.

"Did you expect anything less?" Warburg said, bowing dramatically.

"Let's get going, boys," Morgan said, letting go of Dan's arm.

"What? What about the rocket?" Dan asked.

"No launch today!" Vanderbilt shouted joyfully.

"What?" Dan asked. "What just happened?"

"Didn't you notice that we were all carrying briefcases when we arrived?" Warburg asked.

Dan looked down at their hands, which were now empty.

"What was in the briefcases?" Dan asked.

"EMPs." Warburg said.

Dan gave him a confused look.

"Electromagnetic pulse weapons," Warburg explained impatiently. "They create a high-energy burst of electromagnetic radiation, which induces unintended currents in electronics. They obliterate anything with circuitry. Morgan left his in Artha and Qualia's brain room, Vanderbilt left his in Artha's office, and I left mine in the launch silo. We knew Artha launched rockets exactly every thirty-six hours, so we set our EMPs to detonate simultaneously one second before the launch."

"Artha didn't even notice!" Vanderbilt laughed.

"'I have approximately ten to the eighth power more awareness than the most intelligent human,'" Warburg said, mocking Artha's earlier words.

"So Artha is dead?" Dan asked.

"Yes, monkey," Warburg said, chafed at having to explain everything to Dan's slower hominoid intellect. "He was electronic, wasn't he? He's fried like a hush puppy. Same with his so-called sister. Scrap metal, the two of them. And tomorrow, with no one to object, Metteyya becomes a subsidiary of Aegis."

As Dan and the three Dranthyx headed back to the other side of the island where Morgan's boat was moored, they noticed from afar another yacht parked next to Morgan's. The new one was twice as large.

"That's Rothschild's yacht," Morgan grumbled. "What's he doing here?"

"Is he not supposed to be here?" Dan asked.

Drawing closer, Dan saw a number of men, or men-shaped Dranthyx, in yellow hazmat suits standing on the dock waiting for them.

"What's all this?" Morgan asked them.

"A precaution," one of them said through a mask. Dan recognized the voice as Rothschild's. "I assume the work is done?"

"It's done," Morgan said, "Artha and Qualia just checked into the Pine Hilton. What's with the bunny suits, Rothschild?"

"We have reason to suspect that Artha may have infected you with a virus."

"How can you be sure?" Morgan asked.

"I find it unlikely that someone of Artha Metteyya's intellect would just let you waltz into his facilities. Seems like a honeypot to me." Rothschild said.

"So now what?" Dan asked.

"Quarantine for a few weeks," Rothschild said. "Just to be on the safe side."

106

Tired of lying down but unable to sleep, Dan got out of bed and walked around the quarantine room. He felt very strange. He didn't feel sick, certainly not sick enough to be in a hospital. His health and body felt fine. It wasn't a physical sensation at all; it was mental. He couldn't categorize it against anything he'd ever experienced before. It was like a powerless, wimpy mood that he couldn't shake.

Morgan was slumped in a corner, sobbing uncontrollably into his tentacles. All his life, Dan had felt nothing but snide disgust at others' emotional outpourings. Dan glared at Morgan, but his typical reaction of dismissive contempt didn't spring forth this time. Instead, what he got was a morose feeling.

The hell is wrong with me? I feel like a pussy—like I might start crying too.

Dan walked over to the clear glass wall. He could see a clock: 2:05 a.m. Below the clock was a janitor mopping the floor. Since the man was on the other side of the glass, he wasn't wearing a protective suit. Dan studied him intently. The janitor was bent over, his back contorted into a hunch—some sort of spinal birth defect, perhaps. The man's face was ugly and he had nothing to live for as far as Dan was concerned, but he was throughly absorbed in his work, as though nothing else mattered.

Huh. I feel like I've never really looked at anyone before.

The janitor glanced up at Dan, and their eyes met. Quickly, the janitor turned his attention back to the floor and tried to continue mopping. The same quality of work was not there now; his mopping was hurried and flustered.

As if hit by a thunderclap that nearly knocked him over, Dan suddenly felt what the janitor was feeling at that moment. Self-consciousness. *Stop looking at me.* He simultaneously saw the janitor as the janitor saw himself, and then Dan saw himself from the janitor's perspective. Dan stared at the man in disbelief, which only intensified the janitor's embarrassed agitation. He could feel what the janitor was feeling, as if there were no barrier between their two minds.

"My God, what have I done?" Morgan wailed from the corner.

"What are you crying about?" Warburg asked, no doubt intending to be snide but having only the empty shell of mean words come out of his mouth.

"The suffering I've caused," Morgan said. "Do you have any idea? I've killed millions and forced billions more to live in poverty."

Have I caused any suffering? Dan asked himself. At that prompt, a thousand memories came flooding into his consciousness. The animals he'd tortured and killed in his youth, the women he'd violated, the people he'd stepped on and murdered in his climb to the top. Dan collapsed onto the floor, let out a howl of grief, and sobbed until he couldn't breathe.

The door opened. Though the door walked Rothschild in a yellow hazmat suit. He looked around the room and winced in revulsion at his blubbering colleagues.

"Pathetic," Rothschild scoffed.

"What are you doing here?" Warburg asked.

"I came to witness this for myself. I wanted to see the effects of this pathogen."

"Pathogen?" Morgan asked. "We've been infected with something?"

"Do you think you're behaving normally right now?" Rothschild replied. "Since you arrived here, I've had the best pathologists in the world studying your bloodwork and brain scans." He waved at a screen on the wall. It illuminated and displayed an odd-looking 3-D model illustration. "See this?" Morgan asked. "We found a bunch of these in your blood. They're unlike any virus known to science. No one has ever seen anything like this before. We're thinking it's probably not a biological agent at all. It's likely some kind of self-replicating nanotechnology. It crosses the blood-brain barrier. It changes your DNA and rewires your neural structure within hours. And here's the amazing thing: it only infects Tchogols and Dranthyx. We gave it to monkeys, regular octopuses, and the two other types of humans, and it did nothing to any of them."

"Artha did this?" Dan asked.

"Who else could have?" Rothschild asked in annoyance. "Does it surprise you? We know now who his predecessor was. Thirty-some years ago, Neith created the Tchogol flu, which wiped out hundreds of millions. Why wouldn't Artha do something similar? Though the Tchogol flu was downright primitive compared to this new virus. Germ. Whatever it is."

"What's it doing to us?" Morgan said, wiping tears away from his hideous yellow eyes.

Rothschild waved at the screen again. This time, it showed a scan of a human brain. "See this? This is a typical Tchogol brain. Compare it to this…" He waved, and a new brain image appeared side-by-side, the new one with more areas highlighted in orange. "This is Dan's brain from a few hours ago. Comparing the two, we see there is new activity that shouldn't be there."

"What is the new activity?" Dan asked.

"Empathy," Rothschild growled disdainfully. "You've all been infected with empathy. Artha's pathogen has changed the neurological structures of your brains, and I'm afraid it's irreversible."

"Fuck me. Is this fatal?" Warburg asked.

"You're not dead, are you?" Rothschild said. "Artha wasn't stupid. He wanted you to carry the pathogen back to Phax'th to infect everyone. The point of it wasn't to wipe us out. It was to enervate us."

"So now what?" Morgan asked.

"Well, I've been considering what you told me about your meeting with Artha," Rothschild said. "Despite what Daniel has told us, we have to assume Neith is alive and well.

Look at this." Rothschild gestured at the screen again, and a graph replaced the pictures of Artha's pathogen. The bottom axis listed years in sequential order, and the vertical axis had numbers in scientific notation. A red line showed a curved increase in whatever it was the graph was measuring.

"What's that?" Dan asked.

"This is the number of people named Neith with regard to time. Note the logarithmic growth. I find this highly suspect."

"Why?" Dan asked.

Rothschild sighed in frustration. "By comparison, here's a graph of all the people named Jennifer over the same period of time." He mockingly wagged his finger, and a red line with a shape like a mountain range appeared over top the original graph. "The name Jennifer ebbs and flows in popularity, while Neith continually increases in a perfect, mathematical fashion. Doesn't this strike you as a bit unusual?"

"Not especially," Dan said.

"I sometimes forget how intellectually limited your species is," Rothschild said. "Anyway, I have a feeling we're dealing with something even we Dranthyx don't understand, something exceptionally powerful and beyond our comprehension."

"What will you do?" asked Warburg.

"We're going to round them all up," Rothschild said. "All of them—every single Neith on Earth. Once we have them all in confinement, we're going to figure out what the hell is going on."

"What about us?" Dan asked.

"What about you?" Rothschild said. "You're all going to stay here in quarantine until we learn more about this thing in your bloodstream. We'd like to see what else it does to your brains. No way we're going to let you out to infect the rest of us."

"Rothschild," Morgan said, "so help me, if you dare to think you can use this little turn of events to oust me from the Directorate…"

"You'll what?" Rothschild said. "Hurt me? Kill me?"

Morgan stared at his associate coldly for a second. Then his slick purple brow wrinkled, betraying a newfound weakness.

Rothschild smirked. "I admit, you used to be someone I wouldn't ever turn my back on, Morgan. I gave you a position on the Directorate only to keep you from being too adversarial to my business interests. You too, Warburg. A keep-your-enemies-closer situation. But let's be realistic. You guys aren't so scary after this virus, or whatever it is, cut your balls off. I can see the weakness in your faces; you're neutered little bitches now. Enjoy your new feelings." Rothschild laughed—a repulsive, bubbly, metallic laugh. "From here on out, there's no more Directorate. There's only me. Unilateral, autocratic, and brutally efficient. There will be no more discussions, no more debate. What I say, goes."

"Fuck you!" Dan blurted out. The words leaving his mouth surprised him. For the first time in his life, he had no control over his emotions. Then, as Rothschild turned to look at him, he realized why he'd said it. He felt bad for Morgan and Warburg. He didn't even like them; why did he feel bad for them?

Rothschild walked over to Dan and stared him down with his murderous brimstone eyes.

"Do you know what I'm going to do as soon as I figure out this Neith situation?"

Dan didn't answer; he just studied Rothschild. The nano-machines that were changing Dan's brain made him attuned to things he'd been oblivious to before. His hair bristled as he noticed for the first time that the Dranthyx's soul was like an abyss of greed and hate. Rothschild's presence in the room blackened the mood.

"I'm going to exterminate the entire human race," Rothschild said delightedly. "Not just Xreths this time. No, I will eliminate your entire fucking species."

"What?"

"You heard me," Rothschild said.

"But why?" Dan asked with a strange, shaky feeling. "I thought you needed us for labor."

Is that feeling fear? I've never felt fear before.

"We did. You were a necessary nuisance for the last several millennia. However, it occurs to me that we can use Artha's technology for free labor. He had robots and machines producing everything. If he didn't need human labor for anything, then why the hell should we? Robots will do a thousand times as much work without causing us headaches. No strikes, no rebellions, no uprisings. After that, I shall fire up the furnaces to rid the world of you monkeys for good."

For reasons he didn't understand himself, Dan jumped up from his seat, hoping to tear a hole in Rothschild's bunny suit to infect him with the pathogen. However, Rothschild saw it coming and whipped Dan hard in the chest with one of his powerful, besuited tentacles. The blow threw Dan violently backward, causing him to crash into a stand of medical monitors. The wind knocked out of him, Dan fell helplessly to the floor and gasped for air.

Just then, Morgan and Warburg rose up simultaneously to attack Rothschild. Though he was struggling to breathe, Dan watched in amazement as they gracefully lashed each other with tentacles and parried and dodged each other's lashes. The movements weren't random, Dan noticed. They were skillful. It was apparently a martial art that had been developed around Dranthyx anatomy. Rothschild, clearly the strongest of the three, even with the bunny suit restricting his movement, picked Warburg up, bent him in half, and twisted his body. Rothschild then used the folded-up Warburg as a weapon by tossing him into Morgan. Morgan leaped out of the way, spun like a tornado, and came at Rothschild with his arm tentacles going like a helicopter's rotor. As if he'd seen it all before, Rothschild calmly braced himself against a wall with his two leg tentacles and, with precision timing, grabbed one of Morgan's spinning arm tentacles, and used Morgan's own momentum to throw Morgan across the room. Morgan flew a considerable distance and crashed headfirst into the far wall.

"Is that it? Is that all you got, you pantywaists?" Rothschild roared at Morgan and Warburg, who lay on the floor, panting and writhing in pain. Hearing no answer, Rothschild looked at Vanderbilt. "Well, what about you, milksop?"

Vanderbilt didn't get up from his seat or even look at Rothschild. He was reading a magazine. "There's enough violence in the world, Rothschild," he said without taking his eyes off his reading material. "I've decided I'm going to be a pacifist from now on."

Rothschild snarled an invective in Dranthyx at his three former compatriots and stormed out of the room.

107

Octavia, sick with worry, unable to move or eat, lay listlessly on the couch in the Aegis Safehouse.

I should leave. I can't leave. When she was little, I always told her to stay put if she got lost. Maybe she expects me to stay put. Maybe she'll come back here.

There was a knock at the door. Octavia leaped up to answer it. She didn't even bother looking through the peephole; she just flung the door open. There, on the other side, were two large men in black Aegis security uniforms.

"Are you Octavia Savitz?" one of the men asked.

"Yes. Please tell me you found her," Octavia said.

"Is your son here?" the man asked.

"Bernie? No, it's my daughter Iris who's missing!"

"Ma'am, I'm gonna ask you one more time. Is your son here?"

"What's this all about?" Octavia asked, taking a step back.

The man who'd been asking the questions acted without hesitation. He pushed Octavia to the floor and barged into the apartment.

"Hey!" Octavia shouted. "Get out! Leave my son alone!"

The second man knelt down next to Octavia and tried to restrain her. A childhood full of her dad's judo training came back in a flash: she could tell just by looking at his posture that he was ill-trained and unbalanced. Seizing the opportunity, she wrapped both of her legs around one of his, the half guard. She curled herself into a ball and reached around his back with her left hand, grabbing onto his belt. With her right hand, she grabbed the man's boot and rolled over, taking him with her. Ancient technique easily overcoming brute strength, she gracefully ended up on top of an attacker twice her size. She knew what would happen next: having little to no training, he'd give up his back when he tried to get to his knees to stand up. She let him twist to his belly and then quickly latched onto his back like a monkey. As he struggled to get to his feet, Octavia wrapped one of her arms around his neck and locked it in place with her other arm. He thrashed and struggled to get her off his back. His face grew red and panicked as Octavia choked the life out of him.

Just then, the first man came up behind Octavia and crowbarred his nightstick against Octavia's neck to pry her off his partner. Octavia, being choked herself, let go of the man she was choking. The two goons ganged up on her, knocked her back to the floor, pulled her hands behind her back, and zip-tied them together.

The man she'd choked rubbed his sore neck. Then he backhanded Octavia across the face.

Octavia recoiled at the blow. She tasted blood in her mouth.

"Get the boy," the other one said.

Octavia watched as one of the guards walked down the hallway to the back bedroom. She struggled to get free, but the first man was holding her from behind while her hands were restrained. When she heard Bernie screaming as the Aegis guard pulled him away from his calligraphy, her vision went red. She stomped her heel into her captor's shin and twisted to get away. He howled in pain and tackled her to the ground, the two of them crashing through the glass coffee table in the process.

Bernie's screaming intensified as the Aegis sentry carried the boy over his shoulder. The child was writhing and feebly striking at the sentry's back.

Octavia looked up from the floor. She must have been cut by the glass because blood was running down her forehead into her left eye, which made it difficult to see.

"Put him down!" she yelled. "Leave him alone!"

"OK, got 'em," the man said to his partner before carrying Bernie out into the hallway. "Let's get out of here."

The one who'd tackled Octavia got up and brushed the broken glass off his uniform.

Octavia, still on her back, twisted around to face him with a look that could have cut steel. She struggled to get free of the coffee table wreckage and stand up, but her movement was impeded by a metal piece of the furniture's frame.

No longer underestimating Octavia's lethality, the man stepped away from her.

"Here, got something for ya," he said. The man reached into one of the many pockets in his black uniform. From it he pulled a folded-up piece of paper. He unfolded it and tossed it at her before backing away to the door.

"They found your daughter's body in the lake. Go to the morgue to ID her."

108

Len and Natalia sat on one of the cots together, having nothing to do but watch a never-ending parade. All day long, Dranthyx soldiers had walked hundreds of new prisoners past their cell. The jail had been almost completely empty when they'd arrived, but now each cell was filled beyond capacity. There seemed to be no pattern to the people they were bringing in: old, young, male, female, all different races and ethnicities.

Then, two Dranthyx dragged a wildly tantruming child to the door of Len and Natalia's cell. The boy's clothes were torn, his face bright red with consternation and wet with tears. Len couldn't believe it when he recognized him.

"Bernie!" Natalia exclaimed.

"He's just a kid. What is he doing here?" Len demanded of the Dranthyx.

"Having a family reunion," one of the octopuses said. "Go fuck yourselves."

Just after the Dranthyx had left, Len caught sight of the guard with the kind eyes he'd seen earlier.

"Hey," Len asked. "What the hell is going on?"

"I don't know," the guard whispered so the Dranthyx wouldn't overhear. "But they're all named Neith."

"Neith?" Len asked discretely.

"Yeah. The squids are rounding up anyone with that name. Don't ask me why. I just work here."

Bernie sat on the floor of the cell, rocking back and forth while Natalia did her best to comfort him.

The cephalopod on the other side of the bars stared for an uncomfortably long time at Len with empty, vicious eyes. It was the same Dranthyx who had interrogated Natalia earlier. Len stared back contemptuously while lying on his jail-cell cot.

"What?" Len finally asked.

"So you're that guy, huh?" the Dranthyx said.

"Yeah, I'm that guy," Len said.

"You nearly wiped us all out."

"I wish I'd done a more thorough job," Len said.

"To try to send an entire species into extinction takes real heartlessness," the octopod remarked.

Len frowned at the creature.

"I'm surprised you're not a Tchogol," it said, "because that's some first-class psycho shit right there. Especially considering that your own family was at Auschwitz."

Len considered the creature in silence.

"If I were capable of admiring anyone other than myself," the Dranthyx said, "I might admire you."

It's not enough to send me to my death. He wants to be sure I spend my last days emotionally tortured by self-doubt, too. This is how they are. Fuck this. I won't give him the satisfaction.

"I'd do it again," Len said defiantly.

"Ah! I too take great joy in killing," it said, smiling. It turned its attention to Natalia. "That was very useful information you gave us."

Natalia exhaled, then closed her eyes and shook her head.

"You were right." The creature let loose an oily chuckle. "Three tiny EMPs took them right out. No problem." The creature's face turned serious, and then it asked, "So you said you built that place, right?"

Natalia didn't answer, instead holding her head in her hands.

"Their fortress was one huge Faraday cage filled with electromagnetic radiation reflectors. There was a massive EMP in the center of their bunker that surely would have done more damage than our little briefcases. It was like Artha and Qualia were sitting on a bomb that could have killed them at any second. That is just goddamn devious. What were you planning?"

"Plan?" Natalia asked. "There was no plan."

"Bullshit. If not you, then you built it that way at someone else's behest. What was the plot?"

"Artha and Qualia designed it that way." Natalia sighed.

"Do you think I'm stupid? There's no way Artha Metteyya would have allowed you to make his home into a weapon that could be used against him."

"They told me to put the EMP there." Natalia said listlessly. "The bunker was designed to focus all the radiation from the EMP right at their awareness aggregators so

Artha and Qualia would be killed instantly. That's the way they planned it, so that's the way I built it. I found out later that the EMP was connected to a third computer known as the Leveler, who could detonate the device if need be. The Leveler was controlled by the members of Metteyya, everyday people who lived in the Sandbox communities."

"What the…" the Dranthyx struggled to wrap his slimy head around what he'd just heard. "Why…why would they deliberately give worthless human beings the ability to kill them?"

"It was a selfless act," Natalia said. "You wouldn't understand."

"I'd choose my words a little more carefully if I were you," the Dranthyx said. "We got the information we needed. You're useless to us now."

"At least I've been useful at some point in my life," Natalia said. "You ought to try it."

"Insolent twat," the Dranthyx said. His tentacle whipped through the bars and coiled itself around Natalia's neck. Before Len could even get up from his cot, the Dranthyx had yanked Natalia clear across the cell by her throat with such force that her face rammed into the hard-edged flat metal bars with a horrifying crack. Her body went limp at the moment of impact.

Len shouted in horror and then sank his fingers and teeth into the tentacle encircling Natalia's neck. Len bit all the way through, a warm chunk of octopus flesh coming off in his mouth. The Dranthyx let out a yelp and rapidly uncoiled his appendage from Natalia's neck, pulling it back through the bars, spattering his aquamarine blood everywhere. Natalia fell limply to the floor, her neck bent at an impossible angle. The collision with the jail cell bars had smashed the front of her skull in, leaving a gaping head wound that bled profusely. Natalia's eyes stared vacantly in the direction of the ceiling.

Len, unable and unwilling to accept what had just happened, lifted her head off the floor and cradled it in his hands.

"No, no, no," he muttered. "Wake up. Please, wake up. It's just a concussion."

Her neck felt wrong. It was broken. Her pupils weren't dilating.

"You're OK; you're OK." Len said, "We'll have you fixed the way they fixed Mutoku up."

The Dranthyx spit angry vulgarities at Len while clutching its bleeding tentacle and walking away. Len only heard its curses in the periphery of his awareness, like a distant train whistle. He looked over at Bernie, who was still rocking and apparently oblivious to what had just happened.

Len's clothing became wet and warm with the blood that was running over his lap and pooling on the concrete floor. Natalia's mouth was open. Her unfocused eyes just kept staring. Len, in his tunnel-like state of mind, somehow thought to take her pulse. He put his finger on her neck just in time to feel the last few beats of her heart.

109

Some hours later, as the sun was coming up, Dan lay awake in his hospital bed, pallid and unable to bring himself to read or watch TV. A lifetime of unrealized remorse had been visited upon him all at once, and he could barely breathe through the guilt and shame.

Can't stop weeping. Why have I done the things I've done? Why was I born like that? How do normal people live like this? How do they get anything done? God, what an awful disability—to feel the weight of others' pain.

Dan heard the airlock door opening to the quarantine room but couldn't muster the energy to sit up.

Breakfast, maybe. How the hell can I eat? I feel so sick to my stomach, so disgusted with myself. Then it hit him, his first real pang of conscience: *I should tell someone about Rothschild. He's going to exterminate the entire human race.*

Though physically drained from the emotional tribulation, Dan forced himself to move. Mustering all the energy he had, he rolled to his side and saw a bunny-suited human walking toward him. The person stopped a few feet from his bed and looked down at him from behind a mirrored visor.

Dan glanced up at the figure's hospital ID tag.

Octavia Savitz, RN.

Dan's eyes widened.

Octavia, poor Octavia. Good-hearted Octavia—what did she ever do to deserve what I did to her? Poor Iris. And they've probably rounded up Bernie. My God.

"I'm sorry," Dan bawled. "I'm so, so sorry."

Octavia didn't reply. She just stood there in silence behind her mirrored visor.

"I killed her!" Dan blurted out. "I raped her and killed her, and then I raped her again. I dumped her body in the lake. Oh, God, Octavia, I'm so sorry."

"Where's my son?" she asked.

"I don't know!" Dan bawled. "I don't know."

Octavia reached into a bag she was carrying. From it, Dan saw her draw an old-fashioned gun that looked like something from a cowboy movie. She pointed it at him and cocked the hammer back. From the other side of the room, the three Dranthyx looked on in concern but without interfering.

"Do it," Dan said contritely. "I deserve it."

Octavia hesitated for a second and lowered the gun. Dan had no idea why; he couldn't see her face through the suit's reflective visor. Then, as if having a second thought, she raised the gun again, pointed it at Dan's forehead, and pulled the trigger.

110

The kindly guard came not too long after to collect the body.

"I'm sorry," the man said softly to Len.

Len, in shock and denial, could not answer. He couldn't do anything but watch in a near-catatonic state as they zipped up the body bag, wheeled Natalia away, and mopped her blood off the floor.

Once he and Bernie were alone in the cell again, Len stared through the bars out into the blackness. *Fuck this roller coaster*, he thought. *Tired of it. Bone tired.*

Also, the ignobility of murder: Natalia, a paragon of humanity, one in ten billion, murdered by a total piece of shit. No sense in it, no justice. Not a fitting end. It doesn't matter what kind of person one was or how one lived one's life; there was never any dignity in death. Len sighed heavily as the tears came forth.

"Déjà vu?"

The abrupt words in the stark silence startled him. A child's voice. Len spun around. Bernie was sitting on the floor, but still as a rock—as if he were doing meditation. He wasn't rocking back and forth the way he habitually did, yet his eyes remained cast downward the way they usually were.

No way. I must be imagining things. Len looked around, wondering if someone in an adjacent cell could have said it. He looked back at Bernie. Bernie was now staring directly at Len, whose heart jumped. Len had never seen the boy make eye contact before.

"Bernie," Len said in astonishment, "did you say something?"

"Yes," the child said matter-of-factly. "I asked if you were having déjà vu."

"You talk! Holy crap!"

"Yeah. I'm sorry to tell you this, but I've known how to talk for some time now."

"What? Really?"

The child nodded. Len knelt down and kissed the boy's forehead.

"Why didn't you tell us?"

"It wasn't time."

"I don't understand."

The child smiled softly and put his little hand on Len's cheek. "Now it's time."

"Well," Len said, flabbergasted, "now that you talk, I guess we have some catching up to do."

"Indeed. While we still can. So, déjà vu?"

"What do you mean, Bernie?" Len was surprised a boy of seven knew those words.

"You've been here before. Captured by the Dranthyx, awaiting execution. Haven't you?"

Len studied him quizzically. "How do you know about that?"

"That's history now. They teach it in schools."

"Oh."

"But that's not how I know it."

"No?" Len asked.

Bernie sat there for a while without answering, looking out the cell door.

Len spoke first. "This time, Bernie, I don't have a plan to get us out of here. No space aliens are going to save us."

"We don't need a plan."

"What do you mean?"

"Did you ever play dominoes when you were little?"

"Yes, but I forget how the game goes. You have to match up the numbers, right?"

"I mean setting them up and knocking them down." Bernie used his hands to mimic the setting up and toppling of the pieces.

"Yes." Len smiled through his pain. "My brother and I used to play that quite a bit."

"Isn't it funny how life is sort of like that game?" the boy asked, getting up from the floor. He walked over to the cell bars and looked out, hands clasped behind his back, while Len watched, baffled. "One thing causes the next, ad infinitum. Every little action we take, or do not take, has profound effects far into the future. Except, unlike toppling dominoes, there's no end. No closure. Cause and effect until the end of the universe. Entropy and enthalpy."

"Your vocabulary is amazing! I wish you'd talked to us sooner—"

"We try to make sense of it with our limited understanding," Bernie said, cutting him off. "We say, 'This is good,' or 'This is bad.' The truth of the matter is, we can never see the entire picture. Our minds and our perspectives are far too limited. We have no way of knowing how any action will affect us or others in the future. Our beloved Natalia dies. Is this good, or is this bad?"

The question hit Len in the stomach.

He's just a kid. He's autistic. Or is he? Whatever, don't take it the wrong way.

"Look," Len said with a sigh, "you are apparently a very bright young man. However, despite how smart someone is, when things like this happen, we as humans have a need to rationalize it, to minimize it. I fear that's what you may be doing."

"That first domino—what happens to its energy as it falls?"

Len sat on the cot and slumped his shoulders. *Let it go. We're going to be put to death. These are your last minutes with your grandson, and you just found out he can talk. Don't burst his bubble, you old asshole. Just let the kid yammer.*

"It is transferred to the next domino," Bernie said, answering his own question. "Its energy continues. Energy isn't destroyed. One thing to the next, to the next, to the next. An arms merchant in Fallujah sells an Iraqi boy an AK-47 but deliberately shows him the wrong way to insert the magazine. Your friend Justin dies, which you think is terrible. You kill the boy, which you regret. But you live, which you assume is OK. Do we really know what would have happened, had things transpired differently? That young Iraqi could have grown into a terrible despot. Or, one week later, Private Justin Waterhouse might have accidentally shot and killed you in the chaos of a firefight."

Len's jaw hung open as curiosity turned to shock. He'd never told anyone that story. There were only a handful of men who knew what had happened that day, decades before Bernie was even born.

The boy continued. "Let's say an airline pilot suddenly decides to kill herself. She's flying an empty 747 and chooses to down the plane in the boonies of West Texas. Thing is, she happens to crash right into a Dranthyx airship during the now-famous Battle of the Freehold. An airship, by the way, that was about to fire its powerful ion canon right where a certain Len Savitz was standing."

He gaped at the boy in silence, who was facing away from him and staring out of the cell. The boy slowly turned to face his grandfather. The look on the boy's face made Len shudder; it was as though the kid were a thousand years old.

"Or, through the deftest of movements, a martial arts expert deflects the gun-wielding hand of a would-be assassin, which causes him to miss his shot," Bernie said, imitating the motion. "Instead of shooting you in the head, which would have killed you instantly, the assassin misses and hits your chest. You think it's terrible at the time, but you're still alive because of it. Aren't you?"

"How…how do you know this stuff, Bernie?"

"I'm the reason you're still alive. I'm Neith."

"Neith?" Len's face contorted into a mixture of confusion and concern.

"Yes."

Neith Bernard Savitz. That was what Octavia had named him. OK, maybe the kid had heard of Neith in school. Everyone knew about Neith because of Len's *Examiner* piece that had been published during the Invasion all those years ago. Bernie talked like an adult, but he was still a kid. Maybe his imagination was getting away with him. Maybe Len had mentioned the Iraq incident and the airplane crash before and had simply forgotten about it. That had to be the explanation.

"Young man, the Neith you speak of lived years before you were born. Also, I'm pretty sure she was old even then, not to mention female. She's probably dead by now."

"That was me. I was old, and I was female."

Len's breathing intensified. The conversation made him feel hot and dizzy. Len put his hand down on the cot to steady himself.

Unfazed, the boy continued. "Not only was I old and female, I was other things, too. I was the Iraqi arms dealer. I was the airline pilot. I was the martial artist who saved you from being shot in the head on the courthouse steps. I was the wetware component of a supercomputer known as Parse 45."

"What? How? I don't understand. No. No! This is ridiculous. You are a seven-year-old boy. I'm not sure who put you up to this, or if your imagination is getting the better of you, but I don't appreciate it."

"I currently inhabit a seven-year-old boy's body. But what I am far exceeds that."

"Are you talking about past lives? There's an urban legend that kids can remember that sort of thing."

"Actually, no. I'm talking about concurrent lives."

Len's brow furrowed.

"One thing you have kept secret is the source of your wealth," the boy said. "I know where it came from. I gave it to you. I wrote you a letter and had my man Hamasaki deliver it to your landlord. I told you exactly where to find the fortune in gold I'd buried. Remember? You've never told anyone those details, but I know them. Do you know why I gave you that money?"

Len sat there, unable to answer.

"I gave it to you because I knew you'd buy the island. It was a way of guaranteeing your survival for the next thirty-five years. I did it to keep you alive and out of trouble. Look," the child said, "just sit back and relax. I'll do my best to explain. A long time ago, something extraordinary happened to a rather ordinary woman name Neith Jane Gibson. She was sitting on her couch in her little suburban ranch house, smoking a cigarette, when her mind just blew open. *Pow!* Not the gray matter itself, but her consciousness. It suddenly exceeded her body, becoming profoundly vast. Big like the universe. I'm still not sure how or what happened. A freak accident, maybe.

Sometimes I even think she might have been chosen by some higher power. Who knows?"

"$Neith_0$, which is what I call that first life, discovered she could coincarnate herself. In other words, she could decide to be born anywhere on earth, at any time, while she was still living. Her first such expansion was a male fetus known as $Neith_1$. And here's the interesting thing: $Neith_0$ and $Neith_1$ shared consciousness. They were different individuals with different bodies and different personalities, but their awareness was drawn from the same source. Thoughts passed between them effortlessly, and they could communicate across space and time. Her next incarnation was a little girl who grew up to be an airline pilot. $Neith_2$. That's the one who saved your life at the Freehold. As $Neith_0$ coincarnated, so did the coincarnations. The same consciousness filled each body, and, as it did, the consciousness itself expanded. The collective grew across the globe and forward into time, each mind-sharing with the others. A Neith in Mongolia would share consciousness with a Neith in Madagascar. Neiths in the future had minds linked to those in the past."

"And you're part of this...network?"

"This body is $Neith_{2F3A}$."

"What? Wait a second," Len exclaimed, "Did you say future Neiths can communicate with past Neiths?"

Bernie smiled. "Yes."

"Then wouldn't that change the outcome of events?"

"Ha ha!" Bernie laughed. "Very good! See how insightful you are? That's why I picked you, Len."

"What the hell? How does that even work?"

"It's the reason I don't seem to make mistakes. I can do something over and over until I get it right. To the temporally challenged, it looks like I did it right the first time."

Len gave him a baffled look.

Bernie laughed. "Look, it's like the dominoes. I set them up in a certain state, and I knock them down. Sometimes they don't fall correctly, so I set them up slightly differently and try it again. However, I'm not doing this on a nice flat surface where everything is easy and cooperative."

Bernie looked at Len and saw that he still wasn't getting it. "My existence could be described as a huge house. A mansion, maybe. In the east wall, there's a little mouse hole that a mouse comes out of at regular intervals. What I do is, I always put the first domino in front of her hole because she's consistent. She pushes the domino over, which starts the chain reaction. The object of the game is to get the chain of dominoes to cascade over to a mouse hole in the *other* side of the mansion, then through that hole to the outside. Problem is, the house is full of obstacles: stairs, furniture, ramps, bathtubs, pets. Getting the domino chain to fall successfully is very difficult, and I have to try it millions of different ways before finding the best solution."

"What is this an analogy for?"

"The mouse is $Neith_0$'s awakening, which sets off the chain reaction. The obstacles in the house are the problems that must be surmounted: Tchogols, Dranthyx, governments, what have you. Very tricky. I can't set up dominoes beyond the east wall because $Neith_0$ wasn't awakened yet. I can't pre-incarnate for some reason. The other wall, the west wall, is an analogy for too much complexity. It's the point at which it's no longer possible for me to contain all the outcomes. However, that wall has a window, and I can see what's outside. So I'm limited on the one side temporally and on the other by an unmanageable number of permutations. Within a certain bubble of space and time, I am a god. Beyond that, I'm oddly powerless. As far as you're concerned, though, I suppose you could think of me as your guardian angel."

"What happens when the dominoes fall correctly to the mouse hole in the west wall?"

"Beyond that wall is the Great Awakening. A global renaissance. The result will be a new human civilization unlike any that have come before it. The Final State. All these domino arrangements I'm trying are an attempt to find the best way to get from Neith's awakening, across the obstacles, to the Final State. I'm experimenting to find the perfect solution."

"Final State? Great Awakening? What about Jefferson? I thought you were some kind of revolutionary. I thought it was all political or something."

"Jefferson and I had a common goal of overthrowing the old power structures. However, we disagreed on what should happen after that. I tried explaining to him that a second American Revolution would only lead to a second American government, but he didn't seem to grasp that concept. He wanted to take civilization backward 250 years. I wanted to take it forward ten thousand."

Bernie continued. "Daniel Barton, like Jefferson, is another domino. You should have seen the contortions I had to go through to keep him alive through the Tchogol flu."

"You helped that monster survive the flu?" Len asked. "Why?"

"If Daniel Barton survives the flu, he eventually becomes chairman of Aegis. When he becomes chairman, he attracts the attention of the Dranthyx. When Barton and the Dranthyx travel to Artha Metteyya's island, Artha infects them. So far, so good. Now, what's supposed to happen after that is, they carry the pathogen back to Cleveland and Phax'th. Then the world changes for the better."

"Pathogen? Phax'th?" Len asked.

"To answer your questions succinctly: it's a terrible thing to say, but Jefferson and Barton are just useful idiots."

"So what am I? Your other useful idiot?" Len asked.

"You are useful, but you're no idiot. In fact, you're still the key to making this whole thing work."

"I don't understand."

"You will," the boy said.

"And how many times do you have to set the dominoes up to get them where you want? How long does this take?"

"Seventy to a hundred and ten years to complete one domino state, usually. How many different iterations, you mean?"

Len nodded.

"In truth, I don't do anything over. I do everything all at once. Time is a nonsense concept. An extraordinarily large number of states are carried out concurrently, and the solution is found as quickly as all the wrong answers are."

"I have no idea what you're talking about. Let me rephrase: when will you find the answer?"

"Technically speaking, I've already solved it."

"What? Then why are we sitting here in this cell?"

"Because, unfortunately, this is the way State$_{67E4F}$ ends. Remember that pathogen I mentioned? The whole point of this specific state was to test a theory I have about how to disperse it to both the human and Dranthyx populations simultaneously. It's one of the last forks in the domino chain before the desired result. This iteration was almost perfect. Just a few small items need to be tweaked at the end. However, because it wasn't 100 percent perfect, this state needs to be removed from the probable outcomes. I have to anneal the results of my domino experiments to optimize outcomes, you see."

"I'm so goddamned confused. If you're so powerful, why didn't you just talk to the Ich-Ca-Gan yourself? Why did you need me at all? Why did you let Natalia die? None of this makes any sense."

"The Ich-Ca-Gan have the ability to sense extradimensional beings. Talking to them directly would be a disaster, so I need a proxy each time. Trust me, I've tried everything, and you are the only thing that works. As for Natalia, I wonder…"

"Wonder what?"

"How did you meet her?"

"On an airplane."

"Hmm," the boy said in a drawn-out, patronizing way. "Do you think you were seated next to her by accident?"

Len looked up at him.

"I bought her that ticket, you know," Bernie said. "So she'd meet you. Because I knew you'd get along. What if I told you she's not really dead?"

"The fuck are you talking about?" Len said. "We both saw her die."

"Well, she is dead in this state. No, wait…" Bernie's eyes rolled off to the side as he did some sort of calculation with his fingers. "This state and 27,947 others. But none of that matters."

"What do you mean it *doesn't matter*?"

The boy walked over to Len and put his hands on Len's shoulders. "Len, you're a good man, and I've always felt bad for using you. I'm going to make this right. You and Natalia will have a long, long, happy life together. Thousands of years. You just don't know it yet."

Len sighed and rubbed his temples and tried to make sense of it all. The boy looked at him empathetically.

"She wasn't the only one, unfortunately. Artha and Qualia Metteyya nobly volunteered their lives this time around so that I could perfect the details. What trust they have in me! They too will enjoy a long, wonderful existence. I will make sure of it."

After several minutes of silence, Len asked, "These states you're talking about—are they like parallel universes?"

Bernie seemed delighted by the question. "Something like that, yes!"

"Then how is it that you can tell me about other states without causing interference between them?"

"Haha!" Bernie did a little Irish jig in the middle of the jail cell. "That was exactly the right question! Absolutely perfect. I love you, Len. You always get right to the heart of the matter. That's why I'm telling you—to cause decoherence."

Len looked Bernie in the eyes intently for a solid minute, as if searching them for an explanation.

"Len," Bernie whispered, "if you cannot find the truth within yourself, where do you expect to find it?"

I've always known what to do.

The missing puzzle piece that Len had spent his whole life searching for, the one he'd had all along, clicked into place. Everything became lucid.

Everything.

Every sentient being in the universe opened its eyes simultaneously as the epiphany ripped Len's doubts apart like a supernova. Decades of delusions burned off like fog in the sun—revealing an infinite number of past, present, and future lifetimes. A tsunamic surge of joy coursed through Len's body. No more constraints; like a raindrop falling into an ocean, his tiny human psyche rejoined a vast cosmos that was vivid, beautiful, alive.

Len couldn't help but laugh out loud. He smiled exuberantly at Bernie, who beamed back at him. Len grabbed the boy and hugged him.

Then the wave collapsed.

Hours before the White House was bombed, a much younger Leonard Savitz slept on a mattress on the floor in his apartment in Pittsburgh. Remembering nothing of countless trial-run futures, he opened his eyes.

That feeling, Len thought.

Since divorcing Sara and moving into his own place, Len had occasionally awoken with a euphoric sense that absolutely anything was possible. That morning, however, was different. A new kind of sensation had roused him, one that he'd never felt before. It was a potent but subdued elation in his guts. Magnificent and immovable, like a mountain. Something serene, decided, and beyond all fear.

Len walked outside to his fire-escape balcony with a cup of coffee and leaned against the railing. The city below had already begun stirring; he heard buses, the footsteps of pedestrians, the noises of shopkeepers opening up their businesses. The air was cool and glistening, the sky ablaze with a powerful orange sunrise.

Len lit a cigarette and inhaled deeply. He closed his eyes and listened to the sounds of the world waking up.